SHADOW KISSED

THE WITCH'S REBELS BOOK ONE

Shadow Kissed
Copyright © 2018 by Sarah Piper
SarahPiperBooks.com

ISBN-13: 978-1-948455-06-0

TAROT ACADEMY

ONE

GRAY

Survival instinct was a powerful thing.

What horrors could we endure, could we accept, could we embrace in the name of staying alive?

Hunger. Brutality. Desperation.

Being alone.

I'd been alone for so long I'd almost forgotten what it was like to love, to trust, to look into the eyes of another person and feel a spark of something other than fear.

Then *they* came into my life.

Each one as damaged and flawed as I was, yet somehow finding a way through the cracks in my walls, slowly breaking down the bricks I'd so carefully built around my heart.

Despite their differences, they'd come together as my protectors and friends for reasons I still didn't fully under-stand. And after everything we'd been through, I had no doubts about who they were to me now. To each other.

Family.

I didn't know what the future held; I'd given up trying to predict it years ago. But I didn't need my Tarot cards or my mother's old crystal ball to know this:

For me, there was no future without them. Without my rebels.

"Gray?" His whisper floated to my ears.

After several heartbeats, I took a deep breath and opened my eyes.

I heard nothing, saw nothing, felt nothing but the demon imprisoned before me, pale and shattered, fading from this realm.

"Whatever you're thinking," he said, his head lolling forward, "don't."

Looking at him chained to the chair, bruises covering his face, blood pouring from the gashes in his chest, I strengthened my resolve.

His voice was faint, his body broken, his essence dimming. But the fire in his eyes blazed as bright as it had the day we'd met.

"Whatever horrible things you've heard about me, Cupcake, they're all true…"

"Please," he whispered, almost begging now. "I'm not worth…"

His words trailed off into a cough, blood spraying his lips.

I shook my head. He was wrong. He was *more* than worth it. Between the two of us, maybe only one would make it out of this room alive. If that were true, it had to be him; I couldn't live in a world where he didn't exist. Where any of them didn't exist.

This was my fate. My purpose. My gift.

There was no going back.

I held up my hands, indigo flames licking across my palms, surging bright in the darkness.

The demon shuddered as I reached for him, and I closed my eyes, sealing away the memory of his ocean-blue gaze, knowing it could very well be the last time I saw it.

TWO

GRAY

2 Weeks Earlier...

Don't act like prey, and you won't become it. Don't act like prey...

Whispering my usual mantra, I locked up the van and pushed my rusty hand truck down St. Vincent Avenue, scanning the shadows for trouble.

It'd rained earlier, and mist still clung to the streets, rising into the dark autumn night like smoke. It made everything that much harder to see.

Fortunately it was my last delivery of the night, and I'd brought along my favorite traveling companions—a sharp stake in my waistband and a big-ass hunting knife in my boot. Still, danger had a way of sneaking up on a girl in Blackmoon Bay's warehouse district, which was why most people avoided it.

If I hadn't needed the money—and a boss who paid in

cash and didn't ask questions about my past—I would've avoided it, too.

Alas...

Snuggling deeper into my leather jacket, I banked left at the next alley and rolled to a stop in front of the unmarked service entrance to Black Ruby. My hand truck wobbled under the weight of its cargo—five refrigerated cases of O-positive and three AB-negative, fresh from a medical supplier in Vancouver.

Yeah, Waldrich's Imports dealt in some weird shit, but human cops didn't bother with the warehouse district, and the Fae Council that governed supernaturals didn't get involved with the Bay's black market. The only time they cared was when a supernatural killed a human, and some-times—depending on the human—not even then.

Thumbing through my packing slips, I hoped the vampires weren't too thirsty tonight. Half their order had gotten snagged by customs across the bay in Seattle.

I also hoped someone other than Darius Beaumont would sign for this. I could hold my own with most vamps, but Black Ruby's owner definitely struck me as the shoot-the-messenger type.

No matter how sexy he is...

Wrapping one hand discretely around my stake, I reached up to hit the buzzer, but a faint cry from the far end of the alley stopped me.

"Don't! Please!"

"Settle down, sweetheart," a man said, the menace in his voice a sick contrast to the terrified tremble in hers.

My heart rate spiked.

Abandoning my delivery, I scooted along the building's brick exterior, edging closer to the struggle. I spotted the girl first—she couldn't have been more than fifteen, sixteen at most, with lanky brown hair and the pale, haunted features of a blood slave.

But it wasn't a vampire that'd lured her out for a snack.

The greasy dude who'd cornered her was a hundred percent human—just another pervert in dirty jeans and a sweat-stained henley who clearly thought runaway kids were an easy mark.

"It'll all be over soon," he told her.

Yeah, sooner than you think...

Anger coiled in my belly, fizzing the edges of my vision. I couldn't decide who deserved more of my ire—the asshole threatening her now, or the parents who'd abandoned her in the first place.

Far as I was concerned, they were the same breed of evil.

"Well now. Must be my lucky night." The man barked out a wheezing laugh, and too late, I realized I'd been spotted. "Two for the price of one. Come on over here, Blondie. Don't be shy."

Shit. I'd hesitated too long, let my emotions get the best of me when I should've been working that knife out of my boot.

Fear leaked into my limbs, and for a brief instant, I felt my brain and body duking it out. *Fight or flight, fight or flight...*

No. I couldn't leave her. Not like that.

"Let her go," I said, brandishing my stake.

He yanked the kid against his chest, one meaty hand fisting her blue unicorn hoodie, the other curling around her throat. Fresh urine soaked her jeans.

"Drop your little stick and come over here," the man said, "or I'll break her neck."

My mind raced for an alternative, but there was no time. I couldn't risk going for the knife. Couldn't sneak up on him. And around here, screaming for help could attract a worse kind of attention.

Plan B it is.

"Alright, big guy. You win." I dropped the stake and smiled, sidling toward him with all the confidence I could muster, which wasn't much, considering how hard I was shaking. "What are you doing with a scrawny little kid, anyway?"

He looked at the kid, then back at me, his lecherous gaze burning my skin. The stench of cigarettes and cheap booze lingered on his breath, like old fish and sour milk.

"I've got everything you need right here," I purred, choking back bile as I unzipped my jacket. "Unless you're not man enough to handle it?"

His gaze roamed my curves, eyes dark with lust.

"You're about to find out," he warned. "Ain't ya?"

He shoved the kid away, and in one swift move, he grabbed me and spun me around, pinning me face-first against the bricks.

He was a hell of a lot faster than I'd given him credit for.

"So you're an all talk, no action kind of bitch?" He

wrenched my arms behind me, the intense pain making my eyes water. His sour breath was hot on the back of my neck, his hold impossibly strong, my knife impossibly out of reach. "That ends now."

A few blocks off, an ambulance screamed into the night, but it wasn't coming for us. The kid and I were on our own.

"Mmm. You got some ass on you, girl." He shoved a hand into the back pocket of my jeans and grabbed a handful of my flesh. "I like that in a woman."

Of course *you do.*

After all these years making illegal, late-night deliveries to the seediest supernatural haunts in town, this wasn't my first rodeo. The one-liners, the threats, the grabby hands… Human or monster, guys like this never managed to deviate from the standard dickhole playbook.

But this was the first guy who'd actually pinned me to a wall.

At least he'd ditched the kid. I tried to get her attention now, to urge her to take off, but she'd tucked herself behind a Dumpster, paralyzed with fear.

The man pressed his greasy lips to my ear. "No more bullshit, witch."

You don't know the half of it, asshole.

He didn't—that much was obvious. Just another dude with a tiny dick who tossed around the word "witch" like an insult.

My vision flickered again, rage boiling up inside, clawing at my insides like a caged animal searching for weak points.

It wanted out.

I took a deep breath, dialed it back down to a simmer.

God, I would've loved to light him up—spell his ass straight to oblivion. But I hadn't kept my mojo on lockdown for damn near a decade just to risk exposure for *this* prick.

So magic was out. I couldn't reach my knife. And my top-notch negotiating skills had obviously failed.

Fuck diplomacy.

I let my head slump forward in apparent defeat.

Then slammed it backward, right into his chin.

He grunted and staggered back, but before I could spin around or reach for my knife, he was on me again, fisting my hair and shoving my face against the wall.

"Nice try, little cunt. Now you eat brick."

"Don't!" the girl squeaked. "Just… just let us go."

"Aw, that's cute." He let out a satisfied moan like he'd just discovered the last piece of cake in the fridge. "You'll get your turn, baby."

Okay, she'd saved me from a serious case of brick-rash —not to mention a possible skull fracture—but now she was back on his radar. And I still couldn't get to the knife.

Time for plan B. Or was this C?

Fuck it.

"Hey. I've got some money," I said. "Let us go, and it's yours."

"Yeah?" He perked up at that. "How much we talkin'?"

"Like I said—some."

Lie. At the moment, I was loaded. Most of the $3,000 I'd

already collected tonight was in the van, wrapped in a McDonald's bag and shoved under the seat. I also had $200 in a baggie inside my boot and another $800 in my bra, because I believed in diversifying my assets.

My commission depended on me getting the cash and van back to the docks without incident. I couldn't afford incidents. Rent was due tomorrow, and Sophie had already covered me last month.

But I couldn't—wouldn't—risk him hurting the kid.

"It's in my boot," I said. "Left one."

"We'll see about that, Blondie." He yanked me away from the wall and shoved me to the ground, wet pavement biting into the heels of my hands.

With a boot to my back, he pushed me flat on my stomach, then crouched down and grabbed my wrists, pinning them behind me with one of his meaty hands. With his free hand, he bent my leg back and yanked off my boot.

Bastard.

"I hope you feel good about your life choices," I grumbled.

Another wheezing laugh rattled through his chest, and he coughed. "Choice ain't got nothin' to do with it."

Whatever. I waited until he saw the baggie with the cash, let him get distracted and stupid over his small victory.

The instant he released my wrists and went for the money, I pushed up on all fours and slammed my other boot heel straight into his teeth.

The crunch of bone was pure music, but his howl of agony could've called the wolves.

I had just enough time to flip over and scamper to my feet before he rose up and charged, pile-driving me backward into the wall. The wind rushed out of my lungs on impact, but I couldn't give up. I had to keep fighting. Had to make sure he wouldn't hurt the girl.

I clawed at his face and shoved a knee into his groin, but *damn it*—I couldn't get enough leverage. His hands clamped around my throat, rage and fire in his eyes, blood pouring from his nose and mouth as he spit out broken teeth.

He cocked back an arm, but just before his fist connected, I went limp, dropping to the ground like a pile of rags.

The momentum of his swing threw him off balance, and I quickly ducked beneath his arms and darted behind him, crouching down and reaching for the sweet, solid handle of my knife.

"You can't win," he taunted as he turned to face me. Neither his injuries nor the newly acquired lisp diminished his confidence. "I'm bigger, stronger, and I ain't got no qualms about hurting little cunts like you."

Despite the tremble in my legs, I stood up straight, blade flashing in the moonlight.

"Whoa. Whoa!" Eyes wide, he raised his hands in surrender, slowly backing off. "Hand over the knife, sweetheart."

"Not happening."

"You're gonna hurt yourself, waving around a big weapon like that."

"Also not happening."

"Look. You need to calm the fuck down before—" A coughing fit cut him short, and he leaned against the wall, one hand on his chest as he gasped for air.

I held the knife out in front of me, rock steady, finally getting my footing. Chancing a quick glance at the girl, I jerked my head toward the other end of the alley, willing her to bolt.

Her sudden, panicked gasp and a blur of movement beside me were all the warning I had before the dude slammed into me again, tackling me to the ground. My knife clattered away.

Straddling my chest, he cocked back an arm and offered a bloody, near-toothless smile. "Time to say goodnight, witch."

"Leave her alone!" No more than another flash in my peripheral vision, the kid leaped out from behind the Dumpster, flinging herself at our attacker.

She scratched and punched for all she was worth, eyes blazing and wild. I'd never seen anyone so fierce.

But he simply batted her away like she was nothing. A fly. A gnat. A piece of lint.

She hit the ground hard.

I gasped, heart hammering in my chest, shock radiating through my limbs. She *wasn't* a fly or a gnat. She was a fucking child in a unicorn hoodie, lost and scared and totally alone, and he'd thrown her down.

Just like that.

Still pinned in place, I couldn't even see where she'd landed.

But I would never forget that sound. Her head hitting the pavement. The eerie silence that followed. Seconds later, another ambulance howled into the darkness, nowhere close enough to help.

"What did you do?" I screamed, no longer caring who or what might've heard me. "She's just a kid!"

I clawed at the man's chest, but I was pretty sure he'd already forgotten about me.

"No. No way. Fuck this bullshit." He jumped up to his feet, staggered back a few steps, then took off without another word.

Still trying to catch my breath, I crawled over next to the girl, adrenaline chasing away my pain. Blood pooled beneath her head, spreading out like a dark halo. Her breathing was shallow.

"Hey. I'm right here," I whispered. "It's okay, baby."

She was thin as a rail, her wet jeans and threadbare hoodie hanging off her shivering frame.

"Jesus, you're freezing." I shucked off my jacket and covered her body, careful not to move her. "He's gone now. He can't hurt you anymore."

I swept the matted hair from her forehead. Her skin was clammy, her eyes glassy and unfocused, but she was still conscious. Still there, blinking up at me and the dark, cloudy sky above.

"What's your name, sweet pea?" I asked.

Blink. Blink.

"Hon, can you tell me your name?"

She sucked in a breath. Fresh tears leaked from her eyes. That had to be a good sign, right?

"Um. Yeah," she whispered. "It's… Breanne?"

"Breanne?"

"Sometimes Bean."

"Bean. That's a great nickname." I tucked a lock of hair behind her ear, my fingers coming away sticky with blood. "Hang in there, Bean. I'm going for help."

"No! Don't leave me here. I—" She reached for me, arms trembling, skin white as the moon. "Grape jelly. Grape—"

Grape jelly grape, she'd said. And then her eyes went wide, and I watched the spark in her go out.

Just like that.

"Bean!" I pressed my fingers beneath her jaw, then checked her wrist, desperate to find a pulse.

But it was too late.

Here in the middle of vamp central, the sweet kid in the unicorn hoodie—the one who'd ultimately saved *my* life— was dead.

THREE

GRAY

Murderer.

Guilt flooded my gut, hot and prickly.

She was just a kid. I was supposed to save her.

Instead, I'd gotten her killed.

I puked all over the front of my shirt.

This can't be happening.

Think, Gray. Think.

Wiping my mouth on my sleeve, I returned my attention to her glassy eyes. Empty eyes.

Right now, more than anything, I wanted her alive. I wanted to take her to Luna's Café for a cup of coffee and a hot meal, to teach her how to defend herself against vampires and rogue shifters and bad men hiding out in alleys. I wanted it with a deep and endless yearning, a soul-sucking desperation that felt like it was turning me inside out.

"Please, Bean. *Please*." I stared into her vacant eyes. "Come back."

Silence.

I reached forward again, grabbing her limp hand, but something felt... off. Like I was being watched. Trapped. I whipped my head around and scanned the end of the alley, peering into the misty darkness of the street beyond. An old car backfired nearby, making me flinch. But I saw nothing. Smelled nothing.

I turned back to Bean, my arms erupting in goosebumps. Instantly the temperature plummeted, turning my breath icy with frost.

The alley tilted sideways. I squeezed my eyes shut and felt an old, familiar rush, a pulsing heat gathering deep inside.

No. Not again...

I fought to resist it, but it called to me, warm and inviting where seconds ago I'd been shivering. I opened my eyes, the world spinning and blurring before me.

When it finally stopped, the alley was gone.

I was on my knees in a lush, moonlit forest, my hands full of rich earth.

There were no buildings here, no brick walls or vampires or greasy men. I was alone in the middle of nowhere, the only sound a gentle breeze whispering through a canopy of leaves. The soothing scents of lilac and lavender washed over me.

I know this place.

Rising slowly, I wiped my dirty hands on my jeans.

Several paces ahead, indigo light pulsed, urging me forward along a path clogged with tangled vines and flowers so big their stems had bent beneath the weight.

Picking my way through the growth, I followed the light until I reached a small clearing surrounded by dense trees, darker and more ominous than the forest I'd been kneeling in. Nestled among the blackest branches, a hundred pairs of silver eyes glittered in the night.

Watching.

Not so alone after all…

At the center of the clearing, a chest-high pedestal made of smooth white stones rose out of the earth, vines twining through the gaps between the rocks. Here was the source of my seductive light—a pentacle etched into a stone slab balanced on top, glowing as if it had been carved with living, indigo fire.

Instinctively I reached forward, my fingers slipping into the promise of warmth offered by the light. My skin tingled, but it wasn't creepy or unpleasant; more like getting into a bath that's just a little too hot—a surprise at first, then bliss.

"What is this place?" I whispered.

A soft breeze danced across my hair, bringing with it the lilac and lavender scent I knew so well. The answer was in my head, all around me, everywhere at once.

I knew. Remembered.

This was *my* place. My magic. My source.

The place of calm serenity I'd retreat to, deep inside myself, when my adopted mother Calla was first teaching me how to use my magic.

Some witches drew magical energy by visualizing their bodies extending into the earth, like the roots of a tree— Sophie was like that. Others got energy from the moon, or by raising a cone of power with other witches, or by performing rituals to call on the grace of their deities.

There were as many ways to access energy for magic as there were witches.

Me? I'd always come here to access it.

I hadn't though—not for over nine years.

But now I felt the magic humming through my veins again, waking up after its long nap.

"How is this possible?"

Behind me, the leaves rustled.

It felt so good, so right, such a part of me I wondered how I'd managed to go so long without it. Calla had always told me it was a rare and powerful witch who could generate her own magic energy, but once we figured out that that was my method, she'd done her best to teach me how to care for it, access it, and replenish it.

I'd loved coming here. Always. And for the first sixteen years of my life, I'd known it as well as I'd known my own face in the mirror.

But I was twenty-five now, and this place... It wasn't exactly as I'd remembered.

Beneath the scent of lilac and lavender I'd always associated with my magic, something else lurked—a cloying, rotten scent I couldn't quite place. Where once the path was clear and well-defined, edged in knee-high colorful blooms and ferns as soft as feathers, now it was wild and untamed.

Uncontrolled. Before, there had been no eyes watching, glittering and unblinking in the pale moonlight. And out beyond the stone pedestal, the gentle rolling meadow so bright in my memory was now a gnarled, leafless forest. The trees were enshrouded in mist, their branches barren and broken.

It looked like a great black skeleton army on the march.

Nothing is static, a voice inside me said. *All things must change.*

As I peered into the dark wood, the bare trees began to shift, slowly revealing a new path. Something compelled me forward, though this path was narrower, the trees so closely packed their branches scraped my arms.

I couldn't shake the feeling that I was being watched— not just by the eyes of the forest, but by something else. Something sinister.

I will find you…

Rubbing the goosebumps from my arms, I hurried down the path toward another clearing, stopping before a stone archway choked with black vines and carved with glowing, silver-blue runes.

Enter, the trees seemed to whisper.

An iron gate appeared beneath the arch, and I wrenched it open and stepped through. Stars glittered in the night sky, but soon the shifting clouds obscured the view. The clearing before me darkened.

The trees were closing in.

Dense mist crept out from the forest and swirled around my ankles, and once again I was shivering. The black skeleton army stepped forward, and for the first time, I noticed the black-and-silver threads draped over their branches, swaying in the breeze like tinsel on a Christmas tree.

It was breathtaking.

As I watched, mesmerized, the bare black branches stretched forward, closing in around me. With the same instinctual movement that had guided me into the warm indigo light on the pedestal, I reached for the closest branch, twining my fingers with the cool, shimmering threads. They wound around my hands, instantly tightening, icy cold and wrong, wrong, wrong.

"No!" I jerked backward out of the mist and back through the gate, falling hard on my ass. The forest vanished on impact, the alley reappearing just as quickly. But this time, I was surrounded by a dome—some kind of iridescent shield. It glimmered like a soap bubble, blocking out the mist and the sounds of the warehouse district.

The tinsel-like threads had vanished from my hands, but my skin was streaked an oily black where they'd touched. When I turned my hands over, my palms ignited in dark indigo flames that licked the night air and cast the alley in a blue glow. The flames didn't burn.

I gasped, turning to look at Bean. Silver mist poured from her mouth, shimmering in the darkness like the sheerest gossamer scarf.

Her soul.

On the pavement next to her, a raven appeared. He was more beast than bird, with opalescent black feathers and great golden eyes that held the wisdom of a creature a thousand times his age. I stared openmouthed, my body frozen in shock. I knew the raven wasn't a real bird—not one that I could feel with my hands—but a shadow creature that by all accounts I shouldn't be able to see.

He was a messenger. A ferrier of souls.

And the most magnificent, terrifying creature I had ever seen.

But I couldn't let him take her. She wasn't ready. Wasn't so far gone she couldn't be helped.

Possessed by some ancient, unnamed knowledge, I raised my flaming hands, horrified as they caught the edge of Bean's soul. But instead of igniting, the misty fabric of her essence simply recoiled, slithering back into her mouth.

The raven disappeared.

The flames in my hands died out, the black streaks fading from my skin.

The shield dropped away.

"Bean!" I knelt beside her, pressing a hand to her forehead. She was even colder now. Her eyes were still open, but covered with a sick, milky-white film, shot through with tiny blue veins.

The sound of new breath sucking into her lungs nearly stopped my heart.

Bean gasped and sputtered, her legs twitching. Then she sat bolt upright.

I shot to my feet and stumbled backward, slamming into the wall behind me. Didn't matter. For once I was grateful for the pain. The bricks were reassuring against my shoulders, a piece of solid reality in a night that had gone utterly sideways.

Bean moaned, her curdled-milk eyes staring right through me.

My heart dropped into my stomach. Was she a zombie? A revenant? Whatever she was, I'd made her, and I'd done it with something dark. Other. Something festering inside me that I didn't understand and absolutely did *not* want to fuck with.

Worse, I'd broken my only unbreakable rule. After nine-plus years of lying low—not even so much as a heat spell for my coffee or a money spell to help with rent—I'd just used my magic.

In a series of jerky, disjointed movements, the girl—*creature*—hauled herself up. She pinned me with those rheumy eyes, seething with an unspoken accusation.

You did this to me, witch.

I wanted to bolt—every instinct inside me shouted at me to get away—but I couldn't. I let her approach, shuffling and awkward, my own body paralyzed with a mix of fear and morbid curiosity.

She tilted forward, face close to mine, and inhaled deeply.

But rather than attack, as I'd half-expected—or die again, as I'd half-wished—she simply turned away and shuffled down the alley, disappearing into the misty dark.

Instead of going after her, I did what I do best.

Ran like hell.

FOUR

GRAY

Normally I liked to take the long way home after dropping off Waldrich's van, strolling along the Bay's narrow beach as neighboring Seattle blinked awake. The scenic route was a three-mile walk from Waldrich's dock at the Hudson Marina to the house Sophie and I shared in South Bay, and a good way to unwind after a long shift.

But this morning, as sunrise turned the sky the same milky shade as Bean's eyes, I took the shortest route possible, zipping home to lock myself inside.

A hot shower washed off the blood and grime, but as I leaned against the countertop in our cheery red-and-yellow kitchen an hour later, Sophie's annoying fox clock ticking above the stove, guilt and confusion lingered.

What the hell happened out there?

I'd gone over it a hundred times, played it back from every angle... It didn't make sense. Necromancy wasn't something that just *happened*—it took years of dedicated study and a fondness for the darker arts a thousand miles south of my personal comfort zone.

And if I *had* done it...

No. I couldn't go down that road. That road meant living in fear. It meant running, starting over in a strange city, abandoning the people I cared about.

Again.

For the fourth time since I got home, I checked all the doors and windows in the house. I was pretty sure no one but Bean had seen me use magic tonight, but I wasn't taking any chances.

On my way back to the kitchen, I heard Sophie's keys in the front door.

"About time," I called out as she stepped inside and kicked off her silver platform heels. She was late getting home from her overnight shift at Illuminae, the fae club where she tended bar. "Rowdy night with the faeries?"

My familiar teasing brought me back to reality, grounding me. Suddenly the alley felt like a bad dream.

"Don't even ask." Joining me in the kitchen, Sophie dropped her bag on the table and flopped into a chair, her sequined micromini riding up her thighs. Her normally straight red hair was woven into intricate braids, each one pulsing with light that changed colors as I watched. Whorls of silver, blue, and teal danced across her bare shoulders like a living tattoo of the sea.

The fae loved their parlor tricks.

Sophie caught me staring and looked down at the

oceanic designs undulating across her freckled skin. "It'll wear off soon."

"As if you don't love to sparkle."

She shrugged, a cute smile lighting up her face. "Sparkle *is* my color."

I returned her smile. "All you need is a unicorn, and you're all set."

"If Kallayna thought it would bring in more business, she'd make it happen." Sophie slid her fingers into her hair, trying but failing to unravel the braids. "How was *your* night?"

I took the seat across from her and blew out a breath. Guilt and fear sat heavy on my shoulders, but I didn't want to get into it with her—not until I was certain what *it* was.

From a small wicker basket we kept on the table, I picked out one of the dozens of beach rocks Sophie had painted, a black palm-sized stone decorated with a red-and-purple mandala. On the other side, she'd written *just breathe* in glossy white script.

Rubbing my thumb over the smooth paint, I was so focused on *just breathing* that I'd forgotten my face looked like I'd gone six rounds with a sledgehammer.

Sophie gasped when she saw it. "What happened to *you*?"

I set the stone back in the basket and pulled my hair forward, hiding the messed-up part of my face. "Some guy jacked me on the last delivery."

"And?"

"And nothing." I waved away her concern. "Chased

25

him off."

Sophie reached across the table and grabbed my hand. Her eyes widened, then narrowed, scrutinizing me from beneath several layers of shimmery blue eyeshadow. "Gray Desario, you are completely full of shit."

"Nah." I slipped her grasp and headed to the sink to put the kettle on. "Only *half* full of shit. The other half is pure liquid sunshine."

Sophie grunted. "Doesn't feel like sunshine to me. It feels like magic."

Sophie could sense energies by touching people or objects—emotions, motivations, intentions, history, things like that. She'd always said it was like her intuition dusting for psychic fingerprints. The more intense or traumatic the situation, the stronger the vibe. It meant that all of our furniture came from Ikea—thrift store finds had too much history.

It also meant she was a human lie detector.

Still eyeing me warily, she pulled a deck of Tarot cards from her purse and began to shuffle. "Start talking."

I took our mugs out of the dish drainer and righted them on the counter, then rummaged through our well-stocked basket of teas. "Dreaming of Chamomile, Lavender Honey Sweetness, Chocolate Bliss, or Merry Mint?"

"How about a big mug of Stop Dodging the Damn Question?"

"We're fresh out of that. You're getting mint."

She sighed, cutting and reassembling her cards.

I let her stew. I still wasn't a hundred percent convinced

it'd actually happened. Hanging out with Sophie in our sunshiny kitchen, pouring hot water into the chipped blue mug she'd painted for my birthday last year, the whole magic scene started to feel like a hallucination. A trick of the mind brought on by the stress of being jumped, the fight, the proximity to vampires—yes, that had to be it. Their presence had always made me lightheaded—something about my blood reacting to the threat.

You did this to me, witch.

You.

You did this.

To me.

You.

"Gray? You okay?"

"Huh?"

"What's going on?" Sophie asked, her voice heavy with fresh worry. "Really?"

"I... Nothing."

The silence that fell between us was so complete, I could practically hear the tea steeping. The tension made my insides itch.

"Sophie, seriously. I'm cool." I grabbed our mugs and sat down across from her. "I'm just—"

"Full of shit, like I said." She rolled her eyes, but at least she was smiling again. "Where's Ronan?"

The sound of his name sent a shiver down my spine. The good kind.

"Haven't seen him in a few days."

"God, I hate when he does that," Sophie groaned. "Are

you planning to tell him about this?"

"No. And neither are you." The last thing I needed was an overprotective demon trailing me on my deliveries. It was bad enough he made me spar with him once a week, just to keep my reflexes and fighting skills sharp. If he saw me like this, I'd never hear the end of it.

"He'll find out," she said. "He always does."

"Not from you."

She blew across the top of her mug and arched a brow, steam curling up around her face. "Speaking of your sex life—"

"Nice transition, and no, we aren't speaking of it."

"Exactly my point." Sophie's eyes lingered on a cut above my eyebrow. "You do realize that you've been in more fights in the last month than you've gotten laid in, like, years?"

"Really? I'd totally forgotten about my pathetically lonely nights and desperately unfulfilled longings! Thank God my best friend is keeping track for me!" I nodded at the Tarot cards stacked between us, eager to get back on neutral ground. "Draw your card before I fall asleep. I'm beat."

"Classic Gray Desario redirect." Sophie smirked and pulled a card for herself, setting it face up between us.

Her smile vanished.

I glanced down at the card—Seven of Pentacles. The image showed an apprentice witch using a rusty nail to draw blood from a tree. Seven silver pentacles bloomed on otherwise barren branches.

I knew right away what it meant, and despite the fact that the tree looked eerily similar to the ones I'd seen in my magic place, this card was not about me.

"Sophie," I whispered, "you're practicing magic again." It wasn't a question—just the first thing that popped into my mind. As soon as the words were out, I knew they were spot on.

Using magic was dangerous. It left a signature, and if enough witches left enough signatures, it could create a hotspot—one of the primary ways hunters tracked us. How they'd *been* tracking us—for millennia. The last time they'd rallied a few decades back, they wiped out thousands of witches and drove the remaining covens and solitary practitioners underground.

These days, most witches were firmly in the broom closet, if they admitted their magical heritage at all. Sure, other witches and supernaturals could identify us, but humans? Hunters? No way. Not without the magic.

"I guess I have a confession," Sophie said.

"About the magic, or the fact that you've been keeping it secret?"

Crossing her arms over her chest, she met my gaze across the table, unwavering. "Both."

I felt it then—a crack in the once solid foundation of our friendship, just wide enough for a secret to slip inside.

Seven years ago, in this city of the lost and the damned, Sophie and I had found each other, young and scared, both looking for a safe place to anchor, a safe place to stash our secrets. It was our identity as witches—as magical outcasts

—that brought us together, made us instant friends and perfect roommates. Now, the thing that had so powerfully bound us was the very thing I wanted to shove into a box and lock away.

I'd always thought that's what she wanted, too.

"Hear me out," she said.

I sipped my tea, reining in my anger. "I'm listening."

"No, you're judging. That's not—"

"I'm *listening*, Sophie." Trying to, anyway, which was all I could promise.

She nodded and picked up her mug, eyeing me over the rim. Then, in a soft voice laced with guilt, "I've been meeting with Bay Coven."

"With… I don't… Wow." *Damn it.* I knew she was friends with some of the Bay Coven witches—a few of them regularly hung out at Illuminae, and I'd even gone with Sophie once to a potluck dinner at the leader Norah's house —but I had no idea she was actually *involved* with the local underground.

Practicing magic.

And keeping it from me.

"Why?" I struggled to keep the sting of betrayal from my voice.

"They need me. The witches are strong, but Norah keeps everyone on a leash. If there were more of us, we could—"

"Us?" My head was spinning. I didn't even know Sophie *wanted* to do magic again, let alone with other people. "Where is this coming from?"

Sophie shrugged, her rainbow braids lighting up as they brushed her shoulders. "I want to know who I am, Gray. What I can do."

"What you can do is get yourself killed."

"We're witches," she said plainly. "Hiding our magic doesn't change that."

"No, it just makes it a hell of a lot harder for the hunters to find us."

"You're doing that thing," she said, pointing at my chest. "Putting on your tough bitch act, hoping you can fake it till you make it."

"Whatever it takes."

"Stop shutting me out."

"I'm not the one keeping secrets."

"Bullshit." Sophie grabbed my hand again, her thumb skating gently across my scraped palm. "This wasn't some random fight. There's something inside you, Gray. I can feel it. What happened?"

Heat flickered in my gut, embers from a fire not quite finished burning. I closed my eyes and sucked in a cool breath, willing the feeling to settle. To go away.

"Whatever it is," she said, "you can trust me. We'll deal with it together."

I opened my eyes and met her kind gaze, but I still couldn't bring myself to confess.

Necromancy? No one fucked with that shit. And no matter how desperately Sophie wanted me to open up, I wouldn't lay that on her. She was one of the good ones. If she was smart, she'd turn me in to the Fae Council—not because she was disloyal, but because those were the rules we lived by. The ones that kept our supernatural communities secret and safe.

Putting her in that position, well... Maybe one day it would come down to friendship or morals.

And maybe I didn't want to see which one she'd choose.

I pulled away, wrapping my hands around my mug to keep from fidgeting. "How long have you been using magic?"

She glared at me a moment longer, then relented. "A few weeks. A month? I'm sorry I didn't tell you sooner. I wanted to feel it out first."

"With the coven?"

"Yeah." Sophie's smile brightened. "Haley—you remember her from the potluck, right? She's teaching me blood magic and helping me reconnect with my earth energy. It's amazing, Gray. It's—"

"Dangerous and stupid. The more witches using magic together, the greater the risk."

She frowned. "Togetherness is the whole point. If and when the time comes, we shouldn't have to fight alone."

"We shouldn't have to fight at all. *That's* the whole point. The point of not using magic."

"Is that so?" Shaking her head, she glared at my chest as if she could see the darkness swirling there. "It's destroying you. The more you hold back, the more you repress and deny your true nature, the worse—"

"Sophie? Stop. Seriously. I said I'm fine."

True nature? No way. This morning was a freak accident, that's all. It wouldn't happen again. Period.

I whipped the next card off the top of the Tarot deck and tossed it down in front of me, hoping for a Three of Cups, maybe The Sun, something bright and cheerful to chase away the gloom of this conversation.

But… nope.

On the face of the card, a mother stepped on a small child as he tried to climb back into her pregnant womb. Both figures had sleek, ebony bodies, but their heads were bare skulls, elongated like wild horses. A doomed ship sank into the depths of the oil-black sea behind them.

Trump thirteen. The Death card.

"See? See!" Sophie pointed at my chest again, her mouth stretching into a smug grin. "You are *so* not fine. Even the universe agrees."

"The universe is obviously drunk." I picked up the card for a closer look, suppressing a shiver.

Tarot wasn't magic—it was intuitive. The moment I drew a card, no matter how distracted I was, I always got an immediate message.

But that was just it—there was no message now.

I sensed nothing. Oblivion. A great yawning blankness that stretched on endlessly, devoid of warmth or hope.

Sophie's eyes widened. "Gray, you're freaking me out here. What's wrong? What are you sensing?"

"Nothing. It just means… a transition." I tossed the card back onto the pile, reverting to the Death card's generic book definition. "Big shakeup. It's probably about my job. I need to figure something else out—something safer. Maybe even something with health insurance and profit-sharing and, I don't know, other benefits…"

I was babbling, but Sophie let it slide.

"Being Waldrich's delivery girl *is* taking a toll on you," she said. "That's something else the universe and I agree on. Pretty sure Ronan does, too."

"All three of you are overprotective." I stood up and stretched my arms over my head, forcing a yawn. I had to get out of there, away from the card and the lingering tension. "I need to crash. See you for dinner? Maybe we could try the new Thai place on Fourteenth Street? I got paid today—my treat."

It was my peace offering, and I held my breath, waiting for Sophie to take it.

Please say yes…

"I can't tonight." She glanced at the fox clock, her shoulders slumping. "Everyone's meeting at Norah's before my shift."

A grumpy sigh escaped my lips.

"Instead of huffing and puffing," she said, "why don't you join me? I know they'd love to see you there. And maybe they can help you figure out—"

"I don't need their help."

"Fine, okay, you don't need anyone's help—you've made that abundantly clear. But maybe… Maybe I need yours." Her next words were no more than a whisper. "Please, Gray. Something's going on with them. I can't put my finger on it, but I—"

"Sophie, it's not—"

"God, you're so stubborn!" Her multi-colored hair pulsed brighter, her skin turning pink beneath the freckles. "Will you at least *think* about coming before you shoot me down?"

I didn't *have* to think about it. Any desire I'd had to belong to something bigger, to learn about my origins and my magic, to be a witch... That was taken from me nine years ago, burnt to ash in a house 3,000 miles from here.

My life in Blackmoon Bay was far from perfect. But it was just that—a life. A chance at normalcy—at least at what passed for a closeted witch's normalcy—and I wasn't about to wreck it by delving back into the very thing that had nearly destroyed me.

Not even for Sophie.

The incident in the alley was a wake-up call. Didn't matter how comforting and familiar my magic place had felt, or how much I'd welcomed the touch of that warm, blue light. I needed to stick to the plan and stay far away from all things magical.

Permanently.

"Sure, Soph." The lie left a bitter taste on my tongue even as it brought a smile to Sophie's face. "I'll sleep on it."

"Thank you, thank you, thank you! You're the best!" She stood up from the chair and came around to my side of the table, squishing me in a strawberry-scented hug.

The stack of cards slid across the table, burying Death from view. But I still felt its icy finger trailing down my spine, teasing the darkness inside me to life.

FIVE

GRAY

As far as I was concerned, Death could go to hell.

I'd slept the day away, and now that the moon had risen again, I had work to do.

Starting with Bean.

My mind kept insisting on the most logical explanation —that it simply hadn't happened. She'd hit her head but hadn't actually died. She'd passed out, and after my little trip down magical memory lane, she'd woken up and staggered on home.

Not bad as far as theories went. If I couldn't locate her in the warehouse district or pick up any murmurings of wandering undead teenagers, logic would win out, and I could close the book on the whole ordeal.

And if it *had* happened? If she was out there somewhere in half-resurrected form? I needed to find her. She was the key to unlocking the mystery of this strange, dark power inside me. And unlocking that mystery was the only way to shut it down—preferably before anyone else found out about it.

Before anyone else got hurt.

Back at the scene of the crime, blood stained the alley, a sick reminder that I hadn't imagined the fight. The sound of her head hitting the pavement echoed in my memory.

Grape jelly grape…

"Miss Desario. I might have guessed you had something to do with this."

I jumped at the voice, though I recognized the delicious British accent immediately.

Slowly I turned to face him, tightly gripping my wooden stake.

Darius Beaumont was beautiful. Elegant, tall, and lean, he was dressed in an impeccably tailored black suit that probably cost more than I made in a year. Wavy, chin-length brown hair and a perfectly stubbled jaw stood out starkly against a crisp white dress shirt, the top two buttons undone.

His golden-honey eyes sparked with possibility.

Or hunger.

Dangerous? You bet. But good God, he was sexy. The liquid caress of his voice, the intensity in his eyes, the sheer power locked away in those lean muscles…

In a blur of movement, he tore the stake from my hand and threw it against the bricks so hard it splintered into dozens of useless pieces.

"Now that we've taken care of that nasty business," he said calmly, "care to explain the rest?"

I lowered my eyes in a sign of respect, but I didn't back away or bow or submit to him in any way. Technically, vampires weren't allowed to feed on us without consent, but the Council tended to look the other way for all but the most heinous infractions. My policy with vamps was simple: don't give them a reason to infract.

"Explain?" I asked.

"Your involvement in this." He stepped toward me, looming so close that if he were human, I would've felt his breath on my cheeks. His imposing shadow fell across my face, making me blink as I met his gaze.

Despite the fact that he could end my life with a single touch, everything about him made my mouth water—one of the many reasons I usually avoided him.

"What makes you think I was involved?" I asked.

"Just after closing this morning, I emerged to find my delivery abandoned here and an alley full of human blood. Your scent was..." Darius picked up a lock of my hair and pressed it to his lips, closing his eyes. "Everywhere."

He knows my scent?

A shiver crept down my back, but I couldn't tell whether the idea was terrifying... or a complete turn-on. "Yeah, I... Sorry about your delivery. I got... distracted."

"I see." Darius released my hair. With a light, cool touch, he traced my bruised cheekbone, his eyes dimming. "And this... *distraction*. Was he responsible for this?"

God, I love the way he's touching me...

The erotic caress of a vampire was a dangerous lure. Witches could defend against the power of mental influence vamps used on humans, but it took a lot of energy—something I was running severely low on. And the longer I stared at his mouth, at the way his lips curved at the edges, hinting at a soft smile behind his cool exterior, the more I wanted to give in.

But that was a *terrible* idea.

"To be fair," I said, dragging my gaze away from his lips, "you should see the other guy."

"I suppose that's his blood all over my alley?"

I nodded, toeing the pavement with my boot. "His teeth are around here somewhere, too. Unless he came back for them."

A cool smirk slid across his face. "Quite the little brawler, aren't you?"

I shrugged and forced a confident smile. "Well, nice seeing you again, Mr. Beaumont. I should probably let you get back to your guests."

"Probably." Darius's fingers trailed down from my face to my neck, his touch turning icy as it slid over my pulse points. "Is that all you have to say on the matter, then?"

I nodded, hoping he couldn't sense the tremble inside me.

"Lying to me is unwise, necromancer."

Necromancer...

More than his dangerous touch, the word made me stiffen. Every hair on my neck stood on end.

"Excluding you," he said calmly, his smile vanishing, "two humans bled in my alley this morning. One of them died. Moments later, I sensed her rise. Explain."

My heart sunk.

My so-called logical theory was falling apart. Vampires could sense human life force—it's how they figured out who was worth eating, and who had already gone cold. So if he sensed Bean die, and then rise...

You did this to me, witch...

"You're right—there's more," I admitted. "I... I can't explain it. I don't know..." Tears pricked my eyes. In a whisper only a vampire could hear, I said, "Nothing like that ever happened before. I swear. I—"

"*Miss Desario.*" The warning tone in Darius's voice stopped me cold. I swallowed hard and met his gaze, realizing how weak I must look. Like a scared little girl. Like prey.

His eyes blazed suddenly with red-hot desire. If Darius had been a younger vampire, one with less control over his predatory instincts, I'd already be dead.

He wanted me to know it. And he was giving me about five seconds to do something about it.

I hated the bullshit power games, but not as much as I'd hate being dead.

With all the confidence I could muster, I gritted my teeth, jerking free of his hold. "Message received, *vampire*. Back off."

After a beat, Darius stepped backward and turned away from me, putting some much-needed distance between my throat and his fangs.

Get your shit together, Desario.

Standing up straight again, I took a deep breath and

forced the tremble out of my limbs. Scared and snackable? Definitely not a good look for me.

"Does the coven know about your… extracurricular activities?" Darius asked, still facing the wall.

As if I'd tell those witches anything.

"No one knows. *I* didn't even know I had that kind of juice until last night."

"Juice?" At this he turned around, his eyes still smoldering but slightly less terrifying. "If that was witchcraft, it's not a magic I've ever encountered among your people."

So I'm not just any old freak. I'm a super *freak! Awesome.*

"Okay, let's assume you're right," I said, clinging to the possibility that the darkness hadn't come from me after all. "If it wasn't my witchcraft, what was it?"

"Now *that* is the question, yes?" Darius considered me, his lips twisting into a calculating smile. I could practically hear the gears turning in his head, all the possibilities playing out in his hyper-logical mind. "A witch with a new toy. Imagine if you also had my strength? Speed? Immortality? Ah, the things we could achieve."

Even if I wanted to be an immortal, superstrong bloodsucker—and that was a big if—I wouldn't take the risk.

Witches were biologically human, so turning us vamp required the usual blood swap—he'd drink mine, I'd drink his. But we also had the added complication of magic in our blood, whether we used it or not. Unfortunately, no one knew how vampire blood affected us in the long term.

Because in the short term? No witch had ever survived the change.

"Perhaps we can come to an arrangement," Darius said.

"Thank you for the invitation, but that's a hard pass."

"Regardless…" The hunger in his voice sounded especially menacing out here in the alley, where no one was around to hear me scream. "The invitation remains."

"Noted."

"Come." Darius opened the door to the service entrance and gestured for me to enter ahead of him. "It seems we have some things to discuss."

I took a step backward and raised my hands. "Again, thanks for the invitation, but I—"

"Apologies for giving you the wrong impression, love." Darius clamped a hand over my shoulder, eyes blazing once again. "But *that* was not an invitation."

SIX

GRAY

For creatures of the night, October in the Pacific Northwest usually meant shorter days and more time outdoors. Yet an hour after sunset, Black Ruby was already packed with vampires.

The windowless club was an elevator ride two stories down from street level, dimly lit and cool as a cave. With its exposed brick interior, wooden booths, and mahogany bar, it felt less like a sleek vampire hangout and more like a friendly neighborhood pub—though in my opinion, the things that went on here were anything but friendly.

Sitting on a high-backed stool at the bar, I scoped out the room. Most of the fang-bangers were huddled in dark booths with their blood slaves—some so pale and emaciated it was hard to tell if they were still human. The whole scene turned my stomach, but it wasn't surprising. The port city of Blackmoon Bay was a hub for runaways and transients—easy pickings for the powerful vamps.

Hell, I'd been there myself. Guess it was just dumb luck that when I'd washed up on these shores at eighteen, barely alive after two years on the run, I'd managed to avoid the vamp welcoming committee.

I'd gotten Ronan instead.

Calla would've called that a far worse fate, but then, she'd never trusted demons.

Darius set a cocktail napkin on the bar in front of me, bringing my attention back to the present. "Allow me to buy you a drink."

"Is that an invitation or a demand?"

Darius's golden eyes glinted with amusement. "That depends on whether you'll tell me what you'd like, or force me to choose for you."

I leaned forward across the bar and lowered my voice. "What exactly are we discussing tonight, Mr. Beaumont?"

"Darius. I insist."

"Yeah, I'm starting to realize that's a thing with you, *Darius*."

His eyebrow quirked, but the vampire didn't answer my question—just grabbed a glass from the rack above the bar and poured me a straight shot of Jameson.

He was making me sweat. Fine. As long as he didn't make me bleed, I could wait him out.

I downed the drink, enjoying the burn.

Darius poured me another, then glanced toward the entrance, where a group of particularly menacing vampires had just emerged from the elevator. *Rich* menacing vampires.

He cursed under his breath.

"Problem?" I asked.

"Only in keeping my schedule sorted. If you'll excuse me a moment, I've got a meeting."

"Don't let me stop you."

"I won't be more than twenty minutes." Darius shot me a warning glare. "Don't leave, Gray."

I wasn't sure I had a choice.

"Fine. But if you're not back in twenty, I'm out." I shrugged and left him to it, nursing my second drink and trying to gather my thoughts.

Damn. The vamp had something on me now. Something major. Not that he'd use it—around here, the freaks might not like each other, but we damn well kept each other's secrets. Our survival depended on it. Whether it was human cops poking too closely around our haunts or outside supernaturals looking to take over new territory, none of us wanted to bring scrutiny to the Bay.

Still... I didn't like the fact that knowledge about what I'd done was out there. Vampires were immortal, but that didn't mean they couldn't be tortured.

Everyone had a breaking point, and everyone had a price.

"Hello, sexy."

I turned toward the smarmy voice just as the vamp it belonged to slithered onto the chair on my right. A muscle-bound blond with a nasty scar cutting down his cheek, he eyed me with obvious hunger, making my skin crawl.

I opened my mouth to tell him I was with someone else

—anyone else—when a second vamp took the chair on my left. This one was a skinny, emo-looking dude with greasy black hair and way too many facial piercings.

Scarface wrapped a hand around my thigh and leaned in close. "I've never tasted witch before."

His gray eyes glinted with ice, colder and more deadly than the eyes of any vamp I'd ever tangled with. It was a struggle not to cower or turn away, but showing weakness now would activate his predatory instincts faster than an outright threat.

Darius was nowhere in sight.

I was stuck.

"How about joining us for a little fun tonight?" Emo asked.

"You'll like it," Scarface said.

"No thanks," I said, calm but firm. "I'm waiting for someone."

"Well, I guess that dude's gonna have to learn to live with disappointment." Scarface grabbed my arm, forcing me out of the chair. "Remember where you are and don't make a fuckin' scene."

Emo vamp closed in on my other side, digging his fingers into the flesh on my upper arm.

Panic surged, my mouth going dry. Where the hell was Darius? And worse—what if this was totally acceptable behavior at Black Ruby? Letting the customers get a little carryout for the road?

My skin prickled, and low in my belly, something dark and strange sparked to life. Ignited. Burned.

Don't let them take you, a voice inside me warned. *Kill them...*

"Let me go." I tried to jerk free, but even with the magic roiling inside me, I wasn't strong enough—especially now that Darius had destroyed my stake.

"Shut up." Emo clamped a hand around my neck, squeezing so hard it was a struggle to breathe. They dragged me away from the bar and into the back of the club, shoving me down a dimly lit hallway of what looked to be offices and storage rooms. But halfway down, Darius stepped out from behind one of the doors, his eyes blazing.

Clearly, carryout was not Black Ruby policy.

I'd never been so happy to see a vampire in my life.

"Out of the way, Beaumont," Scarface said with a sneer. "This bitch is—"

"Not on the menu, Mr. Hollis." Darius stepped into the fray and pushed me behind him, blocking me from their reach. Emo backed off immediately, but Scarface—Hollis—let out a low growl, the air around him crackling with electric tension. He and Darius were about the same height, but while Darius was lean and lithe, Hollis was a tank.

Still, my money was on the Brit.

"Are you alright, Miss Desario?" Darius asked over his shoulder, not taking his eyes off Hollis and Emo.

"I'm fine," I said. My arm muscles throbbed from the rough handling, and my neck would definitely be sporting finger-shaped bruises tomorrow, but I was still in one piece.

"Your little pet could use a lesson in manners," Hollis

said. "Teasing us like she did." His threatening glare sent a chill down my spine.

God, I really hoped I'd never meet *him* alone in a dark alley. Something told me he wouldn't soon forget the witch who'd refused his so-called invitation.

Darius continued to stare him down, the picture of grace and elegance. Despite his cool demeanor, raw power emanated from his body, sending a different kind of chill down my spine.

"I presume Miss Desario has not given her consent to this arrangement," he said. "Continuing on your present course could place you in a precarious legal position, could it not?"

"This is bullshit," Emo said.

"If you'd like another opinion, Mr. Weston," Darius said, "I'd be happy to place a call to the Council and let them sort it out."

I wasn't sure what kind of legal trouble they could possibly get into—everyone knew the Council wouldn't bother with something as trivial as vamps taking a witch for their blood slave, even if it *was* against the rules. But Black Ruby was Darius's club, the warehouse district Darius's territory. Council or not, he had every right to intervene.

"I'm outta here." Emo shook his head, slinking off toward a stairwell exit at the end of the hall. "You're on your own with this bitch, Hollis."

"Excellent. Now that we've got that sorted..." Darius stepped back and took my hand, standing right at my side as he glared at the remaining vampire, the challenge in his eyes as terrifying as it was thrilling.

I sucked in a breath. I wasn't totally up on vampire hierarchies and politics, but I was pretty sure Darius's actions indicated that I was under his protection. If that were true, no other vamp could touch me without serious consequences.

Judging from the new fury flickering in Hollis's eyes, my assessment was correct.

"You sure you want to do this, *brother*?" Hollis asked.

"It's already done."

"Since when do you side with witch whores?"

Anger flared in Darius's eyes, but other than a slight tick in his jaw and a quick squeeze of my hand, he didn't move a muscle. He remained stone-cold silent for so long I was beginning to think he might just implode.

But then he raised his chin, his coiled muscles emanating raw power as he stared Hollis down. "I'm not your brother, vampire. You'd be wise to remember that."

"Oh, I will." With no move left to play, Hollis pushed past us, knocking against my shoulder on his way out. Pinning me for just a moment with that icy, terrifying stare, he leaned in close and whispered, "I remember *everything*."

SEVEN

DARIUS

The challenge was over almost as quickly as it'd begun, but I'd be a fool to think I'd seen the last of Clayton Hollis. Tonight's victory would certainly cost me.

The question was how much? And when would he come to collect?

Setting aside further speculation for now, I led Gray back to the bar, where she immediately reclaimed her stool and polished off the drink she'd left.

After everything I'd just witnessed, I couldn't blame her.

Hollis and Weston. Bloody hell, Ronan is going to stake me for this.

"I'm beginning to understand how the events of last night transpired, little brawler." I ducked behind the bar and rummaged for a clean dishtowel, filling it with crushed ice. "Tell me something. Do you always pick fights in which you're seriously outclassed?"

Gray laughed, a sound so warm and soft it melted the

last of my lingering tension. "Only on the weekends, apparently."

"Here. This should help." I handed her the ice pack, wishing I could do more to ease the angry red welts on her skin—not to mention the scrapes and bruises she'd collected last night.

How could someone so small cause so much trouble?

"Thanks." She blew out a breath, pressing the towel to the back of her neck. "I'm sorry you had to get involved."

"I'm the one who's sorry, love." I grabbed the bottle of Jameson and topped off her drink. "If I'd known Hollis and Weston were here, I wouldn't have left you alone. Most vampires know better than to break the rules in my club."

"Not Scarface and Emo, though."

"No." I smiled at the fitting appellations. "They're what I call historically problematic vampires."

Gray wrapped both hands around her glass, staring so deeply into the amber liquid I thought she might fall in.

After a long moment, she finally asked, "Should I be worried about them trying to retaliate?"

I considered her question. Would they *try* to retaliate? Highly likely. Should she be worried about it? Absolutely not. As far as Hollis, Weston, and any other Bay vampires were concerned, Gray was now untouchable. If they so much as looked at her, my associates and I would destroy them, swiftly and completely.

Still, she'd just been assaulted in my club. My assurances probably wouldn't offer much comfort.

"I'll ring Emilio Alvarez tonight," I said instead. "I'll ask him to assign someone to keep tabs on them for a bit."

"Alvarez... the wolf cop?"

"Detective, actually. You're not acquainted?"

"Just by name. Ronan says he's good people, though."

I nodded. Decades ago, when I was still practicing law and he was up-and-coming on the police force, we used to consult together on criminal cases.

More recently—seven years ago, to be precise—Detective Alvarez and I had come together with Ronan and another demon on a more important matter:

The arrival of an extremely powerful young witch in Blackmoon Bay.

Thinking about that night still made me ill. Gray had been so lost, so broken. Not even old enough to drink legally, she'd turned up under a tarp in one of Waldrich's old boats, soaked through from the rain, malnourished, and badly wounded. Even with the ensuing round-the-clock care we'd provided, she'd drifted in and out of consciousness for weeks.

Of the four of us who'd brought her back from the precipice of death, Ronan was the only one she seemed to remember now. It made perfect sense—he'd stayed with her long after her wounds had healed, helping her make a home here in the Bay. The rest of us had agreed to keep watch from a distance until she was ready to bring us back into her life on her own terms.

It wasn't the sort of thing one brought up in casual

conversation. But it still stung to look into the depths of her blue eyes and not find so much as a spark of recognition.

"We're in good hands," I assured her now. "Detective Alvarez is the best in the business."

With fresh tears glittering in her eyes, Gray reached across the bar and took my hand, her touch tentative but warm. Genuine. "Thank you, Darius. This weekend has been… insane, to say the least."

Words failed me.

Not one hour ago, I'd forced Gray to accompany me into Black Ruby when she'd clearly wanted to leave. I'd left her alone in a bar full of vampires, where she'd been assaulted and nearly kidnapped by two of the worst of our kind.

She should despise me.

Yet here she was, offering me genuine gratitude.

I was finally beginning to understand why Ronan had always believed she was so special. That the day would come when she'd need—and deserve—our loyalty and protection.

He'd never told us what, if anything, he'd known about her origins, or how she'd come into our lives on that storm-tossed night, or why he'd been so certain she'd ultimately need us in her corner—only that he *was* certain. The young witch had a purpose, he'd insisted. A destiny larger and more important than any of us.

Like the others, I'd given him my allegiance simply because he'd asked, though his ominous words had felt too much like a prophecy for my liking—notoriously unreliable things, in my experience, and prone to gross errors in translation.

But last night, just outside Black Ruby, our mysterious little witch had called upon her dormant magic and resurrected a dead child.

And though a single-minded vampire like Hollis may not have sensed it, that same magic had surged again tonight, just before they'd taken her. It's what had called me out of my meeting, alerting me to the fact that something was *very* wrong.

Perhaps I needed to rethink my stance on prophecies.

Covering her hand with mine, I looked into Gray's eyes and frowned, wishing I truly *could* protect her, that I could promise her that the fights she'd endured this weekend were the very last of her troubles.

Unfortunately, something told me that the darkness for Gray—for all of us—was only beginning.

EIGHT

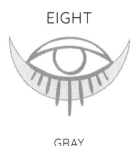

GRAY

"We need to talk about last night, Gray."

The vampire fixed his honey-eyed gaze on me, and the warmth that had risen between us suddenly evaporated.

After everything that'd happened, I'd almost forgotten the real reason I was here tonight—why he'd all but dragged me inside Black Ruby.

"It doesn't matter." I pulled away from his touch and repositioned my ice pack. "It's in the past. Nothing I can do but move forward."

"Gray, I don't think that's—"

"Could I get some water?"

That muscle in Darius's jaw ticked, but he filled a glass for me and set it on the bar, watching me with a calm detachment that told me he was in no hurry.

Immortal beings rarely ever were.

"You claim it was your first time, yes?" he asked.

"First time?"

"Bringing someone back from the—"

"Don't say the D-word."

"Alright." He folded his arms across his chest and leaned back against the shelving behind him, his muscular forearms flexing. "First time calling on your mag—"

"Don't say the M-word, either." I ditched my ice pack and grabbed the glass, chugging down half the water in a few swift gulps. "You said it yourself—it wasn't witchcraft."

"No, I said I'd never encountered anything like it among your people. That leaves room for a whole host of other possibilities." His eyes never left mine as he waited for my response.

It felt like being dissected, and no matter how hard I tried, I just couldn't hold up under the scrutiny.

"Her name was Bean," I said softly, my throat tightening. "She hit her head, and she just…" I squeezed my eyes shut and pinched the bridge of my nose, forcing the tears to stay put. What was done was done. I could no more bring her back than I could my mother, and I'd already cried an ocean of tears for her. "Something took over inside me. I doubt I could do it again, even if I had to."

Darius watched me for a long time, his expression neutral, his body eerily still. His mind was obviously churning, but I had no idea what he was thinking.

All I knew was that necromancy was highly illegal, punishable by death. Darius was required to report me, or he risked imprisonment as an accessory.

And fae prisons? No joke.

"We need to figure precisely out what happened." Darius glanced around the bar, quickly surveying his customers before returning his gaze to me. In a soft but determined voice, he said, "But I assure you—what transpired last night shall remain between us until and unless you deem otherwise. You have my word."

"Your word." Trying to bite back my sarcasm, I said, "And in exchange for the eternal silence of a vampire?"

"Hmm. To be determined." That slow, unnerving smile spread across his face again. "Unless you'd like to come home with me tonight, settle our affairs the old-fashioned way."

"A duel?"

Darius laughed, the sound as deep and warm as his golden-honey eyes. "Of a sort, Miss Desario."

He stretched my name into a sensuous whisper that slipped across my skin, leaving goosebumps in its wake.

I couldn't deny being curious about sex with a vampire —especially a powerful, commanding vampire like Darius. After all, they were strong, never ran out of breath, prided themselves on perfection, and most had had hundreds of years to hone their techniques.

But it was a rare vamp who invited you into his bed without strings attached.

Maybe even handcuffs, too…

The fantasy heated up my insides, but as I looked around at the other humans in the club, my veins filled with ice. Letting him take me like that… Leaving myself vulnerable and helpless, enslaved by the intoxicating plea-sure of his every touch...

"Interesting," he said playfully, and my gaze snapped to attention, my cheeks burning.

"What's interesting?"

Darius leaned forward, his fingers brushing my face, dipping down to the pulse point on my neck. "Your heart rate has gone a bit erratic."

"Because you're making me nervous," I whispered, but I didn't flinch or pull away as he continued to stroke my skin. Truth was, I liked his touch. His smile. His soothing, seductive voice.

"I don't think it's nerves, love." He traced a finger across my collarbone, and a full-bodied shiver rolled through me.

I closed my eyes and slipped into that fantasy again, Darius leading me into his wine-dark bedroom, blind-folding me with a silk tie...

Oh my God, what the hell is wrong *with me?*

I finally pulled back and opened my eyes, severing the connection before my thoughts got any crazier. Sophie was right—it'd been way too long since I'd had sex, and now my libido was getting all amped up at the first sign of a cute guy.

A *really* cute guy.

More like a really cute, really dangerous bloodsucker who knows your secrets, idiot.

Reaching for my water again, I sucked down the rest and wiped my mouth on the back of my hand. "Stop trying to blackmail your way into my bed."

"Technically I'm trying to blackmail *your* way into *my* bed." Laughing, Darius finally backed off. But like the momentary spark between us, his smile faded fast. "You will owe me a debt, then."

I slumped forward on the stool, the reality of my situation weighing heavy as I considered his offer. Accepting it meant three things.

One, I'd be spared an inquiry—and possibly charges and imprisonment, or execution, or other psychological torments—from the Council.

Two, I'd be in his debt, and vampires never forgave their debts.

And three, I could no longer deny what I'd done.

Regret wrapped itself around my heart and squeezed. Whoever Bean was before she'd crossed my path, whoever she might've become, I'd doomed her to an eternity as a monster.

I set down my empty water glass and scrutinized the vampire behind the bar.

How is it that I walked in here a stranger, and now I'm making a blood promise?

No matter. Time was up, and I was ready.

Maybe I was thankful.

Maybe I was just looking for absolution.

I pushed up my sleeve and stretched my arm across the bar. "Do it."

"So quickly?" His eyes sparkled with amusement and a hint of raw desire that went well beyond our earlier jokes.

With the lightest touch, he caressed the pale skin of my inner arm.

But the bite never came.

"What are you waiting for?" I asked.

"Gray. As tempting as you are..." Darius shook his head, still caressing my skin. "This isn't necessary. I already gave you my word."

A blood oath without the bite to seal the deal? No way. Darius may have helped me tonight—and been surprisingly sweet in the process—but I still didn't really know him.

Whatever was going on with me, I needed to stay focused on figuring it out and shutting it down. Looking over my shoulder every five minutes, constantly wondering whether—or *when*—my new vampire friend would stab me in the back? That was a distraction I couldn't afford.

The blood oath would ensure we both kept our end of the bargain—his silence for my future favor.

"Now it's my turn to insist." I thrust my arm closer to his mouth. "I'm serious, D. I'm not leaving until you do it."

Darius let out a low chuckle. "D? Skipping the formalities now, are we?"

"Hey, we're doing some serious bonding tonight. Fighting off historically problematic vampires, sharing a secret... The least you could do is let me give you a nickname."

His lips quirked, rewarding me with another picture-perfect smile.

"Very well, little brawler." He took my arm in both

hands, drawing it close to his lips. Meeting my eyes across the bar, he said, "You're certain?"

"I'm certain."

He pressed his lips to my wrist, firm and cool. I felt the velvet touch of his tongue, then a searing pain as his fangs broke the skin.

In an instant that pain turned to pure pleasure as Darius began to suck.

A warmth that had nothing to do with the whiskey I'd polished off spread up my arm, across my shoulders, and down my back, making me tingle all over.

I was mesmerized, unable to look away as Darius fed on my blood. It was a testament to his self-control that he stopped when he did. We both knew that if he had decided to drain me, there wasn't a damn thing I could've done about it. Hell, it had felt so good, I wouldn't have even tried to stop him.

"Exquisite." Darius finally pulled back and met my gaze, his lips red with blood—*my* blood. For a moment he looked as delirious as I felt.

"All set?" I asked, breaking the spell.

Nodding, Darius swiped his thumb across his mouth, then licked it, savoring every last drop. We were blood bound to each other now—a mutual promise sealed with a bite. Greater vampires like Darius followed the old customs; if he reneged, his life would be forfeit.

And if I reneged, he had my consent—and the Council's —to hunt me. To feed on me at will.

Again, images flooded my mind, raw and unbidden. My

nude body, glistening and pale against his dark, silky sheets. My legs spread for him, trembling, desperate for the press of his cool, sensuous mouth on my thigh...

I grabbed the edge of the bar, forcing myself to take slow, even breaths until my heart rate returned to normal. The wounds on my wrist—two tiny, ruby-red puncture marks—had already begun to heal.

Vampires sure knew how to clean up their messes.

Apparently sated, Darius propped his elbows on the bar, resting his chin in his hands. "Counsel from a friend?"

I pushed my sleeve back down and shook off the last of my lingering fantasies, forcing out a laugh. "Is that what we are? Friends?"

"Hey. There's no going back now. You gave me a nickname."

"Not to mention the fact that you've tasted me."

"Yes, there is that." Eyes turning serious, Darius leaned forward, his lips brushing the shell of my ear. "Get it under control, Miss Desario."

I knew he didn't mean my dirty little thoughts. Darius was talking about something much darker, something much more dangerous.

Sound advice. Advice I had every intention of following. But how could I control something I didn't even understand?

Sophie thought the coven could protect us—strength in numbers—and maybe that was true. But even if I could trust them with this secret, how long would they be able to keep me safe? And how could I be sure I wouldn't hurt *them*? Or Sophie? God, she was my closest friend. My sister, as far as I was concerned. If anything happened to her…

I shook my head to clear the morbid thoughts, then gestured for Darius to pour me another shot of Jameson. Water wasn't cutting it.

This time he left me the bottle.

I laughed sourly. "Is this going on my tab, too?"

"Put it on mine," a deep, gravelly voice rumbled behind me.

I didn't have to turn around to identify the man who'd spoken. This time, unlike with the vampire, the hot pulse of desire between my thighs was as familiar and predictable as the rain in Blackmoon Bay.

As a witch, I could detect other supernaturals based on cues in my body. Vampires made me a little lightheaded. Encountering fae was like being in free fall—a swooping stomach, a strange giddiness in my chest. I had to see a shifter to pick them out—they moved with an instinctual, animalistic grace that was hard to miss if you knew what to watch for. Demons had a fiery scent—smoke and ash, matches, incense, sometimes a chemical kind of burning I could feel in the back of my throat, depending on the demon's particular makeup.

The man standing behind me? My body responded to his presence in a way that had nothing to do with his mysterious demon fire.

A slow smile spread across my face. I'd missed him a lot more than I wanted to admit. "Welcome back, Ronan."

NINE

GRAY

Ronan took the adjacent stool, enveloping me in his cloves-and-campfire scent. I tried not to shiver as his shoulder brushed against mine.

Neither of us made a move to look at each other.

"Desario." Cocking his head toward me, he said, "What's a nice girl like you doing in a blood-sucker dive like this?"

"Looking for my future ex-husband, obviously."

"I brought stakes." Ronan slid a protective arm over the high back of my stool and leaned in, warm breath tickling my ear. "Say the word. I'll save you the trouble of a messy divorce right now."

I rolled my eyes and called to Darius, who'd been watching us with the cool detachment I now realized he could turn on and off like a tap. "Bartender? This boy needs a drink before he hurts himself."

Darius set a cocktail napkin and glass in front of Ronan

and poured a shot from my bottle, nodding a brief acknowl-edgment. Something dark passed between them, but I knew better than to ask about it.

For reasons I couldn't begin to understand, most vampires kept a safe distance from Ronan. Darius didn't though. I wouldn't call them friends—their relationship was antagonistic at best—but something in their shared past had bound them together, cementing their loyalty long before my time in the Bay.

Secrets? You bet. That was something we *all* had in common.

Ronan picked up his glass, turning toward me as he downed the drink. His knees brushed my leg, and that warm, soft spot between my thighs throbbed again.

I felt my body heating up under his gaze and finally turned to face him.

Mistake.

I'd forgotten about the state of my face and neck.

"Before you freak out," I said, watching his hazel-green eyes turn completely black, "I'm totally fine."

Ronan didn't say a word.

I slid my hand over his knee. "It looks a lot worse than it is."

With a gentle touch that belied the demonic rage in his eyes, he traced his thumb along my eyebrow, down my temple, and across my cheek, ghosting over the cuts and scrapes. My heart jackhammered in my chest, but Ronan's face was grim, his jaw tight.

I shrugged away from his touch and turned back to the

bottle, pouring myself another drink. "Ran into some trouble on a delivery last night, that's all."

His gaze cut to Darius. "Bloodsucker?"

I shifted my hand from his knee to his arm, reclaiming his attention. His muscles were tight with anger, warm and rock solid beneath my touch. "That one was human," I said. "And it's handled, so please chill."

"*That* one?" Ronan picked up the bottle, poured himself a double. "Explain."

"Last delivery of my shift, I let some asshole get the drop on me."

"And then you beat his ass? Tell me you beat his ass."

My stomach bottomed out at the memory, filling my mouth with the taste of bile. The booze wasn't helping, wasn't giving me the comfortable numbness I'd been hoping for.

Maybe I just hadn't had enough of it.

"Yep." I poured the rest of the bottle into my glass and downed it before Ronan could talk me out of it.

Not working. I can still feel.

I nodded for Darius to bring me another bottle, but Ronan shook his head. Darius looked at me once more, then turned his back and replaced the new bottle on the shelf.

To me, Ronan said, "What's going on, Gray? Seriously."

"It's happy hour. I'm... getting happy." I tipped my glass back, then remembered it was empty, and slammed it onto the counter. "Working on it, anyway."

"What you're working on is a hangover." He slid off the stool and fished out his wallet, tossing a few twenties onto the bar. For now, he seemed to forget about my injuries. His eyes returned to their normal shade—like dark green leaves turning brown in the fall. "Let's go."

I shook my head, even as I was getting up to follow him. I wanted to go with Ronan, but I wasn't ready to go home yet. Sophie had been asleep when I'd left, but by now she'd be at Norah's, pissed that I'd blown her off. I couldn't explain it, but the idea of going back to the empty house made me feel even more shitty than the idea of getting into another argument with her.

"Ronan, wait." My feet hit the floor harder than I'd planned. The room tilted. Ronan grabbed my shoulders, steadying me.

"Yeah, you're definitely cut off." He flashed me a devastating grin outlined in a trim, sexy new beard—the kind of grin that would get me in serious trouble if I wasn't careful. "Damn, Desario. I leave you alone for two days, and you turn into a lightweight."

"*Three* days, and lightweight? I just drank a bottle of whiskey and I'm still standing."

"Good to know you're keeping tabs on me, and I know *exactly* how much you drank. I paid for it."

"I'm not keeping tabs. And Darius wanted to buy me a drink."

"Yet he didn't." Ronan shrugged. "So who's the better date? My money's on me."

"You," I said, pushing against his chest, "are a *terrible* date. You got me all liquored up, didn't even feed me."

Ronan jerked his head toward the booth behind us,

where a long-haired vampire greedily sucked from the neck of his victim—a willing one, if her blissed-out smile could be trusted. "At least I didn't feed *on* you."

"That a warning?" I pulled back and met his eyes. The booze had obliterated my guard, and my dealings with Darius had left me riled up in more ways than one. Somewhere in the back of my mind, Good Gray—the voice of reason—shouted a warning, but Bad Gray bitchslapped her. Bad Gray was tired of watching every step, every move, every word, especially around Ronan.

Seven years ago, he'd found me on my first night in the Bay, a total mess. Calla had always warned me to steer clear of demons, but Ronan was different. Memories of my first month here were still a little fuzzy, but I knew that he took care of me. Patched me up, fed me, and gave me a place to crash. In exchange, I cooked and kept the place clean, and sometimes I kept him company during his long overnight shifts on the docks, loading and unloading boats for Waldrich. A few months in, the boss finally gave me a job of my own making deliveries. Not long after that, I'd met Sophie, and we'd found a place together, finally moving me off Ronan's pull-out couch.

Those first few years had been so easy between us; just like with Sophie, it'd felt as if Ronan and I had known each other forever. Like we were meant to be friends.

But in the last several months, something had shifted.

Now, being with him was like playing a constant game of tug-of-war, our friendship solidly on one side, with something else—something hot and primal and infinitely more dangerous—on the other. It was clear both of us felt the pull, but we'd been doing our best to keep our feet planted firmly on the friendship side.

But on nights like tonight, when I'd had a few drinks and he was looking at me like all I'd have to do is say the word and he'd have me pinned to the wall, my legs wrapped around his hips, his mouth on my neck... Damn. Bad Gray wanted to see just how hard she could tug that rope.

I slid my hands up over his shoulders, aching to slide my fingers into that mop of silky, light-brown hair. He kept it short on the sides, long on top, perfectly tousled and begging to be touched.

The heat between us crested to dangerous levels.

"What are you *doing*, Gray?" His voice was a low rumble in my ear, but he didn't pull away. He slid his hands down my back, over the curves of my waist, down to my hips. His fingers dug hard into my flesh, even as his thumb ghosted across the bare skin peeking out beneath the hem of my shirt.

"Nothing," I said innocently. "What are *you* doing, Ronan?"

Don't ever stop touching me...

Ronan let out a sigh. His lips were so close to my mouth I could taste the whiskey on his warm breath.

I swayed a little on my feet, pressing closer to Ronan's rock-hard body. He was shorter than Darius, but solid and warm, a man who'd have no trouble holding me down in bed.

I was pretty sure he already had a hold on my heart.

"Ronan?" I dug my fingers into his shoulders, willing myself to be strong. To be brave. "I think... I think I'm in—"

"I think you're drunk," he said plainly. "And as your friend, I'm going to spare you the future embarrassment of whatever it is you're about to say."

He glared at me, his eyes still hot with desire. After a beat, he jerked his head toward the elevator, then released me, stalking out ahead.

A crowd of vampires entering the club parted to let him pass.

My body felt his absence immediately, and I shivered.

Behind me, Darius laughed, deep and silky. "I guess that didn't go as planned."

I huffed. Rejection was one thing. Rejection in front of an audience was a whole 'nother level of mortification.

"Have a lovely evening, Miss Desario," he said. "I'll be in touch."

"Touch *yourself*, vampire." Pouting, I turned away from him and pushed my way through the crowded bar to the elevator, riding it up to street level alone.

Ronan and his devastating scowl were waiting for me outside.

* * *

That night, these were the things I knew about Ronan Vacarro:

I knew he'd taken care of me when I had no one else—that he was taking care of me still.

I knew he would go to hell and back for me, and I'd do the same for him.

And I knew that other than Sophie, he was the only person I trusted with my life.

Didn't mean we knew each other's secrets.

I stole a glance at him as we walked down Denton Street, wishing I could read him the way Sophie could read me. I studied the sharp planes of his face, the purposeful stride of his steps, the hunch of his shoulders. His eyes were hidden in shadow, just like his thoughts.

I'd never worked up the courage to ask about his origins, and he'd never offered to tell. It was one of those things we just didn't talk about, like where he went when he disappeared for days at a time, and what my life was like before I came to Blackmoon Bay, and what the hell had been going on between us lately.

Over the years we'd developed an unspoken understanding: some things were just better left unsaid.

"So," he said now, "You gonna tell me why the fuck you made a blood deal with Beaumont?"

TEN

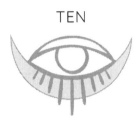

RONAN

I wasn't sure whether it was the cold air or my question, but as we cut through an open-ended alley toward her neighborhood, Gray sobered up pretty damn quick.

"It's nothing." She rubbed the skin on her wrist, the exact spot where the vamp had stuck in his pointy little fangs. "He's helping me with something."

Helping himself, more like it.

I shook my head, trying to put my anger on ice. Beaumont wouldn't do anything to hurt her—I knew that. He also wouldn't let her take a blood oath unless something serious had gone down.

My gut clenched.

"Helping you with what?" I pressed.

Gray shrugged, looking up at me just as we passed under a streetlamp. The yellow glow threw a harsh spotlight on the shiner under her eye.

Fucking hell.

I jammed my hands in my pockets, fighting the urge to touch her face.

To kiss her.

"It doesn't matter," she said.

"Does to me."

"Why?"

I lifted a shoulder. "I just want to know."

"Well, newsflash, Ronan. I'm not a book you can crack open and flip through whenever you feel like it." Gray pushed past me and charged ahead, arms folded stiffly across her chest. Half a block down, she spun around and charged back at me, fire in her eyes. "I don't have to tell you shit, Ronan Vacarro."

"But I—"

"No buts." She jabbed a finger into my chest. "You disappear for days without so much as a text message, then you show up out of nowhere, tracking me down and demanding answers like a jealous boyfriend? I don't think so."

"Jealous? Of a bloodsucker? Come on, Gray. Give me a little credit."

"Then what's your deal?"

"No deal. I'm just looking out for you."

"Well… you can stop. What I do with my body—or my blood, for that matter—is none of your business. Good night, Ronan." She charged ahead again. I let her go, just far enough to give her a little breathing room, but not so far that I couldn't keep an eye on her.

A jealous boyfriend…

Yeah. If only it were that simple.

Much as it pained me to admit it—and I never would, not out loud—Gray could do a hell of a lot worse than Beaumont for company. He made my blood boil on the *best* of days, but he was on the damn decent end of the blood-sucker spectrum, and he'd always looked out for Gray, just like Emilio and Asher had.

We'd saved her life, the four of us. That kind of thing bonded people for eternity. Her memories of that time were murky at best, but eventually, she *would* remember, and she'd find her way right back to them. To that deep, unbreakable bond. And one day on that not-so-distant horizon, if Gray decided Darius Beaumont or Emilio Alvarez or Asher O'Keefe was the man for her—hell, if she decided all *three* of them were for her—I'd never stand in the way of her happiness.

I just wanted to be part of it.

But I was playing with serious fire just *thinking* about crossing that line. One toe over the edge and I'd likely get my ass smoked to oblivion, no chance at resurrection.

A demon guardian falling for the woman whose soul he was charged with delivering upon her death? Forbidden didn't even *begin* to describe it. Hers was a devil's bargain; didn't matter that the contract had been signed in someone else's blood before Gray was even old enough to speak. Didn't matter that she had no idea what awaited her at the end of all this, and if I so much as *hinted* at it, she'd be banished to oblivion, too.

Didn't matter that she hadn't asked for this, or that I

knew—deep the fuck down in my bones—that she was meant for greater things than becoming a demon slave.

How could she not be? Every time she was supposed to die, the woman just kept on fighting her way back from the brink.

Hell was losing patience. I was losing my mind.

If I was jealous of anything, it was this: when the shit finally hit the fan, Beaumont, Alvarez, and even that crazy-ass demon O'Keefe would still come out of it the good guys.

Me? Three hundred and twelve years old, and the only thing I was good at was following orders.

Hell's orders.

Fuck this…

"Gray, wait." I caught up in a few strides, and she finally slowed down, letting me slip an arm over her shoulders. Her scent washed over me—that fruity, tropical shampoo of hers that always made my damn mouth water —and I pulled her close, kissing the top of her head. "Mmm. You taste like a smoothie."

"Shut up." Gray nudged me in the ribs, finally cracking a smile. "Can't you see I'm trying to be mad at you?"

I tugged on one of her curls. "Give it up, Desario. You know you love me."

"Excuse you, Mr. Ego. I *tolerate* you. Subtle but important difference."

She tried to punch me in the arm, but I grabbed her hand and held on tight.

We kept our mouths shut the rest of the way home, but I

could tell her mind was working overtime—she almost missed the turnoff for her street.

When we finally got to her place, she leaned back against the railing on the front porch and sighed, her shoulders slumped with exhaustion.

I tucked a lock of hair behind her ear. "Rough night?"

"Understatement."

"You, ah, wanna talk about it?"

Gray pressed her lips together and closed her eyes, and I backed off. Last thing I wanted to do was crowd her, but seriously—what the fuck was going on?

The woman was covered in scrapes and bruises—a story she'd yet to tell me. She'd made a blood deal with Darius Beaumont. And as much as she tried to hide it, a deep, new worry had settled in around her eyes.

This wasn't just another day in the life of my crazy, badass witch.

"I'm sorry I was so cagey before," she said, looking up at me again. "Something weird happened last night during my shift and my magic kind of… bubbled up."

"Your… what?" My heart rammed against my ribcage, everything else in me going cold. Far as I knew, Gray hadn't touched magic since she was a kid.

It's happening…

"I'm sorry," she said again, pushing off the railing and digging into her pocket for her keys. "I'm not trying to be dramatic. I promise I'll tell you everything. But first I need to talk to Sophie, and she's not even home… God, I really made a mess of things." Gray's eyes misted, and she blew out a breath. "Right now, I just want to lose myself in a hot bath with some tea and a good book. Okay?"

It killed me not to push for details, but she was completely wiped out. She needed to unwind, get some sleep, and start fresh tomorrow.

"How about I bring over breakfast for you guys, and the three of us will figure everything out then." I reached for her hand. "Sound good?"

Gray smiled. "Only if you're not cooking, and only if you make it brunch. Morning is not my friend."

"Brunch it is, night owl. And no, I wouldn't dream of ruining such an important meal with my suck-ass attempts at cooking." I brought her hand to my mouth. Beaumont's scent was all over her skin, but fuck it. I kissed her palm anyway, making another silent vow.

Even a devil's bargain had a way out. I'd do whatever it took to find the loophole that would invalidate her contract.

Until then? Looked like it was time for a little chat with Beaumont and the boys.

Fuck. Sometimes I really hate being right.

ELEVEN

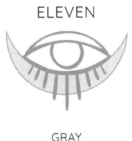

GRAY

Ronan released my hand, and a cool breeze lifted the hair off my neck, bringing with it the salty, briny scent of the bay. The dark clouds that had been hovering in the night sky slithered away, giving us a peek at the quarter moon and a dusting of stars.

It was hard not to dream under a sky like that.

"Don't you ever just want a normal kind of life?" I asked.

"Hmm." Ronan's voice was soft and alluring in the quiet darkness. "Kids and a minivan?"

"Why not?"

"Hate to break it to you, Desario, but I'm not normal. And neither are you."

Ronan laughed, but a deep sadness clung to his features like a mask.

I thought of the Death card from this morning, considering it now with new understanding. Everything changed.

Died. Was born again. Life didn't come with a guarantee—
I'd learned that lesson a long time ago. I knew better than to
think my friends would always be here. That we'd always
be together. No matter what our intentions and feelings,
things ended. Circumstances changed. People went away.

Sometimes on purpose.

Sometimes not.

It was a fact of life, and for the most part, I'd accepted it.
But the thought of things changing between me and Ronan?
It nearly wrecked me.

I slid my key into the front door lock, then turned to face
him, my heart heavy. "Ronan, are we okay?"

He ran a hand over my hair, cradling the back of my
head. I searched his eyes for an answer, a promise that no
matter what happened, no matter what came crashing
down around us, we would always be solid.

But here's another thing I knew about Ronan: he never
made a promise he couldn't keep.

He pressed his forehead to mine and closed his eyes, his
breath tickling my lips. After a beat, he kissed my temple,
then turned away without another word.

I watched him walk down the path to the sidewalk,
feeling like the ground was about to drop out from
under me.

I didn't want it to. Not again.

"Ronan?"

He turned to look at me, and for a minute I lost myself
in those deep, soulful eyes. Every one of my walls came
crumbling down, leaving my heart unguarded, totally

SARAH PIPER

exposed. I opened my mouth to say the words, the right ones, the ones that would make him stay.

The ones I'd been trying to say for months.

But before I could find them, the air around us shifted, and a raven landed on the window ledge outside Sophie's bedroom. Clouds slithered back in front of the moon, bathing us in a darkness so deep and black and all-consuming, it felt like we'd never see the sun again.

Every hair on my neck stood on end.

Ronan's body tensed. "What the hell?"

I took a deep breath, trying to figure out where the bad mojo was coming from.

The night had gone still and silent.

Ronan and I locked eyes for a split second… and then I felt it.

Something in the house was wrong.

Dead wrong.

80

TWELVE

GRAY

I pushed through the front door first, with Ronan right on my heels.

Nothing looked out of place, but I felt it immediately—the heaviness in the air. It was too quiet; even the fridge had stopped buzzing.

A deep sense of dread settled over me, squeezing my lungs until it hurt to breathe.

"Stay here," Ronan whispered. He edged past me and headed down the hallway that led to our bedrooms.

Ignoring his directive, I followed close behind.

My bedroom door was open—nothing amiss in there. Same with the bathroom and the small spare room Sophie used as an art studio.

At the very end of the hall, Sophie's bedroom door was closed.

"Sophie?" I called out softly.

No response.

Ronan turned toward me, pressing a finger to his lips to shush me.

She's at work, that's all. She went to the coven meeting like she'd planned, and now she's at Illuminae with her sparkly tattoos and rainbow hair, right where she's supposed to be.

I closed my eyes and pictured her behind the bar at the fae club, head bopping to the otherworldly beats as she lined up glasses and poured fruity, metallic-colored drinks for the club's flamboyant clientele.

She's at work, she's at work, she's at work…

Ronan reached for the doorknob. As soon as his fingers wrapped around the metal, a bolt of icy fear shot down my spine. Goosebumps tightened my scalp.

"Sophie?" I called over Ronan's shoulder. My voice trembled as he turned the knob and pushed open the door. "You home?"

The lights were off, but her curtains were pulled back, the bedroom dimly illuminated by a streetlight. Both of her windows were open, screens and all. The raven I'd seen outside was gone.

I stepped into the room behind Ronan, rubbing the chill from my arms. It took a moment for my eyes to adjust to the weak light.

That's when I saw her, stretched out on her bed beneath her sunflowers-and-daisies comforter, mouth parted in blissful sleep. Fanned across her pillow, her red hair was almost back to its natural shade, the ends still giving off a faint faerie glow.

I blew out a breath, tears of relief stinging my eyes. Sophie was here. She was safe. Late for work, probably pissed that I'd blown off the coven meeting, but safe. I almost jumped onto her bed with joy.

"Gray?" Ronan clamped a hand over my shoulder, pulling me back.

"She's okay," I whispered. "It's fine. She—"

"Don't move."

"But—"

The room shimmered before our eyes. There on Sophie's chest, right on top of her cheery comforter, a raven appeared—seemingly from thin air.

I stood at the end of the bed, hands gripping the edge of the footboard. It was the raven from outside. The same one, I realized now, that I'd seen in the alley.

In that terrible moment, I knew that my best friend was not sleeping peacefully at all.

Sophie was dead.

No...

Ronan tried to pull me away, but I was paralyzed, watching with numb detachment as the raven slid his beak into Sophie's mouth.

Silver-blue mist curled out from between her lips, glittering in the dim room like a winter's breath.

No, not a breath. A soul. Her *soul.*

The realization set fire to my limbs.

"Leave her alone!" I bolted onto the bed and swiped at the raven, but my fingers passed right through him, like trying to touch a shadow. He leaped away and perched on Sophie's dresser instead.

I lay across her body, my hands clenching her sheets. All around me the bedroom began to fade, replaced with wild trees under a jet-black sky. Indigo light glowed in the distance, and I knew it was like the alley again, my mind slipping into my magic place even as my body remained with Sophie.

I didn't want to leave her. I fought the change, focusing on the feel of her cool sheets in my hands, on the strawberry scent of her shampoo.

It worked. The image of the forested path faded almost as quickly as it had arrived, leaving me right back in her bed.

Though I hadn't ventured all the way into the black forest with the tinsel trees, my hands were once again engulfed in that strange blue flame. I tried to pull back, but instinct pushed me forward, closer to Sophie.

This time, though, the fire didn't chase her soul back into her body. Instead, it turned a lighter blue, encircling her head like a halo. The silver mist of her soul entwined with my flames, and as I took my next breath, it entered me.

A tingling warmth spread inside me.

Sophie's essence, her scent, and every memory we ever shared together crashed through me, wave after wave after wave, until I could no longer tell where she ended and I began. It was as if our souls had merged.

The raven, who'd been watching from his perch on

Sophie's dresser, launched himself into the air, exploding in a tempest of oil-black feathers that swirled and spun above the bed, then crashed violently back together, reforming into a terrifying figure in tattered black robes.

I couldn't see his face, but beneath a black hood, ice blue eyes glowed bright, his presence sucking all the energy out of the room. He hovered above us for only seconds, then lunged for me, hauling me off the bed with inhuman strength.

I was dimly aware of Ronan banging on an invisible barrier—the same shimmery dome that had covered me in the alley. His lips were moving, but his voice was no more than a distant echo.

The hooded stranger curled his pale fingers around my shoulders.

"Do not struggle." His command was everywhere, outside me and within, reverberating through every cell in my body.

He pressed his mouth to mine, breath cool and sweet as he sucked the air from my lungs. Sophie's essence was leaving me as quickly as it had entered, one memory at a time.

He took the first time I met her, delivering cases of absinthe to Illuminae. He took the day we signed the lease on this house, and the one where we busted the door frame moving our new couch into the living room because we were too amped up on girl power to ask Ronan for help. He took the last time I'd cooked us dinner—grilled cheese and tomato soup, not three days ago. I'd burned one side of the grilled cheeses, but she ate hers anyway, insisting that melted cheese made everything good. He took her strawberry shampoo and her laugh and her smile and her Tarot cards, took the painted stones from the basket in the kitchen.

One by one, he took and took and took until there was nothing left.

When he finally stopped, I felt like a dry husk. If not for his hands on my shoulders, I probably would've blown away.

"It is over," he said.

I nodded dumbly, compelled by his strange, otherworldly power to believe him. Obey him.

With one hand still wrapped around my shoulder, he extended his other hand between us, palm up. A single black feather hovered there, spinning in place. He whispered an incantation that sounded as old as the earth, and the feather transformed into a golden-eyed owl.

He blew a silvery breath into the bird's open mouth— Sophie's soul.

The owl flapped its great wings and took off through the open window. The shield I'd inadvertently cast disappeared, and Ronan was at my side in a heartbeat, catching me as my knees buckled.

Death—that's what he was, I knew now—turned his back on us, closing the windows with a simple flick of his wrist.

Ronan's arms wound tight around me. He was the only

thing holding me up, the only thing keeping me tethered to reality.

"What the *fuck*?" Ronan growled at the hooded man, rage rippling through his muscles. "What did you do to her?"

Speaking to his own reflection in the glass, Death said, "The human body is incapable of eternal rest unless its soul passes into the Shadowrealm. Without this passage, the body believes the soul is merely traveling, and will endlessly seek to be reunited with it."

"Say again?" Ronan demanded.

"If I'd allowed the witch to keep that soul, the woman to whom it once belonged would've become a revenant, her body animated but not alive." Turning to me, he said, "A mortal body is not made to carry two souls indefinitely. The souls would eventually fuse, feeding off each other, fighting for sustenance until the body could no longer support them. At that time the body would die, and both souls would be trapped inside the vessel for eternity."

"You had no right," I said, but Death either didn't hear me or didn't care.

As if I were no longer in the room, he looked at Ronan and said, "She doesn't yet possess the skill to—"

"You don't know the first thing about her," Ronan said.

"The skill to what?" I demanded.

Death finally turned his attention back to me, his eyes still glowing faintly. His body, which had initially seemed as shadowy as the raven's, had solidified.

It didn't make him look any more human.

"You're Shadowborn," he said.

Shadowborn?

The word tumbled through my consciousness, snagging on a memory—water? A creek, maybe?—but I couldn't hold onto it. I had no reference for it, nothing to make it stick.

Death put his hand on Sophie's chest and whispered again in that strange, ancient tongue.

"Where is she?" I asked. "Can you bring her back?"

"She is dead. Her soul has passed on to the Shadowrealm, as it should."

"Why didn't she come back? The girl in the alley... I thought... My magic..." I trailed off, confused and scared. I hadn't told anyone but Darius about Bean, and though Ronan was still in the dark on the matter of my so-called necromancy, I was certain Death already knew my secrets.

All of them.

"That is not a fate you wish upon someone you love," he said. "You brought back certain aspects of the girl she once was, but you were not able to properly reinsert her soul. With discipline and training, you—"

"Gray," Ronan said, "what girl? What are you talking about?"

I untangled myself from Ronan's embrace and knelt on the floor next to Sophie's bed, smoothing the hair from her forehead. Her skin was cool to the touch and as pale as her sheets.

"She can't be gone," I said simply, as if that settled things. "We always have tea in the morning after work, and

I don't know if she wants the mint or the chamomile... I mean, I can't just pick for her, you know? She's allergic to cinnamon." I was babbling, but I couldn't stop myself. Stopping meant seeing reality. Stopping meant acknowledging that she wasn't coming back, and that wasn't an option.

As long as I kept talking, kept pretending, I didn't have to accept the fact that she was gone. That I had tasted her soul. That Death himself had removed it, sent it on its way, and was now standing in our home like some kind of invited guest.

You're Shadowborn...

I felt Ronan's hand on the back of my neck and flinched.

"It's okay, Gray," he said gently. Softly. "I'm right here."

Since my arrival in Blackmoon Bay, Ronan had been my rock. He'd picked me up from my lowest point, dusted me off, helped me find my footing again. No matter how strained things had gotten between us, I knew I could always count on him to give it to me straight.

I tilted my face up and looked into his eyes for confirmation that everything really *would* be okay, that somewhere in all this impossible shit, a sane explanation existed. That in a few hours we'd hear Sophie's keys jingling in the front door, and she'd walk in, kick off her shoes, and say, "Oh my God, you guys. Wait till I tell you about my crazy night!"

But when I looked into Ronan's eyes now, they were black and empty, offering no solace.

Instead, he said, "We need to call—"

"No, we don't." I rose to my feet, then pulled up Sophie's comforter and tucked it around her shoulders. I didn't want her to be cold. "Let's go. Sophie doesn't like people wearing shoes in her bedroom."

THIRTEEN

GRAY

Ronan made the call anyway, and fifteen minutes later, Detective Emilio Alvarez arrived with the cavalry, shattering my bubble of denial.

Clutching the *just breathe* mandala stone in my hand, I lay on the living room couch with my head in Ronan's lap, his fingers tracing light circles on my forehead as I watched the muddy boots of half a dozen cops stomp back and forth between the living room and the bedroom of my dead best friend, picking up fibers and dusting for prints and whatever else they did at a crime scene.

That's how they were treating this. A crime scene.

Death had vanished as quickly as he'd arrived, and Ronan hadn't uttered a word about it. I still couldn't get my head around it. Death had said things, revealed things, *done* things in that room that should've left my mind spinning with impossible questions, but all of it felt like a distant memory now, like a story I'd been told a long time ago about someone else.

In Sophie's room at the end of the hall, one of the cops was shooting pictures. I flinched every time the flash sparked, but Ronan remained calm as always, gently trailing his fingers through my hair.

The cops spoke in hushed voices. I pictured them touching Sophie's body with rubber gloves and tweezers, putting her personal things into plastic baggies labeled with black Sharpie, and all I could think was, *They're getting mud all over her carpet. She's going to kill me for letting them in there.*

It was more than an hour before Detective Alvarez finally emerged from the bedroom. He looked like an ER doctor coming to tell the crying family there was nothing more he could do.

I sat up and leaned back against the couch, pulling my knees to my chest. The detective crouched down in front of me, as graceful and powerful in human form as he must've been as a wolf.

Shifter grace aside, everything else about him was totally human. A faded green San Francisco T-shirt stretched across his broad chest, the kind of shirt somebody buys you at the airport on the way home when they realized they forgot to get you a souvenir. His skin was golden and smooth, and his wavy jet-black hair stuck up on one side as if he'd been running his hands through it.

It made him look young and playful, despite the seriousness in his eyes.

"Miss Desario, I know this is hard," he said in his lilting

Spanish accent. "I'm so sorry."

I nodded, letting him get away with that comment because he *did* know. Ronan had once told me once that Alvarez was a lone wolf—that he'd emigrated here from Argentina decades ago, shortly after he and his sister had separated from their pack.

I didn't know the details, but a wolf shifter without a pack was never something that happened by choice.

But Ronan hadn't called him here for his empathy. He'd called him because Alvarez was the only one who cared enough about people like us to do the job right.

"How did she die?" I asked.

He narrowed his eyes on my bruised face, but his scrutiny felt more like concern than suspicion. "Are you okay? That... looks like it hurts."

"Just a scuffle at work last night. I'm fine."

He nodded, and I forced myself to focus on his kind face.

"We don't yet know what killed Sophie," he said, "but there are no signs of a struggle. I don't believe she suffered."

I blew out a breath.

"I need to ask you a few questions," he continued, and I nodded, soothed by the compassion in his warm brown eyes. He flipped open a small notebook and ran through the standard list: approximately what time did we discover Sophie? To my knowledge, had anyone else been in the house tonight? Was it possible she'd gone out earlier, then returned? Did Sophie have any enemies? Did she ever mention any trouble at work, any customers that had crossed the line? Any issues with her boss?

Ronan and I answered his questions as best we could, but there was so much more I couldn't say. So much more I couldn't explain even if I'd wanted to.

Bean, and whatever I'd turned her into. Wherever she'd vanished.

Death. Something told me we hadn't seen the last of him.

Souls. I'd seen two now. *Touched* them. Done things to them that no human—not even a witch—should've been able to do.

What am I? Does Sophie's death have something to do with my magic?

"There's something else you should know." Detective Alvarez jotted down a few notes, then flipped the notebook closed. It felt like a thousand hours before he spoke again, and when he did, his voice sounded strained. "Two other Bay area women were killed today under almost identical circumstances."

I gasped. "What?"

"Witches?" Ronan whispered.

Emilio glanced over his shoulder, confirming that none of the human cops were within earshot before continuing. "Yes. One shortly after sunrise in Rockport, and another just a few hours ago in the Bayshore neighborhood. We haven't officially ruled them homicides, but my gut tells me that's what we're dealing with."

As much as it hurt to admit it, my gut was saying the

same thing. Witches weren't immortal, but we tended to outlast our normal human counterparts. We didn't just up and die at twenty-five years old.

Ronan slid a hand over my knee and squeezed, a little too tightly. "Any leads?"

Detective Alvarez shook his head. "We're still gathering evidence, putting the puzzle pieces together." He and Ronan exchanged a weighted glance. "Be careful—both of you. Whoever did this… He may not be finished."

"You thinking hunter?" Ronan asked.

"Too soon to rule it out," Detective Alvarez said, keeping his voice low. "But we haven't seen hunters in the Bay in, what, thirty years? Not since the covens practiced openly. Plus, they've always hunted in packs. This feels like the work of an individual."

Ronan nodded.

"We're keeping all possibilities on the table right now. I'll let you know if and when that changes." Alvarez capped his pen and headed back into Sophie's bedroom to consult with his colleagues, leaving me to sit with Ronan's speculation.

A hunter…

Could my magical outburst have been enough to create a hotspot? What about the coven's magic? Sophie said they'd all been practicing regularly—earth magic, blood spells, who knew what else. Hadn't Norah taken precautions?

No, it didn't make sense. Magic or not, there was no way a hunter did this. Hunters were vicious, brutal, and above all else—thorough. They didn't leave dead witches behind to tell their tales with fingerprints and fibers and DNA samples.

They burned us, every time.

"How late is it?" I stood up from the couch and rolled my shoulders. Everything inside me ached.

"Just after one." Ronan rose to his full height and stretched, then slid his hand over the small of my back and nodded toward the kitchen. "Come on. You should eat something."

I followed him, not because I was hungry, but because I couldn't stand the sound of all those boots.

I sat at the kitchen table in a daze as Ronan made toast.

Toast was good. Toast was normal, and normal people didn't have the homicide squad in their home in the middle of the night. Normal people didn't have murdered best friends and visits from Death.

Normal people weren't…

"What's Shadowborn?" I asked. The word slithered through my mind again like a snake on a far-off trail, there one minute, gone the next. I tried to hold on to it, but it was just too slippery, and by the time Ronan turned and met my gaze, I'd forgotten what I was even asking about.

We watched each other in silence for a minute, maybe two, the haze of grief settling over us like freshly poured cement, making it difficult to see, to move. We might have stayed like that all night, waiting for someone else to tell us what to do, but the unmistakable smell of smoke cut swiftly through the muck.

"Shit." Ronan popped two charred bits from the toaster and dropped them onto a plate. Tendrils of smoke rose from their blackened edges.

"Shadowborn," I said as it came back to me once again. "He said I was Shadowborn, and you didn't question it. Why?"

The plate clattered to the floor, toast overboard.

"Fuck," Ronan said. "Sorry about that."

I shrugged. "It was burnt anyway."

"I wasn't paying attention."

"You've always been a shitty cook."

Ronan tried to smile, but it was forced and sad, nothing like the mischievous grin I loved so much. It felt like a knife twisting in my heart, and it was that moment—not discovering her body, not the police in Sophie's bedroom, not Alvarez's questions or the stretcher on the front porch waiting to wheel her out, but Ronan's broken, half-assed smile and the blackened toast on the floor—that made me realize nothing would ever be the same again.

Pain crushed me all at once. Everything inside me liquefied, and I slid from the chair onto the floor, unable to move, unable to cry, unable to breathe.

Ronan sat down next to me and gathered me in his arms, holding me against his chest. His heartbeat was the only true thing I knew.

By the time Detective Alvarez poked his head into the kitchen to check on us, my legs had fallen asleep and my neck was stiff.

He pulled out a chair and gestured for us to join him at

the table. Sophie had left her Tarot cards stacked there in a neat pile, and I couldn't bring myself to move them.

The Death card was back on top.

"Here's what we know," Detective Alvarez said. Compassion lingered behind his steely professional gaze, but more than that, I appreciated his efficiency. The sooner he wrapped it up, the sooner they'd all leave. "We haven't recovered a weapon, and there's no sign of forced entry. We—"

"The door and windows," I blurted out, suddenly remembering. "When I got home, the front door was unlocked, and her bedroom windows and screens were wide open."

"Are you sure?" he asked.

I nodded. "The lock sticks—it always takes a few tries. I put my key in tonight, but I never turned it. Ronan and I got this weird feeling that something was wrong, and we ran inside. I don't even know where my keys ended up."

"Here," Ronan confirmed, patting his pocket. "I grabbed them when the police arrived. They were still stuck in the door lock. I didn't think of it before, but yeah, Gray's right —the house was definitely unlocked."

"I know I locked it when I left for Darius's place earlier," I said. "I always do."

"Does anyone else have a key?"

"Just Ronan," I said, "but he was with me at Black Ruby. We walked home together."

"What about the windows?" Alvarez asked, pulling out

his pad to take a few more notes. "They were closed when we arrived."

I glanced at Ronan, then looked down at my hands.

Oh, that? Just Death showing us a few parlor tricks…

"I… closed them," I finally said. "It was cold."

Detective Alvarez wrote all that in his notebook. "So there's a chance if someone showed up here, Sophie invited him inside. Maybe she knew him?"

"Or her," I said.

"Or her." Alvarez nodded. "Alternatively, maybe they came in through the windows and left out the front door. We should know more when we get the prints back."

"You said you couldn't find a weapon," I said. "But you think it's a homicide? I don't understand."

"Neither do I. Right now, I'm working off a hunch." His eyes softened, and he reached out and touched my hand, his fingers warm. "But I can tell you that Sophie likely died peacefully."

It was cold comfort.

"All death is peaceful," I said, my eyes drawn back to the Death card. "It's the whole leading-up-to-it part that sucks."

"You… have a point," he said.

I reached for the basket of painted stones, pulling one at random. This one had a pink rose design. *Stop and smell me,* the white script said.

"What else do you know?" I asked.

It had been a few hours since we'd discovered Sophie's body—since the raven had taken her soul. Even through all of my denial and babbling and pretending, deep down I knew she was gone. But I hadn't really allowed myself to *feel* her absence or think about what it might mean tomorrow or the next day and the day after that when I pulled our two mugs out of the dish drainer and realized that from here on out, I'd only ever need one.

I sat there thinking about it now, trying *not* to think about the fact that I was thinking about it, my fingers wrapped so tightly around the rose stone that the tips had turned white, but still, I didn't cry. Didn't gasp. Didn't break down until Detective Alvarez looked at me once again and said, "They took some of her hair. Several of her braids appear to have been crudely cut with a knife."

It was so gruesome, so horrid, even more so than the death itself because this somehow felt more personal, more intimate. But through the fresh tears that fell, all I could do was laugh. I laughed and laughed and laughed, because in that moment when all things had stopped making sense, the picture that came to my mind was of an evil man walking around the Bay with a handful of glittering, rainbow light.

I was still laughing when Alvarez rose from his chair and put a hand on my shoulder.

"We'll know more after the autopsy and the lab reports, Miss Desario," he said. "I'll keep you posted."

Willing myself to pull it together before he decided to call the psych ward, I nodded, forcing out a thank you. "We didn't know who else to call."

"You did the right thing," he said, then asked to speak with Ronan privately in the living room.

I counted sixty clicks of the fox clock before Ronan returned—one minute that'd felt like an entire day.

He told me that the medical examiner had arrived and they were getting ready to transport Sophie's body to the morgue. Alvarez wanted to know if I needed a moment to say goodbye.

I shook my head. I didn't want my last memory of Sophie to be a bunch of strangers zipping her into a body bag. "I... I have to clean the kitchen floor."

"You sure?"

I nodded once, and that was the end of it. Ronan went back into the living room to deal with the transport.

It was the kindest thing he'd ever done for me.

I stayed alone in the kitchen, scrubbing the floor while they strapped my best friend to a gurney and carried her out our front door for the last time. I tried not to dwell on it, remembering instead her infectious laugh, her all-knowing smirk, the glittery tattoos of the sea that had danced across her chest less than twenty-four hours ago.

By the time Ronan came back into the kitchen, the house was silent. Everyone else had left.

Ronan held out his hand and helped me up off the floor.

When I looked into his eyes, I gasped.

For the first time since I'd known him, my demon—my rock, my shelter in the storm—was terrified.

"Gray," he said urgently. "You need to pack."

FOURTEEN

GRAY

I stripped off my yellow cleaning gloves and followed Ronan down the hall to the bedrooms, averting my eyes from Sophie's door.

Rifling through my closet, Ronan found a duffel bag and a beat-up old backpack and tossed them onto the bed.

"Where are we going?" I asked.

"A safe house Asher set up."

"What are you talking about? Who's Asher?" The only friends Ronan had ever mentioned were Darius and Detective Alvarez, and even then the word *friends* felt like a stretch.

Ignoring me, he ransacked my dresser drawers, pulling out clothes and shoving everything into the bags, stuffing them to capacity.

He zipped up the backpack and tossed it at my feet. It hit the floor with a soft thud.

"If there's anything else you want, get it now," he said. "We won't be coming back."

I picked up the backpack and hitched it over my shoulder, swallowing the lump in my throat. "Ever?"

Ronan was back to ignoring me.

"But... I'm Shadowborn," I said randomly. Everything was rushing at me so fast, I couldn't keep up. I felt like I was underwater, looking up from the bottom of the pool while everyone else swam around on the surface, oblivious. "What does that even mean?"

"We don't have time." There was desperation in his eyes, an uneasiness I'd never seen there before. But he knew me well enough to know that I wouldn't—couldn't—let this go.

Exasperated, he said, "Shadowborn are witches who exist in two planes—the world that you see here, and the Shadowrealm."

"What else?"

"They're extremely rare."

"And?"

"Once they fully come into their magic, they can access powers from both realms."

My stomach tightened. "What powers?"

Ronan stared at me a long time, his lips pressed into a thin white line. It was a look I'd gotten to know well from my stubborn friend. It meant that he had all the answers, but didn't want to share them.

"What powers?" I repeated.

"The strongest among you can manipulate a person's life force," a voice said, but it wasn't Ronan's.

Death was back, his shadowy form taking up all the space in the doorway. His tone was so matter-of-fact, it was like we were watching this unfold on a National Geographic special. "They can become soul ferriers, like my owls and ravens, but infinitely more powerful. They are necromancers in the truest sense of the word. They have the capacity to give life, to save it, or to destroy it. And they are, all of them, bound to me."

"Well I've never heard of it," I said, eager to move past words like *necromancer* and *bound*. "*Shadowborn*. Sounds made up."

Death opened his arms and shrugged. "Yet here you are. Existing."

Ronan, who had been silent through this latest exchange, grabbed the duffel bag off the bed and heaved it over his shoulder. "Gray, I'll answer your questions later— and so help me, you need to be straight with me about whatever the fuck happened to you last night. But please get your shit together. Beaumont's meeting us up there— he's already on his way."

"Wait... Darius?" I pressed my fingers to my temples, trying to slow the churning madness. "Why? Ronan, what is going on?"

"We're wasting time, Gray. Let's go."

"No," I snapped. "I'm not leaving. Not without Sophie." Then, in a much softer tone, "Not until we find who killed her."

"Alvarez is on it. There's nothing more we can do."

"Nothing?" Death made a low, throaty sound that might've passed for a laugh if there was anything even remotely human about him. "How can you be so certain?"

Ronan whipped around to face him. "Why are you still here?"

"I am everywhere. Always."

"Enough with the riddles," Ronan said. "Explain yourself."

"I have business with the Shadowborn. It does not concern you."

"Everything about her concerns me."

"She needs to know who she is. She must be trained. Protected. I will give her that." Turning to me, he extended a gloved hand and said, "Come. I'll take you back to the realm and we'll—"

"Like hell you will." Ronan's eyes turned as black as night. He dropped the bag and stalked toward Death, but Death held up a hand, stopping Ronan in his tracks.

"Careful, *demon*." Death's tone was so soft, so gentle, he could've been instructing a toddler how to hold a butterfly. "Unless you wish to reveal your secrets as well."

Ronan shook with rage, but instead of charging Death, he backed off. When he looked at me again, his eyes had returned to normal.

I had never, ever seen Ronan back down from a challenge like that.

I glanced from Ronan to Death and back to Ronan again, trying to figure out what was going on. Ronan wasn't afraid of him, but there was definitely bad blood between them.

Once again, I wondered about Ronan's origins—about all the things he was hiding—but my mind was already spinning with so many other what-ifs and what-nows, there was little room for anything else.

Ronan said, "We don't know who killed Sophie and the other witches. We don't know what they were after, but Alvarez thinks they might come back for more. I'm not taking that chance with your life. We have to go, Gray. Come on."

"You mean run," I said. "You're telling me we have to run."

Before Sophie and Ronan, I'd only truly loved one other person in my life—Calla, the woman who'd adopted me as a baby after my real mother died.

When Calla was taken from me, I didn't seek vengeance from those responsible, even though I knew who they were. I didn't call the police. I didn't even call the neighbors.

I ran.

I survived. It was Calla's dying wish—her last word. *Survive.*

It was the only thing I could give to her, the silent promise I'd made on the day she died.

I'd always told myself that if I ever got into a dangerous situation—I mean, *really* dangerous—I would run again. Survive, no matter what.

But now that danger had found its way back to my doorstep, I wasn't sure it was the right call. How could I run when my best friend was murdered in our home less than a day after I'd inadvertently used magic and brought a girl back from the dead? How could I run when I'd nearly taken Sophie's soul, nearly condemned her to an eternity as a revenant, just as I'd done to Bean?

How could I run when everything in me was screaming for a chance to stay and fight?

I looked from Ronan—one of my best friends, a man I was pretty sure I was falling in love with—back to Death, shrouded in shadow and a deep coldness I couldn't even begin to fathom.

Both were offering me a way out. A way to survive, just like I'd promised Calla I'd do.

I had every intention of keeping my promise.

But Calla was gone. Sophie was gone.

And I was done running.

"I'm not going anywhere," I said, dropping the back-pack and standing up straight for the first time all night. "I have work to do."

FIFTEEN

GRAY

By the time Ronan and I left the house a few hours later, the streets of South Bay were wet and grey and oily, the morning sky bleached of color. Everywhere I looked people huddled under umbrellas, ducking into cars and shops to escape the rain.

Sophie would've called it a Five of Cups kind of day, like the Tarot card of the same name. On the card, a cloaked woman mourned three cups that had spilled on the road before her, so focused on the loss that she hadn't noticed the two full cups behind her, still upright.

As to the weather, it was the kind of day that soaked you clear to the bone, made you wonder if you'd ever feel the sun on your face again.

I zipped up the sweatshirt I'd taken from the hook on Sophie's door—a ridiculous hot-pink number that I normally wouldn't be caught dead wearing—and soldiered on, trying to visualize those two full cups standing some-where on the horizon.

Trying to visualize hope.

Normally I didn't mind the rain—it was one of the things I loved about the Bay. To me, it'd always meant a fresh start, a great washing away of everything shitty that had come the day before.

There wasn't enough rain in a monsoon to wash away the events of last night, but as I walked the sopping wet streets, I found a kind of clarity.

Sophie was dead. Murdered in her own bed, just like two other witches in the Bay. Detective Alvarez had told Ronan these cases were his top priority, but like all super-naturals trying to hack it in a human-dominated world, he had to tread carefully around human laws. Hell, he'd taken a vow to uphold those laws the day he joined the force. Like Ronan and Darius, I believed he was a great cop, but I had no doubts he'd play by the rulebook, get proper warrants, and ask appropriate questions.

Me? I had no such hangups.

Wiping a pink sleeve across my eyes, I squinted into the rain, trying to remember which block was Norah's.

"This way, I think." I turned down Pierce Avenue, Ronan matching my strides.

He'd spent the better part of the morning trying to talk me out of this, but when it was clear I had no intention of skipping town with him, he unpacked my bags, put every-thing back where he'd found it, and put the kettle on.

He even managed not to burn the toast this time.

Progress.

I still couldn't wrap my mind around everything that had happened, and I was doing my best not to obsess over it. Right now, the only thing keeping me sane and breathing was the idea that I might be able to help track down her killer.

That was my life now. My sacred mission.

"There's the house. I remember it now." I stopped in front of an old Victorian about halfway down the block, three stories high with a huge stained-glass window shaped like a star on the top floor and a sprawling wraparound porch on the bottom. The house was probably once a vibrant red with bright white trim, but salt and time had left its mark, rendering it the color of overcooked salmon. I had only been there one other time—the potluck Sophie had dragged me to last year.

We can't just keep ignoring them, she'd said, already preparing an organic fruit salad to bring. *We should at least pop over and say hello...*

Ronan and I climbed the porch stairs and stopped in front of the door, both of us totally soaked. Under any other circumstances, the incessant pitter-patter of rain against the porch roof might've felt cozy. Romantic, even.

"You're shivering," Ronan said softly, brushing the wet hair out of my eyes with his fingertips. "I'd give you my jacket, but I'm pretty sure it's holding about ten pounds of water."

"It's the thought that counts. How's my face? Makeup holding up?"

Ronan cupped my chin, giving me a quick once-over. "No sign of your newly acquired battle wounds, if that's what you mean."

"Score one for Sophie's waterproof foundation." I took a deep breath, inhaling the familiar scents of Blackmoon Bay: rotting wood, salt, the briny Salish Sea. The air was particularly fishy today, but I was okay with that. It smelled like home.

"You sure about this?" Ronan asked.

At the moment I wasn't sure about anything, but the coven was the only lead I had. I needed to know whether Sophie had come here last night. There was also a chance— as much as I hated to consider it—that Norah, Haley, or any of the others knew something about my best friend that I didn't.

She'd been spending time with them for weeks—maybe months—without my knowledge. She'd been practicing her magic again, and I'd been left in the dark. I couldn't discount the possibility that Sophie had other secrets, too.

"I'm sure," I said.

Ronan didn't look any more convinced than I felt, but when had I ever let that stop me?

I figured Detective Alvarez had already been here to question them, and as I leaned closer to the door, the sounds emanating from the other side confirmed it for me —women speaking in subdued voices, the clink of silverware against china, someone blowing her nose. The whole crew seemed to be in mourning together.

A pang of jealousy pricked my heart.

Before I could talk myself out of it, I pressed the doorbell.

The young witch who answered looked about Bean's age, with a spray of freckles on her nose and a curly mop of dark hair that spiraled down past her shoulders. Her blue eyes lit up when she smiled, but before she could even speak, Norah appeared behind her and took charge.

"Oh, Gray," Norah said, pressing a hand to her heart. "I'm so sorry for your loss."

Tall and stately, with sharp gray eyes and a tight bun of silver-gray hair, Norah Hanson looked better suited to tea with the Queen of England than to leading an underground coven in the Pacific Northwest. I was surprised she recognized me; I'd only met her the one time, and I didn't think I'd made much of an impression.

Norah offered a delayed smile. "I was hoping you'd stop by."

I wasn't buying it.

"Reva," Norah said, and the young witch at her side flinched. "There should be some fresh bath towels in the dryer. Why don't you get one for Gray?"

For Gray. The implication was clear: Ronan would not be admitted.

It wasn't unexpected—just disappointing. In most circles, witches and demons didn't mix. In the judgmental eyes of Norah's coven, my relationship with Ronan was just another thing that made me *other*.

Ronan placed a hand on the small of my back and leaned in close, whispering reassurances I hadn't realized

I'd needed. "You've got this, Gray. If things go south, just text me. I'll be back here in a flash."

"Only if they go *really* south," I whispered back, though I was sure Norah could hear us. "Like, Argentina south."

"I was thinking Florida." With those parting words, Ronan gave me half a smile, then headed back out into the rain, crossing the street toward Bloodstone Park.

"Come in, Gray," Norah said. "Please."

I felt the brief resistance of her wards as I stepped into the foyer, the guardian magic like a giant soap bubble that popped on my skin, then reformed behind me, locking out anyone with harmful intentions.

Or maybe just locking me *in*.

Again I wondered whether she'd done enough to shield their inside magical practices from outside eyes. From hunters. Norah was an experienced witch, but no one was perfect.

"You all remember Gray Desario," Norah announced. "Sophie's friend."

Everyone was gathered in the living room at the front of the house, warm and dry before a crackling fire, huddled together on sofas and chairs, sipping tea and nibbling pastries, blotting their lips with floral-print paper napkins.

Dripping water all over the gleaming wood floors of the foyer, I felt like a feral cat who'd just crashed their pretty little tea party.

"*Best* friend," I corrected.

The women stiffened, and the temperature in the room seemed to drop.

To me, Norah said, "Make yourself comfortable. I'll get you some hot tea. I know Sophie's allergic to cinnamon, but what about you? Any allergies?"

I shook my head, trying not to show how badly her comment about Sophie burned. I didn't like these people knowing personal things about my best friend.

"Okay," Norah said, her smile a little too tight. "Be right back."

I took the chair closest to the fireplace, glad for the warmth. It was the only open seat in the room, and for the briefest second, it felt as if they'd all been waiting for me.

I perched on the very edge of the uncomfortably fancy cushion, hoping I wouldn't ruin the upholstery.

No one spoke. No one even looked at me. When Reva returned with a towel, she kept her eyes averted as she handed it over. I rubbed the water from my hair and wrapped the towel around my shoulders, but still, the witches didn't say a word.

Death did terrible things to the people left behind—I knew that. It robbed us of our words, our gentle smiles, and our simple kindnesses because death was neither simple nor kind—especially not when it took a young person. I understood how it felt when words and hugs seemed inadequate in the face of such cruelty.

I could forgive the witches for that.

But what was going on here had nothing to do with death, and everything to do with me.

"Look, we all know I'm not your friend," I finally said. "But Sophie cared about you guys, and you obviously felt the same about her. Can we just put everything else aside for now and talk? For Sophie's sake?"

They let out a collective sigh. A few of the women nodded at me, finally making eye contact.

"Sophie told me she was planning to meet you here last night," I continued.

"She never showed," one of them said. "I texted her a few times, but she—"

"*Wendy.*" A curvy, dark-haired witch named Haley—the one I thought Sophie was closest to—shot Wendy a warning glare, making her cheeks flush.

"I texted her, too," another witch said. Delilah, I thought her name was. Delilah looked at Haley, who sighed loudly, but eventually nodded, as if giving the other woman permission to speak.

Interesting…

"She didn't text me back," Delilah said.

"Same here." It was Reva this time, the youngest witch among them. Tears gathered in her eyes, her voice breaking as she spoke. "I just figured she got called into work early or something."

I shook my head. It wasn't adding up. Sophie was not a flake. If she'd gotten called in to Illuminae, she would've let them know.

Haley probably would've known that about her, too, but when I tried to catch her eye, she looked away.

"None of you thought that something might be wrong?" I asked.

"Not really." Reva turned toward the kitchen, where

Norah was still preparing my tea, then back to me. "It wasn't the first time Sophie missed a meeting."

"Usually because of you," Delilah grumbled.

"Oh yeah?" I snapped. "This time it was because she was being murdered in her own bed while you guys sat around with your broomsticks up your asses."

"That's not fair," Haley said. She was about to say something else, but the witch sitting next to her on the couch cleared her throat. Norah's footsteps were getting closer. All of the women fell strangely silent after that.

What the hell is going on here?

They were acting like a bunch of kids about to get scolded by the nanny. If that's what joining the coven did to you, I was glad I'd stuck to my instincts and steered clear.

"I'm sorry," I said, softer this time. "I'm not blaming anyone. I'm just trying to figure out what happened to her."

"We all want that, Gray," Norah said, returning from the kitchen with my tea. I wrapped my hands around the offered mug and nodded my thanks.

The witches fidgeted in their seats.

"I know you're probably feeling helpless," Norah continued, "like maybe you need to get out there and do something proactive. We all feel that way. But like I told the girls, now that the police are involved, I think it's best if we let them handle it. Right, girls?"

"Yes, Norah," came the chorus.

Okay... Death made people awkward and uncomfortable in the best of situations, but now I was getting *serious* creepy vibes. Cult vibes. And what did she mean, *now that the police are involved*? Would she have preferred to put these dainty, coffee-cake-nibbling witches in charge? Scare the killer out of hiding with a coordinated floral napkin offensive?

The fire popped and hissed beside me, and I sighed, watching the steam dance across the surface of my tea. I wished I were better prepared for this, but your best friend's murder isn't exactly something you can plan for.

"I'm not helpless," I said. "That's why I'm here. I'm trying to do something more productive than crying."

Norah bristled. "We all cared about Sophie, Gray. We are dealing with this loss the best way we—"

"She's not *lost*," I snapped. "We're not putting her picture on a milk carton, hoping she'll turn up in Iowa with a bad case of amnesia. She's not coming back—ever. She's dead."

The energy in the room crackled, and I looked up to find all eyes on me.

"I'm sorry," I said again. God, how was I screwing this up so badly? "I just wanted to ask a few questions about Sophie and the meeting last night to see if the police may have overlooked anything."

"You don't trust Detective Alvarez?" Concern flashed in Norah's eyes, but like her smile, it didn't seem authentic. "He said you and your... *friend*... called him directly."

Her tone was almost accusatory.

"It's not that," I said. "I'm sure he's great at his job. But he doesn't know Sophie. How her mind worked, who she was. He's not a witch."

"Oh, and you *are*?" Delilah snapped.

"Delilah," Norah warned.

"No," Delilah said. "It's not right. Gray thinks she can stomp in here with her demon pet, insult us, get whatever she wants from us, when all she's ever done is pretend we don't exist. She thinks she's too good for us. She thinks she's the only one who has a right to grieve for Sophie."

"It's not like that! Sophie... She was my best friend," I said. "She's all the family I had."

"Yeah? Whose fault is that?" Delilah asked. "You could've been part of this, Gray. Part of *us*. That was the only thing Sophie ever really asked of you, and you let her down."

Her words hit their mark, slicing through me like a hot blade.

I was out of my chair in an instant, my mug crashing to the floor as I lunged for her.

Before I got within striking distance, the air around me shimmered with magic.

I was flat on my back before I took my next breath.

"I will *not* have you attacking the sisters in my home!" Norah loomed large over me, hand outstretched as her magic pinned me in place. The unspoken warning in her eyes made my blood run cold.

Her hold spell was terrifyingly strong. She'd barely granted me enough room to breathe, and when she finally released me, I sucked in air like I'd been starved of it for days.

Haley held out a hand, helping me up off the floor. A

guilty look crossed her face—almost as if she felt bad about what Norah had done—but it was gone before I could get a true read on her.

"I think it's time for you to go," Norah said. Her tone had softened slightly, but the steel in her eyes had not. "I'll walk you out."

Outside the door, I tried to apologize for going after Delilah and making a mess of the living room, but Norah cut me off, grabbing my arm and dragging me to the other side of the wraparound porch.

Far from the front windows and the prying eyes of the others, she said, "You involved the police. That's why they don't trust you."

"I came home to find my best friend dead in her bed. What was I supposed to do?"

"You should have contacted us first, Gray. There are things we might have tried—other avenues. But it's too late. We risk too much exposure as it is."

"What avenues?"

"Delilah wasn't wrong in what she said."

"What, that I'm not one of you? Or that I'm not a witch at all?" I couldn't bring myself to repeat what she'd said about Sophie. About how disappointing I was.

"As I understand it, you turned your back on your powers a long time ago," Norah said. "What, then, makes you a witch?"

My eyes widened. Sophie must've told Norah all about me.

Anger flared briefly in my chest. I didn't like people

knowing my secrets, and Sophie knew that. But how could I be mad at her for trying to bring us together? She'd thought the witches could help me. That we could help each other.

Oh, sweet Sophie.

"You can't have it both ways." Norah folded her arms across her chest. "You're afraid of your magic, and that's a dangerous place to be. For all of us."

I opened my mouth to deny it, but she was right. I *was* afraid of my magic. I *hated* magic. It was the reason I'd lived most of my life on the run. The reason I wanted nothing to do with the coven.

"You react out of fear," Norah went on, "and that's how people get hurt. That's how witches get exposed."

"Using magic is how witches get exposed. For all you know, that little hold spell you cast on me sent out a beacon."

"One spell is hardly enough to send out anything. And my home is warded, Gray."

"Are you sure?"

"I don't take unnecessary risks with my coven."

"What about necessary ones?"

Norah frowned, her eyes searching my face for a long time. I had no idea what she was looking for, but I was pretty sure she didn't find it.

"I'm very sorry about Sophie's death." Norah put a hand on my shoulder. "But unless you're willing to commit yourself to this sisterhood, to live by *our* code, I can't help you. Not with your grief, and not with your magic."

I jerked away from her touch. "I didn't come here to drink the coven Kool-Aid."

"Then we've got nothing left to say to you, Gray."

I pulled out my phone. "Can I at least text them my number? In case anyone remembers anything about—"

"If anyone remembers anything significant, we will share it with the police, as we've already been instructed." Norah headed to the front door. Without so much as a backward glance, she said, "I have to insist that you don't return here, Gray. I can't have you stirring up the coven and causing problems."

With that, she disappeared inside, bolting the door behind her. Fresh wards vibrated across my skin, much stronger than the others, nudging me away from the house.

The longer I stood in place, the harder the wards nudged, until they finally turned painful. It felt like an electrical current.

The message was clear.

You're not one of us, outsider.

I headed down the porch stairs and out into the rainy afternoon, stopping once I'd cleared the wards to take one more look at the house. Behind the star-shaped window at the top, I caught sight of a pale face framed in dark curls, her hand pressed against the colored glass panes.

Reva.

I couldn't tell whether it was a goodbye... or a call for help.

SIXTEEN

GRAY

Ronan was no longer alone.

I found him sitting on the edge of a mermaid fountain in Bloodstone Park's sculpture garden with a man I'd never seen before. A demon, I realized, catching a faint whiff of his scent—fresh ground cinnamon, hot peppers, and candle flame all woven into one incredibly powerful, incredibly intoxicating package. Despite the rain and the distance between us, I could *feel* the heat emanating from him.

I crept a little closer and ducked behind an adjacent statue, keeping out of sight as I sussed out the situation.

"—so overprotective of her," Hot Demon was saying. "It'll get you smoked."

"I'm handling it," Ronan said.

"Dude. You're emotionally compromised. You can't possibly—"

"I said I'm handling it," Ronan snapped.

"Handling *it*, or handling *her*?" The demon grinned, his implications clear.

"Fuck off, Ash. It's not like that."

"No? So tell me what it's like. Because from where I sit, you're out there risking your ass for a—" The demon cut off abruptly, and for a second I worried I'd been discovered. But then he barked out a laugh, pointing an accusatory finger at Ronan. "Oh, shit. You're in love with her."

My heart skittered, but before I could even contemplate what that might mean, Ronan grabbed the guy's throat, every muscle in his body strung tight as a bow.

"Tread carefully, dickhead," Ronan said, low and menacing. "*Real* carefully."

Sucking in a deep breath, I took a few steps backward.

I shouldn't have eavesdropped. There was no point in assigning meaning to the demon's words, to Ronan's reactions, to the butterfly swirls in my stomach. We had bigger things to worry about now.

Still a little unsteady, I looped back around the outer edge of the park and re-entered the sculpture garden from the other side, coming at them head-on.

Ronan got to his feet when they spotted me, but Hot Demon stayed put. Even from a distance I could see him glowering, making no attempt to hide his disdain as he scanned my body head to toe.

When I reached the statue and he finally met my gaze, my breath caught.

Holy. Hell.

He wasn't just Hot Demon. He was Gorgeous, Mesmerizing, Sex-on-a-Platter Demon. Penetrating dark blue eyes pinned me in place, as fathomless and hypnotic as the deepest part of the ocean. His cupid's bow lips were full and perfect, cocked to the side in what looked to be a permanent bad-boy smirk. My fingers itched to slide into his messy, chestnut-colored hair, pull him close, and beg for a taste of that kiss. I could already feel the soft scratch of his stubble on my chin as his hot, wet mouth claimed mine, my core pulsing with need...

"Are you fucking *serious* right now, Ash?" Ronan punched the guy in the arm, his sharp reprimand snapping me out of the momentary fantasy.

It felt like I'd just been cut free from a giant rubber band, and I gasped for air, trying to get my heart rate under control.

Demons don't have influence powers like vamps do.... So what the hell just happened?

The demon laughed, but just as quickly as that rakish smile had appeared, it vanished, and he narrowed his eyes on me once again. "So *you're* the girl Ronan's losing so much sleep over? Gotta admit—not what I was expecting."

"Happy to disappoint," I said, glowering right back at him. I didn't know why he was affecting me so strongly, but I wouldn't give him the satisfaction of showing it. Or of admitting that I already missed his smile and wished I'd worn something other than a sweatshirt the color of Pepto-Bismol. "Who the fuck are you again?"

"He's nobody," Ronan said, at the same time the demon

said, "The guy who's gonna make sure you don't put a wrecking ball through my boy's life."

Ronan pinched the bridge of his nose as if the whole ordeal had given him a headache. "Gray Desario, meet Asher O'Keefe. Asher O'Keefe, fucking behave yourself."

Asher... Why did I know that name?

"Wait," I said. "Asher—with the safe house?"

Asher grinned. "Whatever horrible things you've heard about me, Cupcake, they're all true."

I had no doubt about that, but unfortunately, I hadn't heard *anything* about him—not really. That was the problem.

Well, that... and the fact that the evidence of my stupid fantasy still lingered between my thighs.

With a mouth like that, I bet he kisses like a god...

Crossing my arms over my chest to hide my suddenly erect nipples, I turned to Ronan. "This isn't really the best time for bringing new friends into the mix."

"Oh, I'm not your friend, sweetheart," Asher said.

"Ignore him. They don't let him out of his cage often." Ronan shot Asher a warning glare, then wrapped a hand around my forearm, his touch comforting and familiar, grounding me as always. "Any progress with the witches?"

"Sure. I progressed clear through to the part where they banned me for life."

"Seriously? What happened?"

I glanced back at Asher, not sure how much I should reveal.

"He's with us, Gray," Ronan said softly.

"Can I talk to you for a sec?" I jerked my head toward a whale sculpture about ten yards away. "In private?"

"You'd better go, Ronan," Asher jeered. "Wouldn't want the witch getting her pointy little hat in a twist."

Ignoring him, I grabbed Ronan's hand and headed for the whale. We were safely out of earshot when I turned to him with a scowl. "Explain."

"Gray…" Ronan dragged a hand through his damp hair, lowering his eyes. In a voice thick with emotion, he said, "Sophie was murdered in your house last night. Alvarez doesn't have any leads. We obviously can't count on Norah."

"That's an understatement."

"The point is you're still in danger. We need backup on this, and Asher's the best demon for the job."

"Best demon for the job? No, screw that. We *are* the backup. You and me. Just like always." I tried to keep my voice steady, but it broke on the last word. After yesterday, I wasn't sure I could put much faith in words like *always* anymore. As badly as I wanted it to be so, *always* just wasn't a promise anyone could keep. Not even Ronan.

He cupped my face and met my gaze again, his leaves-in-the-autumn eyes both gentle and fierce. In a reassuring voice that left no room for argument, he said, "Keeping you safe is my number one priority. I can't do it by myself, and your new vamp-buddy Beaumont is useless during daylight hours."

"Hmm. But not so useless at night, right?"

Ronan shrugged. "He's not a bad guy to have in your

corner. I wouldn't have called him about the safe house last night if that wasn't the case. But you vetoed that plan, and here we are."

"Yeah, I vetoed it, because I'm not leaving." I tugged the sleeves down over my hands, blowing on them for warmth. "So you've decided to trust Darius?"

"Trusting him was never the issue. I just don't like that he…" Ronan grabbed my hands, his thumbs grazing the insides of my wrists. The spot where Darius had fed from prickled.

"Anyway," Ronan continued, "someone out there is taking out witches, and on top of that, you've got the Grim Creeper on your ass. The whole thing is just an epic cluster fuck."

Grim Creeper. I might've laughed at that one if there were anything even remotely funny about this situation.

"Ronan…" I fought off a shiver and looked into his eyes. I really didn't want to talk about what had happened in the alley—what had almost happened again with Sophie—but I couldn't keep him in the dark any longer. "Last night… That thing with Sophie? When he said all that stuff about inserting souls?"

"He's crazy, Gray. He doesn't know what the fuck he's talking about."

"He's Death, Ronan. Pretty sure he's got his finger on the pulse, okay?"

"It's not—"

"Listen to me. Please." I had to tell him before I chickened out again. "The reason he showed up like that… It's because of my magic. Something's wrong. The other night in the alley, a girl got hurt trying to help me fight off an attacker. She died in my arms, and before I even realized what was happening, I tapped into my magic. Somehow I…" I blinked away the images of her milky stare and those jerky, awkward steps as she shambled out of the alley, tears blurring my eyes. "I brought her back."

Ronan went completely still. Through a jaw clenched so tightly I thought his teeth might shatter, he said, "Define 'brought her back.'"

"I mean, one minute she was dead, and then I sort of…" I held up my palms like I had that night, and the slick, watery feeling of her soul came right back to me, making my skin tingle. "I basically—*magically*—pushed her soul back inside. I don't know how else to describe it."

"Like you tried to do with Sophie," he said.

"Yes. Only I wasn't trying—not with either of them. Something took over and it just sort of… happened." I shivered, remembering the ghostly black trees that had infiltrated my magic place. Echoes of that coal-dark wood had stayed with me even now, and as much as I wanted to tell Ronan every last detail, I couldn't bring myself to describe it. Talking about that place felt too much like going back there, and I never wanted to go back to that forest again.

I told him the rest, though. About the man in the alley, and Bean, and how Darius had figured it all out.

Ronan was silent for so long, I was beginning to worry I'd finally pushed him over the edge.

"You can say it," I whispered, my throat tightening. "I'm

a total freak. I wouldn't blame you if you bailed. Or notified the—"

"I can't believe you'd even *think* that."

I shrugged. It's not that I didn't have faith in our friendship—I did. But in my experience, once the first domino fell, they had a tendency to keep dropping.

"Gray, that's not…" Ronan shook his head, blowing out a breath. He reached out and pulled me into a hug, pressing his lips to the top of my head. "I will *never* bail on you. Or do anything to put you in harm's way. Ever."

My heart sped up, everything inside me suddenly warm and buzzing. Words like *safe* and *home* and *real* floated through my mind, and I reached up to brush my fingertips across his lips, wanting to touch him, to feel him.

Wanting to kiss him.

Ronan wanted it, too. I could see it in his eyes, a hundred moments just like this one crashing through his memory, finally pushing us past the invisible boundary we'd both worked so hard to keep in place. None of that mattered anymore. Nothing mattered but this moment, the kiss we could no longer delay…

"Hey, lovebirds?"

Ronan and I jumped apart at the interruption, and I turned to see fucking Asher O'Keefe waltzing into our private moment with another one of his maddeningly stupid smirks.

"Think we could continue this touchy-feely fest somewhere else?" he asked. "I'm freezing my dick off out here."

"Real classy," I said.

"Hey. No one likes a frozen dick, Cupcake."

"How do *you* know?" I snapped. "Maybe *lots* of people like frozen dick."

"In that case, when's your birthday?"

That earned him another punch from Ronan. "Fuck off, Ash. Preferably at least fifty feet away."

"No problem," Asher said, stomping away in a huff. "Fucking off is what I live for."

I rolled my eyes at Ronan, watching Asher's retreating backside. Staring at it, actually. "So that's the guy you want looking out for me, huh?"

"He may be rough around the edges—"

"Not to mention a complete tool."

"That, too." Ronan smiled, but it was clear our tender moment had passed.

It was also clear I would need to find a really good hiding place for Asher's body, because once all this was over, I was going to *kill* that demon.

"I trust him with my life," Ronan said. "And yours."

I searched his eyes, but there was absolutely no uncertainty there. Whatever I personally thought about Asher, Ronan was vouching for him.

I sighed.

"Give him a chance." Ronan looped me into another embrace, and I lay my ear against his chest, inhaling his cloves-and-campfire scent, once again finding my safe place in the steady beat of his heart.

"Fine," I grumbled. "I'll give him a chance. But you

can't make me like him. I've known him all of ten minutes, and I already want to punch him in the nuts."

Ronan laughed, the deep rumble of it reverberating in my ear as he tightened his arms around me. "Gray Desario, you have no idea how fucking *thrilled* I am to hear that."

SEVENTEEN

GRAY

We walked side by side down Pierce Avenue, me in the middle, flanked by the two demons now tasked with keeping me safe.

Unlike Ronan, I wasn't ready to assume I had a target on my back, and I certainly wasn't ready for this to become a permanent arrangement. But for now, I took comfort in their imposing presence, and as we walked back toward my neighborhood, I felt a little better than I had this morning.

"So, the witches..." Ronan prompted, picking up where we'd left off in the park.

"They're definitely hiding something," I said. "It's so obvious."

The rain had let up, and in the sudden quiet of the deserted street, my declaration sounded paranoid and shrill.

Didn't mean I was wrong, though.

"Everyone in this town is hiding something," Asher said, scanning the streets as we walked.

"Even you?" I asked.

He turned toward me and smirked, his blue eyes a striking contrast to the dull gray day. "*Especially* me, Cupcake."

"Well, everyone may be keeping secrets," I said, "but only one person murdered my best friend. And I'm pretty sure those witches know a hell of a lot more than they're letting on."

"Doesn't add up, Gray." Ronan shook his head. "You said it yourself—Sophie was basically part of the coven. Their sister. Why would they cover up her murder?"

I clenched my teeth. *Part of the coven. Their sister.* It still stung to hear it.

"You didn't see them, Ronan. Something about the whole scene was just... off." I had no love for the Bay Coven, nor them for me, but something about Norah's rejection went beyond all that. It wasn't sitting well with me.

Now that I'd had some distance from it, I could see it more clearly. Our conversation on the porch, the tea... In fact, other than my fight with Delilah, and Reva's final goodbye, almost everything about my visit had felt staged.

"A witch was murdered," Ronan said. "One of their own. They've gotta be spooked."

"I could almost buy that, but I'm telling you, there's more to it. It's like... I don't know. Like they're all afraid of Norah."

Ronan shrugged. "She's the alpha, right?"

"She's the *elder*," I corrected. "And it's her house. But witches aren't like shifters. Covens are big on equality—one voice, one vote kind of shit."

"Except—" Asher pointed at my face, his mouth stretched into a smug grin. "—when it comes to you. You get *no* votes."

"Yeah, well. They don't see me as a witch." I smacked his hand away, ignoring the momentary spark I felt at the brief contact. "They've made that pretty clear."

Asher grunted. "Nothing says get the fuck out like the 'Don't Let the Door Hit You in the Ass' ward."

"Thanks. I was wondering what that ward meant." *Asshole.*

Burrowing deeper into Sophie's sweatshirt, I swallowed the lump in my throat, blinking back tears. I had never wanted to join the coven, but maybe some part of me liked knowing the door was open if I ever changed my mind.

Now, I was truly a witch alone.

As if he could read my thoughts, Ronan slid his warm hand around the back of my neck, casting my skin in goosebumps. "You're not alone, Gray."

"Clearly," Asher chimed in. "Ronan can't keep his hands off you for more than five minutes without getting twitchy."

"Keep talking, demon," Ronan warned, "and I'll twitch my boot right up your ass."

I forced a smile. I appreciated Ronan's support in all its many forms, but he didn't understand. Despite his loyalty to our friendship—and apparently to Asher—demons were solitary by nature; I suspected that was why Ronan took off like he did, disappearing for days at a time, or why he sometimes slipped into a melancholy so deep and dark I feared I'd never be able to drag him back into the light.

Sometimes the human world got to be too much for a demon.

Me? I was solitary by circumstance, not by choice.

"Game night!" Sophie announced, bouncing into the living room with a bottle of Absolut. "Drunk charades. Am I brilliant, or am I brilliant?"

"You're totally brilliant," I said. "But I'm pretty sure we need more people to play charades. Also, I have to work in an hour."

"Ooh, I know this one!" Sophie pointed the bottle at my face, her grin lighting up the room. "Boring-ass bitch who desperately needs a fun night off."

"Wow. You really are brilliant."

"Call Waldrich and tell him you're sick. I'll get the glasses..."

Tears clouded my vision as the random memory passed, the reality of her death slamming into me all over again. Half my heart was missing. And she hadn't just died of natural causes, or fallen on a wet sidewalk, or lost the battle to some crazy disease. All of those things would've been terrible, but they were actual reasons.

This? Some senseless murder? Someone had *taken* her from us. They'd come into our home, found her sleeping in bed, and snuffed the life out of her.

The air rushed from my lungs, and my knees buckled beneath me, threatening to send me sprawling. But just before I crashed to the pavement, two pairs of strong hands grabbed my arms and hauled me up.

"Gray?" Asher's face was a blur before me, but I didn't miss the flash of concern in his eyes.

"She's okay." Ronan leaned in close, his strong arms enveloping me, his voice warm and comforting in my ear. "Just breathe, Gray. Just breathe."

I couldn't though. That was the thing.

My chest felt like it had been clawed open, my heart exposed. Even as Ronan rubbed slow circles on my back, I couldn't seem to catch my breath. All around me, the world tilted sideways, rocking and spinning until I could no longer tell which way was up and which way was down.

More memories of Sophie flickered through my mind like a hundred little movies: Eating Chinese takeout on the floor the first night in our rental house, wondering what people without access to Chinese takeout did on moving day. Painting her bedroom a pale lavender and mine a sunny yellow-orange, only to switch rooms when we realized we each liked the other one better. Finding one of her cheerful painted rocks in the pocket of an old coat I hadn't worn in months, wishing me a beautiful day; snuggling together under her sunflowers-and-daisies comforter and binge-watching romantic comedies on her laptop during a rare snowstorm that had kept the entire city indoors for two days. And of course, that first night we'd met during a delivery to Illuminae—the instant connection I'd felt the moment she smiled at me across the bar.

I'm new here, she'd said, signing for the order. *Don't tell anyone I have no idea what I'm doing.*

Since that night nearly seven years ago, I hadn't gone more than a day without seeing her.

Now, I'd never see her again. Never find a rock in my pocket, painted with one of her encouraging Sophie-isms. Never draw Tarot cards with her over a pot of tea after a long shift. Never climb up onto our garage roof at midnight to watch a meteor shower.

Never tell her how much she meant to me.

A tremble rolled through my body, starting in my legs and rumbling up through my chattering teeth. Tears leaked unbidden from my eyes, and I squeezed them shut and tried to follow the sound of Ronan's voice, a faraway beacon in the fog of this wretched misery.

"Just breathe, baby," Ronan whispered again. "I've got you."

I didn't know how long I'd stood there falling apart in his arms, but when the fog finally dissipated and I felt like I could stand on my own two feet again, I looked up into Ronan's eyes and smiled. Not a happy grin by any stretch, but a grateful one.

Grateful for Ronan. Grateful for our friendship and his unwavering loyalty. Grateful that no matter how short Sophie's life had been, the universe had seen fit to give us seven years together.

In that moment, I was even grateful for grumpy Asher—not that I'd share *that* particular sentiment out loud.

"There you are." Ronan returned my smile, then pressed

a kiss to my forehead. "Hey. When was the last time you ate? Toast doesn't count."

"I... don't remember."

He grabbed my hand, lacing our fingers together and giving me a reassuring squeeze as Asher resumed his place on my right. "Come on. We're making a detour."

Johnny's Seaside Pizza was a tiny place on Water Street with a three-stools-wide counter up front, a kitchen in the back, and a side room the size of a shack for placing takeout orders. Despite the meager setup, it was the best damn pizza west of Seattle—and only four blocks from home.

Ronan was buying, so Asher and I waited outside under the awning as another downpour pelted the pavement in front of us. Across the street, two crows huddled beneath a bench, arguing over a soggy pizza crust.

Watching them fight for that scrap of food filled me with deep sadness.

"Hey, Asher? I... Thanks," I mumbled, needing a distraction. "For before. I don't usually..."

I trailed off, not sure how to finish that. In the last two nights, I'd gotten a young girl killed, half-resurrected her, sworn a blood oath with a vampire, found my best friend murdered in her bed, refused an invitation from Death, and gotten myself officially banned from a coven. Something told me there were quite a few more 'I don't usually' moments in my future.

Asher nodded once, but he didn't say anything. Didn't even turn to look at me.

Wow. If Ronan was enigmatic, this guy was downright impenetrable.

When I couldn't take another minute of his stone-cold silence, I turned to him and said, "So, what's your story, Asher O'Keefe?"

"Which one, Gray Desario?"

"Any one. I don't know. How did you and Ronan hook up?"

"Wouldn't *you* like to know?" he teased.

"I was just trying to make conversation."

"Hot tip, Cupcake." He turned to me with a condescending frown. "Maybe you should stick to making your fluffy bunny potions or sparkly charm bracelets or whatever it is you flit around doing all day."

"Potions and charm bracelets? Please." I let out a low chuckle. "I'm more of a poisons girl myself. Never know when you might need a gruesome yet completely untraceable cause of death for that special someone in your life."

Asher cocked an eyebrow, and I swear I caught a flicker of appreciation in his sea-blue eyes.

I was trapped by his beautiful gaze, and again I felt that strange pull, like tendrils of heat snaking around my body and drawing me in. But right as I was about to fall headlong into another totally inappropriate fantasy, he clammed up, grunting once more before turning his attention back to the fighting crows.

"Whatever you say, Cupcake."

And just like that, I was dismissed.

Fucking demons.

The wind kicked up, spraying us both with bone-chilling rain, finally dousing the heat between my thighs. Shivering, I hunched my shoulders and shoved my hands into my sweatshirt pockets, surprised to discover something waiting for me inside the left one—a note scrawled on a floral-print napkin.

Find Jael. Go alone.

"Shit."

"What is it?" Asher loomed over my shoulder, smothering me in his fiery, spicy scent.

"Someone sending a message." I fingered the napkin, turning over the possibilities in my mind. More to myself than to Asher, I said, "Gotta be Haley—she was the only one who got close enough."

I couldn't decide whether I was relieved or completely freaked. Was Haley an ally after all? Why couldn't she say this in front of Norah and the others? More importantly, what the hell did Haley know about Jael?

"Jael?" Asher grabbed the note, his brow creased with suspicion. "What's this Haley chick's involvement with the Seelie prince?"

I snatched it away from him and shoved it back in my pocket. "That's what I want to know."

Because Jael—Prince of the Seelie Court, brother of Sophie's boss Kallayna, and Illuminae's most sought-after deejay—was also Sophie's lover.

EIGHTEEN

GRAY

If witch and demon relationships were frowned upon in the supernatural community, witches and fae were practically a capital offense.

Fae were beautiful, otherworldly, and highly manipulative. Get too close to one, and he might have you revealing your deepest magical secrets, or worse—using your magic to harm someone else at his behest.

Thing was, Sophie could read their intentions, which made weeding out the shady ones easier for her. So, when she came home late from work one morning last year glowing in a way that had nothing to do with fae illusion and everything to do with Jael's touch, I wasn't worried. I was actually happy for her.

Sophie made me swear I wouldn't tell a soul, both of us giggling like teenagers as she spilled all the sweet and sexy details. She and Jael had been flirting for months, all of it reaching a crescendo that night when they'd finally shared a kiss that led to another kiss that led to... well, everything else.

Until I found Haley's napkin, I'd believed I was the only one other than Sophie and Jael who knew.

Now I wasn't so sure.

The only thing I *was* sure about was that I needed to talk to Jael alone. So, when dawn's first light poked through the clouds the following morning, I sent a little prayer up to Sophie and slipped out of the house as silent as smoke, leaving behind the two sleeping, snoring, way-too-overprotective demons camped out in my living room.

If you didn't know where to look, Illuminae was nearly impossible to find. Fortunately, I'd been delivering here for years and had spent enough time on the inside with Sophie to know the club's cloaking tricks.

From the outside, the building looked like an abandoned storefront, its crumbling bricks covered in graffiti, the windows so caked in grime you couldn't see through them.

The entrance was below sidewalk level, down a narrow, seemingly endless staircase hidden under a pair of rotting wooden doors. To anyone else, it looked like a delivery entrance or a storm cellar, and one peek into the dark abyss beyond was usually enough to scare off even the most intrepid urban explorers.

I yanked open one of the doors and headed down the

stairs, pulling the door shut behind me. It felt like an hour before I reached the bottom, and from there I walked straight ahead down an equally claustrophobic corridor, pitch black but for the dim blue light spilling out around the club entrance at the end of the hall.

I recognized the bouncer standing guard—Leila, a friend of Sophie's.

"Gray!" Leila beamed when she saw me. I was glad my first fae encounter of the day was with someone I actually liked. Leila had waist-length, shocking white hair and bright yellow eyes, the exotic combo reminding me of some kind of Arctic cat. Her gossamer slip dress left little to the imagination, but I was seriously digging her thigh-high red leather boots.

I could tell immediately that she hadn't heard the news, which meant that Detective Alvarez hadn't been here yet. Part of me was pissed—wasn't he supposed to be turning over every stone?—but I was also grateful. It meant I'd get a straight, unrehearsed reaction from Jael.

Besides, it'd only been about a day and a half. With three dead witches on his hands, Alvarez probably had lots of other clues to track down first.

"Oh my God," Leila said, "where the hell is Sophie? She blew off work all weekend. No one can reach her." She leaned in close and lowered her voice, her whisper like wind chimes in a gentle breeze. "But don't worry. Kallayna talks a good game, but she'd never fire Sophie. The customers would revolt—she's our best bartender."

"Sophie's… taking some personal time." I didn't have

the heart to tell her the truth—not yet. Right now, I needed all of my strength to talk to Jael, to find out why Haley had sent me here. "I'm actually looking for Jael. Is he around?"

"Sure," Leila said. "Be right back."

I promised to watch the door while Leila went to find him.

Even though it was dead inside at this early hour, the place was still lit up for a party. The club had no windows, though you wouldn't know it to look around. Fae magic bewitched the walls, the ceiling, and even the floor to look like an endless starry night, as if you were floating in deep space. Every few minutes, a comet streaked overhead, and in the distance, a new star was born. The bar itself seemed invisible—a floating collection of bottles and glassware—until you got up close and realized it was just a series of mirrors and tricks.

If you weren't used to it, the whole place could make you feel drunk and disoriented before you'd even taken one sip of fae potion.

Other than absinthe, I had no idea what most of the bottles I delivered here for Waldrich contained, but I was pretty sure it wasn't Jack Daniels and Bombay gin.

Like Leila, Jael was tall, thin, and fine-boned, with the same white hair and yellow, cat-like eyes. He wore his hair pulled back in a loose, low ponytail, which only accentuated the severity of his sharp cheekbones and lush lips. Dressed in dark jeans and a tight black button-down, he looked more like a Calvin Klein model than a club deejay, and even less like a Seelie prince.

Well, aside from the otherworldly beauty.

I couldn't take my eyes off the pair as they crossed the room toward me, gliding through the faux-starry night like a majestic god and goddess.

Leila resumed her post at the door, turning me over to the prince.

"Miss Desario." Jael pressed a kiss to the back of my hand, his eyes never leaving mine. He was definitely pretty, but Sophie had assured me his delicate looks were deceiving. It was easy to see why she'd fallen for his charms. "I'm told you have a message for me?"

"Is there someplace we can talk privately?" I asked.

"Of course." He led me across the club and into a small sound booth the size of a walk-in closet, most of which was full of electronic equipment.

He closed the door and turned to face me, his arms completely still at his sides. He didn't fidget, didn't cross his arms or smooth out his shirt or lean back against the door or do a single thing that would have made me think for even a second that he was a regular guy.

"I presume this is about Sophie?" he asked, cool as ever. "She hasn't returned my calls. I fear she's upset with me."

There was no easy way to say it, and I needed his honest gut reaction. No sugar coating.

"Sophie was murdered Saturday, Jael."

His cold smile didn't falter, but I saw the agony in his eyes—the briefest flash of deep, heart-wrenching pain—and then it was gone.

I exhaled in relief. I hadn't honestly suspected Jael, but

his reaction—however slight—was all the confirmation I needed.

The fae prince was innocent.

I gave him a few more seconds to sit with the bombshell, then said, "I know that you cared for—"

"Come with me," he said.

Okay, so I guess we're skipping the whole bonding-over-our-shared-pain thing...

Just as well. I wasn't really in the mood to cry on his shoulder and reminisce. Sophie may have been sleeping with him, but Jael wasn't the kind of guy you brought home to get to know your roommate over a few beers. We had absolutely nothing in common.

Other than Sophie...

Steeling myself, I followed him out of the sound booth and up a set of nearby stairs to a glass corridor that over-looked the bar and the main dance floor below.

At the end of the corridor, a solid black door with a silver doorknob awaited, shockingly plain compared to its magical surroundings. Jael retrieved a key from his pocket and slid it into the keyhole above the knob.

Looking over his shoulder, he said, "I asked her to return with me."

"What do you mean?" I asked, then cringed. In the small space of the hallway, my voice sounded loud and crass compared to his. "Where?"

Jael frowned and shook his head as if I was wasting his time with my stupid human questions. "To court, Miss Desario. Where else?"

"But… That would mean…" I wasn't as up-close-and-personal with fae culture as my best friend, but I was pretty sure that when a fae prince invited a human to court, it was basically the equivalent of a marriage proposal.

"She declined, of course." Jael pushed open the door, gesturing for me to go in ahead of him, then closing and locking it behind us. He touched the wall just inside, and the room was bathed in a soft glow, no brighter than the light of a full moon, but plenty enough to see by. "She told me she had important work to finish here. And, of course, there was you to consider."

His cat-eyes narrowed, trapping me in a gaze so vicious I worried I might have been wrong about his innocence. But then it was gone, replaced with cool detachment, and I recognized the brief flare of emotion for what it was: jealousy.

Sophie had chosen me over him. That's how he saw it.

"I didn't know," I said. It was another secret between us, another layer in the deep iceberg of my best friend's life. "Sophie never told—"

Jael held up his hand. "That is not why you were sent here. Please, take a seat."

At the center of the room, eight leather executive chairs surrounded a large conference table—again, a touch of normalcy completely incongruous to this otherworldly place.

I took a seat at the head of the table, swiveling in my chair to watch Jael's movements. He was behind me, and I didn't like it.

"Jael, what—"

"Quiet." In a flash, he turned to the wall and pressed his palms flat against it, whispering incantations in a language I couldn't understand. The wall glowed a strangely beautiful shade of deep purple I'd never seen in the human world, then slid sideways to reveal a hidden closet. From the tallest shelf, he retrieved a metal lockbox similar to the kind they used at banks.

"This belonged to her, stored here for safekeeping each night. Do you know what it contains?" he asked, setting it on the table before me. His reverent tone suggested it was important.

My heartbeat kicked into high gear. If this were a movie, the box could've contained anything—money, fake passports, drugs, diamonds, paternity test results. But as far as I knew, there was only one thing Sophie would go to the trouble of locking up in a secret fae vault.

I shook my head, not wanting to admit it. Not wanting to even believe it. "I have no idea."

Jael reached down inside his shirt and pulled out a shimmering chain so fine it was nearly invisible. A tiny but intricate golden key dangled from the end.

Unclasping the chain from his neck, he said, "Sophie instructed me to give you this in the event of her departure from this realm."

I held out my hand, and he dropped the key into my palm. It was much heavier than it looked, warming instantly at my touch.

"The key unlocks the box, but you're the only one who

can unlock what's inside." Jael watched me for a moment, his pale skin luminescent in the dim room. He really was beautiful, and despite his coldness, my heart ached for his loss. He might not be willing—or even able—to show it, but I sensed the depth of his pain. It felt nearly as endless as mine.

He really loved her…

"This room will afford you complete privacy," he said. "Once I exit and close the door, nothing you say, do, think, or cast will echo beyond these walls."

I nodded, grateful for this particular bit of fae magic.

After Jael left, I wasted no time unlocking the box and folding back the lid. That was the easy part.

Accepting responsibility for the contents?

That was another story altogether.

NINETEEN

GRAY

I reached into the box and retrieved the objects nestled inside—a slim silver dagger in a jewel-encrusted sheath and a hardcover book the size of an old encyclopedia, its faded black cover etched with a silver pentacle surrounded by flowering vines.

Hundreds of bright, tiny threads crisscrossed the book, locking it in a cage of light that glowed red and pulsed in time with my heartbeat.

A blood spell.

Jael didn't need to tell me I was the only one who could see those threads.

I set the book on the table and unsheathed the dagger, taking a few deep, shaky breaths.

A witch's book of shadows was more than a diary. It was a reckoning of her life as a witch, an accounting of her days, her magical hopes and dreams, her trials and tribulations, triumphs and failures, and yes—her spellcraft. Other than the clothes on my back, my own book of shadows was the only thing I'd taken from my old life in New York, and even though I'd stopped practicing magic the moment I crossed state lines, the book was still my most cherished possession, locked up in a waterproof safe and buried in our backyard. It was a part of me, just as Sophie's was a part of her.

The fact that she'd secured it inside the club and bound it with a blood spell tuned only to me meant she was keeping even more secrets than I thought.

Part of me—a big part—didn't want to know what lurked behind that black cover. But Sophie had wanted me to know. No matter what she'd revealed to Haley and the coven witches, no matter what intimacies she'd shared with Jael, I was the only one she'd trusted with this.

I owed it to her to press on.

"No more secrets, girl." Holding my breath, I sliced my palm with the blade, then made a tight fist, dripping blood onto the pentacle. My blood filled in its outlines, tiny channels that now glowed deep red rather than silver.

The room filled with the scent of apples and vanilla, and I closed my eyes, letting the warm and gentle touch of what could only be Sophie's magic envelope me. Unlike Haley and the others, I'd never smelled it before; Sophie and I had never practiced together.

When I opened my eyes, I found myself in my clearing again, hands pressed to the stone surface of the pedestal. The barren black forest I'd last encountered here had retreated a bit, giving way to the green meadow I remembered. Sophie's book of shadows lay open on the stone slab before me, a soft breeze rippling through the pages and revealing her collection of herbal and crystal correspondences, custom Tarot spreads and readings, and sketches of plant life and moon phases.

I traced my fingers over a Tarot reading dated from last week, but before I could interpret it, something in the meadow caught my attention—a woman dancing barefoot in the dewy grass, her hair shimmering like a rainbow.

Sophie!

Abandoning the book, I ran to her, heart pounding in my chest.

"You found me," she said, beaming. "I knew you'd come."

She gave me her brightest smile, the one I'd seen nearly every day for seven years. It was almost exactly like the real thing, but not quite.

I pulled her into my arms and held on tight anyway. Deep down I knew it wasn't really her—just the combined effect of our joint magic on the book, my mind conjuring up the image and feel of Sophie to go along with her written words. But at that moment, I didn't care. This connection, this magical bond... It was the closest I would ever get to her again.

"I miss you so much." I pulled back to look at her. Projection or not, I wanted to memorize every detail of her face, catalog all the things I hadn't truly taken the time to look at while she was alive, even if my subconscious had.

Back then, I didn't think I'd need to.

Sophie nodded, but her smile was fading fast. "We don't have much time."

Truer words had never been spoken.

Sophie and I used to say that it'd felt like we'd known each other our entire lives, but that wasn't the case at all.

I'd learned more about my best friend in the days since her death than in the entire span of our friendship. Part of that was because she'd kept things from me, but most of it was my fault. I'd been too stubborn, too proud, too wrapped up in my own shit to think for one minute that Sophie might have secrets. That she might want to share those secrets with me.

There was so much I wanted to say to her, so much I *needed* to say, but just like I knew this projection wasn't really Sophie, I also knew she hadn't entrusted her book of shadows to me just so I could absolve my guilt.

"We need to talk, don't we," I said. It wasn't a question.

She opened her hands before me. Her favorite Tarot deck—the one we'd last used that morning in the kitchen —materialized.

I smiled sadly. "I didn't bring any tea."

"That's okay. Maybe next time."

I followed her to a flat, even spot in the grass, and we sat down across from each other, a black silk cloth spread on the ground between us. The eerie black trees crept closer again, their bare branches stretching endlessly into the sky.

Sophie turned over the first card.

I gasped. It was my least favorite card in the deck—in

any deck. More than the Death card, the Tower struck a chord of fear deep in my heart.

Sophie's grin was almost manic, though. She wiggled her eyebrows, and in a singsong voice, said, "Don't fear the storm, Gray. Be ready for it."

It's what she'd always said about the Tower. It was one of her favorite cards—never mind the sudden, shocking pain the Tower typically heralded. Sophie was all about the aftermath. The inevitable fresh start that came when everything you'd once held so dearly crumbled down around you.

Taking a deep breath, I focused on the imagery of the card. From the depths of a black sky, the moon shot a bright beam of light into a massive brick tower, smashing the top to bits. People jumped from the highest windows to avoid the devastation; one man already lay bent and broken on the ground.

"Something bad is coming, isn't it?" I whispered.

"Something *big*, that's for sure." Sophie shrugged. "Bad is relative."

"You sense this? I mean, you did? Before?"

Sophie nodded. "I think you sense it, too."

She was right. Even before her death and the incident in the alley, something had been feeling... off. Like the calm before the storm, as cliché as that sounded.

And something told me that Bean's resurrection, Sophie's murder, and Death's arrival were still just parts of that calm—that the real stormy shit hadn't even hit the fan yet.

"Draw another card," I said.

The Magician appeared next, and Sophie covered him crosswise with the reversed King of Swords. Normally I liked the King—he often showed up when I was feeling sorry for myself and needed a reminder that I had the power to kick life in the ass. But the reversal gave him a sinister cast, one that spoke of madness, brutality, and domination. With the tyrant King covering the Magician, there was no mistaking the message.

Hunters.

I wrapped my arms around my chest, trying to remind myself that I wasn't alone in this. That I had Ronan. Darius. Asher. That despite Norah's threats, Haley and some of the others might come around, too.

Assuming I could get close to them again. Assuming I even wanted to—jury was still out on that.

"Hunters have been quiet for too long." Sophie traced her fingers over the King's sword. A menacing imp with sharp teeth and even sharper claws sat at the King's feet, clutching the entire earth in his talons. "The witches believe we're on the verge of another Great Hunt."

"Norah, too?"

"Norah prefers to keep her head in the sand." Sophie's eyes darkened. "She can't be trusted, Gray."

Sophie turned over another card—the High Priestess—but she was reversed like the King of Swords.

"Haley and I found out that some of the underground covens back east had been in touch with Norah, trying to share information and unify against the threat. They're all feeling it, Gray. One of the Boston leaders said that the same ripples we're feeling here are stirring up groups in Europe and Southeast Asia, even as far away as Australia. They're all trying to reconnect, but it's hard because there's still a lot of mistrust and fear."

"Are you serious? The covens are talking about unifying?"

If that were true, it was major news. Witches had gone their separate ways decades ago in hopes of avoiding detection by the hunters, who at that time had grown extremely powerful. Splinter groups like the Bay Coven remained, but typically operated underground. These days, an attack on one witch by a single hunter was enough to send the stragglers back into the shadows.

And after a generation with everyone doing their own thing, uniting them under a single purpose seemed like an impossible task.

"Some of them are trying to figure it out," Sophie said. "The stronger, more established groups believe it's time for witches to rise up again, to come out of the broom closet and take on the hunters once and for all. But Norah wants no part of it. When Haley and I confronted her about keeping her communications with the other groups secret, she freaked. She forbade us from getting in touch with anyone outside Bay Coven. She said if she found out anyone had gone against her rule, she'd bind our magic."

"Holy shit. Can she even do that?"

"Does she have the authority? Well, there's no one to

stop her. Whether she has the juice for it is another question, but none of us wanted to test it."

"How could you even stand to be around her?" I shook my head, trying to clear the memories of yesterday's disastrous confrontation with Norah. "How could you put yourself in danger like that? You should've—"

You should've told me, I wanted to say. But of course, she'd tried to tell me. Tried to get me involved, to get my help.

"I'm sorry," I said instead. "I should've listened to you."

"You didn't know, Gray." Sophie reached across the cards and grabbed my hand, squeezing it fiercely. "Just… Stay off Norah's radar. You need to be prepared for whatever's coming, and you can't do it with Norah on your ass. The only one you can trust for sure is Haley, and maybe Reva, but she's pretty new. The others are alright, but some of them still think the sun rises and sets on Norah's face."

"Do you really think the hunters are coming?" I asked.

A breeze stirred, and behind us on the pedestal, the pages of the book rustled.

"The Bay witches aren't the only ones to turn up dead this fall," Sophie said. "Three east coast witches were murdered in their beds last month. Then more in Chicago, Denver, San Francisco—and those are the ones Haley and I found out about. I'm sure there are others."

Turn up dead…

My heart squeezed in my chest. Sitting here in the grass, looking into my best friend's eyes, I'd almost forgotten this version of Sophie wasn't real. All of her words were coming from my own thoughts and projections, or from her book—from the things she'd written about before her death. Things she'd wanted me to know all along.

Her comment about dead witches only reminded me how blind I'd been.

I reached out and squeezed her knee, searching for the words to make things right, but Sophie had already returned her attention to the cards.

She drew the Six of Wands next—a beautiful, moon-faced creature with iridescent wings emerging from a flower bud. Appearing before the creature, five strong hands raised wooden staffs in her honor, clearly willing to follow her to the ends of the earth.

Sophie covered the Six of Wands crosswise with another card—the Four of Swords. This one featured another moon-faced creature, but unlike the winged one in the Six of Wands, this creature was buried in the earth, surrounded by dirt and roses. Three swords pierced the ground above her. A fourth she kept by her side, the blade pointed at her belly.

The Six of Wands usually spoke to me of leadership and victory. The Four of Swords was a little murkier. Sometimes that card was just a message about the importance of rest and reflection, but this time it spoke only of death.

I knew immediately that both cards represented Sophie.

"You were a lot more involved with the witches than you let on," I said.

"I wanted to help them," Sophie said. "I thought if Haley and I could win them over to the side of reason, and start training them in secret, we would eventually be powerful enough to confront Norah. Then we could join up with the other covens and help figure out what kind of threat we're dealing with."

I picked up the Four of Swords, my gaze lingering on a red rose in the creature's hand. "Did you know you were going to die? I mean, did you sense it? Did your cards indicate... anything?"

Sophie watched me for a long time, her face pinched in concentration. The breeze blew her rainbow hair into her mouth, and when she brushed it away, she said, "These cards aren't about me, Gray. They're about you."

Goosebumps prickled my arms.

"But..." I dropped the card. It slid across the others and onto the grass.

"There are four of you." Sophie plucked the card out of the grass and held it up in front of me, forcing me to look at it again. "The swords represent four witches. Three standing their ground, waiting for the fourth to rise, to find them and give them purpose."

"Where? What four? Who are they? From Bay Coven?"

"You have to find the others," she said, shaking her head. "The four of you must unite the covens. You—"

"Four of *who*? Sophie, this is your reading. Your cards. I don't know what you're talking about."

And because I truly *didn't* know, Sophie—this projection of her that existed only in my mind—didn't know either. The real Sophie had done this Tarot reading before her death, recording her predictions in the book of shadows, but she hadn't been certain about it then, either. Otherwise, it would be in the book, and she'd be able to tell me about it now.

"I don't know who or where," Sophie said again. "Only that there are four."

I wanted to scream in frustration. Maybe if she had told me about this when she was still alive, we might've been able to puzzle it out together. To figure out what the cards were trying to tell us about the four, about uniting the covens, about Norah. But I'd been too stubborn to listen, and now Sophie was dead, and all I had left of her was a book of useless spells and guesses.

I hopped up from the grass, suddenly desperate to get away from her. She wasn't my Sophie, not really. Just a cheap imitation that lived in my mind, a two-dimensional caricature rehashing the words from her book.

This entire place existed in my mind, and the longer I lingered, the more time I wasted. I had to get out into the real world and look for clues, figure out what happened. This whole thing—the covens, Norah, the hunters, the new threat—none of it was real. Not to me.

The only real thing was that Sophie was dead and her killer was still out there.

"Are you leaving?" Sophie asked, her mouth pulling into a frown.

"Do you want me to stay?"

"If you can, just for a few more minutes?" The fragile hope in her eyes brought me to my knees. It was the exact look she'd given me the last time I'd seen her alive, right after I'd promised her I'd think about going to the coven meeting.

I settled down in the grass again and reached for her hands, pulling them into my lap. I didn't care that we were messing up the Tarot spread, or that it was getting dark, or that the forest seemed to be encroaching on us, inch by inch.

"Do you know who killed you, Sophie?"

"Eww." Her nose wrinkled, and a smile broke across her face. "Don't be so morbid, Gray. God."

I wanted to laugh with her—it was such a Sophie thing to say—but I didn't have it in me.

"Sorry," I said.

"There's something else you need to know," she said, her smile fading.

"About the four?"

"Maybe. I don't know. I'm sorry I can't be more helpful, Gray." She reassembled the cards and gestured for me to draw.

With trembling fingers, I pulled two more cards from the top. The first was the Three of Swords, a woman whose heart had been run through with three swords. Tears gathered in her eyes, but she was still standing, and no blood stained the blades. In the next card—the Moon—two marionettes danced in the street, the full moon pulling their strings.

"Betrayal." It was the first word that came to mind, and the sound of it sent an icy chill down my spine.

Sophie nodded. "Just remember the message from the Moon. Things are not always what they seem."

I looked around at our meadow, at the shadowy and ever-shifting forest that surrounded us.

"Trust your intuition, Gray. In all things." She held my gaze again, her eyes blazing with renewed passion.

"I'll find him, Sophie," I whispered. "Whoever did this. I promise."

"I know you will." Sophie shuffled the cards back together and wrapped them up in the black cloth, all of it vanishing with a wave of her fingers. "I'm sorry it had to be this way. I wanted to tell you before, but—"

"But I didn't want to listen." I reached up and tucked a lock of glowing green hair behind her ear, grateful that at least in my vision, her hair hadn't been cut.

"Will you listen now?" she asked.

"Always." I meant it, even if I didn't yet understand what she wanted me to hear. "Sophie, I—"

But she was already gone. The forest and meadow faded away, leaving me back in the cold, strange room above Illuminae, Sophie's book of shadows open on the table beneath my palms.

I slammed the book shut. The pentagram was silver again, no trace of my blood left. Seconds later, the book glowed red, locked once again in its magical cage.

Sophie was gone—at least for now.

The moment I left Jael's secure room, my phone chimed with a text.

Detective Emilio Alvarez's name flashed across my screen.

Can you meet me at the station? It's urgent.

TWENTY

GRAY

My skin buzzed with nervous energy as I hauled open the heavy door that led into the police precinct. A grizzled human cop who looked like he hadn't cracked a smile in twenty years escorted me into a colorless room furnished with a cheap folding table and four chairs. The smell of old, burnt coffee permeated the air.

Other than its lack of windows, the room had nothing in common with the room at Illuminae, but my mind kept wandering back there anyway—back to Sophie and her book. She hadn't just left me a diary or a collection of secret spells and rituals. She'd sent me an important message. I just didn't know what to make of it yet.

Even after her death, it seemed I still couldn't figure out how to listen.

My heart ached. Seeing the projection of her vanish before my eyes in the meadow… It was like losing her all over again. There was so much I never got to say to her

while she was alive—so much I never even *thought* to say—
and now I'd never have the chance.

Guilt gnawed my insides. I kept reviewing her Tarot
cards in my mind, waiting for some magic clue to trigger
my intuition, to send me on the right path. But nothing
clicked. I was stuck in the same endless loop.

The part about Norah made sense—it confirmed how
I'd been feeling about the woman. But who were these four
witches? Were they from the coven? Did Haley know
about them? Or were they from somewhere else altogether? Was I one of them, or was I just supposed to find
them?

And what was that Three of Swords betrayal all about?

"Gray Desario, you are in some *serious* shit."

Startled, I looked up into the blazing eyes of the demon
looming in the doorway.

Then I cracked a small, guilt-laced smile and stood up,
propping my hands on my hips. "Ronan. Is that any way to
say good morning to your favorite witch?"

"Hey, um, favorite witch? What part of 'dangerous killer
on the loose' aren't you getting?" He shut the door behind
him and crossed the room, gathering me into a tight hug.
He was still wearing the same clothes as yesterday, one side
of his face lined with faint red marks that could only be
from my couch. "Jesus, Gray. I wake up to a text from
Alvarez to get my ass down here, Asher's passed out on the
floor and snoring like a beast, and you're nowhere to be
found."

"I had some errands to run. And newsflash, bud." I

poked him in the chest. "You *both* snore like beasts. No wonder you didn't hear me leave this morning."

"So you admit it. You snuck out while we were asleep because you knew—"

"That you'd go all parole officer on me? Yes, exactly." I headed to the far side of the room and leaned back against the wall, arms crossed over my chest. "I have a life, Ronan. I can't just hole up in my house. I know you and Asher mean well, but you guys have lives, too. You're not my personal bodyguards."

Ronan shoved a hand through his hair but didn't say another word. Just glared at me across the room, his body tensed for a fight.

After a long, loaded silence, he made his way over to me, eyes locked on mine, frustration simmering between us. The closer he got, the more oppressive the air felt, and by the time he stopped in front of me, the room was so hot and stuffy I thought I might pass out.

Why aren't there any windows in here?

"You don't get it, do you?" His voice was low and soft now, his earlier anger melting into something else—something I wasn't ready to name. Ronan leaned in close, bracing an arm against the wall next to my head. His cloves-and-campfire scent filled my nose and mouth, and my breath caught, my heart skipping into a wild beat so loud I was sure he could hear it, too.

I felt his presence all around me, inside and out, solid and strong, but I couldn't bring myself to look at him.

"I get it," I whispered, focusing on his shoulder, on the

beat-up leather jacket he'd worn as long as I'd known him. "You think I can't take care of myself."

"I know you can, Gray—you always have." His fingers grazed my cheek, tracing the purple and green bruises beneath my makeup. "But being able to take care of yourself doesn't mean you're invincible. It doesn't mean you throw yourself into danger just because you don't want to ask for help."

I blinked back tears of frustration. Ronan was right. No matter how many dangerous situations I'd been in, no matter how many times I'd been forced to learn this lesson, I was still acting like the same reckless, impulsive witch I'd been at sixteen, thinking I knew it all. Thinking nothing bad could ever happen to me or the people I cared about.

"I'm sorry," I said, my heart still pounding at his closeness. His all-encompassing-ness. I finally looked into his eyes, shocked to find them brimming with so much raw emotion.

For the first time in the history of our strange friendship, Ronan had let his guard down, leaving himself completely vulnerable.

"I don't know how else to…" His voice broke, and he shook his head, sucking in a deep breath. "Finding Sophie like that… She was my friend, too, Gray. I miss her like hell."

My heart broke for him. I'd been so focused on my own loss, my own pain… God, Sophie had been Ronan's friend for almost as long as I had.

"I know you do," I said, resting my hand against his

chest. His heart beat strong and steady, his skin warm behind a faded blue Zeppelin T-shirt. Like the jacket, he'd had it since I first met him—probably longer than that—and I knew every hole in the fabric, every snag.

Ronan covered my hand with his, holding it against his chest. "Here's the fucked-up thing, though. This little voice in my head keeps whispering, what if it were Gray? What if I'd walked in there and found the most important person in my life just... just gone?" He squeezed my hand so hard, the cut I'd made to activate Sophie's blood spell throbbed, but I didn't dare move. "I can't... It would end me, Gray."

"Ronan..." I felt everything at once—the weight of those words, the intensity of his gaze, the crush of his fingers, the heat of his breath—all of it making my body hum with desire even as it made my heart ache. I dropped my chin to my chest and tried to slow my breathing, but the twin sensations continued to surge through me, battling for dominance and turning my legs to jelly.

Ronan hooked a finger under my chin, slowly tilting my face up until I had no choice but to meet his eyes. They were more green than brown today, fierce and intense and terrifying and beautiful.

Slowly, agonizingly, his gaze swept down my face, stopping to linger on my mouth.

"The even more fucked-up thing?" Ronan slid his hand up to cup my cheek, his thumb brushing my bottom lip. "Even with all this bad shit happening, I can't stop thinking about what it would feel like to kiss you."

He leaned in close, feathering his lips over mine for a

sweet, short moment. Though it unleashed a flurry of butterflies in my stomach, it still qualified as a chaste, just-friends kiss.

It wasn't enough.

I wanted—*needed*—so much more. I grabbed the collar of his jacket and pulled him closer, stretching up on my toes to meet him halfway, my body melting against his in a way that left no doubts about my feelings on the matter.

His eyes darkened with desire.

There was nothing sweet and chaste about what came next.

Ronan claimed me with a deep, devastating kiss, the silken heat of his mouth sending waves of pleasure straight to my core. He tasted like coffee and cloves and a warm fire on a crisp autumn night, and I couldn't get enough of him, all those pent-up moments and close calls and near misses between us finally crashing together in one intense, perfect explosion.

My lips tingled, and I slid my hands around the back of his neck, teasing and tugging his silky-soft hair. I nipped and sucked at his bottom lip, and a low moan rumbled through his chest, primal and hungry.

It made me instantly, undeniably wet.

I did that. I made that sound come out of him with just a kiss...

Ronan slid a hand inside the back of my shirt, his strong, hot fingers burning a path up my spine. I whispered his name and arched my hips to get closer, desperate for—

The door banged open, ushering in an amused wolf

shifter, his throaty laugh making my cheeks burn with embarrassment.

"Well now," Detective Alvarez said. "Glad to see my lateness didn't ruin your day."

I broke our kiss, but Ronan wouldn't let me go. Not before pinning me with another blazing-hot look, then leaning in to whisper a final promise, breath hot and silky in my ear. "To be continued."

I was still panting when I finally pulled away from him and turned toward the doorway, frantically smoothing my hair. *How had he managed to knot it up so quickly?* "Detective Alvarez. Hi. We were just—"

Alvarez held up a hand. "I'm a detective, Miss Desario. Pretty sure I can figure it out."

"Sorry," I managed, my lips swollen and hot.

Ronan laughed. "I'm not."

The detective grunted, making an effort to look annoyed. But just before he turned to shut the door, I caught the lie in his eyes.

Detective Emilio Alvarez wasn't annoyed at all.

He was turned on.

TWENTY-ONE

EMILIO

Gray looked at me like the proverbial kid caught with her hand in the cookie jar, her cheeks turning a pretty shade of pink to match the beard-burn on her chin.

Ronan looked at me like he wanted to tear my head off for breaking up their make-out session. It was all I could do not to gloat—I'd been calling this for years. Ronan liked to play dumb when it came to his feelings for Gray, but anyone who knew them could see *that* bit of writing on the wall.

The Precinct Seventeen interrogation room wasn't the most romantic place in Blackmoon Bay, but I couldn't blame them for getting cozy. Spend a little time up close and personal with death, and eventually, you'd run hard and fast for the thing that made you feel the most alive.

"Thanks for coming in," I said. The scent of their desire hung heavy in the air, making me wish I hadn't been saddled with the unfortunate combination of wolf senses and the sex life of an eighty-year-old monk.

Ronan folded his arms over his chest and leaned back against the wall, making no effort to hide the bulge in his pants.

Jesus, how long have they been at it?

"I'm assuming no one gets called down here for *good* news," Ronan said. "What's going on?"

I tossed my case file on the table and pulled out a chair, gesturing for them to join me. Ronan stayed put, but Gray took the chair across from me, blinking up at me with those huge blue eyes of hers—the same trusting, expectant look she'd given me the night she'd finally come back to consciousness in my arms, wrapped up in blankets on Ronan's couch all those years ago.

She didn't remember it, though. And until she did, I'd be keeping the warmth of that memory to myself.

"This isn't easy," I said, hating that I'd had to bring her in like this. Thinking about her the other night at her house… It damn near gutted me. She'd been so strong, so brave. But anyone who looked into her eyes for more than half a second could see this was tearing her apart.

"Please," she said. "Whatever it is… Just tell us."

I took a deep breath, then blew it out slowly.

Damn. Sometimes I really hate this job.

"A witch allegedly went missing last night," I said. "Delilah Pannette."

Gray shot out of her chair. "What? How? What happened?"

"Please sit down, Gray." It was an effort to keep my voice level, but letting myself get visibly worked up about the case wouldn't help anyone—least of all Gray.

When she dropped back into her chair, I said, "According to her friends, Delilah left her home at six p.m. for a meeting at Norah's place, but never showed up. No one has heard from her since."

"But... Missing? I just saw her," Gray whispered.

"Yes. Witnesses claim the two of you fought yesterday. Can you tell me what that was about?"

"Alvarez, what the hell are you getting at?" Ronan moved to stand behind her, hands clamping protectively over her shoulders.

"*This* is why you called me in?" Gray asked. "Norah's cronies think I killed Delilah?" She studied my face, her own crumpling in confusion. "Do *you* think I killed her?"

There wasn't a *hell no* loud enough to answer that question, but no matter what I personally believed about Ronan's witch, I still had to do my job by the book.

There was a reason most supernatural crimes investigated by our human counterparts went unsolved, and it wasn't because the fanged, the furred, and the spelled were better at covering up our tracks. It was because once things reached a certain point on the weird and unexplainable shit scale, most humans simply gave up. Most didn't even know we existed, no matter how long we'd been living and working in the same communities, studying at the same schools, eating in the same restaurants. No matter how many uncanny things they'd experienced firsthand.

For all their evolutionary advances, humans still had a staggering capacity for denial, going to great lengths to convince themselves that the so-called "supernatural" was nothing more than a trick of their very smart, very big brains.

Perhaps that was *their* magic power—the thing that kept them safe. But it sure made my job a hell of a lot harder.

So, twenty-ish years ago, the three supernaturals on the force—the panther shifter chief of police, the fae narcotics officer, and yours truly—had agreed to keep our origins in the closet and team up whenever possible, taking on the supernatural cases before the human cops got too involved. Between our arrangement and a decent working relationship with the Fae Council, we were able to handle most supernatural cases without any human involvement at all—something we all strove for.

But witches posed a unique challenge for law enforcement. As humans that could harness and control magic, they had a foot in both worlds, which also meant they had a human paper trail of driver's licenses, social security numbers, and other records that drew human scrutiny.

If I wanted to keep human involvement to a minimum on these witch killings and have a chance at actually solving the case, I had to tread carefully, following up on every lead, interviewing every witness, and backing up every one of my instincts with cold, hard evidence.

"I think," I finally said, tapping the table between us, "you're connected to two different crimes with very similar circumstances. I'm not making any assumptions beyond that."

Gray pressed the heels of her hands into her eyes and groaned. "I didn't kill anyone."

"He knows that, Gray." Ronan glared at me, tightening his grip on her shoulders.

"I do," I said. "And no one is saying Delilah is dead. She was just reported missing last night. But I still have to cross the Ts and dot the Is."

Gray nodded, and I softened a bit. Putting her through this was not something I enjoyed. It was the main reason I'd called Ronan down here, too. They were tight; if anyone could comfort her, it was the demon.

"Can I get you some coffee? Water?" I asked. When she shook her head, I continued. "What were you and Delilah fighting about?"

"Sounds like the witches already told you."

"I'd like to hear it from you."

"She was talking shit about me and Sophie. It escalated from there." She filled me in on the details of their argument. "Norah banned me from the coven. I haven't talked to any of them since."

Norah banned her?

My hackles rose at that, but I schooled my features and pressed on. "The other night, you mentioned that Sophie had made plans to go to Norah's place. Was she a member of the coven?"

"No. I mean... Sort of. She'd been spending more time with them recently. She was friends with Haley, I guess."

"You *guess* they were friends, or you know?"

"No, they… They were friends. But I don't know how close." The tip of her nose reddened as she fought to hold back tears, and I kicked myself for not bringing tissues. It was all I could do not to lean forward and wrap her in a hug.

"Sophie and I didn't talk much about the coven," she continued. "It was kind of a sore point. I didn't even realize she'd been hanging out over there. I don't think she was a member though. Not officially."

"And you?"

"Not my scene."

"As far as you know, did any of the coven witches have any problems with Sophie or Delilah? Grudges, arguments, anything like that?"

"Like she said, it wasn't her scene." Ronan finally took a seat. "Come on, Alvarez. It's been two days. You must have a theory other than coven infighting by now."

He was right—I did.

I hadn't planned to share the prelims on the labs yet, but Gray was digging in too deep. She'd already questioned the witches on her own, and I'd be a fool to think she wasn't following up on other leads, putting herself in further danger. I needed her to trust me on this, to back off and let me do the work. And the only way she'd trust me was if I kept her in the loop.

More than that, I wanted to ease her pain. If giving her a few details about the case would help her sleep at night, I was all for it.

She looked at me now, a spark of hope shining through the sadness in her eyes.

Oh, Gray…

I'd been a cop in this city for decades, and I'd seen a lot of horrific shit. But this was quickly becoming the hardest, most personal, most important case I'd ever worked on, and no matter what the outcome, I sensed it would bind me to Gray for the rest of our lives.

In some ways, it already had.

And maybe this time she'll actually remember it…

"What I'm about to tell you does not leave this room." I flipped open my case file and scanned the report inside. "All three cases are almost identical. No signs of struggle, forced entry, or sexual assault. All three victims were killed at home in their beds. All missing sections of hair approximately two inches in length. And all showing puncture marks and bruising in the crook of both arms consistent with injections or blood draws."

Gray wrinkled her nose. "The killer took blood samples?"

"Seems like it. We also found…" I flipped past the reports to the gruesome photos beneath, but quickly changed my mind about sharing them. Gray didn't need to know about the runes carved into her best friend's skin. I was already digging through my lore books for a match, and I'd reached out to a demon friend who taught ancient languages at U of Seattle.

"Also found what?" she asked.

I slammed the folder closed, pressing my hand flat

against it as if that alone could keep the awful truth inside. "Other evidence suggesting the crime may be magical in nature."

"What actually killed my best friend?" Gray's voice cracked on the last word, but she held her chin high, determined to get answers.

"Officially? Blood poisoning," I said. "All three cases."

"And unofficially?" Ronan asked. Despite his controlled, pillar-of-strength demeanor, I sensed he was getting antsy —not the best emotional state for a demon.

"All the women were injected with vampire blood," I said. "I scented it in each of their bedrooms, and my tests confirmed it. I'm still working on identifying the particulars, but that seems to be the cause of death." I looked up at the ceiling, wishing there was an easier way to say this. Wishing I didn't have to say it at all. "It seems our killer wanted to turn the witches into vampires. None of them survived the change."

Gray gasped, the sound of it piercing my heart. "But... That makes no sense. Why would a vampire *inject* his blood?"

"I'm trying to work that out." I rose from the table to pace the small room, diving into the familiar routine of police procedure, the logic and reasoning that so often kept my sensitive heart from imploding. "Scenario A: Our vamp was simply in a hurry. In a successful change, injection would theoretically work faster than ingestion."

"No way," Ronan said. "Doesn't fit a vamp's M.O."

"Agreed," I said. Vamps were predators and bloodsuckers. They enjoyed the hunt—or pursuit, in the case of a willing donor—and were rewarded with the sensuous pleasure of the feed. We didn't have to travel farther than Darius's club to see that dynamic in action. "Which brings us to scenario B: The killer isn't a vampire, but for whatever reason wanted to turn witches. Injection would be a good option."

"Assuming he had access to vampire blood," Gray said. "But then he'd also need to inject the witch blood into the vamp sires, right? To finish the blood swap?"

I nodded.

"If the killer had access to the sires," she went on, "they wouldn't need to do an injection. No vampire would sit there passively when he could be feeding."

"The killer could've injected the vampires off-site," Ronan said.

"True," I said, "but then he'd only have about fifteen minutes to do it before the effects faded. And what vampire would agree to that, anyway?"

"Hostage?" Gray offered. She seemed to be puzzling something out in her head, but before she shared her conclusions, she reached for her phone. "I should talk to Darius."

"Gray, you need to let me conduct this investigation on my own terms. I'll get in touch with Darius when the time is right."

"But he..." Her eyes widened suddenly, her skin turning ashy. "Oh my God. Hollis and that other vampire."

"Weston?" I asked. "They're not involved in this."

"How do you know those assholes?" Ronan asked her.

"I don't." Gray pinched the bridge of her nose, avoiding his gaze. "They just... They were giving me a hard time at Black Ruby the other night. Darius tossed them out."

"Jesus Christ." Ronan looked up at the ceiling, shaking his head. "Fucking bloodsuckers. I can't believe Beaumont let them get anywhere near you."

"What if they showed up at my house that night looking to retaliate?" she asked. "They would've found Sophie instead of—"

"No," I said firmly. "Retaliating against you wouldn't explain the other nearly identical murders that happened before Sophie's."

"So maybe it wasn't retaliation, then. Maybe they just went on a witch-killing spree."

"Time of death for all three victims rules them out," I said. "One happened just after sunrise—daylight—and the time of the others puts them at Black Ruby. I've had a tail on them ever since. Hollis and Weston are guilty of a lot of things, but killing Sophie and the others isn't one of them."

She nodded, but she didn't look entirely convinced. Unlocking her phone screen, she said, "I still think I should text Darius. I can ask him to meet me as soon as the sun goes down."

Ronan and I exchanged a loaded glance. When had she and Darius become text buddies? As far as I knew, the vampire didn't even know how to *use* his cell—a fifteen-years-long source of frustration for the rest of us.

"Gray, listen to me," I said. "This case is getting more

complicated by the hour, and solving it is going to take a lot more digging and a lot more time. I can't do my job with you conducting your own vigilante investigation in the background."

"But I can help."

"I know." I gave her a small smile. "You're highly motivated, incredibly smart, and great at thinking on your feet. But you're not a detective, Gray."

Gray bristled, her defenses going up, closing her off. "Sophie was my best friend. I knew her better than anyone. I *want* to help."

"Help by staying out of the way."

She flinched like I'd wounded her, and I took my seat again and reached for her hand, giving her a reassuring squeeze. "I can't put you and the other witches in this city at risk by drawing too much attention to the supernatural aspects of this case. I have to color inside the lines on this one."

"But—"

"I'm sorry, Gray. I can't cross that line."

She pulled out of my grasp, shoving her hands into her jacket pockets, glaring at me with fire in her eyes. "Can't or won't?"

"Both." I looked to Ronan, imploring him to step in.

He glared at me, but I suspected he understood where I was coming from.

After a beat, he blew out a breath and crouched down in front of her. Tucking a lock of hair behind her ear, he said,

"Alvarez is right, Gray. Your priority right now is staying out of harm's way."

Gray huffed. "Sounds an awful lot like sitting back and doing nothing."

"It's not nothing," I said, and Ronan nodded. "Your safety—you getting out of this alive and unscathed—is the absolute most important thing."

Gray lowered her eyes, and her shoulders finally relaxed. "If you say so, Detective Alvarez."

"I say so. And since you're in such an agreeable mood, I'm going to need one more thing from you." I took a chance and reached for her hand again, and this time she rewarded me with a small but genuine smile. In that moment, I knew there was nothing I wouldn't do to keep her safe. To make sure her smile never faded. "Call me Emilio."

TWENTY-TWO

GRAY

Ronan was infuriatingly silent on the walk home.

Me? I was crawling out of my skin, my body pulling me in a dozen different directions. My brain wanted to rehash our conversation with Emilio. My fingers itched to call Darius, to see if he had any insight about the vampire blood.

But the rest of me? The rest of my body belonged to the surly demon walking by my side.

My mouth was stuck on that kiss, replaying the soft feel of his lips, the hot slide of his tongue, the clove-and-coffee taste of him that lingered deliciously, even now.

My skin still burned where he'd touched me, my face and my back and my stomach, every nerve ending longing for the exquisite pleasure of his caress.

And every time my heart beat, I heard the echo of his whispered promise.

To be continued...

To be continued…

To be continued…

"You gonna be okay for a bit here? I have to work a double tonight," he said suddenly, and I looked up, shocked to find that we were already standing on my front porch. My feet were aching and tired, but I barely remembered the walk home.

"I'm good." I dug the keys out of my pocket and jimmied open the door, stepping inside. A stack of mail sat untouched on the small table just inside, and I rifled through it, focusing on the junk catalogs and bills rather than Ronan's beautiful hazel eyes. It hurt too much to look at them now, reminding me only of the way he'd looked at me at the station. The way he'd kissed me. The whispered promise, yet to be fulfilled. "I have to work tonight, too. I'll stop by the docks and check in before I pick up the deliveries."

I felt his heat behind me as he stepped over the threshold. "Gray, you're off tonight. You're off… indefinitely."

"What are you talking about? I've got four shifts this week, a double on—"

"Waldrich knows the situation. He's got someone filling in until you're ready to come back."

"Waldrich knows?" I dropped the mail on the table and spun around to face him. "You talked to my boss about me? Behind my back?"

"He's *our* boss, you haven't slept in days, and I'm not about to let you walk around the warehouse district alone in the middle of the night—at least not until Emilio has a better handle on what's going on."

"*Let* me?" A flare of anger shot through my chest, but it petered out just as quickly, his earlier words echoing.

"*What if I'd walked in there and found the most important person in my life just... just gone?*"

Ronan had always been overprotective of me, and honestly, I'd always kind of liked it. Yeah, it got a little overbearing sometimes, but it also made me feel safe. Special. Loved.

Right now, it just made me feel helpless.

But I couldn't be mad at him.

Not when he was looking at me like that, all sweet and concerned and just... Ronan. And definitely not when he put his hands on my face, stroking my cheeks with his thumbs.

"I'm sorry I overstepped," he said.

I allowed a tiny smile to peek through my scowl. "No, you're not."

Ronan grunted, but he didn't deny it. "I just want to keep you safe. And you need sleep—you're exhausted."

"I know. I get it. It's just..." I glanced over to that stack of mail, anxiety bubbling in my stomach. "I wish I could hide out until all this blows over, too. But life doesn't come with a pause button. I have responsibilities. Bills."

Twice as many, now that Sophie was gone. This place only worked with the two of us bringing in money. Sometimes she covered me, sometimes I covered her, but together we'd kept it going.

I was only just starting to consider all the practical aspects to what'd happened. Losing my best friend meant losing the home we'd shared, too; I couldn't afford to stay here by myself, and even if I could find a roommate I trusted, I just couldn't imagine living here with anyone other than my Sophie.

I hadn't even started sorting through her things yet. I couldn't bring myself to go into her bedroom and pack up her clothes, knowing she'd never wear them again, or give away her art supplies, knowing she'd never paint again. Even the fox clock I'd once found so annoying had become a cherished possession, reminding me of her.

My eyes welled up, and Ronan wrapped me in his strong, comforting embrace. Burying his nose in my hair, he said softly, "Don't worry about covering your shifts or your bills. I've got you. I've always got you."

I pulled back to look at him, my hands curling around his biceps. Gratitude warred with frustration as the new realization dawned. "You're Waldrich's temp. You're working my shifts so he doesn't fire me."

Ronan was silent.

"I can't ask you to do that," I said.

Ronan shrugged. "I know."

"Ronan, you can't just... Why? You have your own job, and—"

"I... I can't bring her back to you, Gray. I'm a goddamn demon and I don't have the power to bring her back." His eyes blazed with new fire, his muscles tensing beneath my touch. "I can't take that terrible pain

185

out of your eyes or patch up the hole in your heart or make any of this okay. But I *can* cover for you with Waldrich. I *can* pay a few bills while you're getting back on your feet."

Ronan sighed and shook his head, some of the fire fading. "Just let me do this for you," he whispered. "Please, Gray. I'm going out of my damn mind."

I closed my eyes and rested my forehead against his chest, the last of my resistance crumbling away. "Okay. But I'm only taking a week off, and I'm paying you back for every cent as soon as I catch up again. *With* interest."

"Two weeks, and you can pay me back by taking care of yourself and promising me you won't sneak out on your own again."

"God, you're impossible."

"You wouldn't want me any other way."

"No, probably not."

"Just do me a favor and call Darius or Ash if you need something tonight, okay?" Ronan grabbed my hand, pressing a kiss to my palm.

The touch of his lips sent a zing across my skin, and when he lingered there and closed his eyes, inhaling my scent, memories of our earlier kiss rushed through me once again.

That kiss had surprised the hell out of me—maybe it'd surprised us both. But it hadn't been some caught-up-in-the-moment mistake. It was *real*. I knew he felt it, too—then *and* now.

But for whatever reason, Ronan was backing off.

"I should head out," he said. "Promise me you'll stay put unless you've got backup?"

Disappointment washed over me, head to toe. Maybe he didn't want to screw up our relationship. Maybe he felt guilty for snatching some small moment of pleasure in the wake of our friend's death. Maybe he thought it was too trivial, too distracting with everything else we had to face.

Maybe, maybe, maybe... I could think of a hundred more of those, but none of them outweighed my convictions that what we shared was right. That it was special, just like he'd always made me feel in his arms.

But when I looked into Ronan's eyes now, all traces of his earlier vulnerability—of his earlier heat—had gone.

"Okay. I promise," I said.

"Good. Lock the doors and windows. Get some rest. Once it gets dark, I'll have Asher and Darius check on the house a few times. I'll try to swing by on my break."

Great. Darius was one thing—I wouldn't mind a visit from him, actually. But Asher was the last demon I needed showing up on my doorstep.

"You guys don't need to stop by on my account," I said. "Seriously."

"I'm not doing it for you, remember? I'm doing it for me." Ronan grinned, brushing a lock of hair from my forehead. "What can I say? I'm a very selfish demon."

You don't kiss like a selfish demon. You kiss like the kind of man who takes his sweet, delicious time, touching and teasing and caressing every part of me until I'm weak and trembling...

Heat crackled between us, but when Ronan leaned in

this time, it was only to brush his lips across my forehead, a once comforting and familiar gesture that now left me cold and wanting.

"Later, Gray. Be good."

Ronan headed out the front door and down the porch steps, and for the first time in the history of our friendship, I didn't watch him go. I turned away and shut my door before he even hit the sidewalk, my lips longing for his kiss, my core aching with unmet need, and my heart heavier and more confused than ever.

TWENTY-THREE

GRAY

My bed had never seen so much action.

And by action, I meant my butt planting itself snugly in the middle of the lumpy Queen-sized mattress and remaining there for three days, waking only to pee and gulp down some water and send a few texts to Ronan.

He was right—I'd been totally exhausted. I had no idea whether Asher or any of the other brooding supernatural men who'd become part of my life had stopped by, but when I finally dragged my butt out of bed tonight, the sun had already gone down, my house was still standing, and I was pretty sure no one had tried to kill me in my sleep, so I was counting that as a win.

Then again, maybe I'd just scared them off with my eye-watering smelliness.

Hey, whatever works.

After a much-needed shower, I dressed in clean pajamas and turned on my phone, returning a few texts to let everyone know I was rejoining the world of the living. There were a bunch more from Ronan, just checking in, and a couple from Emilio—he didn't have anything new to share about the case, but he wanted me to know he was around if I needed anything.

There was also a voicemail notification, but I didn't recognize the number.

I hit the playback button.

"Hello, love," Darius said, the smooth caress of his voice sending a spark of awareness low in my belly. "I despise the impersonal nature of this black magic they call voicemail, so I hope you'll forgive the brevity of my message. I am so sorry for your pain, Gray. So, so sorry. And I do hope you know I am available should you need anything at all, whether it be a drink, a midnight stroll, or just some intelligent conversation—something I'm sure you're sorely lacking, given the demonic company you keep. Nevertheless, I understand you may prefer your privacy at this time, so no worries at all about returning my message. But again, if there is anything you need, do get in touch. Either way, I shall ring you again soon, love. Oh—this is the number to the club. You already have my cell. Call me on either line, anytime. Though you're more likely to reach me in the evenings." He let out a low chuckle. "Well, so much for brevity. In any case, thinking of you. Be well."

I smiled and saved the club's number to my contacts, surprised and touched by his thoughtfulness. The message included several more minutes of muffled crowd sounds and clinking glassware before he came back on again with a flustered huff. "Bloody hell, I thought I'd... Where is the damn button? Yes, I realize that, but it's a new... Here, you do it, then."

By the time he finished grumbling and the message cut off, I was actually laughing out loud. The sound took me by surprise; it'd been so long since I'd heard it, and I couldn't remember the last time I'd felt those muscles in my abdomen tighten.

Thank you, Darius. Truly.

Feeling lighter than I had in days, I headed into the kitchen to make tea, steeling myself to face the ritual alone for the first time since Sophie's murder.

The faint smell of bleach still lingered from when I'd cleaned up Ronan's burnt toast, and the only sound came from the second hand ticking away on the fox clock.

"What time is it, Mr. Fox?"

I couldn't look at the clock without hearing Sophie's voice. How many times had she asked that very question?

"Time for you to come home for tea," I whispered, touching the painted mugs we'd left in the dish drainer that morning. I hadn't been able to put them away, and in that empty, silent moment, with no texts or voicemails to occupy my thoughts, I felt her absence as if it were another person in the room.

She'd left a void, heavy and solid, a loss composed of a hundred tiny things: The smell of paint emanating from the spare bedroom. The click-clack of her platform heels in the hallway as she left for work. The kitchen trash overflowing with spinach stems from the green smoothies she loved.

I closed my eyes and inhaled deeply, my senses reaching out for her even though my brain knew she was gone. The house was already starting to lose her scent—strawberries and cream, like the best kind of summer sweetness.

When I opened my eyes again, my gaze drifted to the kitchen table, where Sophie's Tarot deck still sat.

"Don't erect a shrine on my account!"

Her voice playfully scolded me in my head, and I smiled, flicking on the overhead light and taking a seat at the table.

After a quick shuffle, I fanned out the cards and pulled one from the center, flipping it to reveal the Page of Cups, a vibrant, ebony-skinned girl walking barefoot along the beach, carrying a fish inside a golden cup. She wore an opulent tunic and cape the rich blue-green colors of the sea and a headdress shaped like a fish.

The page had always reminded me of Sophie—her joy, her brilliance, her creative spirit, the way she lit up the room with her laugh—and seeing the card now felt like a hello from my friend.

"Oh, Soph." My eyes glazed with tears as I traced the image on the card. "What am I supposed to do without you?"

"Answer the door, girl."

Her voice echoed in my head again, mere seconds before a knock rattled the front door.

Great. It figured the demons would choose now to check in on me, while I sat there in all my braless, frizzy-haired glory. At least I smelled pretty.

I grabbed a sweatshirt from my bedroom, tugging it on as I peeked out the front window, wondering which demon I should prepare for.

But my visitor wasn't a demon at all.

Haley Barnes stood on my front stoop, coat pulled tight around her neck, her dark brown hair slicked into a high ponytail that set off her stellar cheekbones. It looked like she'd been crying.

I opened the door, not bothering to hide my shock.

"Gray," she said, a much softer version of the woman I'd tangled with at Norah's the other day. "Hi. I was hoping we could talk? I brought a lasagna."

She forced a smile and lifted her hands, showing off a glass pan covered in foil.

"Lasagna? Seriously?"

"I'm Italian." She shrugged as if that explained everything. "When someone dies, we bring food."

I didn't know what to say to that, so I just stood there, letting things get awkward.

"She was my friend too, Gray," Haley finally blurted. "So was Delilah. And now one of them is dead and the other is missing, and none of us knows who's next, and our coven leader is sitting on her ass and letting it all fall apart. And this is my Nona's secret recipe and I spent all day chopping and simmering and baking and it's really fucking awesome. So if we could set aside our differences for one night and focus on what's important, like eating good food and not getting killed, that would be *super*."

I leaned my head against the doorframe, considering her

offer. "Did you say you chopped *and* baked? As in, from scratch? The old-fashioned way?"

Haley held up three fingers, scout's honor style. "No spells or microwaves were cast in the making of Nona's lasagna. The woman would rise up from the grave and beat me with her meat tenderizer if I even *thought* about using magic on this."

A whiff of the food's mouthwatering aroma crept up to my nose, garlicky and delicious. My stomach rumbled, and despite my best efforts, I couldn't help the smile tugging at my lips. "You should probably come in, then. Before Nona rises up and beats *me* for refusing her lasagna."

"Why did you send me to Jael?" I handed Haley a glass of Merlot and settled in with mine at the opposite end of the couch. Saucy, cheesy goodness scented the air as the lasagna warmed in the oven, along with a loaf of Texas toast garlic bread.

I might not have liked her, but the girl sure knew the way to my heart.

"A couple of months ago," she said, "Sophie started having these strange dreams. They weren't specific—more like emotional impressions, you know? Those feelings she'd get?"

I nodded, trying not to bristle at the fact that Haley knew so much about Sophie's gift, or the fact that we were talking about my friend in the past tense. Maybe in time I'd get used to that. I didn't want to, though.

"Anyway," she continued, "she said she felt like something big was coming, and that it had to do with you. She didn't share much else—she was still trying to put the pieces together herself."

I sipped my wine, letting her words roll around in my mind along with the things I'd learned so far from Sophie's book of shadows.

These cards aren't about me, Gray. They're about you...

"She made me promise that if anything happened to her, I'd send you straight to Jael," Haley said.

"Do you think she knew she was in trouble? Was someone after her?"

"I don't think so. She never said anything like that. I think she just wanted to be prepared." She swirled the wine in her glass, then took a long sip, draining it. "So, did you talk to him?"

"About?"

"About Sophie."

"What about Sophie?"

"Anything."

When I didn't respond, she sighed and said, "I already know about the book, Gray. I helped her with the blood spell."

Again, my skin prickled with the sting of betrayal, but I let it roll off. Deep down below the petty surface, I was actually glad Sophie had found someone to practice magic with.

My own reasons for holding back my magic had never wavered, but that didn't mean Sophie wasn't allowed to change her mind. Clearly, she had. And as much as magic scared the living hell out of me on the best of days, I'd never *really* wanted to stand in the way of Sophie exploring her heritage and connecting with her people, no matter how those people might have felt about me.

"Any news on Delilah?" I asked, reaching for the bottle I'd left on the coffee table and topping off our glasses.

"Nothing. The cops won't even do anything until she's missing forty-eight hours. Whoever took her is probably long gone by now." Haley shook her head, her glossy pony-tail swishing across her shoulders. "They're such assholes sometimes."

I pictured Emilio's kind face and immediately jumped to his defense. "Not all of them. Detective Alvarez is a good guy. He cares about the Bay, and—"

"This is bigger than the Bay, though. Witches are turning up dead all over the world." She told me about the communications she and Sophie had found at Norah's. "I know my coven—most of us would gladly fight for our sisters. But Norah thinks it's too risky. As powerful as she is, she'd rather bury her head in the sand and hope everything blows over. Good strategy, right? Ignore the problem, and maybe it will go away."

"Yeah, that never works."

"Nope. Unfortunately, that's the example she's setting for the younger members."

I took another sip of wine. "You mean Reva?"

Haley nodded. "She's a runaway. Norah took her in a couple months ago."

"She's lucky, then." I sighed, thinking of all the young girls who ran away to the Bay, bailing on one horrible situation only to end up in another.

Since that night in the alley, Bean was never far from my thoughts, but she flashed through my memory now in vivid color, trembling in her unicorn hoodie, eyes wide with fear despite her own quiet bravery. My heart broke for her. I'd wanted so badly to help her—to save her.

Instead, she'd saved *me*, and I'd cursed her. As far as I knew, there had been no sign of her since.

"I used to think we were *all* lucky," Haley said, bringing me back to the conversation at hand. "Norah seemed like such a great leader. She helped us get in touch with our gifts, with each other. Now it's like she's just… I don't know. Turning off the tap."

I was no Norah fangirl, and the woman was definitely hiding something. But I couldn't fault her for wanting to lie low during an international witch hunt, or to try to protect her coven—especially young witches like Reva.

"You don't think Norah's got a point?" I asked. "Maybe you *should* sit this one out."

"And let the others fend for themselves, knowing how much power we have together? I couldn't live with myself, Gray. None of us could."

Wrong. I could.

I opened my mouth to say it out loud, but in that moment I realized it was no longer true.

I'd stayed off the radar for seven years, denying who I was, pushing away witches like Haley and the others as if that alone could keep me safe. Alive. The only witch I'd let into my life was Sophie, and now she was gone.

In the end, isolating myself hadn't kept me safe, and it hadn't been living—not really.

"I went to see Jael on Monday," I finally confessed. "Sophie left the book for me, but I'm still trying to figure out what it means. I just... I need a little more time."

"I understand." Haley's face softened. "I can't even imagine what you're going through right now. I was just getting to know Sophie, but you... You were everything to her." Her eyes shone with emotion, her smile warm and genuine. "All that stuff Delilah said... God, I love Delilah, and I really, really need her to be okay. But she was way out of line."

"I wasn't exactly on my best behavior, either."

"Sophie was never disappointed in you," Haley said. "She looked up to you, Gray. She said you were the closest thing to a sister she'd ever had."

I wanted to tell Haley how much that meant to me, how those words melted some of the ice from my heart. But when I opened my mouth, all that came out was, "Hungry?"

Haley beamed. "*Starving.*"

With most of the tension between us finally easing, Haley followed me into the kitchen, taking a seat while I dished up piping hot lasagna and opened another bottle of Merlot. Sophie's bartending job had kept us well-supplied in booze, and I poured a glass for my best friend as well, setting it on the table between us.

After we clinked our glasses and drank to Sophie's memory, Haley gestured to the ever-present Tarot cards. "Sophie told me you guys used to draw Tarot every day after work."

I smiled warmly, picking up the Page of Cups I'd drawn before Haley's arrival. "It was one of our rituals. Tea and Tarot. Catch up on the events of the night. Look ahead to the next one."

"That's so cool. I never learned Tarot. I'm more into the blood magic." Haley laughed. "I know, not creepy at all, right?"

"Only slightly creepy. But hey, if you keep showing up at my door with food, I might offer to teach you Tarot." I set the Page back on top of the deck, face up. "You can keep the blood stuff to yourself, though."

"It's a deal."

Eventually her smile faded, her gaze shifting back to the Page of Cups. "Whatever happened to Sophie and the other witches, I feel like it's connected to something so much bigger. The other covens, other cities… Something major is happening."

"I agree." If what they'd learned from the other covens was true, the killings weren't isolated to the Bay, and they probably weren't just the work of a lone psychopath. "What are you thinking?"

"I'm thinking I want to find who did this," she said. "Who's *doing* it. Who they're working for. Who else is involved. And I want to continue what Sophie and I started at the coven."

"Strength in numbers—that whole thing?"

"It's important work, Gray. Reaching out to the other witches, reconnecting. Reclaiming our power."

She sounded so much like Sophie in that moment, I wondered once again if my little Page of Cups was stopping by to say hello.

"I know you don't have many reasons to trust anything I've said." Haley reached for the wine, pouring us each another glass and tilting the bottle back up without spilling a drop—a trick I'd never mastered. "And we didn't exactly get off on the right foot at Norah's place. But Sophie believed in you, and she believed in me, and she was an awesome judge of character. So I say we team up on this."

Team up...

I was distrustful of most people by nature—a policy that had served me well in the years since I'd fled New York. If I'd been more cautious as a teenager, I might've avoided the betrayal that had led the hunters straight to our doorstep.

But I was just a kid back then. Scared, alone, ashamed, on the run for my life.

Friendless.

When you built concrete walls around your heart, most people didn't stick around long enough to find out what was on the other side—and I didn't blame them. It was exhausting work trying to chip away at another person's defenses. But Ronan and Sophie were different. In their own ways, they'd each given me the space and understanding I'd needed to find my way into our friendships at my own pace. And they'd never given up on me, no matter how often I'd pulled away, kept things from them, or closed myself off.

They'd always believed in me. Believed that my friendship was worth the trouble.

So maybe this was my chance to prove that their faith in me wasn't misplaced.

Maybe I wasn't ready to join a coven or start practicing magic again. And I wasn't about to spill all my secrets— especially not about what I'd done to Bean in the alley, or the strange darkness that seemed to be corrupting my magic place, edging in on the corners of my reality.

But for a chance to honor Sophie's memory and prevent other witches from dying the same gruesome death? To give girls like Reva a fighting chance at growing up without the constant threat of hunters or whatever other killers lurked out there?

I could accept Haley's olive branch. I could make an effort. I could try to put myself out there, just a little.

"You're right," I said, lifting my glass. "I *don't* have many reasons to trust you. But you make a kick-ass lasagna, and that's something I can definitely get on board with." I winked, offering a quick but genuine smile. Then I touched my glass to hers and met her eyes, all traces of humor vanishing. "I'm in, Haley."

"Yes!" Haley smiled, shoveling in a forkful of hot, gooey pasta. With a full mouth, she said, "Okay. What's our first step? I'm pretty much open to anything that doesn't violate my somewhat questionable moral compass."

I tore off a hunk of garlic bread and popped it into my mouth, still processing everything Emilio had shared about the case, which wasn't all that much. He knew the witches had been injected with vampire blood, but he had no way of identifying the origins of that blood.

I, on the other hand, knew exactly who could help with that.

"If there is anything you need, do get in touch…"

And just like that, a plan sprang forth from the dark and dusty recesses otherwise known as my mind.

Emilio wouldn't be happy, but sometimes it was better to ask for forgiveness than permission—especially when it came to tracking down your best friend's killer.

"Tell me something, Hay." I grabbed my wine glass, holding it up to the light and admiring the deep, blood-red liquid inside. "How do you and your somewhat question-able moral compass feel about breaking and entering?"

TWENTY-FOUR

GRAY

After I'd been booted out of Norah's house, if someone had told me that one day Haley Barnes and I would be standing in front of the building that housed the morgue and medical examiner's office dressed like twin hookers, I would've asked them to share whatever drugs they'd been smoking.

But a few nights after hatching our plan over Nona's infamous lasagna, that was exactly what Hay and I were up to.

"Are we good?" she asked.

"Almost. You need more cleavage." I tugged down the zipper on Haley's leather jacket, revealing the tight white V-neck underneath. "And more lipstick."

"Pushy witch, aren't you?" Smirking, Haley pulled a tube of Rebel Red from her purse and reapplied. She'd worn her long, straight hair down tonight, bangs framing her face and making her light green eyes pop. "Happy now?"

"Oh, I'm *thrilled*." I snagged the Rebel Red from her and applied another coat to my own lips. "After this, maybe we can run around shifter territory in dresses made of raw meat."

"You know I could do a memory spell on the guy, right?" she asked. "Totally herbal. No side effects."

"I know all about your skills." I returned her lipstick, smacking my lips together to set the color. "But you're not using magic on him. It was hard enough to convince Darius to hold off on the vamp influence."

"Okay, setting aside the fact that the most powerful vampire in the city is taking orders from you—"

"Not even close," I said, but a warmth rose to my cheeks just the same.

It turned out Darius had really meant that whole "any-thing you need" bit, because when I'd asked him to meet us here tonight, he didn't even question me.

"You're blushing," Haley teased. "Methinks someone around here has a little bitty vampire crush."

"It's not a crush," I insisted, but I couldn't meet her eyes, and my fingers kept drifting to my wrist, gently rubbing the spot where he'd bitten me.

"I don't know how you do it, girl." Haley checked out my hair, pulling my curls over my shoulders and giving them one last fluff. "Sexy Brit vamp, sexy brooding demon... I can't even work up the courage to post my

Tinder profile, and you've already got two insanely hot men wrapped around your little finger."

"It's not like that," I said, but there was no conviction in my voice.

I wouldn't call them wrapped around my finger, but there was definitely something—some *things*—going on there.

My feelings for Ronan were a tangled knot of confusion. That kiss had been epic—the kind of kiss that had made my toes curl—and though he hadn't said another word about it, I knew he'd been thinking about it. Haley and I had been hanging out again last night, reviewing the finer points of our plan, when Ronan stopped by for a beer.

We'd both seen the way he'd looked at me. The way he'd touched me.

As for Darius? I hadn't seen him since that night at Black Ruby, but my stomach was suddenly fizzy with anticipation. There was something about him that captivated me, and I was pretty sure it wasn't just my vampire curiosity.

Crazy as it sounded, I couldn't help feeling like I was *meant* to meet him. That he was meant to be part of my life here in the Bay, just like Ronan was.

"It's weird, don't you think?" I asked, surprised at the dreamy tone in my voice. "Liking two guys. I mean, not that I *like* them, like them. But... You know?"

"Oh, I know." Haley smirked. "And hey, maybe they're into sharing."

I smacked her arm, but I couldn't deny the flush of heat

that filled my chest at that idea.

"Okay," she said, getting back to business. Darius was already waiting inside—we needed to get rolling. "I think we're as hot and slutty as we're gonna get. You sure you don't want me to work my magic on this guy?"

"Your *feminine* magic, yes. Witchcraft, no."

I wasn't budging on that point. An innocent security guard didn't deserve to have his memory messed with. And despite Haley's casual attitude about magic, no one could convince me that doing it out in the open was a good idea—not as long as hunters existed.

And they always will...

"Darius shouldn't need much time," I said, tugging the leather miniskirt down over my butt. I'd borrowed it from Sophie's closet, and it was a little on the snug side. "Just long enough to get in there, do his thing, and get out. You ready?"

Haley readjusted her boobs and squared her shoulders, linking her arm in mine as we headed up the steps. "Let's do this."

"Okay, there's the guard," I whispered as we passed through the doors and slinked toward the desk at the end of the entry hall. A human sat behind it, scrolling through his phone. Other than his generic gray rent-a-cop uniform, he was actually kind of cute. "Here we go."

"Leave it to me." Like flipping a switch, Haley turned

on the charm, forcing out a giggle as we approached the desk.

The man finally looked up, eyeing us with a twenty/eighty mix of skepticism and lust. Hopefully, Haley could nudge him even further in the lust direction.

"Hi-yeee!" She waggled her fingers, her eyes widening in confusion as she took in our surroundings. "Is this two twenty-eight Marchetta Street?"

Robocop crossed his arms over his muscular midsection, his gaze settling on her cleavage. Haley leaned forward on the desk, and his lips twitched with a grin, revealing a brilliant smile.

Wow. Who knew security jobs had such good dental benefits?

"It is," he said.

"No offense," she said, tossing her glossy hair like a professional vixen, "but this doesn't look like a nightclub. I don't even hear any music."

"This is the municipal district, hon. No clubs down here. But, ah, if you're in the mood for a dance, I could put on some music for you."

"That's sweet, but we're meeting someone at..." She glanced at her phone. "Yep. Two twenty-eight Marchetta. They said that's the address."

"Told you those guys were messing with us, Jenny." I frowned, pulling out my phone and pretending to check my texts. "Mike's not answering any of my texts, and Niles just keeps sending poop emojis."

Haley cringed at my improv, but quickly reined it in. "Oh my God, Gabby. I think... I think we just got punked."

Her voice cracked, crocodile tears spilling on cue. "What the hell? I really thought they liked us."

"Aww, don't cry, sweetheart." The man rose from his chair, genuine sympathy filling his eyes. I almost felt bad for what we had to do. "Guys like that aren't worth it —trust me."

Haley pouted. "But our ride is gone and we don't know the area and now we're totally stranded."

At this, he came around the front of the desk and put a hand on the small of her back. "Why don't you two take a seat, and we'll figure out this ride situation together."

"Really?" Haley brightened. "You're too sweet."

"It's nothing." He slid his arm up around her shoulders, his gaze focused so intently on that stellar cleavage I worried he might dive right in.

And there's my chance...

Before I could rethink it, I leaned in and reached for the carabiner hanging off his belt, deftly freeing the attached keyring. *Score!*

"Hey, do you have a restroom?" I palmed the keys and forced a bright smile, bouncing on my toes. "I have to pee. Like, *super* bad."

"Right around the corner. Just don't be too long, okay? This one here looks like trouble." He laughed, his gaze still lingering on her chest.

You okay? I mouthed to Haley.

Go, she mouthed back, and the glint in her eye told me she was actually enjoying this.

That makes one of us, anyway.

208

TWENTY-FIVE

GRAY

Deep in the bowels of the building where most Blackmoon Bay residents had never ventured, Darius waited outside the door to the morgue, still as a statue and just as beautiful. As always, he was impeccably dressed, wearing charcoal gray dress pants and a black cashmere V-neck that clung to his lean muscles, pushed up to the elbows to reveal some serious forearm porn.

He turned toward me, silently watching as I descended the basement stairs. Any earlier reservations I'd had about going overboard with the outfit—tight red tank under a cropped denim jacket, Sophie's leather mini, knee-high black leather boots—disappeared in the wake of his desirous gaze.

Maybe they're into sharing...

Darius smiled as if he could read my thoughts.

"No demon entourage tonight?" His smooth British accent rolled over my skin like warm water.

"Ronan and Asher are not my *entourage*," I said, a little defensively. Then, in a softer tone, "Thank you for coming."

"Of course." He stepped closer, his scent floating on the air—like really good leather and expensive whiskey and a richness that was *all* Darius. "I was glad you rang. Although, I do wish it were under better circumstances."

I nodded, grateful he hadn't extended further condolences. I appreciated his voicemail the other night so much, but right now we had to stay focused on the mission: get in, check the bodies (Darius), check the files (me), and get out —preferably before the guard noticed his missing keys.

"We don't have much time." Beneath a frosted glass pane etched in gold with the word MORGUE, I shoved a random key from the guard's ring into the lock and turned. *Bingo.*

"On the first try? You're charmed, love." Darius followed me into the dark room, shutting the door behind us. It took a few seconds for my eyes to adjust, but Darius didn't wait; vampires could see in the dark, and in the time it took me to fumble around for my phone flashlight, he'd already begun working his way down the rows of drawers at the back of the room.

"What are you looking for, exactly?" I asked.

"Traces." Darius slid one drawer closed, then opened another, apparently unfazed by the dead bodies inside. "Scents. Evidence left behind."

I scanned the room, taking it all in. A row of four identical metal tables bisected the room, with the body storage drawers running along the back wall and two desks set up in front. One side of the room held the sinks, scales, and storage cupboards. A row of tall file cabinets loomed on the other side.

The metal tables gleamed under the thin beam of my flashlight, and though they appeared to have been recently cleaned, the one closest to the front was covered in surgical tools neatly arranged on a blue cloth: scalpels, pliers, needles, a huge metal blade that was probably made for sawing through bone.

I swallowed hard, suppressing a shiver.

"Ah, here we are," Darius said. "October the first. Marisol Cates." He hauled open the drawer without ceremony.

I glanced up just in time to see a lock of dark hair spill out from beneath a rumpled white sheet, and my stomach lurched.

I sucked in a deep breath and started counting backward in my head, but it was too late for calm thoughts. Oily black smoke clouded my vision, and my legs turned to lead, as though some great evil were fighting to suck me under. Darkness roiled inside me, sweeping away my queasiness as quickly as it'd arrived.

In its wake, there was only anger. Only rage.

So many dead witches. Dead women. *Brutalized at the hands of men in their senseless quest for power.*

Bring them down.

Burn them all...

"Gray? Are you quite alright?" Darius's firm grip on my upper arms pulled me back to reality, and I blinked up at him in the darkness, waiting for his features to come into focus.

Strong, lightly stubbled jaw. Lush, full lips. Eyes the color of honey, framed by thick, dark lashes.

Wasn't he just working over by the drawers? How long was I out?

"Darius?"

"Hello, love." He smiled briefly, but it wasn't a happy one. Cursing under his breath, he said, "I never should've allowed you in here."

"You can't cut me out of my own plan."

"Gray, that's not what I meant." He slipped a cool hand around the back of my neck, thumb stroking my skin. His touch was soothing, and I felt my nerves settle, my entire body relaxing in a way it never before had in the vampire's intimidating presence. "I didn't think about how difficult this would be for you. You've just suffered the death of your dearest friend."

I inhaled sharply, the sincerity in his words piercing my heart.

"Would you like to wait outside?" he asked. "I'll just be a few more moments."

"No, I... I'll be okay." As much as I didn't want to be in this room containing the bodies of my dead best friend and the others, I'd rather be in here with Darius than out there in the empty hallway. What if that soul-sucking feeling returned? What if it happened when I was alone, and I couldn't find my way back?

"Are you certain?"

"Yes." I turned away from him, rubbing the sudden chill from my arms as I glanced out the frosted glass window in the door. The guard upstairs had been smitten with Haley, but how long could she keep up the act before he got suspicious? "I just need to find the files. You finish… whatever it is you're doing."

Darius returned to the body—to Marisol—and I headed for the tall file cabinet closest to the door. Each time I heard another body drawer open, I flinched, but I forced myself not to turn around. Seeing Marisol's hair had been hard enough. If I saw even one bright copper lock of Sophie's…

The phone buzzed in my hand—a text from Haley. It'd been fifteen minutes since I'd left her.

Clock's ticking, Gray. Kyle's asking what's taking you so long in the bathroom.

Tell KYLE I have my period, I replied. *That will shut him up. Also, first name basis, huh?*

What can I say? I move fast. :-)

You okay otherwise? I asked.

More than okay. I have a date next weekend. Score!

Haley's bubbliness reached through the airwaves, giving me just the boost I needed to keep going.

The files were organized by date, so it didn't take long to find what I was looking for—three manilla folders, each tagged with the names of the victims and the dates of their murders.

I flipped through Sophie's first—various lab reports, handwritten notes scrawled with medical jargon, a copy of my and Ronan's statements—nothing Alvarez hadn't already shared.

But there, behind all that paperwork, I felt a stack of slick, shiny eight-by-tens.

Oh, Sophie…

I squeezed my eyes shut and thought of my best friend the last time I'd seen her alive—the real Sophie, not the magic version from the book of shadows reading. I pictured her rainbow hair and the swirling ocean tattoo dancing across her chest. *That* was my Sophie, just how I wanted to remember her always. I knew the moment I looked at those photos—really looked at them—I would never be able to unsee them, never be able to think of Sophie without recalling those gruesome images.

Bile rose in my throat, the darkness nipping once again at my heels, but I forced it down. I had to do this. For Sophie. For the others. For anyone else this maniac was thinking about hurting.

Taking a deep, steadying breath, I opened my eyes and looked at the first photo, trying to evaluate it with clinical detachment. I pretended I was a student, that these were mockups created in some fucked-up graphic design lab by sadistic cops who wanted to scare kids away from the profession. I pretended I was a movie director looking at someone's special effects portfolio. I pretended I was trapped in an endless nightmare, begging for the alarm clock to rescue me.

But I wasn't fooling anyone.

Nothing could've prepared me for the sight of my best

friend's nude body stretched out on a metal table in this very room, pale and lifeless.

Breathe. Just breathe…

Across the top of her chest, from one shoulder to the other, the killer had left his mark in a series of what looked like ancient runes. They weren't Norse or Celtic—not that I could see. Each one was precisely drawn, deep enough to draw blood to the surface, but not enough to spill it.

This is what Emilio didn't want me to see.

It was too late to stop now. I flipped through the other folders and found Marisol's photos. Sophie's had been taken here at the morgue, but Marisol was still in her own bed, her black hair fanned out on the pillow, her eyes closed. She was nude already; maybe she slept that way. Her cheeks were still pink. If not for the gruesome carvings in her flesh, I might have thought she was still sleeping.

The photos of Helene—the other witch—were similar to Marisol's, though where Marisol was full and dark-haired, Helene was slight, with white-blonde hair and pale brows and lashes.

My heart ached for their families. For their friends. For anyone who may have loved them. For anyone who never got the chance.

Blinking back tears, I flipped through each woman's photos again, trying to puzzle it out. In all three cases, it seemed unlikely to me that a vampire would have the willpower to resist feeding on these beautiful, bleeding women right then and there.

"It still doesn't make any sense," I said. "Who ever

heard of vampires injecting blood into their victims instead of forcing them to drink?"

"Must you use words like 'victims' and 'forcing'?" Darius sighed. "Anyway, I can't imagine why a vampire would do it, either. It's not very satisfying, and we don't turn people just to turn them. Most believe our numbers are too high as it is—we're simply too many competing for too few resources."

"But there's evidence," I said, turning to face him.

Bad idea. He was standing over one of the bodies—not Sophie, thankfully—and when he sensed me watching, he tugged the sheet back into place.

I clenched my jaw, refusing to let the bile rise, and told myself it was someone else on that cold metal slab. Some other woman, someone else's best friend, an elderly person who'd enjoyed a full life and died of natural causes.

"Someone tried to turn these women into vampires," he confirmed. "That much is clear."

"But not through the usual methods," I said.

"And not through the usual vampires." He slid the drawer closed. "There are runes—"

"I know. I found the photos." I glanced down at Helene's picture, trying to decipher the ancient symbols the killer had carved into her skin.

Spellcraft had been one of Calla's specialties. I'd spent more nights than I could count hanging out in her study, peering over her shoulder while she transcribed her spells into her book of shadows.

"Words and symbols have power. More than any potion,

amulet, or charm. Written or spoken, even a thought. We must always choose our words carefully..."

Tears of frustration blurred my vision. Why couldn't I recognize these spells? Why couldn't I help Emilio and his team solve this? I'd broken into this awful place, looked at these horrific photos, imagined the things the killer had done... Yet I remained completely useless, just like I'd been the night Calla was killed.

"This was a bad idea." I snapped the folder closed and tossed it onto the desk. "I don't know how to—"

In the blink of an eye, Darius was behind me, his hand clamping over my mouth, one arm snaking around my midsection.

"Do you trust me?" he whispered, low and urgent in my ear.

The door to the morgue banged open, and Darius wrenched my head to the side, exposing my neck.

Before I could even answer his question, his fangs pierced my tender flesh.

TWENTY-SIX

DARIUS

Despite all evidence to the contrary, I hadn't meant to make Gray tremble—not like this. But circumstances being what they were…

"Good evening, little plaything." A vampire I'd never encountered before—a stocky man with a shaved head, dressed in a white three-piece suit—stalked toward us, flanked by an equally well-appointed man and woman.

Pulling back from Gray's exposed neck, I made a show of licking her blood from my lips. "Find your own blood bank," I warned. "This one's already claimed."

"I see. Well, we're not from around here," the leader said. His accent marked him as an American southerner— from one of the Carolinas, or possibly Georgia. "Perhaps you would be so kind as to explain why *claiming* prevents you from offering fellowship to out-of-town guests?"

"She is my claimed property," I said. "I do with her as I please. And you are not my guests. So if you don't mind…"

I cringed inside, hating the sound of my words. Hating that Gray had to hear me speak about her as though she were nothing but a meal. But the last thing I wanted was to start a battle with three unfamiliar vampires and risk her getting hurt—or worse.

The vampire on his left—a woman with an auburn-colored braid and a row of rings piercing her eyebrow—slithered closer. "Do you make a habit of bringing all your claimed pets to the morgue? Not very romantic, is it?"

I wrapped my hand around Gray's hip and squeezed, hoping the touch would reassure her. She was still shaking, her blood scented with a mix of raw fear and adrenaline as her body shifted into attack mode. I was still hoping we could avoid that particular scenario.

Hang in there, little brawler.

"Oh, I beg to differ," I said coolly. "It's quite romantic. Out of the way, usually private, nice and quiet. So if you'll kindly see your way out, I'd like to finish my snack."

I pressed my lips to Gray's ear, my tone menacing. "Relax, sweetness. This will be over before you know it."

I'd said it for their benefit, but there was a truth to my words I could only hope she understood.

Gray nodded stiffly in my arms, her muscles relaxing just a fraction.

Her trust felt like a gift. One I wouldn't squander.

"The three of you would be wise to move on," I warned. "Your lives are not worth one anemic female."

"No need for threats, bloodsucker." The leader appeared before me in a blink, his gaze drinking in every inch of the woman in my arms. I could practically feel Gray's blood revolting.

"There's plenty to share," he purred. "Isn't that right, lovely?"

He reached out to touch her hair, but I yanked her backward, one arm wrapped protectively across her body, holding her close.

Her frantic heartbeat hammered right through my skin.

I glared at the man. "Touch what's mine again, *bloodsucker*, and rest assured it will be the last time you touch anything."

He bared his fangs and hissed.

And the bloody prat reached for her once again.

Wrong move.

I wasn't certain who'd seen it first—Gray or the vampire himself—but she was the only one to make a sound.

Not a scream, not a shout. Merely a gasp.

His severed hands hit the floor, blood slogging out from his wrists. The metal bone saw vibrated in my hand for just a moment before I swung it in another powerful arc, decapitating him.

His body dropped, his bald head rolling toward my feet.

"D!" Gray's shout was all the warning I had before the other male—a mustached blond considerably larger and more muscular than his bald friend—slammed into me, rocketing us into the storage cabinets.

The bone saw clattered to the floor, leaving me weaponless but for my teeth and hands. Near-evenly matched, the vampire and I attacked each other with punishing fists and fangs that flashed like knives, tearing flesh and splintering bone and spilling blood until the walls around us shook with our shared fury.

The female watched from the sidelines, grinning as she awaited her turn.

But she'd never get it.

Gray, who appeared to have been forgotten in the heat of our vampire battle, slammed a wooden stake into the woman's back, paralyzing her before she could even scream.

Her companion hadn't seen it; he'd been too focused on me. Somehow, he'd gotten hold of my saw, and he sliced my thigh clear to the bone. I had just enough time to knock the tool from his hand before he could do more damage. It spun out across the floor, once again out of reach.

My leg tingled, then went numb.

Still, I didn't relent. I wouldn't—couldn't—let him get to Gray. I hit the man with an uppercut, then launched myself at him, biting an ear until I tasted more blood.

I glanced up to search for Gray, hoping she'd taken cover. But I couldn't see her, and for my momentary distraction, I was rewarded with a punishing blow to the head, my skull ricocheting off a metal sink pipe. The room spun before me as I sank to the floor.

Finally noticing the immobilized state of his female, the male turned back to me with renewed fury.

"You die here tonight," he spat, dropping to the floor and unleashing a storm of punches to my head. Blood poured from the lacerations in his face, his ear torn clear off, but he was a powerhouse, relentless in his quest to pulverize me. "And your little blonde bitch? She'll be no more than a smear of blood on my shoe, not even worth the time it would take to lick clean."

My vision swam with red, and I channeled all that rage, that fear, that primal need to protect Gray into a deafening roar. Shoving him off, I pulled my good leg to my chest and kicked hard, launching him into one of the examination tables.

He was up again in an instant, charging right for me.

"D!" Gray shouted again, and I chanced a quick glance up—just long enough to spot another wooden stake sailing through the air.

I caught it in midair with one hand.

And I slammed it straight into his heart.

The vampire gasped, then collapsed on top of me, eyes rolling back into his head.

"Gray! Are you alright?"

"I'm good," came her call, loud and clear.

I nearly wept with relief.

Shoving my unconscious vampire aside, I slumped back against the wall and closed my eyes, giving my flesh and bone a moment to mend. It didn't take long; the attack had taken a toll on me, but now that the beating had ceased, my body could focus on knitting itself back together.

After a moment, I got to my feet, frantically searching for Gray.

My eyes found hers across the room.

Her hair was a mess of tangled curls, her eyes wide with fear. But she was otherwise unmarred.

I took in the sight of the two staked vampires on the floor, then smiled at Gray.

"Are you always so well-armed, little brawler?"

She shrugged, a small but tired smile lighting up her face. "Why do you think I wore these boots?"

Because they're sexy as sin, and you're *sexy as sin, and I don't care if we* are *standing in the middle of a morgue surrounded by carnage and death. If I stare at those exquisitely creamy thighs any longer, I'll have no choice but to kiss you...*

"So what do we do about these two?" She nudged the woman with the toe of her boot. Unlike decapitation or incineration, stakes wouldn't kill our visitors, but they did poison them. Hawthorn was especially toxic to vampires, considerably slowing our innate ability to heal. If Gray and I left now, we'd have a few hours' lead on them, at least.

But leaving them incapacitated wasn't an option.

"Gray, you know we can't leave them alive."

Despite her deftness with the stakes, Gray looked seriously pained by the idea of finishing the job. "But... Isn't there some kind of dominance rule? We kick their asses, they run away with their tails between their legs, never to rise up and bite the hand that feeds them again? Or... something?"

"No one likes a mixed metaphor, love." I stepped over the pools of spilled vamp blood, finally locating the bone saw. "I have no idea where they came from, but unless we take care of them now, they'll almost certainly come after us again. Probably with reinforcements."

Gray's brow creased, her eyes glazing.

Bloody hell.

She may have been a witch—a very powerful one, even if she hadn't yet realized it—but underneath all that magic and fire and those *seriously* arse-kicking boots, she was still a human. A beautiful, vivacious, twenty-five-year-old woman with hopes and dreams and a soft heart, no matter how badly she tried to convince herself—and the rest of us —otherwise.

She deserved better than this. Every witch in this room —Sophie, Marisol, Helene—deserved better.

When I touched Gray's shoulder, she flinched, but I held firm. "I'll finish it, Gray. Clean up as best you can, then wait for me upstairs. Your friend is probably worried."

"Did you know," she said, her voice suddenly devoid of warmth, "Ronan was the one who taught me how to kill monsters? No offense."

"None taken." I winked to let her know it was okay, hoping to bring back a bit of her spark. Her face had gone so pale, her eyes glassy. "It's basically a required skill in this city, isn't it?"

"He was my first friend here," she said, her voice still strangely detached, "and almost before I knew his name, he was drilling it into me about never leaving home without weapons. About identifying the entry and exit points for any room or closed-in space." She smoothed her hands over the front of her short skirt. "I know the fastest ways to kill a fae with an iron blade—and the slowest. I've memorized the Achilles Heels of every kind of creature in the Bay, and some that've only appeared in mythology books, because you never know. I might be outmatched, out magicked, outpaced, and I might not stand a chance against three vamps or a rabid shifter or winter fae magic, but even then, I'd never go down without a fight. But you know something, Darius?"

"What is it, love?"

She picked her way through the carnage and stood before me, turning her blue eyes my way. In the span of thirty seconds I watched her age a hundred years.

"All of that is just knowledge in my head," she said. "Monster or not, I've never actually killed anyone. I've always found another way."

"There's *still* another way, Gray. Let me—"

"No. I can't keep letting everyone else clean up my messes. You fought for me, and I just… It's time I… I have to do this."

"But you don't."

"No. I really do." She took the blood-stained bone saw from my hand, a brutal contrast against her pale skin, and approached the woman still lying unconscious on the floor. I listened to the beat of her heart—one, two, three, four, five —and then she took a breath and dropped to her knees, blade in hand, and began.

It was bloody, messy work, but Gray was determined to see it through. When she finally finished, the woman's head rolled to the side, her auburn braid glistening with dark blood.

Gray got to her feet. "One down, one to go."

I stopped her as she approached the vampire I'd staked, prying the saw from her hands. "You've done enough for tonight, Gray. Truly."

She held on for a moment, but eventually relented, heading for the sinks while I finished the job.

After scrubbing her hands raw for a full five minutes, she finally shut off the water and turned to me, wavering on her feet. Her skin was deathly pale. "Darius? I'm not... Something's... off."

I rushed forward on instinct, catching her just as she collapsed.

"Oh, Gray. It's alright, love." I scooped her into my arms and carried her out of that wretched place, away from the blood and destruction, away from the reminder of what she'd done. Pressing a kiss to her temple, I said, "We had no other choice. Don't feel bad for this."

"That's the thing, D. I *don't* feel bad." Her voice was faint, her body trembling with exhaustion and leftover adrenaline. When she looked up at me again, her eyes were utterly flat. "I don't feel anything."

TWENTY-SEVEN

GRAY

"Jonesin' for a caffeine hit?" I eyed Darius from the passenger seat of his custom Aston Martin Spitfire as he pulled in behind Luna's, a funky little coffee shop at the edge of Hudson Marina.

We'd just dropped off Haley, who deserved a medal for keeping that guard distracted while Darius and I waited for his "people"—a group of shadowy vampires that arrived within minutes of his call and wordlessly swept into the morgue, cleaning up our mess and eradicating the evidence that tied us to the deaths of those bloodsucking fuckwaffles.

I'd lost the case files in the melee, but at the moment I didn't think I could look at them again, anyway. Right now, all I could see was blood.

All I could smell, all I could feel, all I could taste was blood.

Murderer...

You did this to me.

Witch.

This is who you are.

I shook my head against the barrage of voices. No—it *wasn't* who I was...

Right?

No matter how I felt about magic, I could accept the fact that I was a witch. I could even accept that I'd taken a vampire's life in self-defense. But a person who killed another being without remorse? Without hesitation? With-out... anything? Was that really me?

Whether the vampire had deserved it, hers was the first life I'd ever snuffed out. Darius and I had cleaned up and changed clothes at Haley's, but the woman's blood was still caked under my fingernails.

I should be devastated. Or at least freaked out.

So why was I numb inside?

What the hell is wrong with me?

"I thought you could use a bit of normalcy after... everything." Killing the engine, Darius leveled me with a piercing gaze, his eyes a bright gold contrast to the black button-down he'd changed into. While his body had quickly healed, the lovely cashmere sweater he'd worn earlier had not.

I already missed the soft feel of it against my cheek.

"I should've found a way to de-escalate the situation," Darius said. "If I hadn't attacked first—"

"They might've killed me. Case closed." I turned away and looked out the window, trying to pick out the boats docked in the distance. From here they were no more than silhouettes bobbing on the water, moored until someone decided to set them free.

"I wouldn't have let that happen, Gray. I *won't* let that happen. *Ever.*" Darius laced his fingers through mine and squeezed, but more than his touch, the certainty in his voice sparked something inside me. I turned to face him again, searching his eyes across the dark, intimate space of the car.

"We're connected," he said softly. "I care for you. No matter the circumstances that led to our bond, that bond exists. I know you feel it, too."

My heart rate kicked up in response, but something about his words stung, threatening to dampen my desire. "So this... whatever this is between us. It's just because of the bond? Like some kind of magical... obligation?"

"Ah, love." He brought my hand to his mouth, lips brushing my palm. "If you think that's all this is, you are sorely mistaken."

He grazed the skin inside my wrist with his teeth, and I gasped as a current of unbidden pleasure rippled through me, stronger and more intense than what I'd felt that night at Black Ruby.

His fingers trailed up my arm, and his mouth followed, lips tracing a light path along my veins.

Just like that, my entire body relaxed, muscles unclenching, bones melting into goo.

He was kissing my *arm* for God's sake. How could something so simple feel so utterly amazing?

"I don't... I don't know how you... do that," I breathed, all the stress from tonight's ambush floating away.

"Do what, love?"

"It's like you know exactly how to touch me. How to make me feel…" I gasped again as his teeth scraped the sensitive spot just inside my elbow. "Like that."

"I've tasted you," he said softly, his lips lingering on my arm a moment before moving up to my neck, lightly brushing the spot where he'd bitten me tonight. The memory of that sharp, exquisite pain sent a little thrill down my spine, and I shivered.

"I can smell the blood running through your veins," he whispered. "Hear the tempo of your heartbeat." He tapped his fingers gently against my thigh, mimicking the precise beat of my heart, as frantic as a frightened rabbit.

I wasn't frightened, though. Not of Darius. Not anymore.

Darius leaned close, his scent enveloping me, eyes dark with desire. "I can feel where you *ache*."

His mouth closed over mine, stealing the breath from my lungs, and I parted my lips, taking him in deep. The taste of him exploded over my tongue, like sweet wine and dark chocolate, and despite the coolness of his lips, my entire body was on fire, blood racing through my veins as if everything in me had fallen under his command.

We were parked in the shadowed back corner of the lot, close to the shoreline, but I didn't care if anyone walked by the car anyway, shined a light inside, caught the whole thing on video. Darius felt so good, so right, there was nothing left to do but lose myself in this delicious, intense pleasure for however long it was destined to last.

I pulled him into the passenger seat, maneuvering so that he was on the bottom and I was straddling him.

"You're absolutely enchanting," he breathed, kissing my chin, my jaw, then dipping down to my collarbone.

Nestled between my thighs, his steely length strained against his pants, igniting a fire in my core that blazed out through my limbs, urging me to rock against him, desperately seeking that friction, that pressure, that sweet release.

With nimble but impatient fingers, he pushed up my borrowed tank top, revealing the black lace bra beneath. My nipples ached for the touch of his mouth, but Darius held back, blowing a cool breath across my skin, his thumbs teasing the bottom curve of my breasts as my skin pebbled with goosebumps.

"Please," I whispered, burying my face in his silky hair.

Darius moaned softly, palming my breasts with a too-light touch, unleashing an urgent whimper from my lips. At this, he finally lowered his mouth, tonguing one of my stiff peaks through my bra, soaking the lace. I gripped his shoulders and arched my back, pressing myself against his mouth, desperate for his kiss on my flesh. His bite.

The gentle lick of his tongue turned wicked as he sucked me between his lips, nipping and grazing, and those nimble, dextrous fingers finally slipped inside the waistband of my yoga pants, ghosting down over my underwear and stroking my clit. The damp press of fabric felt cool against my skin, and I sighed as a new rush of pleasure coursed through me.

He must've sensed the change in me, the desperation,

because without warning he slid his hand down the front of my underwear, dipping two fingers inside me. I was already so wet for him, so eager for his touch, and I arched my hips in response, urging him closer.

His teeth grazed my nipple again, and he stroked my core, slow at first, then faster, deeper. My head rolled back as the pressure built between my thighs, intensifying with every perfect thrust.

"Let go, Gray," Darius whispered, and I rocked forward on his hand, my thighs beginning to tremble, heat coiling low in my belly…

"That's it, love." Darius palmed my clit, fingers curling inside me, thrusting harder and deeper. "Let me feel you come undone."

"Darius!" I shattered, my body clenching hard around him, wave after wave of white-hot pleasure washing over me as I rode out every last ripple, every last hot, tingling sensation.

Breathless and dizzy, I finally collapsed against his chest, waiting for the aftershocks to fade as the muffled sounds of the marina filtered into the car: the foghorn of an arriving ferry, bells clanging on the boats in the harbor, the mournful cry of a lone seagull wandering the shoreline.

When I finally got my bearings again, I looked up into Darius's eyes and smiled, dark and devious, reaching for the button on his pants, eager to feel his hot, hard length inside me.

"What's this? My little brawler isn't yet sated?" he asked playfully, eyes darkening with lust as I unzipped his pants.

In the steamy cocoon of the car, his voice was thick and seductive, and the intensity in his eyes made me feel alive and sexy and powerful in a way that magic never could.

"I'm *mostly* sated," I teased, scraping my fingernails over his lean, hard abs, following the dark line of hair that led down from his belly button. "But I seem to recall something about repayment of a debt? A settling of our affairs the old-fashioned way?"

I'd meant it as a joke, a nod to our first meeting at Black Ruby when he'd agreed to keep my magic a secret in exchange for some future favor, but Darius frowned, and something wounded flashed in his eyes.

I regretted my words immediately, but before I could apologize, his devilish smile returned, a threat and a promise all wrapped up in one.

"No, love." He grabbed my hands, pulling me away from his rock-hard body. "When it comes time to have you in my bed, it will not be a debt collection." Then, in a voice so fierce and commanding it almost made me come again, "And you will *beg* for it."

I held back a shiver, not doubting his words one bit. It'd only been a few minutes since he'd sent me over the blissful edge, and my body was already begging for it again, urging me to reach for him, to finish what we'd started.

But Darius was already zipping up, the lusty haze clearing from his eyes.

"So," he said cheerfully. "I'd love to treat you to coffee, but obviously if you're not keen on that, we could go elsewhere. A drink, perhaps?"

The playful tone and abrupt subject change lent an adorable nervousness to his cool, you-will-beg-for-it demeanor, and I laughed, relieved he wasn't holding a grudge. Incredible chemistry aside, I was *really* starting to like Darius. As crazy as it sounded given my intense feelings for Ronan, something about the whole thing with Darius just felt… I don't know. Right. Different, but right.

Having feelings for more than one man was a new and complicated world I wasn't sure I was ready to enter, but I'd been judging myself so harshly about everything else— my screwed-up magic, the way I'd treated Sophie, all the mistakes I'd made—why not give my heart a break?

Unlike the rest of me, maybe my heart actually knew what it was doing.

"No. I mean, yes," I said, beaming. "Coffee sounds great. That's really sweet of you."

"Sweet?" Darius sighed. "Oh, dear. Don't let *that* get out."

I touched my thumb to my wrist, tracing the invisible seal of our strange but no longer uncomfortable bond, feeling the last of the adrenaline leak from my limbs. Tonight's vampire bloodbath would certainly come with consequences, but one thing was certain: I was safe with this man.

"Don't worry, D," I whispered, pressing a quick kiss to his cheek. "It'll be our secret."

TWENTY-EIGHT

GRAY

By day, Luna's Café served black coffee and bacon-and-egg sandwiches to rough-and-tumble dock workers, and over-priced scones to tourists lining up for their whale-watching charters.

Nighttime, though? That's when all the freaks came out. Vampires, shifters, fae, me. Not that humans would notice or care, but Luna's was situated on an energy vortex and served as a 24/7 safe zone—neutral territory for all. No fighting. No killing. No magic.

And the coffee was pretty damn good, too.

"Venti vanilla latte, extra foam," I told the barista, a cute and bubbly fox shifter named Ella who'd been working there a few months now.

"Gray!" She smiled, dimples showing. "Must be your lucky night. I've got two of those chocolate macadamia cookies behind the counter. Interested?"

"When am I not interested in chocolate macadamia?"

Darius slid his credit card across the counter. "We'll take them both. And a double espresso for me. Extra hot."

"Thank you," I said to him, the rich, warm scents of the café wrapping me in a much-needed hug. "This was actually a *really* good idea."

"Don't sound so surprised, Gray. I've been known to have them at least once per century."

We grabbed our order from the bar, then found a table in the back behind a bookshelf stuffed with tattered books and old board games. My gaze landed on Othello, and tears stung my eyes. Sophie loved playing that stupid game. I'd never once beaten her.

God, I wish I could talk to her about this. About Darius. Ronan. Everything going on inside me...

Swallowing the lump in my throat, I settled into the chair Darius had pulled out for me and reached for a cookie from the plate, putting my faith in the healing power of chocolate.

"Do all vampires like cookies?" I asked as he sat down next to me and reached for his.

"I suppose not." Darius brought the cookie to his lips, but he didn't take a bite. He seemed to be appreciating it first. *Really* appreciating it. "But they're certainly one of *my* many vices."

Is he licking *that?*

"What are your other vices?" I asked, my thighs clenching involuntarily as I imagined his response. *Sex. You. Long, slow sex on a Sunday, preferably with you...*

"Cheeseburgers and sweet potato fries." He finally took

a bite, chewing slowly and deliberately, savoring every second of it.

Oh, to be that cookie…

My cheeks burned, a mixture of lust and embarrassment pumping through my blood.

One orgasm from the man, and now I'm jealous of a cookie?

"Are you alright, love? You look a bit flushed."

"What? Great. I mean, good. I'm *fine.*" I broke off a big piece of my cookie and shoved it into my mouth.

When my breathing returned to normal—at least, as normal as it was going to get in the presence of Darius—I said, "Not to be a total buzzkill, but we need to talk about tonight."

Darius smiled. "Why talk? Actions speak *much* louder than words, and after we've finished our coffee, I was thinking we might go back to the car and resume those actions. Yes?"

"As tempting as your invitation sounds, I wasn't referring to *that* part of tonight." I reached for his knee under the table, giving it a squeeze. "I'd like to know what you found before the out-of-towners crashed our search party."

His smile faltered. "Gray, all of that can wait. You don't have to—"

"I *do* have to," I said softly. "Darius, I know things didn't go as planned tonight, but Sophie was my best… She was…"

She was everything to me. Absolutely everything. And I'd let her down.

As much as I appreciated the chill café vibe, the healing

power of chocolate, and the sultry, unexpected moments Darius and I had shared in the car, I was still on a mission. I wouldn't *truly* be able to relax until we tracked down the monster who'd stolen my beautiful friend from this world.

"Tell me," I said. "Please."

Darius considered me a moment, then leaned forward, his voice dropping to just above a whisper. "For starters, Alvarez was right about the vampire blood—I scented it almost immediately. Identical in each case."

"Was it one of the vamps who ambushed us?" I asked.

"No, although it's likely they were involved—perhaps sent by our guy to make the evidence disappear. I'm not sure what else would explain their presence. The Bay is an out-of-the-way place as it is, and the morgue isn't exactly a tourist attraction."

I nodded. His theory was sound.

Darius continued. "The blood is from the Grinaldi line— one of the original European vampire families to settle in America in the seventeen hundreds. They've been here ever since."

"You could tell all that just from the scent?"

"Only because I've crossed paths with them before." Darius scowled, anger flickering in his eyes. "I'm not sure what a Grinaldi-sired vampire would be doing on the west coast, though. To my knowledge, the elder hasn't left his home in decades, and he keeps an extremely tight rein on his family."

"But how? There could be thousands of vamps carrying his blood."

Darius shook his head. "Only twenty."

Twenty. The number of the Judgment card in Tarot. My mind served up the image from Sophie's deck—an angel surrounded by a dark cloud, one side of his face a silver moon, the other side blue. He heralded Judgment Day with a great horn, calling the dead to rise and repent. The card often showed up in a reading when it was time for a major transformation—a great burning of the old so that the new could rise up from the ashes.

I shivered, then wrapped my hands around my mug, taking comfort in the warmth that seeped into my palms. "Always twenty?"

"Only when one dies do they create another. It doesn't happen often—they're well protected. And they've got a strict code about siring. Anyone who breaks it is eliminated."

"And you said they're still here in the states?"

Darius sipped his espresso, then nodded. "Just outside New York City—an estate in Tarrytown."

My stomach flipped. Tarrytown was three thousand miles from the Bay, but less than a hundred from where I'd grown up. From where I'd spent my entire childhood— from the time I was adopted as a baby, right up until hunters attacked our home when I was sixteen.

Yes, New York was a big state, populated by millions of people across hundreds of towns and cities.

But any witch worth her spell book knew there was no such thing as coincidence.

"I'll arrange for one of my east coast associates to track

down the elder and request a meeting," Darius said. "But it won't be easy. Like I said, he's quite reclusive, and he's not keen on strangers."

I sipped my latte, letting this new info settle in. As far as I'd known as a kid, there'd been only one vampire family in my hometown, and outside of an English class I shared with the oldest daughter, we'd hardly ever crossed paths. Chances were the Grinaldi family had no connection to them, or to my past.

But still, I didn't like it. It felt too close for comfort.

"What are you thinking?" Darius asked.

I set down my mug, reaching for another piece of cookie. "Let's assume for now this plays out logically. Setting aside the possibility of coercion, it stands to reason that a Grinaldi vampire broke the rules and tried to turn the witches, or he broke the rules and sired the vamp who did the crimes."

"That's the easiest explanation."

"So... why? Why would he go against his family and risk elimination like that? And what was his motive for trying to turn witches? If he'd just wanted them dead, there are easier ways."

"Indeed."

"And what about Delilah? Her disappearance *has* to be connected to the murders, but why was she taken rather than turned? Who's next? And is the next witch going to be kidnapped, killed, or what?" I closed my eyes, the thoughts swirling in my brain and turning it to mush.

"It's a start, Gray. A good one, but just a start." Darius

reached for my hand, his touch surprisingly gentle. Calming, just as he'd been in the middle of tonight's chaos. "We've still got a lot of work to do."

I opened my eyes, meeting his gaze across the table. "We?"

"All for one, one for all, the more the merrier, etcetera." Darius's lips stretched into a grin. "Surely you didn't think I'd let *El Lobo* and the demons have all the fun?"

"*El Lobo?*" I wrinkled my nose.

"It's Spanish for The Wolf."

I blinked at him. "*You* gave him that name?"

"He's from Argentina," he explained. "Spanish is his native tongue."

"No, I get it. It's just kind of… weak."

"Says the woman who calls me D?"

"Touché, vampire. Touché." I smiled as Darius's words found a soft spot inside my chest, nestling in close.

All for one, one for all, the more the merrier…

For so long, Sophie had been the center of my world—my best friend and a bright light in my life. No matter what I'd gone through, Sophie had always found a way to make me believe in hope. To believe that things could always get better. That we could *choose* better.

Ronan was her counterbalance, dark and brooding and intense, yet grounding me with his deep well of strength whenever I felt myself pulling apart at the seams.

In a blink, Sophie had been taken from us. Just like that, she was gone.

But Ronan was still by my side, no matter where our

kisses led. Darius had become an unexpected friend. Emilio was also in my corner—I felt it every time I looked into his deep, compassionate eyes. Asher had my back, too, if only because he was loyal to Ronan. And Haley? Where had *that* come from?

Just when I'd thought my life would fall to pieces, that everything had been taken from me, that nothing would ever be okay again, the universe was doing its damnedest to convince me otherwise.

Maybe it was working.

I rose from my chair and stretched. "I need to use the restroom. Be right back."

"Take your time, love." Darius pulled out his phone. "It'll give me a moment to check in with my associates about our cleanup operation—assuming I can figure out how to turn this thing on again."

"Button on the bottom, remember?" I moved to head for the ladies' room, but stopped just before I passed his chair, touching his shoulder. "Hey, D?"

"Yes, G?" he teased.

Tears misted my eyes, but they weren't tears of sadness or frustration, and I didn't bother blinking them away. "Thank you. For the coffee, and for looking out for me tonight, and just... everything."

Darius turned his face toward mine and smiled, broad and true, and my heart nearly stopped from the dazzling beauty of it. He reached for my hand gave it a squeeze. "You're not alone in this, Gray. I know it feels that way sometimes, but you're not."

TWENTY-NINE

GRAY

Darius had left me reeling, my body and mind buzzing from so much more than the caffeine in my latte. It was a lot to process, and right now, I just needed to get some air before my brain short-circuited.

After I finished up in the bathroom, I slipped out the back exit and headed over to the railroad ties at the edge of the parking lot, still within the protective boundary of Luna's property. I was pretty confident Darius's people were taking care of the situation at the morgue, but that didn't mean whoever had sent our would-be assassins didn't have more fanged friends lurking in the shadows.

Out beyond the lot, I took in the view of the water, lulled as always by the gentle sound of the lapping waves.

The shoreline wasn't grand or majestic by any means—just a rocky stretch of beach between the marina and the ferry dock—but it was ours, and if I squinted and looked out over our namesake Blackmoon Bay, I could almost see Sophie out there in the springtime, wading into the chilly waters with her jeans rolled up to her knees, searching for the perfect painting stones.

"They don't always wash up on shore, Gray. You have to be willing to work for your art. Dig deep, woman!"

"I don't do art."

"Oops. Did I say your *art? I meant* my *art. You have to dig deep for* my *art. Now get out here and help me dig! I'm freezing my ass off!"*

Laughing, I kicked off my shoes and waded into the frigid waters, holding out a plastic bag to collect Sophie's treasures. "We need to find you a warmer hobby. Preferably something with fire. Something like... glass blowing! That's it..."

"—done doin' overtime without pay. Fuck that."

The gruff voice startled me out of the vision, and I peered down along the beach, picking out the silhouettes of two men heading my way from the boat docks. They looked a bit unsteady on their feet.

"How'd they take it?" the other dude asked, passing a bottle of booze to his friend. He spoke with a lisp, but that could've been the booze talking.

"How ya think? Fired my ass on the spot."

I relaxed. Just a couple of dockworkers blowing off steam. I was about to head back inside Luna's when the response from the other guy set my teeth on edge.

"You shittin' me?" he slurred.

That voice... The lisp... How do I know this guy?

"Nah. Fuck 'em, though, right?" Jobless polished off the

last of the booze, then chucked the empty bottle into the Bay. "You're lookin' at a free man now, T."

"Guess you ain't buyin' the next round, then." The "T" dude laughed, the rasp of it skittering across my skin like cockroaches.

"Not this weekend, anyway." Jobless gave T a fist bump, then headed up to the street alone, leaving T to wander the shoreline.

Less than ten feet from where I stood, the cockroach paused at the water's edge, reaching into his pocket for a pack of smokes. He shook one out and jammed it between his lips. Flicked the lighter. Sucked until the end crackled and glowed.

A wheezing cough rattled his lungs.

Recognition slammed into my chest like a fist.

So you're an all talk, no action kind of bitch?

You got some ass on you, girl.

Nice try, little cunt...

It was *him*. The asshole who'd jumped me outside Black Ruby, threatening to do all sorts of nasty things to me. He would've done the same to Bean, too, if he'd gotten the chance.

Instead, he'd left her to die in my arms.

And I'd turned her into... God, there wasn't even a word for it. My stomach churned just thinking about it. I couldn't close my eyes without hearing her sweet voice —*grape jelly grape*—corrupted now by all the thoughts that haunted me.

You did this to me, witch.

It was his fault. This piece-of-shit excuse for a human standing in front of me, cigarette dangling from his greasy lips, limp dick in his hand as he pissed into the Bay.

The man was drunk.

Alone.

Defenseless.

Inside me, the blackness flamed again, roaring to life with new intensity. Instead of resisting it, I welcomed it, letting it fuel me, letting it fill me up like a battery getting an overdue recharge.

My entire body vibrated with magic.

"Hey," I called out, stepping over the railroad tie, outside the neutral boundary of Luna's. "Can I bum one of those smokes?"

Cockroach flinched at my words and whipped around to face me, pissing on himself in the process.

He narrowed his eyes, but he didn't seem to recognize me, which pissed me off even more. I could live another hundred years and I wouldn't forget the face of the man who'd terrorized me and Bean. But to him I was just another faceless, nameless dock rat washing up on the shore.

"You looking for company, sweetheart?" He grabbed his dick and winked, stroking himself. "Look, I already whipped it out for you."

"Wow. You come prepared." I stepped forward, meeting him at the water's edge.

"That's right, baby." He flashed his near-toothless smile. "Come on over and see what ol' Travis has for you."

"Actually, ol' Travis…" I grinned and held up my hands, power crackling across my palms. "This time, baby's got something for *you*."

THIRTY

RONAN

Beach behind Luna's. Now.

I stared at the text on my cell in disbelief. Fifteen years since we'd all started carrying cell phones, and the stodgy old vampire had never once texted me.

Even without his warning, I knew something bad was about to go down—I could feel it. And it had Gray's name all over it.

Abandoning the shipment I'd been unloading for Waldrich, I hauled ass up to the beach, following Darius's order and the tug in my gut that always led me to Gray.

Sure as hell, I found her there, kneeling in the sand next to some human meat sack. The dude was on his back, bloodied and unconscious, his limp dick hanging out of his pants.

What the fuck?

Beaumont was standing over them, useless as a statue. Not that he could've done much, anyway—they were surrounded by that damn shield again, some strange side effect of Gray's magic.

"What happened?" I demanded, automatically scanning the beach for a raven or an owl or any other sign of Death. Last time she'd called up her powers, he'd shown up out of nowhere and tried to lure her back to the Shadowrealm. Fuck if *that* was happening on my watch.

Beaumont lifted a shoulder as if he didn't have a care in the world, but his eyes told a different story. Mr. Ice-for-Blood, Stick-Up-The-Ass was seriously worked up.

"We were having coffee inside," he said, his calm demeanor forced. "She went to the restroom. Moments later, I sensed a surge of her magic, and here we are."

"How long has she been like this?"

"Five minutes, perhaps? I texted you as soon as I found her out here."

The two of us circled the iridescent dome, but I knew there was no way in. Gray was less than five feet away from me, her head tipped backward, eyes rolling into the back of her head, and all I could do was watch.

She moved forward, hands sliding up his chest, and the guy finally stirred. He cracked open his eyes and gasped for air, revealing a big black hole where his front teeth should've been.

I blew out a breath. At least she hadn't killed him. And if he wasn't dead, she wouldn't get a chance to mess with his soul. With any luck, she'd give him a good scare and burn herself out, no permanent damage done. Darius would have to jack the guy's memories, but hell, he'd be doing him a favor as much as he'd be covering Gray's tracks.

No human wanted to remember this kind of shit.

"We'll have to wait her out," I told Darius. "Last time this happened, it was—"

"Last time? So this is a regular occurrence?" The vampire fumed. "And you didn't deem it worth sharing?"

"I'm handling it, Beaumont. Gray doesn't need you to start—"

"Oh, spare me. I understand you think you have some kind of *mystical* connection to the woman, but—"

"Did… Did you seriously just make air quotes at me?"

"Look. I know you care for her a great deal—we all do. But it's time you level with us." The vampire glared at me, clearly unsettled. It wasn't a good look on him. "Who *is* she?"

I didn't even know how to begin answering that question. Even if I wanted to, I couldn't. It's not like she'd come with an instruction manual. All I had were a bunch of hunches and guesses about her potential, and the fine-print contractual bullshit I wasn't allowed to discuss without damning her eternal soul.

Mine, too.

"Why does it matter?" I snapped. "Knowing the answers wouldn't change how you feel about her. About how *any* of us feels."

"Of course not. But it might allow us to help her through the—"

"I said I'm handling it."

"Yes, I'm quite familiar with your refrain, but—"

I cut him off with a hand in the air. It was an old argument, one we revisited whenever we got worried about Gray, which seemed to be happening a lot lately.

I stalked over to the water's edge, giving us both a minute to cool off. When I returned to the scene, I gestured at the toothless fuck-up sprawled out before our girl. "So who's the asshole, anyway?"

Sarcasm dripped off Beaumont's smug face. "Well, Ronan, I didn't quite catch the gentleman's name, but I'm certain there's a logical explanation. Gray wouldn't attack someone unprovoked."

"Oh, you're the expert on her now?"

"Careful, demon. Your jealous streak is—Christ." His icy grin suddenly flatlined. "What the bloody hell is *that*?"

I snapped my attention back to Gray. Silver mist slithered out of the dude's mouth, curling around her fingers like smoke—same shit I'd seen the night we'd found Sophie.

But this time, Gray wasn't trying to bring a friend back from the dead. She was stealing his soul, yanking it right out of his body while the guy—still very much alive—watched helplessly, eyes wide, scared out of his fucking mind.

He was right to be scared.

Gray was killing him. *Worse* than killing him.

My heart dropped into my fucking boots. She might not have known what she was doing, but if it worked? Game over. Do not pass go. Do not collect two hundred dollars.

Stealing this man's soul—willingly trapping it in the Shadowrealm while he was still alive—would be a violation of the natural world order.

If she succeeded, the punishment for such a heinous crime—Gray's eternal fate—would make demon enslavement look like a trip to goddamn Disney World.

I fell to my knees and pressed my hands against the shield, sending a desperate plea to all the gods of men and demons and witches and fae and anyone else who might've been listening.

Please don't take her from me.

THIRTY-ONE

GRAY

Blood dripped from my hands, soaking into the dirt as I made my way through the meadow.

It was becoming a thing with me, the blood on my hands.

The soul slithering through my fingers was starting to feel familiar, too.

But unlike the beautiful gossamer of Bean's and Sophie's life forces, Travis's soul was tattered and flimsy, full of holes. It was such a ragged excuse for something so precious, I doubted he'd even miss it. I stretched my hands apart and felt the taffy-like pull as it tried desperately to return to his body.

Sorry, T. Not happening.

The eyes of the surrounding forest blinked awake as I marched onward, glittering and eerie. Beyond the meadow, thorny black vines choked my path, leaving it even more treacherous than it had been on my last visit.

I trampled them.

I needed to get to my stone archway. To the black wood and the Shadowrealm beyond.

For that's what it was, I now knew. The Shadowrealm. The source of my strange, soul-altering power. My fate.

Logically, I understood my actions weren't normal. Weren't right.

But my heart—that place inside me where all the deep, ancient things lived—wanted this soul banished, and I knew my magic would stop at nothing to see it through.

I was almost there.

A hundred feet.

I could already see the top of the archway.

Fifty feet. Twenty-five.

A stiff breeze nudged me onward, encouraging.

Ten feet. Five. One…

"It will not bring you peace." Death crept out of the black wood, blocking my entry through the gate.

"What are you doing here?" I demanded.

"I need to speak with you," he said.

"Ever hear of a phone?"

"I've not much use for them in my line of work."

"Cute." I didn't bother meeting his glowing blue eyes— just kept my attention on the archway. The runes, once faint, now burned with fiery intensity, the shadows beyond the gate calling to that primal part of me.

Home…

As if sensing its impending demise, Travis's soul writhed in my hands.

I wouldn't let it escape.

"Well. If you're here to kill me," I said to Death, "take a number."

"I'm afraid I've been greatly maligned in popular culture," Death said. "I do not kill—merely collect. And it's not your time." His attention shifted to the soul in my hands. "Not his either, I'm afraid."

I thought of the things Travis had said and done in the alley. The things he'd probably done in his past. The things he'd likely do again, if given the chance. My mind was made up. "He deserves to die."

"Maybe. But do you want the responsibility that goes along with that decision?"

"Isn't that what you do? Decide who lives and dies, who gets a second chance?"

"Gray." He placed a hand on my shoulder and I flinched instinctively, but instead of the icy grip I'd expected, his touch was warm and comforting, his energy pulsing through me like hot soup on a sick day. "Search your heart. Look past all the anger at what this man did to you. All the confusion and hurt over the death of your friend. All the frustration that the killer has not been apprehended."

Travis's soul slithered. I gripped it tighter.

"Look past your fear, Gray," Death implored.

"I'm not afraid."

"Look into my eyes and tell me that."

I lifted my chin, but the moment my gaze locked onto his, I wavered. His eyes were infinite, full of a thousand secrets times a thousand years times a thousand worlds, each one more vast and incomprehensible than the last.

I felt instantly tiny, instantly insignificant. A speck. A mote. A fucking atom.

He was right. I didn't want to do this. Maybe I could've convinced myself that the vampire woman's death was justified—she would've killed me otherwise. But Travis? Despite his many faults, despite the fact that he was a human stain, this wasn't right.

Dark magic pulsed in my veins, whispering encouragements to hold on. To see it through. My hands turned black with that oily smoke again, tendrils of it coiling up my arms.

Do it. Do it, Gray. This is who you were born to be.

It wasn't, though. I had to believe that. To *know* it.

Tears rolling down my cheeks, I finally closed my eyes and released my grip, envisioning the tattered soul traveling back into Travis's body. *Willing* it back. It slipped through my fingers like a gush of water, and then it was gone.

I was hollow inside, with no more strength to hold me up. I dropped to my knees in the dirt, staring at my blackened, blood-stained hands, watching the smoke dissipate. "What's... what's happening to me?"

Death knelt before me in the dirt, meeting me at eye level.

A shadowy dude with glowing eyes and tattered black robes lurking around your magical realm wasn't exactly comfort food for the soul, but his appearance wasn't quite as startling as it'd been on that first visit, and for once, I was glad for his presence. Here in this strange, magical place, there was something almost human about him, and when he spoke again, I found myself truly listening, turning to him for answers.

He ran a gloved finger along my palm, tickling the skin.

"The man's blood is literally on your hands, Gray," he said softly. His otherworldly echo had vanished, leaving only a man's voice in its place. "And you had control of his soul. The two are intimately connected."

"I don't understand."

"The combination of blood and soul is like a magical key to a very ancient, very complicated lock. In possession of both, Shadowborn have the ability to banish the souls of the living to the Shadowrealm."

"I almost… I almost went through with it."

"Be glad you reconsidered." Death rose, helping me to my feet. The black forest beyond the gate seemed to take a step back, giving us room.

"Tearing a soul from a living being and trapping it in the Shadowrealm is the worst kind of crime," he went on. "The punishment is instantaneous and irreversible."

"What is it?" I asked.

"Like his, your soul would also be trapped eternally, along with everything that makes you *you*—personality, memories, passions, love. Yet your physical body would retain its most primal awareness, even as it began to decay. And though your vitals would go undetected by even the most advanced medical technology, and your friends and family would presume you dead, you would not be. You'd be buried and mourned, yet forever trapped."

A shiver rippled through my body, starting at my toes and vibrating all the way up to my scalp. "Why didn't you tell me?"

"You have choices before you. Always. It is not my place to interfere, then or now or later."

"But you *did* interfere. You stopped me."

"I merely asked you to search within yourself."

"But this... this sick magic, this thing inside me... It's part of me, isn't it? Corrupting me." Another shiver rolled through me, and I hugged myself tight to stop the trembling. "It's pure evil. I want it out of me."

"If only it were that simple," he said with a sigh. "It's not evil, Gray. Just another facet of you. Some people are born with green eyes, some with heart defects, some with a predisposition to like chocolate. You don't get to choose those things, but once you accept them, you can make other choices from that place of truth and courage."

He gestured toward the path, and together we walked back the way I'd come, the arch fading behind us.

"What am I?" I whispered.

"Among other things, you're a necromancer. A very powerful one at that."

Among other things...

Something deep in my gut stirred at his words, my vision flickering. Black vines crept over my feet, and I gripped his hand, sucking in air, desperate not to let it take me...

"Don't fight it!" he said. "That's your magic calling to you. It's who you are. It's—"

"No." I didn't care what he thought about choices and truths. If my magic was responsible for my actions, for that black desire twisting around my heart, I wanted no part of it.

It took all my strength and concentration, but eventually I yanked my feet free, breaking through the vines and stomping them all down.

When they finally retreated, I looked at Death and said, "It's *not* me. You said it yourself—that's not what's in my heart."

"The desire to banish the soul of a living man is not in your heart. But this magic, this power? This *is* you, Rayanne."

Rayanne...

I'd never planned on changing my name. My first two years living on the streets, relying on odd jobs and the kindness of strangers, I'd gone by Rayanne to anyone who bothered asking.

When Ronan had first asked my name, I'd told him the truth, but I'd just regained consciousness after weeks of drifting, and my mouth was so cracked and dry, it'd come out sounding like Grayanne instead.

Ronan smiled and immediately shortened it to Gray, and it made me feel happy and warm and safe for the first time in two years. Though I eventually told him my real name, by then we'd both gotten attached to the new one.

"Rayanne died a long time ago," I said now. "My name is Gray."

"Your name is ultimately unimportant. Your destiny, however, is quite another matter."

"Destiny? What happened to choices?"

"The two are not mutually exclusive. But there are things about your path you must learn, must accept, no matter how difficult."

His ominous tone did nothing to inspire confidence. I didn't want to learn how to bring people back from the dead, and I certainly didn't want to encourage whatever dark terror was going on inside me.

"But I'm *not* evil," I said. It felt necessary to point that out, but Death remained unfazed.

"I've told you evil has nothing to do with it. You have a gift, and you weren't taught how to use it. You've abandoned this place, let it become overrun. And if you don't reclaim it, someone else might do it for you."

A cold finger of dread slithered up my spine, but I ignored it. So what if someone else reclaimed this place? I'd loved it as a child, as a teenager, but just like me, my magic place had changed.

"It doesn't even feel like mine anymore."

"You can't fight this, Gray," Death said, exasperated. We'd reached the clearing near the stone pedestal, and I sensed it was time to go. For both of us. Turning to me, he said, "When you're ready to accept yourself, call me."

He vanished in a puff of thick, oily smoke, and a single black feather swirled before me.

"Hey!" I shouted. "I don't even have your number!"

But of course he didn't come back. Didn't respond. Just left me alone at the pedestal, the eyes of the forest looking on.

I reached up and snatched his stupid feather out of the air, crushing it with my fingers.

Everything went black.

THIRTY-TWO

GRAY

The barista had served me a sand cookie and a venti sand latte topped with extra sand. Right?

It was the only explanation for the crunchy grit coating my tongue. My head wasn't doing much better; a sharp pain lanced my skull with every beat of my heart.

Where am I?

I cracked an eyelid. The room spun so fast I couldn't even tell what color the walls were.

Squeezing my eyes shut again, I focused instead on the voices coming from another room—tense, masculine voices quickly escalating into an argument. Darius and... sounded like Emilio?

"—should've brought me in on this earlier," Darius snapped. "I don't give a damn about protocol."

"I noticed," Emilio said. It had to be him, though I'd never heard him so angry. His accent was stronger than usual. "Hence all the evidence you and Gray contaminated tonight."

I cringed inside. So he knew about that, then. So much for Darius's associates cleaning up our mess without a trace.

I did a quick mental check on my body, scanning myself for any injuries. Other than a bad case of beach-mouth and a throbbing head, all systems checked out.

"...rogue vamp operating in my territory," Darius was saying. "You don't think it's relevant? For fuck's sake, Alvarez. It could've been her."

"It wasn't," Emilio said.

"If you can't see the urgency here, your head is even farther up your arse than I thought."

Emilio said something in Spanish—probably a string of curses.

What are they talking about?

"D?" I sat up too quickly. The floor rushed up to meet me.

"Easy, Gray." Another man's voice enveloped me a split second before his arms did.

Ronan.

Relieved by his presence, I leaned into his touch, letting him guide me into a sitting position. He knelt on the floor in front of me, hands on my thighs, and I kept my eyes open, determined to ride out the spins until I could figure out where we were.

My... living room? Okay, so I was at home. With Ronan, Darius, and Emilio. But how had we gotten here?

"You blacked out," Ronan said softly, squeezing my legs. Concern laced his tone, and as his face came slowly into focus, I noticed tight lines around his mouth, hiding behind his trim beard. "Outside Luna's."

Luna's. Right. Darius had taken me there for coffee. For normalcy.

"Where's Darius?" My voice cracked, and I coughed, sand still coating my mouth.

"Kitchen," Ronan said. "With—"

"Fuck your rules and procedures!" Darius shouted.

"Alvarez," Ronan said, just as Darius stomped into view.

"*El Lobo* needs to learn a few lessons about communication," Darius said. "He can't just—Gray! You're awake!"

Rushing to my side in an uncharacteristic display of relief, he dropped to his knees next to Ronan and pressed a cool hand to my forehead.

The fact that they were sitting shoulder to shoulder and not trying to kill each other should've been a clear sign that something was seriously jacked.

"What... what happened?" I searched their faces for a clue, but all I could find was worry.

"We were hoping you could tell us," Darius said. "What do you remember?"

"We had coffee and I... I went to the bathroom, right?"

Darius nodded, brushing a lock of hair off my forehead. "You ended up on the beach. You attacked someone."

"Physically and magically," Ronan said.

"Attacked?" I looked down at my hands. Sure enough,

they were swollen and red, my knuckles cracked and bloody.

Nothing hurt, though. Was I in shock?

"I think I… I just went outside for some air, and…" *Oh, God. The man from the alley.*

Memories slammed into me, one by excruciating one. The man pissing into the bay. Me, tackling him to the sand and pummeling his face with my fists.

The rage. The desperate darkness surging up inside me, consuming everything in its path.

The magic crackling across my skin.

The silver-blue mist of his soul…

My stomach lurched, and I clamped my mouth shut to keep my latte and cookie from bailing.

"Breathe, Gray." Ronan got up to sit on the couch next to me, his hand curling around my neck and squeezing gently. "Just breathe."

I closed my eyes and did as he said, waiting for the rest of tonight's shitty movie to play out in my memory.

My magic place. Death. The Shadowrealm…

But, no… I'd put his soul back. Let the man walk away with little more than a broken nose and a bruised ego.

"Where is he now?" I asked, opening my eyes. "Is he…?"

I wasn't sure how to finish that question. Hurt? Hospitalized? Permanently damaged from the psychological torment of what I'd done?

"I'm sorry, love," Darius said. "I know how you feel

about mental manipulation, but I couldn't let him walk away with those memories."

I nodded, grateful. As much as I'd wanted Travis to suffer… No, not like that.

"Gray. How are you feeling, *querida*?" Emilio emerged from the kitchen carrying a cup of hot tea.

"Better, I think. Is that for me?"

"Merry Mint." Nodding, he handed it over. "I found it in the pantry. I hope you don't mind."

I smiled and took the mug, his kind face calming the war inside me.

"What's *querida*?" I asked, hoping it didn't mean something like, *you ridiculous, evidence-contaminating idiot.*

Emilio lowered his head, the tips of his ears turning red. "It's just a term of endearment. If it bothers you I—"

"No, I… I like it. Thank you for the tea."

"Did you know him, love?" Darius asked. "The man on the beach?"

"It's… complicated." I closed my eyes, inhaling the clean, minty scent of the tea.

Where did I even begin? When it came to Travis and the incident in the alley, Darius and Ronan knew most of the story, but not all of it. Emilio knew even less. Other than Death, no one knew the full extent of what I'd done—what I was still capable of doing. Once I told them—once I opened that door and let the beast out—there'd be no putting it back in.

But these men were my friends. They had a right to

know who—or what—they were dealing with, no matter how frightening it was to say it all out loud.

"He's the guy from the alley," I finally said, taking a shuddering breath. "The one who attacked me outside Black Ruby the night before the witch murders. He killed a young girl, and I... I brought her back. Sort of."

I paused to take a fortifying sip of tea. My hands shook, but somehow I managed not to spill it.

"We're right here, Gray," Emilio said, as if he could sense my reluctance, my fear that they'd all think I was some crazy, evil psychopath gearing up to take over the world. He sat down on my other side, opposite Ronan. "Nothing you say could change that."

Shifters didn't have the power of mental influence, but the effect of his kindness was the same.

I looked from Emilio's warm brown eyes, to Darius's golden-honey ones, to the lush hazel in Ronan's, and knew they weren't judging me. They were offering me compassion. Openness. The kind of security that came from knowing someone else had your back, just like you had theirs.

"Something is seriously wrong with me," I whispered. It felt like a confession, but I pressed on, telling them the rest of the story. The magic place, how it'd changed since my last visit into something I barely recognized. The unfamiliar darkness simmering inside me, even now, and my fear that it was somehow related to the witch murders.

The black trees, the souls, the Shadowrealm. How I'd

brought Bean back from the dead, and how I'd almost brought Sophie back, too.

The way I'd killed that vampire at the morgue. The awful things I'd done to Travis. How close I'd come to damning him tonight—to damning us both.

I even told them about my conversations with Death, and though they exchanged an ominous glance at that bit, they didn't freak out, or leave me, or threaten to call the Council.

By the time I finished speaking, my tea had gone cold, but my hands had finally stopped shaking.

"There's nothing wrong with you," Ronan said, his warm touch on my knee an anchor in this wild storm. "Whatever's going on—whether it's connected to the killings or not—we'll deal with it."

"All of us," Emilio said. "You have to know that, *querida*."

I nodded, blowing out a breath. Crazy as it sounded, I *did* know that. I'd never doubted Ronan, but Darius and Emilio had only been part of my life for a short time.

It hadn't felt like a short time, though. Not even that night in Darius's club, or when Emilio had first shown up in my living room to investigate Sophie's death. Looking back on my interactions with them, I felt a strange sense of familiarity, like finding a favorite childhood toy tucked away in a box many years later. You didn't always remember playing with it, but somehow you knew it had belonged to you. That it was part of your history.

"What is it, love?" Darius asked. He was still kneeling in

front of me, the other two on the couch at my sides, and a feeling of complete contentment settled over me. I knew it would pass, but for now I let it comfort me like a fuzzy fleece blanket on a cold night.

"This might sound crazy," I began.

"Crazier than being a necromancer with secret powers who has regular chats with Death?" Emilio asked, his eyes twinkling.

I gave him a playful smack on the shoulder, and he grabbed my hand, holding it tight.

"I just… You know how they say people who share traumatic or intense experiences sometimes feel like they've known each other for years, even if it's only been a few days? Well, I kind of feel like that with you guys, but it's even more intense. Is that weird?"

The three of them exchanged a glance, but it wasn't scary or judgmental.

It was warm. Nostalgic, even.

Ronan nodded, and Darius squeezed my calf.

"Not weird at all," Darius said. "We've, ah… We've known you a bit longer that our recent interactions would suggest."

"A *bit*?" Emilio laughed.

I stared at them, waiting for the punchline.

"They saved your life, Gray," Ronan finally said. "The night I found you on that boat."

THIRTY-THREE

DARIUS

For a full minute, Gray seemed shocked into silence, her lips frozen in a tiny pink "o" as she blinked at us in disbelief.

"You guys were *there*?" she finally asked.

"Yes." I closed my eyes against a fresh cascade of horrid images—the bruises on her arms and legs, the fear in her eyes, the way she'd screamed when Ronan had carried her out of that boat. I could live another three hundred years and still not forget that sound.

Just like I'd never forget the sounds she'd made in the car tonight, her body coming alive at my touch. I'd much rather focus on remembering *those* sounds. Perhaps even coaxing them from her again sometime in the very near future.

"So you guys are, like, pals?" she asked, a warm smile gracing her face like a sunrise. It'd been too long since I'd seen either, and it was hard not to stare.

"Pals might be a bit of a stretch," Ronan said, at the same time Emilio said, "More like brothers."

"Yes," I agreed. "The kind who fantasize about beating the hell out of one another, but pulverize any outsider who actually attempts it."

Ronan cracked a smile at that one, the cheeky bastard.

"A demon, a vampire, and a shifter hanging out together?" Gray lifted a brow. "That's pretty rare, even in this town."

"What can I say?" Emilio grinned. "We've always been rebels."

"Sounds like it."

"You weren't speaking," I told Gray, continuing the story. "We weren't even sure you *could* speak—all you'd done so far was scream. But after a day or two, you simply slipped into unconsciousness."

"Asher managed to swipe some medical supplies," Ronan said, "so we ran an IV to keep you hydrated. And we all just took turns doing what we could, hoping it would be enough."

"Wait… *Asher*?" Gray shook her head, clearly trying to process all of this. "I can't imagine Asher caring about anyone other than himself. Well, and maybe Ronan." She looked at the demon in question. "You guys seem pretty tight."

"Thick as thieves, those two," I agreed. But despite my general distaste for most demons, I wanted Gray to know the truth. "For various reasons, Asher O'Keefe is not an easy man to—shall we say—*connect* with. But beneath his brash demeanor and ridiculous tattoos, the hellspawn twat actually does have a heart."

"Wow. I don't even know what to say." Gray leaned forward and hugged her knees, resting a cheek against her thighs. Her hair slipped in front of her face, and I ran my fingers through it, tucking a section behind her ear.

I wanted to see her eyes.

"Once you started to regain consciousness," I continued, "our big, tough wolf fed you homemade chicken soup with a syringe. Every night for nearly a week, he'd warm up the pot for you, adding more vegetables and broth, never letting any of us near it."

Gray smiled again. "Really?"

"I would've made empanadas," Emilio said, "but those are harder to get into a syringe."

Gray laughed and glanced my way. "Did you make me soup, too?"

Now it was my turn to laugh. "Heavens, no. I don't cook, Gray. I have a staff for that. But before you think me a heartless brute, you should know that while your precious *Ronan* did little else but brood like a sullen teenager—"

"Not true," Ronan said. "I also sulked."

"I stand corrected," I said. "While your multi-talented demon boy practiced his dark cloud routine, I read to you every night without fail."

"Bedtime stories?" she teased. "Like, Goodnight Moon?"

"Legal briefings from my defense attorney days, if you must know. It's what I had available at the time."

"Seriously?" Gray laughed again, and in that moment I was certain I'd give up immortality if it meant I could keep hearing that music. "No wonder I was unconscious for so long."

"Now you know why I sold my practice and went into the bar business."

She sat up again, continuing to stare at us in wonder. "I feel like I'm starting to remember some of it—like the taste of the soup, maybe? And the reading. And some kind of... singing?"

"Singing?" I asked.

Ronan turned away, but not before I caught sight of the blush on his cheeks.

"You?" I asked him. "Really?"

Ronan shrugged. "Guilty." He turned back to Gray with a wink. "But I'll never tell you which song. Not even if you torture me."

"That's funny," I said, "because I'd wager that hearing you sing is its own torture."

Everyone had a good laugh at that—even Ronan.

"I wish I could remember more," Gray said. "I feel like I should thank you guys."

"It will come to you in time," Emilio told her, rubbing a hand down her back. "And you *do* thank us. Just by being here. Just by being you."

Gray turned her gaze back to me, her blue eyes bright. "I can't believe you guys never said anything. Especially you, D. God, all that time making deliveries to Black Ruby, I was totally scared of you."

I nodded. "I understand, love. I am an apex predator after all."

"Hello?" Gray rolled her eyes and smirked. "You're *all* apex predators. It's just that *you* happen to have the sharpest teeth."

Her gaze lingered on my mouth, the heat of that penetrating stare sending an inconvenient surge of desire right below the belt. Thankfully I was still on the floor, the—*ahem* —hard evidence not quite in view of the others.

Gray blew out a breath, the lightness of the moment evaporating. "I don't even remember getting on that boat. One night I was in Portland, and then I just… ended up here." She shook her head, and her eyes grew cloudy. "It's all just a big blank."

Silence descended, and I wished more than anything I had the right words for this—the ones to ease her suffering. But of course, I didn't. None of us did.

"Anyway," Ronan finally said, "after all that, you stayed with me, and the other guys backed off. We didn't want to overwhelm you. Figured it'd be better to let you remember things on your own."

"But you didn't," I said, "and eventually it just became easier not to dwell on it. You and I had our brief interactions at the club, but it's not the sort of thing you bring up when signing for a delivery, is it?" I shook my head, clearing the images of her shivering, broken body. "None of us like revisiting those days, Gray. You were badly wounded, and… Well, you're obviously fine now—strong enough to take on vampires and men twice your size, and who knows what other foul beasts."

"Oh, yes," she teased, flexing a toned bicep. "I'm *super* hardcore."

"Clearly my chicken soup worked its magic," Emilio said.

"Or perhaps it was my soothing voice, coaxing you back from the brink." I winked at her, but our story had come to an end, and I needed to call it a night. I still had a few errands to run before sunrise.

I got to my feet, the rest of them following suit. Gray looked a bit tired, but otherwise okay, despite her ordeal tonight.

She stretched up on her toes, wrapping her arms around my neck and hugging me tight. "Thank you. Again."

When she pulled back to meet my gaze, I took her face in my hands and kissed her, slow and deep and delicious, the sweet taste just enough to get me through the hours until I could kiss her again.

Ronan stood behind her, hands wrapped protectively around her shoulders, but when I broke our kiss and met his steady gaze, I found no challenge there.

Only respect.

"Take good care of our little brawler," I told him.

Ronan nodded. "Always do."

"And take care of yourself, too." I headed for the front door with Emilio, but turned around one last time to add a final word—one I hadn't said to Ronan Vacarro in many years. "Brother."

THIRTY-FOUR

GRAY

"I'm just saying it's complete bullshit," Ronan grumbled. "What dude would bail on his band, sell his guitar, and open a bakery just because some woman told him she liked cake?"

"Um. A dude who wants to get laid? And I gotta say, that would absolutely do the trick for me." I hit pause on the rom-com we'd been watching and headed into the kitchen in search of snacks.

The other guys had left a while ago, and though Ronan was doing his best to keep me calm and relaxed, the tension between us kept mounting. It was the first time we'd been alone together since our kiss last week, and when I'd suggested a movie, Ronan was quick to jump on board.

Movies meant no quiet space. No dead air. No chance of talking about what happened.

No chance of it happening again.

But compartmentalization only worked for so long.

"Nothing soothes the soul like a giant scoop of peanut butter rolled in popcorn and M&Ms." I prepared a big spoonful for Ronan and handed it over. Then, I went for the jugular. "Now tell me what's really bothering you."

Ronan wrapped his hand around mine, lifting it to his mouth and shoving the spoon inside. His lips brushed my fingers, the touch of them warming my entire hand.

"I can smell him on your skin," he finally said.

"Who, Darius?"

Ronan nodded.

"Okay, first of all? *Beyond* creepy, Vacarro. Second of all, is that seriously what's bugging you, or are you just making a general observation?"

"Both."

I scooped up my own spoonful of peanut butter deliciousness, but unlike Ronan, I savored mine, one lick at a time. "What is it with you two, anyway? You go from mortal enemies to nearly cuddling. And now I find out you've been partners in crime all along?"

Ronan shrugged. "We've known each other a long time. Sometimes it's... suffocating."

Maybe it was a product of my being alone for so long after I'd left home, but I couldn't imagine feeling suffocated by a genuine relationship like the guys seemed to have. No, nothing was perfect, but true friendship—mutual respect, authenticity, shared history—that wasn't always a given with people. You couldn't throw that away just because you needed a little space sometimes.

"Is it possible you're overreacting, just a little?" I asked.

Ronan stared me down for a long moment, his autumn gaze unwavering. I was beginning to think he'd given up on the conversation when he finally blurted out, "No. Is he a good kisser?"

I laughed. I actually laughed, because the question was so far out of left field, I didn't know what else to do.

But Ronan just stood there, waiting for an answer.

I crossed my arms in front of my chest, glaring right back at him. "Would it bother you if I said yes? Is *that* what you're pissed about?"

Maybe they're into sharing…

"It's—no. Not really." Ronan closed his eyes, blowing out a long breath. "Not at all, actually."

"Ronan, seriously. What is going *on* with you tonight? Is it me? Did I completely freak you out?" I didn't want to talk about my magic again, but if that's what was upsetting him, I'd drag it all back out in the open and sift through every black bit of it until he felt okay.

But Ronan shook his head, guilt flickering in his eyes. "It's not you, Gray. Never."

"Then what's your deal?"

The muscle in his jaw ticked. "Darius made a promise that night we found you—we *all* made a promise. No matter what came between us, no matter how many years passed or what fucked-up shit went down in the Bay, no matter what you ultimately remembered about that time in your life, we'd always look out for you."

"Okay," I said. "How is that a problem?"

"He's supposed to have your back, and look what

happened. That vamp attack? You never should've gotten in the middle of that shit."

Was he serious right now? Darius's actions tonight had been the very definition of having my back. And my front. And every other exposed part of me that would've made a perfect snack for the bloodsuckers if he hadn't been there to protect me.

"You are *truly* impossible. You know that, right?" I tossed my spoon into the sink and stalked down the hall to my bedroom.

He followed me, looming in the doorway as I dug through my dresser for a sleep shirt and boxers. I needed to go to bed. To shut my door and lock him out and crawl deep into a blanket cave until all this shit blew over.

"It shouldn't have happened," he said. "Period. He shouldn't have agreed to meet you at the morgue, especially without me and Emilio. Failing that, he should've found a way to get you out of that mess without a fight. And don't even get me started on Hollis and Weston."

Ignoring the barb about Scarface and Emo—ancient history, as far as I was concerned—I slammed my dresser drawer and said, "But it *did* happen, Ronan. And now you're, what? Ready to stake him? Everything with you is so all or nothing!"

"Where you're concerned? Absolutely." Ronan stepped into my room, barging into my personal space, his presence overloading every one of my senses. The cloves-and-campfire scent of him, the heat rolling off his body, the red-hot memories of our kiss… All of it conspired to lure me closer, even as I tried to resist.

"What happened tonight got way out of hand," he said. "It's just another reminder that I'm not always going to be there to—"

"But every time I turn around, you *are* there. Looking out for me. Bringing in backup. Paying my bills. Doing my job. Fighting my battles for me. Why?"

Ronan bristled. "What the hell kind of question is that? You're my best friend, Gray."

"*Why*, Ronan?"

I knew it wasn't just about our tight friendship or the promise the guys had made all those years ago. I also knew it wasn't a simple answer; I had my own complicated feelings on the matter.

But for once, I needed to hear his.

The silence between us was unbearable, stretching on for so long I was beginning to think he'd just storm out of the room without answering. But then he let out a groan, his guard dropping long enough to reveal the raw, vulnerable emotion in his eyes.

When he finally spoke, his voice was low and gentle. Fragile. "Why do you *think*, Gray Desario?"

The look in his eyes had the power to melt me like a dish of ice cream left in the sun. But I was tired of over-analyzing every look, every gesture, every touch. I needed the honest truth to back it all up.

I needed to know, one way or the other, where I stood with the man.

"It doesn't matter what I think," I said, breaking our gaze and sitting on the edge of my bed. "It matters what you feel. It matters what's true."

"You wanna know what I feel? What's true?" Ronan sat down next to me, our legs touching from hip to knee, hot even through the fabric of our clothing. "Seven years ago, I watched you claw your way back from near-death. And every day since, I've watched you fight for everything you have. I know the Bay isn't an easy place—not for any of us —but you made a life here, Gray. You earned it. So when I think about someone taking it away from you—someone like the sick motherfucker who killed Sophie…" He closed his eyes and took a deep, shuddering breath. "Losing you just isn't an option. *That's* the truth. That's what I feel."

When he opened his eyes again, they shone with unshed tears.

"Who *are* you?" I whispered.

I'd been dying to ask that question since we met, and now that it was out, the words hung heavy and uncertain between us.

The wrong answer could destroy everything we had. Everything we'd built together. Everything that might still come.

But I couldn't take them back.

Ronan shook his head. "You don't want to know the answer to that. You think you do, but trust me—"

"That's the thing. I *do* trust you. Even when you're driving me crazy. Even when every instinct is screaming at me to get as far away from you as I can."

"Every instinct, huh?" Lifting a hand to my face, he slid the pad of his thumb across my lower lip, sending sparks of heat cascading across my skin. "At least now I know I'm not the only one whose advice you completely ignore."

He flashed his sexy, crooked grin, but it couldn't hide the sadness in his eyes. The regret. The secrets.

He lowered his hand from my face, and I knew in that moment he wouldn't kiss me tonight. Not now. Maybe not ever again.

The thought nearly devastated me.

Closing my eyes, I leaned my head on his shoulder and sighed. "Ronan, I..."

I'm in love with you. Can't you see that? Can't you feel *it?*

"Get some sleep, Gray." He kissed the top of my head, then rose from the bed. "If you need me, I'm right out there on the couch."

I need you. I always *need you.*

So many thoughts. So many unsaid words. All I had to do was give them a voice and set them free, and he'd climb back into this bed and kiss me so hard I'd never eat or drink again without remembering the taste of his hot, hungry mouth.

All I had to do was say the words that would finally make him understand what he meant to me—whether he was ready to hear them or not.

But the space around me had turned cold, and by the time I found the courage to open my eyes, Ronan was gone.

THIRTY-FIVE

GRAY

I wake up in my meadow.

Sophie's there in the distance again, the same place where I last saw her, only this time she's naked. Her skin is marred with runes—not just across her chest like in the evidence photos, but all over her body. Each one pulses with fiery red light.

"Sophie?" I jump to my feet and run toward her, but the closer I get, the farther away she feels. I continue to chase her, running until my body burns with exhaustion.

But the trees are closing in. I just can't catch her.

"Tell me what to do!" I scream. "Tell me who did this to you!"

Sophie finally stops running and turns to face me, a frown marring her beautiful face. "I think you already know, Rayanne."

"What? What do I know? I can't—"

A branch snaps in the black forest around the clearing, startling us both.

"You should go," Sophie says. "It's not safe for you here."

I try to reach for her hands, but she's already out of bounds, vanishing into the mist beyond.

I hear the snap again, closer this time, and whirl around to face my assailant. At first, I see nothing but mist and shadow, but eventually, a dark shape emerges from the trees.

A great canine beast with glowing red eyes looms before me.

His fur is coal-black, bloody and matted in parts, torn away in others. Cracked yellow ribs poke through a festering wound on one side of his body, but if he's in pain he doesn't show it. Those glowing, wide-set eyes burn like smoldering embers in an otherwise empty skull.

Beneath an elongated snout, the creature opens his mouth, revealing two rows of razor-sharp teeth dripping with blood and rotten flesh. The sound that erupts from that black cave is beyond primal, as if it were tortured out of him by the devil himself. Every hair on my arms stands on end.

Something else crunches in the forest behind me, and the massive creature before me springs to its hind legs and lunges, two massive paws crashing into my chest. The force knocks me to the ground, and the beast pins me with monstrous paws, his sharp claws piercing my flesh.

Desperate for a rock or a stick, I scratch at the ground around me, but there's only soft dirt and dead flower petals. The scent of rotting lavender filling my nostrils.

I'm bleeding out, which is total bullshit. I'm a witch, my closest friends are demons and a vampire and a wolf, Death himself is practically stalking me... You'd think someone could figure out how to get me out of this mess. Yet here I am, lying in a pool of my own blood, pinned by a gruesome beast in serious need of a mercy kill — not to mention a doggie breath mint.

I don't want to die here. Not in the place of my magic — a place I once held sacred. Not without saying goodbye to the ones I love.

"Please," I whisper, but there's no one to hear me, no one to save me from the beast. The thing won't look at me, but its ghostly jaws snap above my face, foul breath and blood and rot raining down on my skin.

There's nothing left to do but scream.

The crash of a wooden door splintering against the wall jolted me out of the dream, and suddenly Ronan was at my side, hauling me out from under the beast's powerful haunches.

Only… it wasn't a beast. It was a blanket. And I was no longer in my grove, but hunkered down on my floor, moonlight streaming through the windows, casting everything in an eerie blue glow.

The cracked bedroom door hung half off its hinges.

Ronan's body curved around me, shielding me from my invisible attacker. His skin was hot, his muscles tightly bunched and ready to pounce.

"Where is he?" he demanded, jerking his head around to scan the empty room. "What happened?"

"I'm not… I thought I was in my realm." I disentangled myself from the cage of his arms, and we both stood up, peering into the shadows. Bed, dresser, bookshelf, a chair that served as a clothes rack. Nothing out of the ordinary.

"I guess it was just a nightmare," I breathed, though my skin was still tight with goosebumps. And my T-shirt was…

We noticed it at the same time, both of us looking down in sick horror. The once yellow fabric was torn and bloody, sticking to my abdomen in dark, wet patches.

"A nightmare with claws?" Ronan grabbed the bottom edge of the shirt, slowly lifting it to reveal three thin slashes across my abdomen. "Jesus."

What the fuck?

I pulled the shirt back down, trying not to wince. "It doesn't hurt that bad."

Ronan wasn't even listening. His eyes were black as night.

He stalked out into the hallway, fury rolling off him in waves as he ransacked the linen closet for the first aid kit.

"Bathroom," he said. "Come on."

I sat on the edge of the tub with my shirt pulled up, trying to describe the beast from my dream as Ronan cleaned me up. The gouges weren't actually that deep, but they stung like a bitch, and when he finally pressed the gauze to my skin, I sighed in relief.

"I'm okay," I said, trying to reassure him. But Ronan was in his own world, quickly losing himself inside his silent rage. "Ronan, I said I'm—"

"Stay inside," he ordered, snapping the first aid kit shut. "Don't open the door for anyone but Asher."

"Why? Where are you going?"

"No one but Asher, Gray." He shoved the first aid kit back into the closet and stomped into the living room, jamming his feet into his boots. Without another word, he wrenched open the front door, and then he was gone, storming out into the endless dark of Blackmoon Bay.

I didn't even have time to be shocked. Minutes later, a motorcycle rumbled to a stop out front, and I peeked out the window to see Asher dismounting and sauntering up my path, looking for all the world like the prodigal son returning home from some epic carnal conquest.

When I opened the door, he was already standing on the porch, helmet in one hand, a paper bag in the other. His hair was matted, but not even a serious case of helmet head could dull Asher's infuriating good looks.

"Whiskey or tequila?" He held up the bag, sea-blue eyes flashing in the moonlight, grinning that maddening grin of his. "Pick your poison, Cupcake. 'Cause you and me? We're in for a long night."

THIRTY-SIX

RONAN

I hated the fucking desert. Felt too much like hell, which was probably what Sebastian liked about it.

Well, that and the hookers.

"You look hungry, baby." A dark-haired woman with fake tits and pointed red nails ran one of her talons down my chest, hooking a finger in my belt loop. "I can take care of that for you. Fill you up until you're *more* than satisfied."

"I'm good, thanks." I removed her hand from my pants and sidestepped her, stalking over to the floor-to-ceiling windows that overlooked the Vegas strip. Beyond the glittering lights of the city, the wind tore through the dark desert, but I didn't feel it up here on the forty-second floor.

Not for the first time, I wondered how long it would take for nature to reclaim this place, bury it all under an ocean of sand and time.

I closed my eyes, pressing my forehead against the glass.

Sebastian loved making me wait. Making me sweat.

I'd been here twenty minutes already. Turned down three of his favorite women. Ignored the mahogany bar set up in his office.

I was about to throw a chair through the windows and fuck up his ten-million-dollar view when the bastard finally strolled in.

He was a scrawny fuck, with thinning gray hair he slicked back over a head shaped like a potato, a greasy gray goatee trying hard to cover his pockmarked skin. Dressed in a three-piece pinstripe suit and dripping with more gold than the Federal Reserve, the man looked every bit the casino boss he fancied himself.

His accent, though? That shit was peak Colonel Sanders right there.

"Ronan Vacarro," he drawled, shooing the woman out and shutting the door in her face. "To what do I owe the pleasure?"

"Gray was attacked by hellhounds last night," I said. After wasting my fucking time all night, the Prince of Hell wasn't getting the pleasure of small talk. "I want to know why."

Sebastian's mustache twitched. "Attacked? Impossible. She—"

I slammed my fists against his desk, splintering the polished wood. "She woke up screaming and bloody. Her shirt was slashed across the middle. And she described your precious pets to a fucking T. So don't stroll in here and tell me what's possible."

He raised an eyebrow, but showed no other reaction to my outburst.

I hated his mind games. He beat me every time.

"Would you like a drink?" he asked, heading for his bar.

"No."

He grabbed a glass decanter and poured two drinks anyway, passing one to me. "Have a drink, boy. It'll calm your nerves."

I took the glass, set it on a filing cabinet behind me.

Sebastian ignored the slight.

Settling into the leather executive chair behind his now-demolished desk, he sipped the bourbon, nodding his appreciation. Shit probably cost more than this whole building was worth, knowing his flashy tastes.

"My hounds are trained to protect my investments," he said, waving a hand in the air as if my fears were just minor annoyances fucking up his otherwise perfect night. "If she got hurt, she brought that on herself."

I leaned back against the windows, arms folded over my chest to prevent myself from reaching over and choking the shit out of him. "Do you actually believe the bullshit you're spewing?"

"Why wouldn't I? Unlike the rest of you, hounds don't go rogue. They don't let their feelings cloud their judgment. They don't even *have* judgment. I say jump, and you know what they say?"

"How high?"

"No. They don't say a damn thing because they're too busy following orders."

"So you're telling me there's another threat?"

"The beasts wouldn't be there otherwise."

I considered this. The hound had attacked Gray—or protected her, depending on whose story you believed—in her magic place. I didn't know the exact mechanics, but my understanding from other witches who'd accessed magic that way over the years was that a being could only manifest in another witch's magical realm if that being shared a deeply personal or spiritual connection to the witch, had the advanced ritual skills to open magical gateways, and possessed something physical that contained the witch's DNA, like blood or hair.

For that reason, most of the witches I'd known in the past had been very careful about properly disposing of things like hair from the shower drain or fingernail clippings or anything else that could've been used in dark spellwork against them. The practice had fallen out of favor after most of the covens were forced underground. I didn't know any witches that still followed it.

"Do you have any idea what's hunting her?" I asked.

"Many things are hunting her, boy. Always have been, always will be. Why do you think she's so valuable to me?"

"You don't believe in that prophecy bullshit."

Sebastian took another sip, then stroked his goatee. "Doesn't matter. Other people do. And as long as people believe she's packing that kind of mojo, they'll hunt her. Everyone wants power, Ronan."

"And you don't?"

"I'm simply carrying out my end of a binding contract."

"Gray doesn't even know that contract exists." I shoved a hand through my hair, knowing the argument was pointless, but trying again anyway. "If I could tell her the truth, maybe she'd have a shot at protecting herself."

"You know the rules, oathbound."

Yeah, I knew the rules. Memorized them. Every contract, every soul, every demonic order may as well have been tattooed on the inside of my eyelids. Didn't make them go down any easier.

"Break the contract," I pushed. A risk, sure. But what choice did I have? I couldn't just stand around with my dick in my hand while Gray's eternal future went up in smoke over some bullshit deal she had nothing to do with.

Sebastian rose from his chair, crossing back to the bar in search of the ice bucket. "How long have you been in this business, Ronan?"

"Long enough to know there's always a loophole."

"Not this time." He dropped a few cubes into his glass, then topped it off with more booze. "Here's the problem as I see it, son. You're allowing your emotions to cloud your reasoning, and those emotions are confusing you on a very important point: You're not human."

The comment wasn't surprising, but it still stung. "I *was.*"

Sebastian frowned, deepening the pits in his cheeks. "This again? Ronan, you really should see someone about these issues. There comes a time in every man's life when he must stop blaming his adult problems on his difficult childhood."

I was smart enough not to take that particular bait.

"There is no loophole," he said. "Make me a better offer, and we'll talk, but there's no loophole."

"Fine. You want a life? Take mine."

"I already own yours." He tipped his glass back, polishing off the drink. Bourbon dripped from his goatee. "Lighten up, boy. The contract isn't all bad—it offers her certain protections. She'll be my responsibility soon enough, and you can move on to a new deal, help me get through some of this backlog."

"You're assuming she'll die soon."

"Sources tell me she's getting closer every day."

I felt my eyes go black, my rational mind shutting down, my body preparing to lunge. *I will tear out your throat, Prince...*

Sebastian must've sensed my intentions, because when he looked at me again, his eyes were glowing red.

A silent fucking threat that got the job done every time.

He was the boss, after all. The master.

"Now, if that's all, I have other pressing matters to attend, like ordering a new desk and sending you the bill." He opened the door, dismissing me.

"My best to Gray," he said as I walked out, his demeanor as calm and cool as a desert oasis. "Oh, and Ronan?"

I turned to look at him over my shoulder, already dreading what would come next. He'd said it every fucking time we parted ways.

No wonder I had issues.

Sebastian grinned, his eyes glinting with the sick plea-sure he took in lording his eternal hold over me. "Don't forget your place, boy."

THIRTY-SEVEN

ASHER

Ronan's witch was everything I hated in a woman.

Total pain in the ass. Too smart for her own good. Gorgeous as hell. And a hundred and fifty percent off fucking limits.

Hands on her hips, she squared off with me in the living room, refusing to give an inch. "Do you know where Ronan went?"

I let my gaze roam over her curves, right down to the bloody slashes in her shirt.

Jesus.

My fists tightened, nails digging into my palms. No wonder Ronan sounded so blitzed on the phone. *Get here,* he'd said. *Fucking now.*

I pointed at her shirt. "I suspect he's having a chat with whatever did *that.*"

She folded her arms across her midsection. "*That* was a nightmare."

"Whatever you need to tell yourself, Cupcake."

I had no idea what the hell had happened. All I'd managed to get out of Ronan was that she'd been attacked in her sleep, probably by a hellhound.

Ignoring me, Gray turned away and stalked down the hallway, disappearing into her bedroom. When she came back, she was wearing a baggy, ugly-ass Seattle Seahawks sweatshirt, hiding everything *woman* about her.

Made me miss that pink-and-white sweatshirt she'd been wearing in the park that day. The one that'd made her look like a cupcake.

Good enough to lick off all the frosting...

"So are you just going to stand there staring at me like an idiot all night?" she snapped.

"Would you like that, Cupcake?"

She laughed. "Is this the part where you tell me I need a real man in my life and invite yourself into my bed?"

"Is that a challenge?" I asked.

"Is that a yes?"

"*Mmm.*" Made my dick hard just thinking about it, but... Nope. Bad idea. Terrible. The worst. "Your boy Ronan would lock my ass in a devil's trap faster than you could say *abracadabra*, little witch."

Her cheeks flamed, and she stormed off into the kitchen, giving me no choice but to follow.

Reaching up into a cupboard over the sink, she pulled down a couple of shot glasses, then set them on the table, gesturing for me to sit.

I hung my helmet off the back of the chair and pulled the booze out of the bag.

"Hungry?" she asked. "I've got some leftover chicken fajitas from El Sarape if you're interested."

"Yeah?" My stomach rumbled, and I smiled up at her, my first real one all night. "Sounds good. Thank you."

"You want me to zap it?"

"Nah. Cold is just fine."

She got out a plate, set it all up for me.

Taking the chair across from me, she said, "He's not my *boy*, you know. Ronan and I are... We're just... We've known each other a really long time."

"That so?"

"Nearly a quarter of my life." She folded her arms across her chest and leaned her chair back on two legs, her smile smug and adorable. "Seven years."

I shoved in a forkful of chicken stuff, then said, "Well, I've known him for a hundred and eighty, and you don't see me blushing every time someone says his name."

Not that I minded that sweet little blush. Not at all.

"I'm not blushing," she said, dropping her chair back to the floor. But now she was biting her lip, too, trying to hold in a smile.

Damn, she had it just as bad for Ronan as he had it for her. *This can't possibly end well...*

"So," I said.

"So."

I glanced around the kitchen, taking in the girly decor.

Yellow walls with red accents, cutesy little bird knick-knacks on the window sill, fox clock on the wall, a basket of painted stones in the middle of the table.

You can never really know love until you know yourself, one of them said.

Next to the basket, I spotted a deck of Tarot cards, but that was the only thing that screamed *witch* about the place.

Last time I'd been here with Ronan, I hadn't really given it much thought, but something was definitely off about Gray's house.

No witchy shit.

"Not very mystical in here," I said.

"How do you mean?"

I shoved in another bite of food. "You know, little statues, incense, pentacles. I thought witches were into all that woo-woo shit."

Gray shrugged and lowered her eyes, running her thumbnail along a crack in the table. "I don't practice magic anymore."

"Since when?"

She stopped messing with the table and looked up, lasering me with an icy glare that made my dick shrivel. "Since hunters butchered my mother right in front of me."

I dropped my fork, and she flinched. Total accident, but damn.

Son of a bitch, Ronan. Why the fuck didn't you say something?

I'd met Gray the same time Darius and Emilio had—on her first night in the Bay. But Ronan had known her longer, had known she'd come with baggage. Couldn't talk about it though—all part of the gig for a demon like him.

All I'd known about her at the time was that she was one of Ronan's contracts. A witch. Powerful as hell. And eighteen years old.

That she'd suffered some kind of fucked-up tragedy was obvious; kids like her didn't just show up in the Bay starved and beaten if they had money and a nice, cozy family somewhere.

But hell if I'd ever asked for the details.

Ronan had said she was important—that she needed our protection. That one day she might need more than that. And we'd all agreed to look out for her, no questions asked. Blood or not, that's what brothers did.

Now, I'd barely been back in her life a week and I was already hurting her. Breaking my promise to take care of her.

"Alright, Cupcake," I said, more than ready to see her smile again. "Here's the plan. I'll pour the drinks. You shuffle up your little deck of magic cards and tell Asher his future."

I grabbed the bottle of tequila and poured two shots, but Gray looked downright scandalized.

"I don't read Tarot for people who refer to themselves in the third person. And I certainly don't read when I'm drinking. It interferes with my intuition."

"I can solve both of those problems for you right now." I downed the shots myself, then grinned. "Gray. Will you please give me a reading? Me, as in, first-person me?"

She rolled her eyes, but she was already reaching for the deck.

* * *

"So this card represents your past." She turned over the first card—a tormented creature crammed into a wooden box, ten swords shoved right through it. Right through *him*.

Felt like a kick in the nuts, but I kept right on smiling. "Damn, girl. Tell me how you *really* feel."

"This has nothing to do with how I feel and everything to do with the energy and events in your life."

"So what's this energy saying? Don't play hide-and-go-seek with sharp objects?" I picked up the card for a closer look. Thing gave me the creeps.

"With the Ten of Swords in the past position, there's likely something in your life you haven't dealt with yet. Whatever it is, it's major, and it's been haunting you for a long time. But this card is all about endings. Whatever happened, it's done. You need to let it go or it's going to destroy you."

Guilt rippled in my gut, and I dropped the card. This was supposed to be a fun distraction for us both, but Gray was a little too good at this Tarot shit. I hadn't meant for her to dig that deep.

"No comment?" she asked.

"Let's, ah, leave the past in the past. Shall we?"

She narrowed her eyes, but thankfully didn't push it.

She laid down another card in the present position, a

grin lighting up her face. "Knight of Swords," she said, pointing at the image of an armored knight riding a demonic horse, sword out and ready to rock. "*Very* mercurial. Talks before he thinks. Quick to rush into everything and make a big ol' mess. Does that strike a chord with you?"

"I don't rush into *everything*, Cupcake." I glanced down at her mouth. "Some things are worth taking a very long, very deliberate time to do."

She squirmed in her chair, and I'm not gonna lie—that new blush on her cheeks made me hard as fuck.

What was it about this girl? It's not like I'd never been alone with an attractive woman before, but something about Gray was quickly taking hold.

I wasn't sure if I liked it. I wasn't sure I should even *think* about liking it.

"Moving on," she said quickly. "Let's see what lies beneath—the essence of the matter, you might say."

She set down another card, this one showing a naked couple on the beach doing exactly what naked people on the beach were supposed to do.

Thing was, a serpent had just sunk its fangs into the guy's leg.

"The Lovers card," she said, flipping the next one and laying it crosswise over the sex card. "Crossed by The Devil."

I stared at the new card—a winged demon that looked a lot like a guy I used to know, dancing on scorched earth. "That... can't be good."

She studied the cards a minute longer, brow furrowed in concentration.

And then she gasped.

My heart kicked me in the ribs. "What was *that* for? Is my dick about to fall off or something?"

She looked up at me, her pretty blue eyes wide with shock. "You're an *incubus*?"

Relief rushed in, and I bit back a smile. "Cards told you my secret, huh?"

"Not specifically, no. But that's the message I'm picking up, loud and clear. And you're not denying it, so..." She reached for the bottle of tequila, pouring a healthy shot and slamming it down in a swift gulp.

"Thought you didn't drink and read?"

"New policy." She wiped her mouth with the back of her hand, staring at the cards as if they might come back to her with some other outcome.

When she finally looked up at me again, her eyes were full of a hundred questions.

I gestured for her to spit it out. "Go ahead. Ask."

Her cheeks pinked up again, but to her credit, she didn't shy away. "So you survive on... How do you... I mean, how does it work? You're sitting here eating fajitas. That doesn't do the job?"

"Not entirely. It's not much different from vampires," I explained. "I eat and drink regular stuff, but I still need to take in a certain kind of... let's call it *energy*... to survive."

"So basically you need to have sex constantly or you drop dead?"

I downed another shot to keep from laughing.

Yeah, sex definitely kept the spring in my step, but I could get by for long stretches without it. In fact, it'd been a few months since I'd had time to pursue that kind of steady sustenance—it took a lot of planning, since a partner who wasn't prepared for the energy exchange could get seriously fucked up. But as long as people were getting down and dirty in the vicinity, my body could absorb that excess energy without hurting anyone.

Not that I'd be sharing those special little details with her.

Raising a brow, I said, "If I told you yes, would that change your plans for the evening?"

"Oh, absolutely." The woman didn't miss a beat. "I'd make you sleep outside so I wouldn't have to spend tomorrow cleaning the dead body stink out of my couch."

I full on cracked up at that. Cupcake had a way of throwing me off balance, I'd give her that.

I picked up the bottle and tipped it toward her. "You want another one?"

Gray shook her head, the smile already fading from her lips. The chill moment between us seemed to be passing.

I tried not to let it get to me.

"Do you know when Ronan's coming back?" she asked.

The question was like an ice bucket dumped on our momentary fun.

I really, really didn't want to get into this with her. Ronan was her demon guardian—I got it. But he was already in way too deep.

And she seemed perfectly happy to let him fall.

"If you're so concerned about Ronan's whereabouts all the time," I said, "maybe you should learn how to fight your own battles."

"Right," she scoffed. "Have you *met* Ronan?" She had a point, but she couldn't just let it go at that. "He fights for me because he cares about me, Asher. Because he's my friend. Maybe you've heard of the concept?"

Was she *serious* right now?

Ronan and I had gotten into—and out of—more shit together, had traversed more levels of hell together, had fought in more demonic battles together, and had saved each other's lives more times than this fluffy bunny could ever hope to imagine in her short, human, blink-of-an-eye lifespan.

And she wanted to know if I'd heard of the *concept*?

"Sorry, Cupcake." I shook my head. "He fights because you let him. He fights because he's too hung up on you to know he's in serious fucking danger. And unfortunately for him, you're too damn selfish to notice and too damn weak to do anything about it even when the truth jumps right up and bites you on that perky little ass."

Hurt flickered in her eyes. I'd hit the soft underbelly with that little barb.

So why didn't I feel vindicated?

I sat back in my chair and waited for her to punch back. To tell me off. To put me in my fucking place, just like she'd been doing all along.

But Gray had gone silent. She wouldn't even look at me

—just swept her Tarot cards into a neat little stack on the table and bailed, leaving me alone with my booze and a big-ass pile of steaming hot guilt.

My gaze landed on the basket of stones again.

You can never really know love until you know yourself.

Yeah. More like, you could never really know love until you stopped acting like a flaming bag of dicks.

I poured another shot, toasting to my pathetic eternal bachelorhood.

Drink up, asshole.

THIRTY-EIGHT

GRAY

As much as I would've loved to slam my door, Ronan had torn it half off the hinges in his mad rush to save me from my nightmare with claws.

So I did the next best thing and turned off all the lights, climbed into bed, and pulled the blankets over my head, blocking out the world.

But even as I burrowed in deep, I could still feel Asher's presence in my house. His heat. It hovered around me like a fine mist coating my skin, making me hot and sticky and completely wound up.

It wasn't even his incubus "vibe" or whatever they called it. He'd given me a taste of that the first time we'd met, the sensation like the physical pull of an elastic band stretching and snapping back.

Unlike that day in Bloodstone Park, he wasn't messing with me now. No, this was all me and my stupid Benedict Arnold sex drive.

I didn't know what the hell was up with me lately—
why after coasting on cruise control for the past ten years
my libido had suddenly kicked into hyper-drive, right
along with my magic—but it was becoming a serious
nuisance.

Now was not the time for indulging in fantasies.
Certainly not about that cocky, infuriating, crazy-making,
asshole excuse for a demon—pardon me, *incubus*—drinking
himself into a stupor in my kitchen.

Yet half an hour later, when my hand drifted lazily
down my belly and slipped inside the front of my sweats,
the name on my lips wasn't Ronan or Darius, and the eyes I
imagined glazing with lust as they watched me trace slow
circles over my clit weren't hazel or honey.

They were the fathomless, hypnotic blue of the deepest
part of the ocean.

THIRTY-NINE

GRAY

I was still awake when I felt it—the magic tingling across my palms. My heart rate spiked, sweat breaking out across my forehead, but I didn't resist this time, didn't allow the fear to take hold.

Not even when the oily black smoke swirled around the end of my bed, slithering up my sheets in the moonlight, dragging me down, down, down...

Just breathe...

When I opened my eyes, I found myself in the meadow, lying in the grass beside the stone pedestal.

"Shall I assume you're ready to accept your true nature?" Death loomed over me, his shadowy presence blotting out the stars in the sky.

Again, I refused to let the fear take hold.

After all, why should I fear him? He wasn't my enemy. He was a force of nature. *The* force. As much as we were taught to cower in his presence, to believe we might outrun our inevitable end, Death himself was not that ending. He was the great transformer, the renewer. Just like the Death card in Sophie's deck, the child sought to crawl back into his mother's womb, but couldn't. He had already grown and changed, and she was already pregnant with new life.

In that way, maybe nothing ever truly ended. It just transformed.

For the first time since our acquaintance, I looked up at him and grinned. "Hi there."

Death said nothing. Did nothing. Showed no signs of acknowledgment. Just stared down at me with those eerily glowing eyes.

I rose from the ground, dusting off my palms. The whole cloak-and-dagger bit was getting a little old. "So, Death. Listen. No offense, but..." I reached out and touched the edge of his robe. It was more substantial than a shadow, but not quite as solid as real fabric. It felt almost like a spiderweb. "Do you ever wear anything... normal?"

He looked down at my fingers, still visible through the sheer blackness of his garb. "Normal?"

"As in... less creepy?"

"I am Death. Showing up in khaki pants and a white polo shirt might, shall we say, lessen the impact."

Okay, that was kind of funny, picturing him like that. I laughed, and I thought he might, too, but then he just... vanished.

Great. I've just offended Death.

"I'm sorry!" I called out, my voice echoing across the black forest. Night creatures skittered through the underbrush, but otherwise, I heard nothing. Saw nothing. "I didn't mean—"

"Is this better?"

I whirled around at the question, shocked at the sight before me—a man in his early thirties, wearing dark jeans and a long-sleeved red henley pushed up to his elbows. He was fairly tall, with broad shoulders, narrow hips, and a full head of thick, perfectly messy blond hair that fell in front of his eyes.

It was Death. I wasn't sure how I knew it, but I did.

"You... You're, like, a normal new guy," I said, leaving out the part about how smoking hot this normal new guy was.

"I thought you might be more comfortable this way." He ran a hand through his hair, revealing electric blue eyes that reminded me of Arctic ice. A little uncanny, maybe—not to mention the most ancient-looking eyes I had ever seen—but at least they'd stopped glowing. "Yes?"

"Yeah. I mean, yes. Definitely."

"Good. Because if we're going to work together, I'd prefer you not think me creepy."

I couldn't hide my smile. "I don't suppose this normal, non-creepy guy has an actual name?"

"Liam James Colebrook," he said plainly.

I laughed. "Been saving that one up, have you?"

Death—rather, Liam—shrugged. "That was his name."

"Whose—oh." I clamped my mouth shut as the realization hit. Normal new guy wasn't just a glamour Death had invented for my comfort. He was a vessel, a human whose body Death now inhabited.

"I didn't kill him," he explained. "It was merely his time."

"So you're... hijacking his body?"

"I prefer the term borrowing." He ran a hand through his hair again. It wasn't just blond, I noticed now, but copper too, streaked lighter in places by the sun. His skin was tan, and I wondered where human Liam had lived. California, maybe.

And then I wondered how he died. Who he'd left behind. Why such young, vibrant people had to die at all.

"If you prefer someone different," Liam said, "I can—"

"No, Liam's fine." One presto-change-o was about all the excitement I could handle. Besides, Liam Colebrook wasn't exactly hard on the eyes. If the goal was to make me more comfortable, Death could've done a lot worse in his vessel choice.

He was quiet for a long moment, taking in his surroundings as if he'd never seen them before. The change to solid form—to Liam—seemed to unsettle him a bit. I wondered if he'd ever done it before.

"Can you do—" I gestured from his head to his feet, indicating his newly solid form. "—on the physical plane?"

"Yes, but only for short intervals of linear time. A few hours. A day, perhaps."

"So you never just drop in for a few weeks? Spy on us mere mortals?"

"I can't." He slid his hands into his back pockets,

rounding out his shoulders in a gesture so human I nearly forgot his real identity. "Rather, I *could*, but doing so would... complicate things."

I nodded, not sure I was ready for a deep dive into that particular can of worms. I was having enough trouble figuring out how my own magical realm worked, let alone the metaphysical mindfuck of Death manifesting in human form on Earth.

Magical realms. Magic power. Demons. Vampires. Witches. Hunters. It was my world, my universe, but sometimes it seemed like a crazy dream—the kind where you're just the observer, watching someone else's life play out on the big screen.

"Something is troubling you," he said, perceptive as always.

"It's just... Witches are known for our magic. For channeling that energy and manifesting changes on the physical plane. So why do I always feel like my magic is controlling *me*?" I walked over to the stone pedestal, tracing the grooved pentacle carved on the slab. "I used to come here as a teenager. *Willingly* come here. Now it seems I just *end up* here."

Liam shook his head. "This is your place, Gray. You can access it any time you wish."

"Not anymore."

"You've suppressed your natural magic for many years. You're just out of practice."

I considered his words, trying not to fan the flames of hope kindling inside me. If I could find a way to control it, maybe it wouldn't be so bad. Maybe I could reconnect with this place, get rid of that creepy black forest. Open myself up to the joy I used to feel with Calla, long before my magic turned dark.

"It's a matter of stilling your mind," Liam said. "You need to learn to be fully present, casting your mind here while you can still feel—and be in complete control of—your body on the physical plane."

"So… meditation?"

"Some call it that, yes."

It made sense. Calla was big on meditation, too. She used to say a quiet mind was a witch's sharpest magical tool. I'd never fully understood that as a kid.

"Can you teach me?" I asked him.

Liam smiled, and the sight of it took my breath away. He really was beautiful, and not just physically. His otherworldly presence lent an almost imperceptible glow to him, a richness that radiated outward, drawing me in.

"I thought you didn't want any part of your magic," he teased.

"I'm not sure the universe is giving me a choice."

At this, he turned serious, his Arctic-ice eyes brightening. "There is always a choice, Gray. But if you don't make it, others will do it for you. So…" He spread his arms before me. "Who's going to make *your* choices?"

* * *

"You're doing great, Gray. See? This isn't as foreign as you feared."

I beamed, inhaling the fresh lavender- and lilac-scented air around me. Liam and I had only been practicing for an hour, but already I felt the transformation inside me. I was reconnecting with my magic place, our bond manifesting in the crisp spring air and the lushness of the meadow, everything blanketed with new growth.

The black forest around us had remained still and silent. It hadn't encroached further, but it hadn't retreated, either, and the path that led from my stone pedestal to the archway and the Shadowrealm beyond still beckoned.

Liam noticed me eyeing up the dark path. "That is just as much a part of you as the flowers and the grass, Gray. The sooner you accept that, the sooner you can tap into the rest of your gifts."

A shudder rippled through my body, and deep in my gut, an ember of magic ignited. I closed my eyes, neither resisting it nor encouraging it, and the ember sparked another, then another. Soon it roiled and bubbled inside me, sending heat and electric tingles to my limbs.

"That's it," Liam said. "Welcome it. Connect with it. Bring it in to—"

"No!" I opened my eyes and sucked in air, forcing the embers to cool. I didn't want that all-consuming feeling, that complete lack of control, the mysterious power that had compelled me to kill a vampire without remorse, to take Travis's soul, to become someone I no longer recognized.

But even though the heat inside me had subsided, black vines crept over my feet again, pulling and tugging...

"You must not fear it," Liam said, frustration edging his tone. "You must learn to control it. You must—"

"I'm not ready for all those musts." I tore away from the vines, stomping them down again. "I just—wait. Do you feel that?"

A new sensation crept across my skin, cold and icy. The hairs on the back of my neck stood on end.

"Someone's here," I whispered, narrowing my eyes and peering into the trees. I'd gotten used to the silvery eyes that lurked there, but this was different. This was wrong. "I can feel a presence. He's watching me."

Liam seemed unconcerned about this latest development. "You must learn to use your magic, Gray. Or rest assured, it will be used against you."

I nodded. He was right. I knew it intellectually. I *felt* it. But learning how to pop into my magical realm on command was very different from calling up that strange, dark power. Liam kept telling me it was my birthright, that it was a gift. But no matter how many ways I tried to look at it, I only ever saw a curse.

"I want to accept this," I said, clenching my fists to keep the fear at bay. Magic pulsed through me again, calling to the black vines at my feet. They twisted closer, teasing me. "But I—"

A blur of black fur streaked across my vision. Before I could figure out what it was, something knocked me flat on my back.

It'd happened so fast—no more than a blink.

My chest heaved under its weight. The smell of rot and ruin clogged my nasal passages.

The beast was back for blood.

No. Not like this.

If this unholy monster was going to tear me to shreds, so be it. But I wasn't going out without a fight.

I slammed the heel of my hand into the bottom of its jaw and grabbed a fistful of bloody, matted chest fur...

"Don't move!"

"I'll get it!"

Voices filtered in from some faraway place, slowly pulling me toward consciousness.

"Haley!" someone shouted. "Don't get near that thing!"

"Ronan, she's awake."

"Back off!"

My eyes snapped open at Ronan's sharp command, and I took in the chaotic scene. I was back in my bedroom, covered in mud and sweat and grime, surrounded by four familiar faces.

Asher. Haley. Ronan. And Death—rather, Liam—solid in his new human form.

All eyes stared down at me.

And at the rotting black beast I'd dragged into my bed.

FORTY

GRAY

Liam struck first, leaping onto the bed and wrestling the beast to the floor.

I bolted upright against my headboard, panting and trembling. My shirt was torn again, the bandages Ronan had patched me up with last night soaked through with fresh blood.

"Do what you need to do, demon," Liam warned Ronan. "I can't hold him much longer."

Ronan placed his hands on the beast's head, whispered some demonic incantation, and then the monster was gone, vanishing into nothingness. Liam got to his feet and dusted himself off, and then he was gone, too, leaving the signature black feather in his wake.

"Gray, you okay?" Ronan asked. "What happened?"

"It attacked me in my realm again," I explained. "I tried to fight back, but somehow it ended up… here." I looked around in disbelief. It was daylight now, probably late morning. How long had I been asleep? How long had that beast been in my bedroom? What if it'd attacked one of the guys? Or Haley?

"It wasn't attacking you, Gray." Ronan slumped onto the edge of my bed, shoulders sagging with exhaustion. I had no idea when he'd gotten back or where he'd been, but it was obvious he hadn't slept since I'd last seen him. "It was protecting you."

Haley came around the other side of the bed, inspecting my torn, bloody shirt. "That's not protection, Ronan. It's mutilation."

Ronan's jaw ticked. "They're not the most conscientious creatures."

"I don't understand," I said. "Protecting me from what?"

"From whom, more likely," he said. "If you're encountering these creatures in your magical realm, someone is there that shouldn't be."

I rubbed my arms, trying to shake off the lingering feeling of being watched.

The beast had shown up right after I'd sensed that other presence in my realm. Now that I thought about it, I realized it *hadn't* actually attacked me; despite the sharp teeth and claws, all it had really done was pin me down, slicing up my skin in the process.

"But… what the hell *is* it?" I asked.

Ronan held my gaze for a beat, then glanced at Haley.

She seemed to get the hint.

"I should probably go," she said, looking from me to

Ronan and back again. "I just dropped by to leave you some stuffed shells and to tell you that Norah and Reva left."

"What do you mean, they left?" I asked.

"I don't know much—just what Norah said in her voicemail. She's worried about Reva and decided to get out of Dodge for a while."

"What about the coven?"

"We're on our own." Haley frowned, her normally bright eyes dimming. "What's left of us, anyway. After we heard about Norah, a few of the others shipped off, too."

"So much for strength in numbers," I said.

"I can't really blame them," she said. "It's not safe here right now. I'm just not sure it's much safer anywhere else."

I reached for her hands, giving them a squeeze. "You can't lose hope, Hay. You're in charge of the hope in this operation and you need to keep it going. For both of us. For Sophie, too. Okay?"

She gave me a soft smile, her green eyes lighting up again. "Yes, ma'am."

"We'll figure this out—I promise." I pulled her in for a hug. "And thanks for the stuffed shells. Another Nona special?"

"You know it." She winked and started to head out, but Ash stopped her.

"You need a ride? I've got a few errands to run."

Haley nodded. "That would be great."

Asher glanced at me, our eyes locking. Memories of my late-night fantasy flashed in my mind, and in that moment I realized he must've known about it. He'd probably sensed the surge of sexual energy when I'd finally...

Oh, God.

"You okay?" he asked.

"Fine!" I blurted out, forcing a smile. "Totally fine. Why do you ask?"

"You slept for two days, Cupcake." A flirty challenge flashed in his eyes, sending a spark of desire straight to my core. "Guess that tequila was stronger than I thought."

"Yeah, I guess it was." I lowered my eyes, though the hot flush of my cheeks was probably a dead giveaway. "Thanks for... holding down the fort."

"Not a problem. Sorry about..." He trailed off, waiting another awkward, supercharged moment before finally speaking again, his half-formed apology apparently forgotten. "Anyway, yeah. I'll take Haley home, give you two a chance to catch up. Be back in a bit."

* * *

After a quick shower to rinse off the mud, I put fresh gauze on my belly and clean sheets on my bed, tossing the dirty stuff into the wash.

"It's a hellhound," Ronan said, anticipating my question before I even reached the living room. "They shouldn't bother you again. But until we know who they're protecting you from, you should probably steer clear of the magic realm."

"I can't always control it, Ronan."

"You have to try. The hounds can't be trusted. They aren't after you, but they're still dangerous."

"Okay," I said, trying to take it all in. "So that thing I brought back was a hellhound, and you banished it. That makes you... what? The hellhound whisperer?"

I'd meant it as a joke, but when Ronan turned and met my gaze, there was absolutely no humor in his eyes.

In fact, if I didn't know him better, I'd say he was nervous. Not about the beast I'd pulled from my realm. Not about the fact that Death had manifested in my bedroom as a human. Not about any of the other crazy shit going on in the Bay.

But about me. About us being alone. About whatever it was he needed to tell me.

"Something like that," he said.

"So a hellhound is protecting me, and you're..."

Holy. Shit.

My eyes widened, and I stumbled backward, dropping onto the couch. Every one of my memories of Ronan rearranged itself to make room for this new realization.

"You're a *crossroads* demon?" I nearly choked on the word.

His nervousness changed to anger in a blink, and he fought to keep his eyes from going black. "Are we really comparing freak flags, Desario? Because last time I checked, *you* bring people back from the dead."

The comment should've stung, especially coming from him, but I was too shocked to feel it.

"You're a crossroads demon," I repeated, closing my eyes and dropping my head into my hands.

I'd always known that Ronan was powerful, but I had no idea that he held the fate of souls in his hands.

When someone made a deal at the crossroads, it was an act of pure desperation. Crossroads deals were for the cursed and the damned, for those who'd lost everything, for those who feared worse things than death.

No matter what the bargain, the payment was always the same: a soul, sold into demonic slavery for eternity.

Crossroads demons kept watch over the damned, and at the end of the promised term—ten years, twenty, two—they brought in their hounds and collected, delivering the poor bastards straight to hell.

No one fucked with them, because even without a deal, crossroads demons still had the power to imprison your soul in hell, even if your greatest offense was stepping on their toe and scuffing their shoe.

And for the last seven years, the crossroads demon standing in my living room had been spending almost all of his time in the Bay with me, watching over me.

Since I'd never made a deal myself, it could only mean one thing.

I was part of someone else's. Some bargaining chip Ronan had been tasked with guarding until it came time to cash me in.

Fisting my damp hair, I opened my eyes and looked up at the man I'd always considered my friend. The man I loved.

It was all a lie.

"This changes nothing, Gray." He stalked over to the couch, and I stood up to face him, jabbing my finger into his chest.

"It changes everything," I said. "You lied to me. You—"

"I never lied to you. I never would. Please, Gray." He reached for my face, my name no more than a sigh on his lips, but suddenly I didn't want his hands on me. I didn't want him anywhere near me.

Channeling all of my rage, all of my anger, all of my sadness and desperation, I shoved him as hard as I could into the wall. I screamed until I had no voice, pounded on his chest with my fists so hard my hands ached, and still Ronan took it, immovable as an oak tree.

When I was all out of fire, I finally sagged against his chest, my whole body trembling. Saying nothing, Ronan slid his hands into my hair and tipped my head back, forcing me to meet his eyes.

I saw his age then—his real age, not the human mask. Hundreds of years of regret darkened his autumn-colored eyes.

Eyes that had seen so much pain. So much loss.

"You should have told me," I whispered, tears spilling down my cheeks.

He slid the pad of his thumb across my lips, making me ache. "I'm sorry. I didn't want to lose you."

"You can't lose me. It's your *job*."

"It was never that simple for me. You have to believe that."

"At least tell me why you're here. Tell me why you've been sent to me. Tell me…" I trailed off, knowing that asking for further details would be pointless; even if Ronan wanted me to know, crossroads demons physically *couldn't* share the terms of a deal. Doing so would obliterate him, banishing him to non-existence.

"None of that matters, Gray." His voice broke on my name, but his pain only served to enrage me all over again.

"Then what does?" I shouted. "What matters? What are we even doing to—"

Ronan's mouth closed over mine, cutting me off with a kiss I felt all the way to my toes.

I melted instantly.

There was more—so much more he wasn't telling me. Everything in me wanted to resist, wanted to turn my back on him and our friendship and everything I'd ever felt about him.

But no matter how upset I was, no matter how wounded and afraid, his kiss told me more than his words ever could.

His kiss was a promise, and Ronan never made a promise he couldn't keep.

"You… You're everything to me," he breathed. "It never should've happened, but I can't… I'm just… I'm completely unraveling over you, and I don't want to stop."

My heart galloped in my chest, my eyes blurry with tears. Nothing had ever felt so real. So inevitable.

"I don't want you to stop, either." My confession was no more than a whisper as I snaked my arms around his neck and pulled him close, closer, closer still. His tongue slid between my lips, devouring me with every stroke.

I was done waiting with bated breath, done with all our to-be-continueds. I trailed my hands down the front of his chest, over the firm ridges of his abs, hooking my fingers into the waistband of his pants. I fumbled with his belt buckle, and he grabbed my sweatpants, both of us yanking and tugging off clothes until we were finally free of all the layers that separated us.

I stood against the wall in front of him, naked and hot, my nipples hardening as he swept his gaze over me, drinking me in.

"You take my breath away," he whispered. He waited only a heartbeat before he kissed me again, grabbing the backs of my thighs and lifting me up, guiding my legs around his hips. Ronan backed me up to the wall, the hard, velvet-smooth length of his cock pressing eagerly against my hot, wet center.

I felt him hesitate.

"It's okay," I said. "I can only get pregnant by a human." Calla had drilled those lessons into me from a young age. And like all supernatural creatures, demons couldn't catch or spread any human sicknesses, so that wasn't going to be an issue either. "We don't need a condom."

Ronan kissed my shoulder, a smile curving his lips. "I know how it works, Gray. I just…" His expression turned serious again. "I need to know you're okay with this."

"I'm more than okay with this." I arched against him,

my core slippery with need. "Can't you feel how much I want this?"

"Is that a trick question?" He grinned, his eyes blazing with desire. With love.

His smile gave way to another kiss, and then he let out a soft groan, eyes closing in sheer pleasure as he sank into me, his deep thrust so perfect and delicious it made me ache in the best possible way.

"Ronan," I breathed, digging my fingers into his powerful shoulders as he rolled his hips, slowly finding our rhythm. The wall was ice cold against my back, but everywhere our bodies touched, my bare skin burned for him, for this man, for this demon I loved with everything in me.

What we had... It *had* to be real. It had to be true. I refused to accept anything else.

Fresh tears stung my eyes, and again I pressed my mouth to his, kissing him fiercely. It was the kind of kiss to remember me by, the kind of kiss he'd look back on in a hundred years and still feel. Still want. Still dream about.

With one hand spanning my back, Ronan slid his other hand between us, fingers stroking my clit, setting off a chain reaction that started with his touch and radiated throughout my core. I wouldn't last much longer, but no matter how hard I tried to prolong the inevitable, he simply felt too good, too perfect.

Seconds later, my body clenched hard around him, and he growled, low and primal, burying himself inside me with one last powerful thrust.

All the magic inside me, all the darkness and the light,

and I'd never felt so powerful as I did right now, making this demon—*my* demon—come.

The desperate sounds he made sent me over the blissful edge, and I finished with a shuddering cry that left my throat raw, my legs shaking. Ronan held me up through it all, his mouth blazing a trail of hot kisses down my throat, and when I finally stopped trembling and the heat of my orgasm receded, I opened my eyes and found him watching me with a look that could only be described as pure devotion.

"What?" I smiled, feeling a little shy at the intensity of his stare.

Touching his forehead to mine, he closed his eyes and whispered, "There is nothing I wouldn't do for you, Gray Desario."

And no matter how many secrets he'd kept, no matter how many secrets he was *still* keeping, I believed him.

FORTY-ONE

GRAY

We slept through the rest of the morning. Made love through the afternoon. Stopped only long enough to scarf down Haley's stuffed shells. And then we slipped right back into bed.

By the time I stirred again, my room was dark, rain pattering lightly against the windowpanes.

I opened my eyes and turned toward Ronan.

He was awake, head propped up on his hand, his eyes tracing the contours of my face.

Something was wrong. I saw it in his eyes—a subtle change from devotion and wonder to sadness and regret.

My heart sank.

"Gray, there's something I need to—"

I pressed my fingers to his lips, cutting him off. I didn't need to hear that this shouldn't have happened, that it couldn't happen again, that it changed everything.

He was right. It *shouldn't* have happened. It *couldn't* happen again. And it *did* change everything.

But it was done. And despite the ache blooming in my chest, despite what the future held, despite the details of whatever crossroads deal had brought him into my life, I wouldn't say I regretted it. Not for a minute.

I sat up in bed, clutching the sheet to my chest. "What time is it? Have you heard from Asher? We should probably check in with those guys."

"Please don't go," he whispered. "Not yet."

I felt his hand on my shoulder, warm and solid, gently urging me back to bed.

Staring up at the ceiling, I lay back down beside him, trying to brace for whatever he was about to tell me.

"I didn't choose this life, Gray. I need you to know that." The dark tone of his voice leant a sense of grave importance to his words.

"Okay," I said tentatively.

Outside my window, a flash of lightning streaked the sky. I counted seven seconds before the distant thunder rumbled, and still Ronan hadn't spoken.

His arm brushed alongside mine, and I wrapped my pinky around his, nodding for him to continue.

"Centuries ago," he finally said, "I woke up in a place I didn't recognize, no clue where I'd come from or how I'd gotten there. I didn't know my name, my age, my country, none of it."

My breath caught in my throat, and I rolled onto my hip to

face him. In all our years as friends, he'd never talked about his past. His origins. I'd always been too scared to ask for details. Even after what I'd found out earlier, I still didn't have the courage to ask for any more than he'd already offered.

Now, I bit my lip, waiting for him to fill in the gaps.

"I was in a castle," he said. "In the countryside of an unfamiliar land I later learned was Ireland. I searched every room until I finally found a man sitting alone in a stuffy formal dining room. It looked like he'd been waiting for me.

"He poured us each a glass of bourbon and told me he was my father. Said I'd been born a demon, but had suffered a magical attack that had screwed with my memory. He told me that just before my attack, I'd chosen to fulfill my destiny as a crossroads demon, just like he and his father had done."

"Did you believe him?"

"I had no real reason to doubt the guy, but the story never felt totally right. Almost from the beginning, I hated the work. All the contracts, the souls, the lives... It haunted me in a way it shouldn't have—not if it were truly my chosen path. But what could I say? I had no memories of my own. No place to go. All I had was this man and his legacy—one I didn't want to taint. So yeah, I chose to believe him. And I went *on* believing him for... for a long time."

"But not anymore?" I asked.

Thunder rattled the windows, much louder now. Ronan

shivered, and I scooted closer, our legs tangling together for warmth.

"About fifty years ago," he said, "I refused a deal. A kid was involved, and I just... I couldn't. So I let the family off the hook—tried to help them go undercover, get new identities, the whole thing. It worked for a few years, but eventually hell caught up with them." Ronan closed his eyes, the memories deepening the lines around his mouth.

"My father flew into a rage," he continued. "But rather than beating me or locking me in a dungeon or sending me to oblivion, he decided the most severe punishment he could dish out was the truth."

I reached up and traced his brow, wondering how long he'd been carrying this burden, wishing more than anything I could take away his pain.

"The man who'd been calling himself my father was not my father at all," he said, "but a high-ranking demon prince named Sebastian. Turned out I hadn't always been a demon. I was human once, Gray. Thirty-one years old. Ronan Michael Vacarro—that part has always been true."

"But... How did you end up there? You don't remember selling your soul?"

The rain picked up outside, lashing the windows, and I grabbed Ronan's hand and turned over, wrapping his arm around me as I pressed my back against his chest. I wanted him to know that I was right here. Solid and real. Not going anywhere, no matter what he said next.

A deep sigh escaped his lips, and he pressed a kiss to the

back of my neck, nuzzling close. After a long moment, he finally said, "My parents—my human parents—they weren't good people. Long story short, my old man made a deal at the crossroads to buy ten more lousy years on their miserable lives. You know the going rate on ten more years?"

I closed my eyes, tears leaking onto my pillow. He didn't have to spell it out for me.

"It was the first thing Sebastian ever told me that rang true," he said. "And for so long after, I blamed my birthparents—people I couldn't even remember. They were the ones who'd made the deal, right? But all that blame was misplaced."

"How so?"

"Sebastian could've let me spend the rest of eternity in the dark about my human origins, but he'd wanted me to know that I wasn't good enough. That my own parents—my fucking *parents*—cursed my soul to hell."

I turned back to look at him again, taking his face into my hands and pressing kisses to his brow, his cheeks, his mouth, trying to show him everything his parents hadn't—that he was loved. That he was cherished.

"I wish he'd never told me," he whispered, closing his eyes.

"But then you wouldn't know the truth," I said. "You'd be living a lie, always wondering why you felt so haunted."

"I used to think that." He opened his eyes, meeting my gaze in the moonlight. "The truth shall set you free—that's how the saying goes, right? But here's the thing about the truth. Yeah, sometimes it sets you free. But sometimes it just fucking destroys you."

"I would rather be destroyed by the truth than build my life on a lie." The words came out harsher than I'd intended, but Ronan didn't flinch—just claimed my mouth in another searing kiss.

When he finally broke away, he brushed the tears from my cheeks and smiled. "I meant what I said. There's nothing I wouldn't do for you."

"I know." I traced the line of his jaw, strong as ever beneath his soft beard. "I just wish we—"

The phone on my nightstand buzzed with a text.

"You should check that," Ronan said, sitting up. The moment between us had faded, the tragedies of the past giving way to the realities of right now. "They're probably wondering if we're still alive."

As much as I hated to leave the warm, safe cocoon of this bed, of this man's arms, Ronan was right. We needed to check in with Haley and the guys, find out if Darius had had any luck with his contacts in New York. Hopefully, he and Emilio were working together on that part of things now.

I sat up and grabbed the phone, figuring it was just Haley saying hi, or Asher being annoying.

It was neither.

The text—a photo—had come from an unknown caller, but I recognized the man in the picture immediately.

Inside a bruised and bloodied face, tormented eyes the

color of the deepest part of the ocean stared right through me.

Oh, Asher.

He'd been chained to a chair, shirtless, metal biting into his skin. Blood ran red over a series of black tattoos on his chest, dripping onto the hardwood floor and activating the magical symbols painted there. The whole thing was surrounded by a circle of salt.

They'd put him in a devil's trap, a powerful demonic prison that could only be destroyed by its maker. Eventually—hours, maybe a day—it would drain him, sucking the life out of him until there was nothing left but a husk, and his soul was banished to oblivion.

Behind him, moonlight filtered in through a stained-glass window in the shape of a star.

"Gray?" Ronan's hand on my naked back jarred me out of my shock. "Everything okay?"

"Call Darius and Emilio," I said, jumping out of bed and snatching up my clothes. "We need to go. Now."

FORTY-TWO

GRAY

Fifteen minutes later, I was stuffed into Waldrich's delivery van with Ronan, Emilio, and Darius, parked on a dead-end side street halfway down the block from Norah's place.

"It might be a trap," Emilio said, peering through his binoculars into the stormy night. I was surprised he'd agreed to our breaking-and-entering rescue mission without a proper warrant, but when it came to saving Asher's life, I wasn't about to ask questions.

"It's definitely a trap," Ronan said. "But we're not leaving Ash in there to rot."

Headlights cut through the rain, and the four of us ducked down until the car passed by.

"So what's our plan?" Darius asked as we sat up again.

No matter how many different ways we'd tried to attack this problem on the drive over, no matter how many ideas we'd bounced around, deep down I knew the truth: there was only one person in this van who could get Asher out of the devil's trap.

I sucked in a steadying breath, hoping I could make them understand. Hoping their faith in me was as strong as my faith in them.

"Darius, you and Emilio will go in the front door," I said. "Ronan and I will take the back. With Norah out of town, I shouldn't have any trouble with the wards. Once we're inside, I'll need to get to the attic as quickly as possible—that's where they're holding Asher. So whatever's waiting for us in that house, you guys need to deal with it. I'll get Ash, and hopefully we can all regroup on the main floor."

All three pairs of eyes turned to me in the dark space of the van, heavy with apprehension.

"Hopefully?" Ronan asked.

"I don't like it." Darius shook his dark head. "Asher may not be the only one waiting in that attic. There has to be another way, love."

"We don't even know if you'll be able to break the devil's trap," Ronan said.

"I can break the trap. You guys will just have to trust me on that."

"What if I take the attic?" Emilio asked. "I'll shift before we head in. If anything's up there, I'll be able to sense it."

"Guys." I held my hands up, quickly losing patience. "We've already been over all the options. This is our best shot. Asher doesn't have time—"

Lightning split the sky, and the crash of thunder that

followed rattled the van windows and set off several car alarms on the block.

It felt as if the whole world were conspiring against us.

"Gray, the safest place for you is here in the van," Emilio said.

Ronan and Darius grunted in agreement.

"You're right," I said plainly. "The van *is* the safest place for me."

"Good," Darius said. "So we'll—"

"Sitting out, staying out of harm's way, letting other people fight my battles," I said. "Definitely safer than jumping headfirst into a trap. But sorry, guys. That's not what family does."

Ronan opened his mouth to argue, but I held my hands up again, cutting him off. "Not up for debate."

I expected more arguing, but surprisingly, they backed off.

"Okay, little brawler," Darius said. "You say you know how to help Asher, and I'm willing to trust you on that. But you need to trust us, too. That means recognizing when you're outclassed and not doing anything to put yourself or the rest of us at risk."

"My main objective is Asher," I assured him. "I'll leave the carnage and mayhem to the pros."

Darius smiled. "That's all I wanted to hear, love."

"Okay. Everyone clear on the plan?" Ronan asked, and we all nodded.

I still wasn't a hundred percent sure *how* I was going to spring Asher from the devil's trap—there hadn't been a lot of prep time—but a hazy idea had begun to take shape in my mind the moment I'd seen his picture.

A demon's soul was bound to hell, but the demon himself was still in physical possession of that soul. Basically, it "lived" in the demon's body.

Liam had once told me that a person's soul was his very essence. So if that theory held true for demons, then it was Asher's soul—not his body—that made him a demon.

A few more pieces clicked into place in my mind as I followed the logic. Devil's traps only worked on demons, and demons were only demons because of their souls. So the only thing keeping Asher locked in that trap was his soul.

Remove that, and there'd be nothing holding him there.

After my experience with Travis, I was pretty sure I could get Ash's soul *out*. The trouble would be getting it back in.

But… One crisis at a time. Too much longer in that trap, and Asher wouldn't have a body left to return to.

"Alright. Let's go," I said, and we filed out of the van into the sopping wet night.

After a quick scan of the street to confirm we were alone, Emilio stripped naked, tossing his clothes back into the van and shutting the door. His golden skin gleamed in the moonlight, slick with water as rain ran in rivulets down his muscled chest and seriously cut abs, finally disappearing into the dark black hair below.

He was… impressive. And I wasn't just talking about his towering height and broad shoulders.

"*¿Que pasa?*" he said when he caught me looking. "No need to ruin perfectly good jeans. They cost a hundred bucks."

I shook my head, biting back a smile. Emilio had to have known I was checking him out, which meant he'd made that comment about the jeans to cover for me.

Ever the gentleman...

Without further ceremony, he crouched down on the ground, and I watched in awe as his muscles bunched, then elongated. Bones snapped and reformed, and thick, black hair grew over his golden skin, transforming him from man to wolf.

Power clung to his body, sleek and muscular beneath the thick coat of hair. I'd seen other shifters before, but Emilio was just... Wow. His beauty made my breath catch.

He nudged my hand with his wolf head, and I rubbed behind his ears, enjoying the feel of his coarse fur on my skin.

"Ready to roll?" Ronan asked, and I nodded, lowering my hand. The touch of Emilio's fur lingered, and my throat tightened with emotion.

Don't say goodbye, I reminded myself. *You'll see them again soon.*

We went our separate ways, Emilio and Darius taking the street entrance while Ronan and I cut through a neighbor's yard and hit the house from behind. Just past a cemented area set up with a grill and patio furniture, we found the back porch steps and headed on up. I'd brought my stakes and hunting knife, and now I pulled out the knife, holding it close to my hip.

As expected, Norah's wards were nonexistent in her absence, but so were the locks. We walked right through the back door and into the kitchen without issue.

Yeah. Definitely a trap.

Inside, we waited for my eyes to adjust, then swept the room. This was an old Victorian house, notorious for creaky floorboards and banging pipes, yet the silence was so all-consuming we could've heard a spider cross the room. Even the rain outside had quieted, despite the fact that it was still streaming down the windows.

That was eerie enough on its own, but something else was bothering me, too. I couldn't put my finger on it. It was just... off.

We continued through two other rooms, finding nothing but that odd soundlessness until we finally met up with Emilio and Darius in the dining room.

Darius shook his head, indicating that their search had yielded the same results. Gesturing to his nose, he mouthed, "No scent."

That was it, I realized. The thing I hadn't been able to put my finger on. Last time I'd been here, the house had smelled lived in—Norah's perfume, coffee and cooking aromas, cleaning supplies.

Now, it was just... a dead zone.

"Cloaking spell," I mouthed back, finally figuring it out. The magic tingled my nose, skittering over my scalp. It was definitely witchcraft, designed to camouflage the scents of any creatures a shifter or vamp might've detected.

Perfect. So not only were we going in blind, we were going in without smell. And we had no idea who'd cast the cloaking spell—Norah? Or some other traitorous witch?

I tightened my grip on the knife and jerked my head toward the stairwell. Whatever creatures waited in ambush, Asher was running out of time.

The men circled me, scanning the room as I took the stairs, one agonizingly slow step at a time.

From the top landing, a long hallway branched off in two directions, with several rooms on each side and a large window on each end.

I tugged on Ronan's arm, gesturing toward the right branch. The two of us crept along the hallway while the other two went left.

I'd just spotted the glint of a metal chain dangling from a hatch in the ceiling—the door that must've led to the attic —when the window at the opposite end of the hallway exploded.

"Get down!" Ronan shoved me to the floor as two blood-suckers crashed into the hallway in a storm of glass and terror, lunging for Darius and Emilio. I'd barely caught sight of them when two more crashed through, and Ronan took off toward the commotion, ordering me to stay back.

I got to my feet, ready to ignore him. To throw myself into the fight.

But then I remembered my promise to Darius.

I was not built for carnage and mayhem.

I was built for magic.

I'd asked them to buy me time, and that's exactly what they were doing. The best way for me to honor that—to help them—was to keep my promise.

It almost tore my heart in two, but somehow I managed to turn my back on the fight. On my family.

I sheathed my knife. Then I reached for the chain and pulled, catching the ladder that slid out from the hatch. Behind me, a wooden door splintered, and the yelp of a wounded wolf filled me with a primal fear.

But even as the battle raged, I refused to turn back. I climbed the ladder, hauled myself into the attic, and pulled the hatch closed behind me.

I'd just gotten to my feet when a broken voice spoke, cutting through the muffled sounds below.

"Admit it, Cupcake," Asher slurred. "You missed me."

FORTY-THREE

GRAY

Hope sparked in my chest. If Asher was flirting, maybe he wasn't as far gone as I'd feared.

"Save your strength," I said, crossing the dim, dusty attic to reach him. Other than the chair they'd chained him to and all markings on the floor, the room was bare. Even the walls were blank—nothing but studs and wooden slats.

I circled the devil's trap, trying to find some other way to break it. But whoever had done this had used powerful dark magic; I could feel its signature whenever I got close. It didn't have the same effects on me as it did on Asher, but it was poison just the same. After less than a minute at close proximity, I was already weak and nauseated.

"Looks like we're going to have to do this the hard way," I said.

Asher tried to speak, but all he managed was a bloody cough.

Bracing myself for another wave of sickness, I reached forward to touch his bare shoulder. His skin was feverish.

"I'm going to get you out of this," I said. "Just... hang in there. And trust me."

He didn't respond, but I saw the hope flicker in his sea-blue eyes.

Backing a good six or seven feet away from the trap, I sat on the unvarnished wood floor in the lotus position, just like Liam had shown me. Somewhere below, someone crashed down the staircase, Emilio growled, and Darius let loose a string of curses. I had no idea what was happening, who was winning, or who was wounded, but I had to trust that they could hold off the vampires. That nothing would get through that attic door.

Clearing my mind, I centered myself and slowed my breathing, gently reaching out for my magic.

It came to me immediately, the now-familiar tingling across my skin. Though my eyes were closed, I sensed the tendrils of black smoke swirling around my legs. I didn't fear it. Didn't resist. Just accepted.

When I opened my eyes, I was in my meadow by the stone pedestal. It still smelled like fresh lavender and lilac, and I took a deep, steadying breath.

Beyond the pedestal, the trees parted again, revealing the path that would take me to the gate and the black skeleton-tree forest beyond. I hurried along until I reached the archway, the silver-blue runes glowing brightly once again.

Passing through the iron gate, I reached for the closest branches, their black-and-silver threads reaching back, sliding across my skin, closing around my hands and pulling tight.

I took a deep breath as the fear surged inside me.

But then it retreated.

This is my magic. There is nothing to fear.

I lifted my hands before my face, watching with a steely calm as they turned black, then ignited, burning with dark indigo flame.

"Gray? What are you doing?"

I turned to find Liam, dressed in the same jeans and red shirt I'd last seen him in. Beyond his usual all-knowingness, his Arctic ice eyes held a mix of curiosity and something that looked a lot like pride.

"Magic," I said, smiling and reaching for his hand. "And I need your help."

FORTY-FOUR

LIAM

Gray Desario was full of surprises.

During her brief lifetime, I had already envisioned a thousand upon a thousand upon a thousand different destinies for her, each one equally possible until she made a choice, and then those destinies altered again, presenting a thousand upon a thousand upon a thousand different outcomes, beginning the cycle anew.

But perhaps—in all those millions and billions of possibilities—there was one even I had missed.

As she told me her plan, I was beginning to think that maybe we had all missed something. That maybe this witch was even more powerful, even more magnificent, even more incomprehensible than any of us could have predicted.

"So where do I fit in, necromancer?" I asked, very curious indeed about my role in this new potential outcome.

"Once Asher's soul is completely inside me," she said, "I need you to pull his body free of the devil's trap. Then you'll have to Hoover his soul back out of me, just like you did with Sophie's."

"Hoover?"

"Suck it out, or whatever you call it."

"Ah. Extract."

"Yes, that. You'll have to extract it from me and put it back inside him. But not until he's out of the trap. Okay?"

"I understand your intent," I said, "But demon souls aren't like human souls. Unlike Sophie's, which sought to connect with yours, Asher's soul could possess you. It could destroy you. Or you could destroy him. We just don't know, Gray. The risks are too great, the possible outcomes too many."

Gray considered all of this, her lips pressed together in a thin line. After only a moment's pause, she said, "That's not a reason not to try."

"But, Gray—"

"Liam. You keep telling me this magic is a gift, not a curse." She raised her hands between us, her dark blue flames surging into the night, flickering the same shade as her determined blue eyes. "Well, this is our chance to find out."

My human mouth curved into a smile, and a feeling inside my chest I couldn't name sparked to life. "Indeed it is, little witch. Indeed it is."

FORTY-FIVE

GRAY

I was back in the attic.

"Gray?" His whisper floated to my ears.

After several heartbeats, I took a deep breath and opened my eyes.

I heard nothing, saw nothing, felt nothing but the demon imprisoned before me, pale and shattered, fading from this realm.

"Whatever you're thinking," Asher said, his head lolling forward, "don't."

Looking at him chained to the chair, bruises covering his face, blood pouring from the gashes in his chest, I strengthened my resolve.

His voice was faint, his body broken, his essence dimming. But the fire in his eyes blazed as bright as it had the day we'd met.

"Whatever horrible things you've heard about me, Cupcake, they're all true..."

"Please," he whispered, almost begging now. "I'm not worth…"

His words trailed off into a cough, blood spraying his lips.

I shook my head. He was wrong. He was *more* than worth it. Between the two of us, maybe only one would make it out of this room alive. If that were true, it had to be him; I couldn't live in a world where he didn't exist. Where any of them didn't exist.

This was my fate. My purpose. My gift.

There was no going back.

I held up my hands, indigo flames licking across my palms, surging bright in the darkness.

The demon shuddered as I reached for him, and I closed my eyes, sealing away the memory of his ocean-blue gaze, knowing it could very well be the last time I saw it.

Acting purely on instinct, I guided my magic forward, searching for his soul. There was no fear this time, only decisiveness. Only hope.

"Gray…" Asher was fighting me with everything he had.

Fortunately, he didn't have much.

I nudged harder, seeking his boundaries, pushing past them, trusting that Liam was with me. That he'd follow through.

Seconds later, Asher's resistance finally broke, and I opened my eyes.

He was unconscious, his body slowly shutting down.

The mist of his soul slithered out from between his lips,

dark gray and hauntingly beautiful, points of light sparkling inside it like stars in a stormy night sky. Slowly, carefully, I drew it inward, feeling it slide into me as it sought its mate in my soul.

Asher's sweet-and-spicy demon scent surrounded me—ground cinnamon, hot peppers, candle flame—calling up the memory of the day we'd first met at the park. But that memory was quickly chased away by others—memories we *hadn't* shared. Memories that belonged to Asher and Asher alone, from a time long before I was even born.

A girl with raven-black hair and dark brown eyes, laughing as he chased her through a golden field.

The love and devotion in her eyes as she looked up at him through thick, dark lashes, pulling him close for a kiss.

I felt everything about that moment as if I were living it myself—his heart hammering, his love for her. His desire.

Their lips met again. The kiss deepened.

And then those tender feelings turned to dread.

I tried to stop the memories, to close my eyes, to break the connection, but I couldn't. It was private, it was painful, and I shouldn't have been there, yet I was—forced to watch the raven-haired beauty's skin turn the color of ash as the light faded from her eyes. Forced to scream her name. Forced to feel that soul-sucking loss as I tried over and over to bring her back, to take back what I'd done...

"Release him, Gray. Now." The commanding voice broke through the fog, shattering the memory like glass. Slowly, the attic came back into focus. I was dimly aware of

Liam's hands on my shoulders, his mouth lowering to mine.

I felt the press of his lips, but my soul resisted, clinging to Asher's. His hold on me was fierce, the connection nearly unbreakable, and though I knew it was wrong—knew it would likely doom us both—part of me wanted to let it happen…

"Gray Desario, release him at once!" Liam had transformed into the shadowy darkness of Death once again, his voice reverberating through me, forcing me to obey. I felt my soul shrink back, and with a searing pain like nothing I'd ever felt before, Asher's soul finally left my body, taking with it the memories I'd seen, the scent of him, the feel.

Death's eyes glowed bright blue, and then he released me.

I dropped to my hands and knees, barely able to keep my eyes open.

"It is done," Death said. And then he was gone, disappearing in a swirl of black smoke and raven feathers.

My insides ached. My outsides ached. I was wrung out and all used up, and all I wanted to do was collapse on the floor and sleep for a month.

But when I lifted my head and opened my eyes, I saw my demon lying on the floor, limp and lifeless.

"Asher!" I crawled over to him and checked for a pulse. It was faint, his skin now cold and clammy, but he was still alive. With a surge of adrenaline and determination, I stripped off my hoodie and covered his torso, quickly rubbing heat back into his arms.

When his eyes finally fluttered open, a sob escaped my lips.

"Cupcake," he whispered. He lifted a trembling hand to my face, but he didn't have the strength to hold it there. "Haley... They took Haley."

"Shh." I smoothed the matted hair from his forehead. "Don't worry about that. We'll find her. Right now, I just need you to be okay."

I looked around the attic for something—a blanket? Food? First aid kit?—but the bare room held no hope.

I wanted to scream. I'd manipulated his soul—risked both of our eternal lives—to save him. I couldn't let him die now.

"Asher, I need to know how to help you. I—"

Oh, Gray. You dummy.

A smile spread across my face as the solution came to me, fully formed.

"You're not going to like this," I teased. "Not at all."

I leaned forward, slowly lowering my mouth to his.

"Don't," he said, trying to swat me away. "You could... get hurt..."

"Asher, you're a goddamn incubus. If you don't let me try, you're going to die. Do you understand me?" God, did he seriously have to fight me on *everything*?

He shook his head, his eyes fluttering closed.

"What the fuck? You don't want to kiss me?"

"Not... not like this," he whispered.

"*Yes* like this, or there's never going to *be* another time." Why was he so infuriating? I straddled him and leaned forward, pinning his wrists to the ground. He tried to push back, but he was wasted. Utterly spent. All he could manage was to turn his face away.

I leaned in close again, kissing his cheek, his jaw, his ear, disregarding the blood and the grime and putting every ounce of sexy, sexual energy I possessed into bringing him back.

Finally, he turned his face toward me, our lips brushing, soft and silent as falling powder.

An electric current sparked across my lips.

Asher's eyes blazed with sudden heat. It surged through his limbs, warming my skin where our bodies touched.

It was working.

With renewed strength, he broke free from my hold and grabbed the back of my head, pulling me down again, smashing his mouth against mine in fevered passion.

I felt the power of that kiss all the way to my toes, and I let out a soft moan of pleasure, the taste of cinnamon filling my mouth as Asher grew hot and hard beneath me…

"Feeling better, asshole?"

Ronan's voice broke the spell, and I turned to see him standing at the top of the attic entrance, arms folded over his chest, his face almost as bloody as Asher's.

But that grin told me everything I needed to know.

FORTY-SIX

GRAY

Limping but alive, Asher leaned on Ronan and me as the three of us hobbled down the main stairwell. The brief but intense kiss had given him just enough energy to make it down to the living room, where he unceremoniously collapsed onto a mostly-intact couch.

He was smiling though. Waving us away when we tried to fuss over him.

Without sex, it would take him longer to recover, but the important thing was that he *would* recover. Without sex. Without me having sex with him. Without us together, having sex…

Head in the game, Gray. Head in the game.

Shaking off the memories of that sizzling kiss, I leaned back against Ronan's chest and took in the scene on the main floor. Most of the furniture had been overturned or destroyed, and broken glass littered the once-gleaming hardwood floors, but all was quiet.

And it looked like my boys had won.

"Alvarez?" Ronan called out. "Beaumont?"

"In here," Emilio replied, back in his human form.

We followed the sound of his voice into the kitchen, where not so long ago, Norah had fixed me a cup of tea.

How did it come to this?

Just like the rest of the house, the kitchen was torn apart, an explosion of dishes and drawers and silverware and tea towels covering every flat surface. But one vampire remained upright in the chaos, chained to a wooden chair and guarded by two of the fiercest, most frightening, most beautiful men I'd ever seen.

Whatever wounds Darius might've suffered, he'd already healed. Emilio was still a little roughed up, but he was in good shape overall, dressed in a pair of hilariously tight, hilariously pink sweatpants he must've snagged from one of Norah's closets.

Behind them, the decapitated bodies of five blood-suckers lay in a heap.

I didn't want to know where the heads had ended up.

"I see we still have a guest," I said, unable to keep the smile from my face. I was just so happy to see them, to know that they'd survived. That we'd all survived.

The vampire turned his head toward me and sneered. He was bloody and broken, but his familiar gray eyes radiated pure evil.

My gut twisted.

Clayton Hollis, a.k.a. Scarface. My old friend from Black Ruby.

"Miss me, sexy?"

Darius grabbed a fistful of his hair, wrenching his head in the opposite direction. "You don't look at her. You don't speak to her. You don't foul the air she breathes. Understood?"

"Fuck you, Beaumont." He spat, spraying Darius's dark blue shirt with blood. "I should've filleted that bitch when I had the chance. Slowly."

Darius and Emilio exchanged a glance. Darius nodded. Emilio headed out the back door toward the grill area.

Moments later, he returned with a bottle of lighter fluid.

"What the fuck?" Hollis shouted. "Are you fucking crazy?"

Darius grabbed the bottle and uncapped it, then squirted it all over Hollis's clothes. His hair. His face.

Then he retrieved a box of wooden matches from a shelf near the stove and lit one, holding it close.

"I didn't kill those witches!" Hollis shouted. "I'm telling you, you got the wrong guy! Jesus fucking Christ, Beaumont!"

"But you know who did," Ronan said. "You wouldn't be at the coven headquarters otherwise."

"Come on, man," Hollis whined, finally losing some of his bluster. "I'm dead if I talk."

"You're dead either way," Darius said. "But you can decide whether you want that death to be quick and pain-less, or… something else."

His match went out. He lit another.

Growling in frustration, Hollis flexed hard against his chains, but it was pointless. He was out of options.

"Talk," Emilio said, and Hollis finally caved.

"Couple weeks back, some human showed up—an out-of-towner, seemed pretty low on the food chain. I heard he was lookin' for some dirt on local witches in exchange for cash."

"Let me guess," Darius said. "You offered your services?"

"He was already getting some good leads—lots of witches in this town, and lots of loose lips. But it just so happened I'd seen a bit of that *real* hoodoo-voodoo, abra-cadabra shit right outside Black Ruby the night before."

I felt the ice of Hollis's glare as he turned toward me, the viciousness still lingering in his eyes.

"So I named my price," he continued. "Told him what I knew and collected my pay."

My stomach flipped as I realized what his confession meant. I'd been so certain no one else had seen me in the alley that night, but apparently he'd witnessed the whole thing.

It also meant that Hollis had recognized me at the bar the next night when he'd harassed me with his emo friend. He was screwing with me. By that point, he'd probably already signed my death warrant.

Only, it hadn't turned out to be *my* warrant at all. It was Sophie's.

I didn't need dark magic to fuel my rage now. Without

thinking, I lunged for him, ready to tear him apart limb from limb.

But Ronan's arm hooked around my waist, hauling me back before I even made a scratch.

"Not yet," he said, holding me tight. "We need more information."

The solid, familiar warmth of Ronan's chest against my back calmed me, and I took a deep breath, nodding for Darius to continue his interrogation.

"So you sold her out?" Darius asked.

Hollis cracked a smile. "We all gotta eat, brother."

Darius cuffed the back of his head. "I'm not your brother, you filth. Keep talking. How'd he find her?"

"Tracked her, most likely. Seemed to know a lot about witch magic. Signatures. I didn't really get all the details—I was too busy countin' the cash."

"Did you see him again after that?"

"Not till a few days back. He showed up again, asked if I wanted to earn a little more green by making a blood donation for his cause. Said his current connection was getting cold feet, and he couldn't finish his plans for the witches without more vamp blood. One of the panthers on the west side told me he was after shifter blood, too. Don't know what that was all about."

"And tonight?" Ronan asked. "How'd you end up here?"

Hollis shrugged. "A little more cash in exchange for an ambush. Take out everyone but the witch—that's what he said. Should've been easy money for me and my crew."

Darius nodded toward the pile of vamp bodies behind them. "Next time, I might suggest a better crew."

"Let's go back to the blood for a minute," Emilio said. "He wanted your blood for the witches, but did he ever say anything about you taking *their* blood? Turning them?"

"Nah. If you ask me, the guy was a little unhinged. Ranting about wars and elemental magic and rightful guardians. Real crusader, that one."

At those words, a creeping doubt crawled across my skin, slowly worming its way into my mind. I'd been trying so hard to convince myself that the killer wasn't a hunter. Other than the end result—dead witches—nothing about the crimes seemed to fit a hunter's M.O.

But the stuff Hollis was talking about? Hunter propaganda at its finest.

According to the lore, when humans first crawled out of the pond and started showing survival potential, the Elemental Source had selected the strongest human bloodlines to become witches and mages—female and male guardians of Earth's magic. They were given equal power and equal responsibility, but over time the mages became assholes, stripping the earth of much of her innate magic, hoarding power for themselves. The Source finally revoked the mages' duties, leaving witches the sole guardians—and wielders—of Earth's magic.

The neutered mages could still sense the magic though —a connection that just couldn't be severed. Eventually, it drove them mad, and their once honorable bloodline evolved into a vicious order of men determined to eradicate witches and reclaim the magic they believed was rightfully theirs.

These days, we called them hunters.

"What else can you tell us about this man?" Darius asked. "What did he look like?"

"Eh, built about like you," Hollis said. "Guy was a fucking ginger, too. Greenish eyes. Wore some charm around his neck—got real touchy anytime someone asked about it. That's all I know. I swear."

Greenish eyes? Ginger? Charm?

Fear gripped my spine, and I felt the blood drain from my face. My hands and feet began to tingle as panic took hold.

I sucked in another deep breath, trying to feel the beat of Ronan's heart against my back, trying to steady myself.

It *couldn't* be him. It *had* to be a coincidence.

You don't believe in those, remember?

"What kind of charm?" Emilio asked, and somewhere deep in the brittle bones of my heart where only the blackest memories lived, I knew what was coming next.

"Some witch bullshit." Hollis sketched shapes into the air. "Sideways crescent moon on the bottom, an eye made out of shiny shit on top."

"Shiny, like silver or gold?" Emilio asked.

"Nah. More like—"

"Opal," I said, my hands completely numb now, my heart jackhammering. Magic tingled in my gut, slithering around my heart. I closed my eyes, every intricate detail of that gleaming eye coming into sharp focus in my memory.

"With topaz and black onyx set in silver, cradled in a silver crescent moon."

Hollis snapped his fingers, then pointed at me. "Bingo. Looks like we've got our witch killer right here, Beaumont. How else would she know about the—"

Darius didn't give him a chance to finish. Just lit another match and tossed it at him.

Hollis ignited so quickly, he didn't even scream.

I squeezed my eyes shut, but it was over in seconds. Emilio found a fire extinguisher under the sink and doused the charred mess.

"Gray? What's going on?" Ronan's hands gripped my upper arms, but his voice sounded far away. When I opened my eyes again, the room went dim.

"What's wrong, *querida*?" Emilio asked, reaching for my hands. To Ronan, he said, "She's cold as ice."

Darius turned to me, concern pinching the space between his dark brows.

"Your heart rate is too high, love," he said softly, brushing his knuckles across my cheek. "You need to calm down. Do you understand?"

I tried to nod, tried to tell him that I heard him, but a searing pain split my skull. Brick by agonizing brick, the wall I'd spent nearly a decade constructing crumbled into dust. A tsunami of my most horrific, traumatic memories rushed through my body, wave after wave of pure, white-hot pain.

I squeezed my eyes shut again, but still the images

came, a horror movie I could temporarily forget but never truly escape.

"What happened?" Darius asked Ronan.

"I don't know. Hollis was describing the charm, and she just freaked."

I finally managed a nod.

"Gray?" Darius cupped my face, tilting it up toward him, his eyes frantic with worry. "What was Hollis talking about? What is this amulet?"

My legs gave out, and Ronan caught me, holding me tight against his chest.

When I finally managed to speak the words, I barely recognized the sound of my own paper-thin voice.

"It's a death sentence."

FORTY-SEVEN

GRAY

Phoenicia, New York
9 Years Earlier...

Boom. Boom. Boom. Boom.

A fist pounded on the front door like a drum beat, rattling the cinnamon broom that hung inside.

It was Thanksgiving, but we weren't expecting company. We lived in a heavily wooded area on several acres of land at least a mile from the closest neighbor, and we never had people over to the house—a policy that had allowed Calla to continue practicing her solitary witchcraft in relative peace.

Still, Calla didn't seem all that surprised by the visitor.

She didn't seem happy about it, either.

Across an oak dining table littered with remnants of the feast we'd just finished, she watched me for a long moment.

Neither of us moved to answer the door; food coma had already set in, and we hadn't even started on dessert.

The knock came again. Four times, just like before.

I pushed out my chair. "I'll get it. Probably just—"

"Listen to me very carefully, Rayanne." Calla removed the napkin from her lap and folded it on the table in front of her, her eyes never leaving mine. Though she spoke calmly, there was an edge to her voice I'd never heard before. "I want you to get your book of shadows and all the money from the tea canister on my dresser. Take it and go into the cellar. No questions. Do it now."

I rose from my chair, panic spreading throughout my limbs like fire ants crawling on my skin. There was only one reason she'd send me to the root cellar with my book of shadows, but... No. It couldn't have been them.

Hunters never knocked.

"What about you?" Some part of me still hoped it was a drill, some weird new ritual she wanted to try out on me. "Should I get your book?"

"No, that's not necessary. I'll be right behind you."

I darted up the stairs to my bedroom and grabbed the book of shadows from my altar, then the money from her tea canister—a wad of bills and some loose change.

When I got back downstairs, the front door was open. Out on the porch, Calla spoke in hushed tones to a man I couldn't see.

I crept closer to the door, straining to hear.

"—have ten minutes, tops," the man was saying. "Do what you can to protect her."

Calla thanked him and came back inside, looking at me as if she'd known I was there the entire time. Eavesdropping was against the rules in our house, but she didn't look angry.

Terror clouded her light brown eyes.

"Aren't you going to invite him in?" I asked, still hoping for a logical explanation. "It's Thanksgiving. There's still tons of food."

A warm smile spread across her face, and for a minute I thought everything would be okay. But then she pulled me to her chest, and my last hope shattered.

She hugged me like she knew it would be the last time.

"You are going to be okay." She smoothed a hand over my braid, an intricate style I'd mastered for the holidays with the help of a dozen YouTube tutorials. "You're strong, you've got a beautiful soul, and there are many things you'll accomplish in your lifetime, magical and mundane."

I opened my mouth to ask her why she was being so morbid, but a chunk of ice cracked and fell from the gutter out front and startled her into action. Without another word, she ushered me down the stairs into the damp basement, straight to the root cellar—no more than a musty, glorified closet beneath the kitchen. The only light came through a half inch gap in the kitchen floorboards directly over my head.

Fear pooled in my gut, making my knees wobbly. I wanted her to hug me again. I wanted to bury my face in her wild, curly gray hair. I wanted to follow her back up to the table, serve up a piece of pecan pie with too much ice cream, and laugh about how sick we would feel tomorrow morning.

She handed me a bottle of water and a hastily assembled bag of leftovers. Then, she pressed her hand against the eye-and-moon amulet at her throat—a charm she'd worn for as long as I could remember—and whispered incantations I didn't understand. My skin heated, a gentle pressure squeezing my chest. At first it'd felt like a hug, like strong but gentle arms encircling me and holding me close. But too quickly, the arms tightened. It was hard to breathe. My heart hammered behind my ribs, but still Calla didn't stop.

Just when I thought I would suffocate, she released me. Gasping for air, I stumbled backward, landing on the floor with a soft thud. When I looked up at Calla, her eyes were filled with tears.

"I have loved you as my own. I hope one day you'll forgive me for my secrets."

She slammed the door shut and bolted it. I heard her run up the main stairwell to the bedrooms upstairs at the same time the front door crashed open. I was powerless on the floor, winded and paralyzed with fear. I closed my eyes and forced my heart rate to slow, taking deep breaths of dank air that smelled of rotten apples and wet earth. I willed myself to go to my source, knowing that magic was the only way I could help Calla face whatever had just crashed through our door.

But for the first time in my life, I couldn't get there.

Overhead, the house shook with the boots of at least half a dozen men, each set louder and more powerful than the last. They barreled through our home, destroying everything in their path—framed photos, flowers, Calla's goddess statues, all the things I'd grown up believing would always be there. Would always be part of my home.

It didn't take them long to find Calla. She'd been upstairs. I pictured her there kneeling before her altar, lighting white tea lights and praying to her goddesses to keep us safe. When they found her, they dragged her down the stairs and into the kitchen. Through the gap in the kitchen floorboards I watched her lips move silently, but whatever spell she was attempting to cast failed.

The men tormented her, kicking and prodding, beating her with fists and elbows and homemade clubs until she finally dropped to her knees.

"Beg, witch." A short, broad man with a dirty blond beard fisted Calla's hair, jerking her head back to expose her throat. "Beg for your life."

Calla didn't beg. She laughed.

"Filthy hunters," she spat. "All this hatred, all this violence. Thousands of years spilling blood, and you're still as impotent as kittens."

Dirty Beard pressed the blade of his knife to her throat.

In the movies, the bad guys always gave nice long speeches about their diabolical plans, giving the good guys plenty of time to plot their escape.

But real life didn't work that way. There were no long speeches, no last-minute second chances. There was only the hunter and his cruel blade.

"You and your kind will burn, witch," he said.

At that, I found my voice.

"Calla!" I screamed. "Mom!" I'd never called her that before, but I knew in my heart that she *was* my mother—biological or not. I called to her, over and over and over until my throat was hot and raw, every breath like fire. The men didn't seem to hear me, but she did.

Calla met my gaze through the gap, her eyes unwavering as I watched in horror, unable to move or to find my magic. Unable to do anything but look on, totally helpless.

"Survive," she ordered.

I watched them slit her throat, watched them shove her face to the floor, watched the wood run red with her blood. I watched them yank the amulet from her neck. I watched the light leave her, knowing that I should have been able to save her.

My magic failed her.

I failed her.

My only hope was that when our souls met in death—soon, judging from the heavy footsteps clomping down the basement stairs—she wouldn't be disappointed in me.

"Find the kid." Dirty Beard shouted from the kitchen. "She's in here somewhere."

The root cellar door rattled on its hinges as the men on the other side—two? Five?—pounded it with fists and boots, a crowbar, an ax. The door was made of flimsy wood held together with rusted metal brackets; I had no idea how it was still standing.

"Damn thing's warded," one of the men shouted. "We can't get in."

I heard them rummage through the rest of the basement. Shelving crashed to the floor, glass jars of peaches and tomatoes and rhubarb from the garden shattering. I wanted to scream, to roar like a lioness, to crash through the door and tear them apart one by one.

But I couldn't move. I opened my mouth, and no sound came.

Whatever the men were looking for, they must've found it. Cruel laughter rushed through the basement like water from a broken pipe.

"Problem solved." Another bout of laughter sent a chill to my bones. Seconds later, I smelled the gasoline. Heard the metallic flick of a Zippo lighter. And knew with utter certainty that wards or not, this was the end.

My pants were warm with piss. I didn't even have the strength to close my eyes.

The man tossed the lighter, then bolted up the stairs with the others. A wall of bright orange light rose up on the other side of the door, crackling as it took its first taste of the old, damp wood.

Curls of smoke licked along the bottom and sides of the door, but the flames didn't penetrate. The root cellar remained cool.

Footsteps thumped overhead again, and a guy not much older than me crouched down, suddenly noticing the gap in the floor.

"I can see her!" He shouted, leaning close to glare at me. His eyes were the color of new spring grass, set off by a mop of dark red hair.

The sight of his familiar, once-sweet face shattered the last beating part of my heart.

"The fire isn't working," he snapped. "She must be protected." Something like remorse flickered in his eyes, but when Dirty Beard spoke again, that look was quickly replaced with anger. With rage.

"Handle it," the older man said.

The boy shoved his fingers through the gap—fingers that had once touched me so sweetly, so tenderly—but he couldn't get any closer.

Tears tracked my cheeks, but I didn't move, didn't back away. They couldn't kill me with fire, couldn't break down the door, but now I wanted to die. I couldn't imagine a life without Calla. Wherever she was going, I wanted to follow. I stretched up on my tiptoes, willing those desperate fingers to reach in, close around my throat, and crush my windpipe.

But no matter how hard I stretched, no matter how badly he wanted to hurt me, the boy couldn't get to me.

"I can't," he told the man—his father, I realized.

Boots stomped across the kitchen. Through the gap in the floor, Dirty Beard glared at me, his eyes full of a deep hatred I didn't think was possible for one human being to feel toward another.

I'd never met him before.

I wished I had. Maybe I could've changed his mind about us.

"Last time I expect a boy to do a man's job." He cuffed his son on the back of his head. By now smoke had clawed its way up the basement stairs, chased by the angry fire, and the man coughed. "Leave her, fool boy. Unless you want to burn."

For a moment the rage in the kid's face turned to fear, then sadness. But when he caught me staring, pleading, the mask of rage reappeared.

He hissed at me through gritted teeth. "I know your face, witch."

He spit at me through the gap, his warm saliva hitting the corner of my mouth, not far from the very spot he'd once told me was his favorite place to kiss.

The green-eyed, ginger-haired boy I once loved, the boy who'd promised me the stars and taken everything I had to offer in return, rose to his feet.

"Her magic protects you now," he said, "but that'll fade. When it does, I'll find you." Then, in a rabid voice that would haunt my nightmares for the rest of my life, he peered down one last time and made his final promise. "And when I find you, I will burn you."

FORTY-EIGHT

ASHER

She was only a kid. How the fuck had she survived?

The more Gray told us about her mother's murder—about the horrors that had brought her to the Bay and into our lives all those years ago—the deeper her words clawed into my chest, igniting a rage that damn near tore me in two.

One side was desperate to hunt down the filthy beasts that had destroyed her life. To brutally torment them for eternity.

The other part of me just wanted to wrap her in my arms and erase every bit of that pain she still carried.

Despite all the animosity between us, despite how I'd treated her, despite all the doubts I'd had about her place in Ronan's life, she'd saved me tonight. And that kiss? Hell, she hadn't just given me a hit of energy. She'd riled me up, gotten under my fucking skin.

And I couldn't stop thinking about it.

We were all in the living room now, Gray next to me on the couch, the others leaning against walls or broken furniture. She was exhausted, clearly traumatized by having to live through this nightmare again, but the guys were strung tight as drums, the energy in the room crackling with barely contained fury.

We might not have always agreed on everything, but we were on the same fucking page about this.

The men who'd done this to her would pay.

"I stood in the root cellar," she continued now, voice shaking like an earthquake but still fierce as fuck, "frozen with fear as Calla's body burned. Her hair singed and disappeared. Her eyes melted. Eventually, all that was left of the mother I loved was a pile of charred black bones."

Fucking horrifying. There were no other words for it.

Fiery rage surged through my limbs again, pushing me off the couch and into pacing mode. I was still pretty weak, but that was fading by the second.

No kid—wait, screw that. No *person*—should ever have to go through something like that. Yet Gray had. She'd faced that brutal attack, lost her only family, and fought her way across the country. Fought her way here to Ronan. To all of us.

She might not realize it, but the thing that had always been so apparent to Ronan had just become crystal clear to me, too. Our girl Gray Desario was so much more than a witch.

She was a fucking warrior.

"You survived, Gray." Emilio crouched down in front of her, squeezing her knees. "You damn well survived."

"But I didn't," she said. "That wasn't my doing at all. Calla's spell was like a bubble around me. I never even smelled the smoke."

Jesus.

I glanced over at Ronan, but he was leaning against the hearth now, a million miles away, no doubt struggling with his own thoughts on all this. He'd known. All this time, he'd known exactly what had happened to her, exactly how it'd all gone down.

He'd been there.

No wonder he was so damn tormented all the time. So protective of her. Yeah, he loved her. But it was so much more than that.

I got it now. He'd seen her face down death—probably more than once. All these years, he'd just wanted to make it okay for her, to stop this from ever happening again.

But he couldn't.

All he could do was be there for her when it *did* happen again. Fight by her side through the battles, help her patch up her wounds, hold her when the tears fell.

And one day, he'd have to let her go. Likely, she'd never forgive him.

Such was the nature of a demon at the crossroads.

My fucking heart hurt for him. For both of them. Hell, for all of us.

"How did you finally manage to escape?" Darius asked.

"I waited," she said. "Days, maybe? My body went into

survival mode. I rationed out the water and food Calla had given me, not sure how long I'd be down there. It was Thanksgiving break—no one would even miss me until school started again on that Monday. I had no idea if anyone had seen the smoke—we lived out in the middle of nowhere. I didn't know if the man who'd knocked on the door to warn us would come back."

Emilio shook his head, shock and disbelief written all over his face. "You must have been terrified."

"I think I was more numb than anything else," she said. I just knew that Calla had ordered me to survive, so that's what was in my head. Survive. I kept repeating it, over and over, even though my voice was shot and my throat burned."

Ronan disappeared into the kitchen, returning a moment later with a bottled water for her. She twisted off the cap and took a long swallow.

"Eventually," she continued, "the fire died. The cellar door had finally collapsed on its own, but when I got out of there, I realized most of the stairs were gone, too. I found some metal shelving in the basement and used it to climb up to the first floor. When I got outside, it was night time, and so quiet. Everything was blanketed with snow, and the moon made it all sparkle like diamonds. I remember being angry, then—like, how could anything have the nerve to be so beautiful after all that? It was, though. I stood there for a moment, and I felt Calla's presence move through me."

Gray wiped away a tear, then leaned her head back

against the couch and closed her eyes. Emilio sat down next to her, taking her hand in his.

"After that, I just… I ran," she said. "I made it into town, got on a bus to New York City with the cash I'd taken from Calla's room. It was less than two hundred bucks, but I stretched it as far as I could, taking on odd jobs until I could afford to hop on another bus, then another, never staying in one place more than a month or two. I stopped using magic, but I learned how to make myself look younger or older, to become whatever I needed to become in order to get fed at night, or to find a warm place to crash. For two years, I just kept running."

"And you kept *surviving*," Darius said. "Through all of it, love. Do you know how amazing that is? How amazing *you* are?"

Gray lifted her head off the couch, those crazy blonde curls brushing her shoulders. I fought not to reach for her, not to tangle my hands in her hair and pull her to my mouth again.

"I kept *running*," she said. "That's not the same thing."

"Running," Darius said, "was the means to a *very* important end. Your mother told you to survive, love. She didn't tell you how. You figured that part out on your own."

"And now you're here," I blurted out. I hadn't meant to, and the words came out brash and clipped. Ronan glared at me, and Gray just…

Damn. Her eyes flashed with anger, even as her face crumpled in pain.

"Sorry to inconvenience you, *demon*," she snapped. "Sometimes life doesn't go according to plan."

Fuck.

I opened my mouth to explain, to apologize, to promise her that I'd spend the rest of my damn existence tracking down the monsters who'd done this. But unlike the vampire, I'd never had a way with words.

"So are we getting out of here," I said, "or what?"

FORTY-NINE

GRAY

You'd think ignoring Asher would've been second nature by now, but he had an uncanny ability to push every one of my buttons, including some I didn't even know I had.

I'd just saved his life. Just shared an explosive kiss. Just seen a glimpse into his past…

No. I couldn't go back there. Not now.

Shoving that memory aside, I finished my water and thought again about the amulet. About what it meant. About my own past.

There were things about that night I'd never forget—the fierce protectiveness in Calla's eyes. The hunter's cruel words. But there were other details, long since lost to the recesses of time, sharpening now as I told the entire story out loud for the first time.

I knew now that my magic hadn't failed me. Calla had temporarily bound my powers to keep me safe. She must've known I would've tried to save her magically, and I probably would've died in the process.

She'd also cast a very potent protective spell over me.

And someone had warned her that the hunters were coming. Calla seemed to be expecting it.

With a final bolt of pure-white clarity, the last piece clicked into place, and I snapped my gaze to Ronan, my eyes wide with sudden shock. "It was you."

"What?" he asked.

"The man at the door that night. Calla made some kind of deal for my life."

Ronan lowered his eyes. His silence was all the confirmation I needed.

Everything about that night shifted in my memory, making room for this new knowledge.

I gasped. "Her soul—"

"Was never part of the deal."

I breathed a sigh of relief. "Then what—"

"I can't, Gray." He looked at me again. The raw pain in his eyes matched the regret in his voice, and though it cut deep, I knew he was telling the truth. "I'm sorry."

Ronan had shared so much with me tonight, so many secrets and personal demons. But he'd still never be able to share the details of the deal that had brought him into my life.

"You're her… guardian?" Emilio asked. "All this time?"

Darius wore the same shocked expression. Only Asher, clearly more steeped in hell's politics than the rest of us, seemed unfazed.

Ronan remained silent.

I closed my eyes as other pieces of my life's puzzle methodically clicked into place.

When I'd met Ronan here in the Bay, I'd felt an instant spark of familiarity, though I could never place it.

Turns out he'd been with me all along.

It explained so much about my time on the run. Life had been a shitshow back then, but despite the rough circumstances of living on the streets, I'd always been strangely fortunate—a narrow escape from a mugger here, an offered cot in a spare room during a storm there, a job turning up just when I'd run out of cash.

"So it was always you," I said to him now. "Saving me."

"You're strong all by yourself, Gray," Ronan said, neither confirming nor denying my statement, tiptoeing around the specifics of the deal. "Always have been. There's nothing you can't survive on your own. The point is you don't have to."

I looked down at the water bottle in my hands, gingerly peeling off the label, a million questions rushing through my mind. Ronan had arrived at—or possibly been sent to—Calla's house to warn her of the impending attack, giving her just enough time to protect me. Somehow, he'd kept an eye on me for two years as I slowly made my way across the country.

And at the end of all that, we found ourselves in Blackmoon Bay—a city where he already had friends. A life. The guys.

I wondered if he'd somehow guided me here, nudging me along the path from the east coast to the west.

But deep down that didn't ring true. My gut told me that despite Ronan's connection to the Bay, I'd found my own way here. I wasn't saying it was coincidence—it never was. But Blackmoon Bay had called to me for other reasons, all on its own.

Despite everything, I truly believed I was meant to make my home here. To reconnect with Ronan, to make these friends, to bond with these fiercely protective, incredibly loyal, and yes—sometimes wildly infuriating men.

To become part of something bigger than myself.

"So what comes next?" Emilio asked. "The killer is still out there, and chances are it's the same perp who trapped Asher and took Haley Barnes. He might have Delilah, too."

"I couldn't get a visual," Asher said. "We'd just pulled up to Haley's place when the guy jacked me from behind. He stabbed me with a syringe—I was out before Haley even got off the bike. I woke up chained to that chair, already beat to hell, some asshole in a mask snapping my picture."

"What about your connections in New York?" Ronan asked Darius. "Anything on the Grinaldis?"

"Not yet," Darius said. "And I'm still not sure about the vamps that attacked Gray and me at the morgue. But I'm thinking that the rogue Grinaldi vamp is the connection Hollis mentioned—the one who'd gotten cold feet and backed out of his arrangement with the hunter. It would explain the blood I scented on the first three witches."

"Makes sense," Ronan said. "If we could track that vamp down, he might have a lead on our man."

Our man. They were talking about the hunter. The boy I once loved, now a man I feared. A man who'd stop at nothing to carry out his demented vengeance.

In nearly ten years, the hunter's threat had never faded. It had always lingered in the back of my mind, whispering from every shadow and dark corner of the Bay.

But I'd learn to live with it. To *survive* with it, just as Calla had asked me to, because ultimately that's all it was—a threat. Words.

Until now.

When I find you, I will burn you.

But not before he toyed with me. He'd asked those vamps to leave me alive tonight. Why?

How long had the hunter been in the Bay? How many more witches would suffer or die before he finally took his revenge on me?

Would I be the last, or was this only the beginning of a much more sinister plot? The vampire and shifter blood, the kidnappings, the devil's trap... The more I thought about it, the more I realized we were still just scraping the surface.

Murder? That was just the tip of the iceberg.

"Hunters have been quiet for too long... The witches believe we're on the verge of another Great Hunt..."

The words from Sophie's book of shadows danced through my memory, mingling with the things Hollis had just shared.

"Ranting about wars and elemental magic and rightful guardians. Real crusader…"

I closed my eyes, wishing I could ask Calla for advice.

But I didn't have Calla anymore.

"There's nothing you can't survive on your own. The point is you don't have to."

Ronan's voice echoed, too, grounding me once again. Bolstering me.

Whatever his secrets, whatever the terms of the contract that had bound us, I trusted him. I loved him. And I believed that he was my true guardian, that he'd always have my back.

And now I had a whole *pack* of guardians.

Being here with them like this, working together, looking out for each other… If I'd brought my Tarot cards, I knew without a doubt the Ten of Cups would turn up. Just like the people in that card, we were a family.

Even Asher, for all his stupid outbursts.

Being with them… It just felt right.

It felt like home.

If the hunter thought he could take that from me now, he was even more deranged than he'd been back then.

So, *how* many more witches would die?

Easy. Not a single damn one.

"I know how to find the hunter," I said suddenly, a renewed sense of purpose giving me strength. "But there's something I need to take care of at home first. Will you guys come with me?"

Ronan smiled. "We'll go anywhere with you, Gray Desario."

Darius nodded. "You don't even have to ask, love."

"We've got your back, *querida*." Emilio reached for my hand and squeezed.

Asher met my gaze, a brutal storm raging in his eyes. I held my breath, waiting for him to scold me, to remind me how I'd put them all in danger, how it was somehow my fault that he'd ended up in the devil's trap.

But with a sudden flash of that bad-boy grin, he opened the front door for me and stepped aside, gesturing for me to go ahead. "Lead the way, Cupcake. We're right behind you."

FIFTY

GRAY

The shovel pierced the earth with a satisfying *thwack.*

"Please tell me it's not a dead body," Asher said, leaning against the back fence.

"It's not." Liam, who definitely would've known if we were digging up the dead, repositioned his flashlight, shaking the blond swoop of hair from his eyes. "And what is a so-called *dead* body, anyway? The body is simply a vessel, never quite alive in its own right. It's the soul that makes it so."

Asher grunted and shook his head, jerking a thumb toward Liam. "Is he always like this?"

"You get used to it," I said, biting back a grin.

Liam had shown up in my backyard just after the rest of us, arriving in a dramatic explosion of smoke and feathers that I was beginning to think was all for show.

Still, I was grateful for the support. I knew it was risky for him to be here in human form, and something about his presence comforted me, especially after he'd helped me with Asher tonight.

"You sure I can't do that for you, love?" Darius asked, his own flashlight bobbing.

"Nope. I have to do it." I drove the shovel into the soft earth, churning up the dirt. After a few minutes of hardcore digging, the spade finally hit something solid. "Bingo."

I cleared away the rest of the dirt, revealing a water-proof safe about twice the size of a shoebox. My heart thumped wildly in my chest, adrenaline making my fingers tingle.

No, not adrenaline. Magic.

I clenched my fists, still getting used to the feel of it. Still recognizing that I had a choice in the matter.

So often in life, our choices were taken from us. Sometimes we never even had choices at all, maybe because of the life we were born into, or because of deals made before we were born, or because of people in power who believed that our choices—our lives—belonged to them.

No matter how long I'd lived on my own before coming to the Bay, I realized now that my life had never truly belonged to me. For millennia, the lives of witches had been shaped by corrupt men—men who would see us driven away in fear or killed in their endless quest for power.

Me? Crossroads deal or not, I was done letting other people decide my fate. Done giving away my power, living in fear. Done letting other people write my story and make my choices and decide who I was meant to be.

It was time to start choosing for myself.

I tossed the shovel to the ground and dropped to my knees, reaching into the hole and hauling out the safe. I turned the combination dials on the front, then popped open the lid.

There in the center, right where I'd tucked it so many years ago, was my book of shadows. I reached for it, the triple moon design on the cover immediately responding to my touch and warming the air around me, filling me with the sense of rightness and wholeness I'd been missing.

I pulled the book out of the box and opened the front cover, and a Tarot card slipped out—one I didn't remember putting in there.

It was the High Priestess from Calla's favorite deck, a beautiful winged woman with waist-length black hair, dressed in sky-blue robes and holding a scepter topped with a crystal ball. She stood on a crescent moon that pointed upward like the one in Calla's amulet. Butterflies danced in the air around her.

Warmth filled my chest. Calla was still with me. She would always be with me, just like Sophie. Just like my vampire, my wolf, my two demons, and even my strange, enigmatic Death, who had somehow become as much a part of my story—my destiny—as the others.

There was still so much we didn't know. Why the hunter was trying to turn witches into vampires, and why he'd killed some and taken others. Why he'd set the traps for us at Norah's, only to vanish with Haley before we'd even arrived. Whether the vamps who'd ambushed us tonight were truly just goons-for-hire or part of a larger conspiracy.

For all I knew, Norah had been part of that, too. Something about her packing up and leaving town right before the attack wasn't passing the smell test.

I was still struggling to make sense of Sophie's Tarot predictions, and there was so much left to study in her book of shadows.

And my heart still ached for Bean, desperately wondering if I'd ever find her again, if her part in this story was over.

But I didn't have to face all these challenges tonight, and I didn't have to face them alone. I had my rebels now. We had each other.

I tucked the High Priestess back into the book and got to my feet, nearly overcome with gratitude.

"We're going to bring that hunter down," I said.

"I hear that," Emilio said.

"It won't be easy, love," Darius said. "He's operated right under our noses the entire time, and we never even caught his scent. May as well be a bloody ghost."

Liam shook his head. "Ghosts don't bleed, vampire. If you consider the inter-dimensional properties of—"

"Guys. He's not ghost," I said. "He's just a man. He's got weaknesses just like the rest."

"Okay," Ronan said. "That still doesn't tell us how to find him. If anyone has any ideas, I'm all ears."

"We don't have to find him," I said. "He'll find us."

They all watched me, waiting patiently for my plan. Trusting that I had one.

"There's one thing he wants more than anything," I said. "And I have it."

"Yeah?" Asher pushed off the fence and stepped closer, his eyes flashing in the moonlight. "What's that, Cupcake?"

I clutched the book of shadows to my chest, and a fresh wave of warmth slid over my skin, pulsing in time with my heartbeat.

I'd tried for so long to outrun this, to repress it, to deny it. But now it felt like I was coming home to an old friend who'd been right there waiting for me all along.

It was mine, my birthright, woven into my very fabric with the same genes that'd made my hair curly and my eyes blue.

From now on, there would be no more running from it. No more hiding. Only accepting and embracing. Only becoming.

I looked at each of my rebels in turn, that feeling of rightness settling deep into my bones as I finally reclaimed the words I'd almost lost.

"My magic."

Gray has reclaimed her magic, but as supernatural tensions heat up in Blackmoon Bay—and *other* things heat up with her sexy, devoted guys—does she stand a chance against the twisted hunter bent on her destruction? Find out in

Darkness Bound, the second book in the Witch's Rebels series. **Get Darkness Bound now!**

* * *

If you loved reading this story as much as I loved writing it, please help a girl out and **leave a review on Amazon!** Even a quick sentence or two about your favorite part can help other readers discover the book, and that makes me super happy!

If you really, *really* loved it, come hang out at our Facebook group, Sarah Piper's Sassy Witches. I'd love to see you there.

XOXO
Sarah

ORIGINS OF THE WITCH'S REBELS

I was primarily inspired to write this series by three things: my fascination with Tarot, my love of all things witchy, and my desire to see more kickass women telling stories for and about other kickass women.

I've always enjoyed books, movies, and TV shows about witches, monsters, and magic, but I never found exactly the right mix. I wanted a darker, grittier Charmed, an older Buffy, and most of all—as much as I love the brothers Winchester (who doesn't?)—I *really* wanted a Supernatural with badass bitches at the helm, hunting monsters, battling their inner demons, and of course, sexytimes. Lots and lots of sexytimes.

(Side note: there's not enough romance on Supernatural. Why is that? Give me five minutes in that writers' studio...)

Anyway, back to The Witch's Rebels. We were talking about badass bitches getting the sexytimes they deserve.

Right.

So I started plotting my own story and fleshing out the character who would eventually become our girl Gray, thinking I had it all figured out. But as I dove deeper into the writing, and I really got to know Gray, Darius, Ronan, Asher, Emilio, and Liam, I discovered a problem. A big one.

With so many strong, sexy guys in the mix, I couldn't decide which one would be the hero to win Gray's heart. I loved them all as much as she did!

I agonized over this.

It felt like the worst kind of love triangle. Er, love rhombus? Love—wait. What's the word for five of them? Pentagon! Yes, a love pentagon.

Pure torture!

But then I had my lightbulb moment. In the face of so much tragedy and danger, Gray fights hard to open herself up to love, to trust people, to earn those hard-won friendships. Her capacity for giving and receiving love expands infinitely throughout the story, so why the hell *shouldn't* she be able to share that with more than one man?

There was no reason to force her to choose.

So, she doesn't. And her story will continue!

You, dear reader, don't have to choose either—that's part of the fun of reverse harem stories like this. But if you happen to have a soft spot for a particular guy, I'd love to hear about it!

Drop me a line anytime at sarah@sarahpiperbooks.com and tell me who's winning your heart so far! I'll tell you mine if you tell me yours! *wink wink*

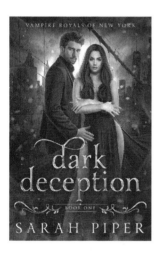

ABOUT SARAH PIPER

Sarah Piper is a Kindle All-Star winning urban fantasy and paranormal romance author. Through her signature brew of dark magic, heart-pounding suspense, and steamy romance, Sarah promises a sexy, supernatural escape into a world where the magic is real, the monsters are sinfully hot, and the witches always get their magically-ever-afters.

Her works include the newly released Vampire Royals of New York series, the Tarot Academy series, and The Witch's Rebels, a fan-favorite reverse harem urban fantasy series readers have dubbed "super sexy," "imaginative and original," "off-the-walls good," and "delightfully wicked in the best ways," a quote Sarah hopes will appear on her tombstone.

Originally from New York, Sarah now makes her home in northern Colorado with her husband (though that changes frequently) (the location, not the husband), where she spends her days sleeping like a vampire and her nights writing books, casting spells, gazing at the moon, playing with her ever-expanding collection of Tarot cards, binge-watching Supernatural (Team Dean!), and obsessing over the best way to brew a cup of tea.

You can find her online at SarahPiperBooks.com and in her Facebook readers group, Sarah Piper's Sassy Witches! If you're sassy, or if you need a little *more* sass in your life, or if you need more Dean Winchester gifs in your life (who doesn't?), come hang out!